JUSTIFIED

J.M. Kennedy

KenWhit
PUBLISHING

ISBN: 978-1-9168981-0-3

For The KenWhitts

Contents Page

Children are the anchors that hold a mother to life

Sophocles

ONE
A Rude Awakening

I should have left the sodding phone charging in the kitchen. Like a demanding toddler, it refused to sit quietly. I snatched it up before it woke Peter, checking the time as I placed it to my ear – 2.30am… great… 'Connelly…' My husky, woken-in-the-middle-of-the-night rasp, alien to my sleepy ears. Peter stirred.

I listened to my Sergeant – in mirrored whispered tones – convey the basic information of a body found in Victoria Park. He knew to relay enough detail to impart the level of urgency and get my butt out of bed. Peter resettled as I slid from beneath the duvet. Twenty years' experience, having conditioned his body to remain in the realms of deep sleep: a throaty, guttural grunt in place of a parting kiss.

Duly pissed off at being dragged out of bed with no intention of changing my mood, I crept along the hall and spied a light escaping from Emilia's room. I held my breath as I pushed open the door, in vain hope that she was asleep but again confronted with the reality of her teenage nocturnal world. 'For God's sake Emilia… it's 2.30 in the morning.'

'I don't have to go in until the afternoon for maths. That's what I'm doing now…' She moved her laptop and dug out a Krispy Kreme from her not-so-secret stash.

'Won't help your spots…'

'Go save the world Mum… Love you…'

'Love ya Spotty…' Picking my battles – the mother of all being next month when she was to be grounded to make sure she revised for her mid-term exams.

After a quick splash in the bathroom, I shuffled along to Jude's room, doubling as a dressing room since his departure to Uni. A dual-purpose sanctuary, minimising the disruption caused by my own night-time comings and goings and my covert shrine to my eldest, where I could sit and reflect on where the hell had the last twenty years gone?

His musky presence lingered. As I sat on his bed, struggling to find my feet to slip on some socks, I closed my eyes for a moment until a powerful twitch made me realise, I had dozed off again. 'O sod off...' I told the urban warrior on his Banksy poster – not for the first time.

Suitably attired in wellies and multiple layers, I headed out onto the deserted streets of Wanstead and shuffled to the cab office by the station – already notified to have a car waiting.

'Alright lads...?'

'Morning Josie... He's outside. Where you off ta?'

'Vicky Park...'

'Well didn't think you were going dancing in them boots.'

I smiled in appreciation that he could even be bothered to be so cheery in the middle of the night, in contrast to my resentment, even after all these years. The team – by now gathered in the park – would know this and any newbies would have been briefed by my Sergeant. My cab driver knew the brief, leaving me in peace with my thoughts.

The photogenic array of autumnal trees, illuminated by the brittle streetlamps – was lost on me. I dug my hands deeper into my pockets, nuzzled into my scarf and squelched through the boggy turf, grateful for the thick pair of Jude's socks I'd nicked from his room. The glaring lights from the Incident Tent, guided my way to The Rose Garden.

My Sergeant, Josh Hughes, looking irritatingly perky and smelling suspiciously of Red Bull, handed me my white paper suit so I could join the other polar bears inside the igloo.

As I strained the zip over my remaining layers, Josh ran through what we knew so far, dispensing with any niceties that would irritate me at this stupid O' clock hour.

'Young female... late thirties to early forties... well

dressed... can't find any identification yet.'

I stood at the entrance of the tent stifling a yawn mid-question, 'do we know how long she's been dead?'

'Monroe's in there now…'

That was a relief... Dr Ewan Monroe's rotund form was a welcome sight. His paper suit bursting at the seams from more anatomical reasons than my own. A blunt exchange of facts was all I could tolerate at this time of night and Monroe was an impatient D.C.I.'s dream. One of the few pathologists who also managed a forensic team, reducing the number of jobs-worths I had to deal with. A bonus, alongside the fact that our similar direct manner, ensured we rubbed along nicely. I approached the edge of the trench created around the body. Monroe did not flinch from his crouched position. I knew to wait patiently until he finished and had something to say.

He was working around the head of the body, obscuring the face but from what I could see, she was a well-dressed woman – albeit under-dressed for a walk in the park. The body seemed to be laid out rather than in a natural position from falling. 'Who found her?' I asked Josh, now towering close by my side.

'A group of pissed kids... They'd been to Gucci's on Victoria Park Road. Jumped the gates... thought they'd pick some roses... got carried away... Swear the spade was already here and started digging up the bushes. Got more than they bargained for... They're in a bit of a state so Angela's down at the cafe now, attempting to interview them. Didn't think you'd be in the mood for their hysterical gibberish.'

'I'm sure I don't know what you mean.'

'The Parkie's arrived and he's down there as well.'

Monroe rose uneasily from his crouching position and stretched before acknowledging my presence. 'Josephine...'

'Ewan... What secrets can you divulge?'

Josh had his notebook ready, his uncharacteristic, unkempt stubble, doing nothing to mature his perpetual-teenager looks. I wondered how much it bothered a man turning thirty-five.

'Deceased about twenty-four to thirty-six hours...' Monroe kicked off, hammering out the facts in his no-nonsense Welsh Chapel intonation. 'Multiple blows to the back of the head with a blunt object. Dust and fragments around the wound, suggest a rock but will confirm. No sign of the weapon yet. No outward signs of sexual assault. No defence wounds on first inspection.' He pointed to an area away from the body as he continued, 'blood splatter has been found, suggesting location of death. Body positioned after death.'

I could see Josh eager to butt in with a question but Monroe pretended not to notice. 'The grave was relatively shallow but I think the local wildlife had a go – attracted by the freshly-turned earth – exposing part of the body before the yobs arrived. Multiple shoe prints in the soil around the rose beds so we'll take samples from the witnesses for elimination. As you know we have an extensive shoe print database. I can schedule a post-mortem tomorrow around 1pm if you'd like to join me?'

'How can I refuse? Thank you, Ewan, I'll keep out of your way.'

With his hefty bulk no longer blocking my view as he strolled off to instruct his team, I was able to scrutinise the face of the victim for the first time.

Monroe had brushed away the soil, exposing a youthful, but over-processed appearance. I crouched down. Below the bright-blonde highlights, matted with soil and decaying leaves, flashed eyelash-extensions, plump lips and when examining the hands – manicured nails. 'Check out misperps from South Woodford to West Essex.'

'Based on what?'

'She's too coiffured to be a Hackney resident... definitely an Essex bird.'

'Stereotyping? Women do spend money on themselves

in Hackney you know. Haven't you heard about The Gentrification?'

He had so much to learn about the natives. 'And have you seen the Hackney Gentry? The Islington-Leftie-Lovies overspill. Eco-warrior, Guardian reader, Birkenstock-wearing...'

'Well South Woodford isn't Essex.'

My knees creaked as I struggled to stand. 'No... But "The Look" starts there. You'd better include Wanstead. Let's hope she's not from Essex otherwise we'll have to test some of that famous inter-force goodwill, we know doesn't exist.' Josh was a fastidious note-taker so I was happy to continue my brain dump. 'Find her bag – an Essex woman wouldn't be seen dead without one.'

'Did you really say that?'

I did because these were the type of people I lived amongst. Once past The Greenman roundabout in Leytonstone: kebab shops and all night supermarkets made way for Blo Dry Boutiques, Nail and Brow Bars. I steered Emilia's tastes away from this look all her short teenage life and hoped she hadn't noticed and would thank me one day. 'Get down to the cafe and help Angela with the interviews and find out all you can from The Parkie.'

I left the tent and stripped off my suit, reapplying the longed-for layers against the bitter night air. Looking back at the path alongside the Rose Garden, I decided to retrace the victim's steps.

With these late autumnal, short days, the likelihood was that they walked through here in the dark but the park closed at dusk so the Parkie wouldn't have known they were here. Was she followed? Was she with a friend? Nothing would be seen in this tree-lined pathway.

I reached a junction – left to go further into the park, right to the gate. I followed the path to the gate. Exposed lawns on either side. Somebody must have seen them. Through the black ironmongery, out onto Victoria Park

Road, stood rows of three-storey, Victorian townhouses in various states of dilapidation or refurbishment: renovated, work in progress, tenement dump. A third in equal measure. The local boozers were now gastro pubs, selling tricksy-named micro beers. The road that ran halfway through the park was similarly packed with trendy restaurants: organic this or organic that. Poverty bumped up against affluence, against the natural order. I pulled my vibrating phone from my pocket, *bag found*, lit up the screen.

When I returned to the tent, Josh was placing the large tote bag inside an equally large evidence bag, held open by one of Monroe's team. An envelope-shaped purse was retained by Josh.

'Where did you find that?' I asked.

'Stuck in one of the rose bushes... must have gone flying when she fell.'

'A Michael Kors bag... That confirms it... unquestionably Essex.'

As he was still wearing his gloves, I left him to go through the contents of the purse. I called back the Forensic tech, 'can you check if there are any car keys in there. Thanks...'

I returned my attention to Josh, 'bet ya a tenner it's a Range Rover.'

'You might be wrong...'

'Na... It's part of the uniform. They're clones... competing for a bigger and better version of the same thing. If we find the Range Rover, the model will tell us something about the victim's status and how she lived her life.'

'There's plenty of money around here but no Range Rovers.'

'That's because Josh – The Hackney Gentry are ashamed of their wealth.'

'Sounding a bit bitter...' he said.

'I guess I prefer the honesty of the Essex lot, wearing

their wealth unashamedly.'

He pulled out a driver's licence card, 'well technically, she's West Essex borders: Mrs Fiona Anderson, 14 The Drive, Woodford.'

'Mrs... Did she have a wedding or engagement ring on?' I asked.

'No... But from what you've told me I'd expect it to be a bit of a rock. A mugging that went wrong perhaps?' He suggested.

'Perhaps...' but it didn't feel like it. 'Did you have any joy with info from those kids?'

He flicked through his notebook, 'not much... timings mainly. I let them go. We'll get them back in tomorrow. I did the same for The Parkie, although he did confirm that the tool shed was broken into and he identified the spade as theirs. Forensics are down there now.'

Morning arrived soon enough. At 8.30 am and wired on a couple of espressos, I had an update with Josh at the station before heading off to the victim's family.

'Spatchcock's asked to see you,' he mumbled as I headed for the car park.

'Then say you haven't seen me.'

'Would do... but he saw you come in...'

'Shit...' I said, turning back to the station and took the walk of shame to the Chief Superintendent's office.

'No need to sit,' he instructed as I stepped into his power base, bulging with trophies, certificates and sycophantic photographic reminders of his powerful connections. I kept my gaze on his pampered face.

'Sir...'

'I believe you've picked up a murder in Victoria Park last night and not our usual clientele.'

'No Sir... a well-to-do Essex resident from what we've gathered so far. I'm on my way now to inform the family.'

‘Ah...’ He punctuated his build up with knowing nods. ‘I believe the date for your disciplinary hearing is soon...’

No... not believed... he knew... for a fact. ‘Yes Sir... I believe it’s in your diary.’

The knowing nods continued... ‘This could prove to be a high-profile case so if it clashes with any conflicting outcome from your hearing, it may need to be reassigned.’

‘I’m sure that won’t be necessary.’

‘I’ll give Detective Inspector Golding the heads up in case things don’t pan out.’

Thank you for your confidence Sir and fuck you. ‘As you wish...’

‘Close the door on your way out.’

I sat in front of the victim’s family in their roomy house on The Monkhams estate: a tick on the aspiration checklist. Informing the family was a process I guarded religiously: observing the authenticity of the initial reactions was priceless and these came in all guises. Before me, the mother, there to look after the children since her daughter disappeared. Now manic on hearing the news that her only child was gone, sobbing uncontrollably in a collapsed heap on a silver velvet sofa. Even through the ugliness of her howls, I could see she was as preened and pampered as her daughter. There could not have been more than twenty years between them.

The husband appeared shell-shocked – for now, appearance was all we could presume. Not as processed as the wife and mother-in-law but manicured enough to tip a toe into vanity.

‘Is there anything you can tell me about her disappearance Mr Anderson?’ I kicked off.

He looked poised to spring out of his seat, ‘I’ve already told those idiots from Woodford. If they’d believed me, she’d still be alive...’

I let him calm down as his rantings were making the

mother worse. 'Unfortunately, it looks like she was dead before you even reported her missing Mr Anderson, although the post-mortem will confirm this. If you could take me through all the details of the day she went missing, it would help us to track her movements.'

He closed his eyes and made a show of taking a deep breath, 'straight after school on Fridays, Fiona takes Alice to a stage school over near Victoria Park. It's run by one of those soap stars and the kids get a lot of casting-extras opportunities or something... She normally goes with another mum who lives quite locally. They take turns in driving.'

'Did she drive this time?'

'No... That's her Range Rover Evoque on the drive.'

'Go on...'

'Sometimes they go for a coffee together while the girls are there or sometimes Fiona would go for a massage at a local holistic centre she liked. The other mum said that Fiona had gone off for a massage but never returned. She brought Alice back for me and dropped her off at Sue's.' The mum nodded confirmation through her sobbing. 'Fiona wasn't answering her phone, so I shot down there to start looking for her.'

'Were you worried at this point?' I asked.

'Of course, I was... It was bloody Hackney. I don't care how much money has moved into the area, it's still gang warfare down there after dark. Wasn't there some kind of gang shoot-out down at London Fields last month – in broad daylight?'

He was right, but I needed him to stay focused, 'where did you look?'

'I headed straight for the holistic centre but she hadn't been there that afternoon. I went into every restaurant and pub around the park. I rang the Hackney Police and the Woodford Police – both useless. I even slept for a bit in the car near the park and she was there... lying there and I didn't find her...' He broke off as he attempted to contain a breakdown as his mother-in-law stretched over and wrapped her arms around him.

I gave them their moment, slyly observed and snuck the opportunity to absorb the room. Everything sparkled, from the glitter-encrusted feature-wallpaper to the high-shine, ceramic floor tiles. Family pictures adorned the room: a halo of blondes, most in exotic locations, the latest showing their daughter to be around ten and a young teenage son.

Anderson pulled away as he regained his composure. My cue to continue, 'do either you or your wife know Hackney well?'

'Some...' He mumbled.

'We're originally from Stepney,' the mum spoke for the first time, revealing her cockney origins, stronger than her son-in-law's. 'Left... before it turned into down-town Bangladesh.' Anderson touched her arm as though to say – not now...

'Do any of the family know anyone in Hackney? Were there any other friends she'd made at the theatre school that she may have visited?'

He shook his head. 'No... Not that she'd mentioned and to be honest, she literally mentioned everything.'

'Yeah... couldn't shut her up...' The mum gave a little hysterical laugh. 'Loved to chat did Fiona. You may not've listened all the time Darren but I did. No... No mention of any mates in Hackney.'

'What is it you do Mr Anderson?' I asked with multiple intent.

'I'm a Trader... in Canary Wharf...'

'Yeah... They've done well for themselves, haven't ya Babe?' The mother began in a manic pitch.

Anderson fumbled with his wallet as his mother-in-law went on. He pulled out a card and handed it to me. 'Here... my details... In case Woodford Police have mislaid them.'

I stole a glance of a Panerai watch on his extended arm.

'Mr Anderson... Do you remember if your wife was wearing any jewellery on that day?'

'She always wore her engagement and wedding rings and her watch. A rose gold Rolex...'

'Could you provide pictures of these please and if I could have any recent pictures of her, I'd be grateful.'

The flush of agitation climbed up his neck, 'are they gone? Are you telling me she was murdered for her jewellery? Jesus Christ...'

'No... I'm not saying that. We need to rule out every possibility.' He seemed to calm down. 'How are your children? We can arrange for some professional support.'

He fiddled with his own wedding band as we continued. 'Nathan's taken her disappearance hard. They were having a tough time, so he blames himself...'

'And little Alice misses her mummy...' This set the mum off again.

'I'll leave you in peace Mr Anderson. A family liaison officer will be in touch. But do think about accepting some help.' He followed me out into the hall. 'We'll need you to come down for a formal identification. One of my officers will pick you up.' He nodded absently. 'The post-mortem will be later today so we'll update you on the findings and have another meeting with you in case we've missed anything.' I hung on a while as he seemed to want to say something else.

'Was she... you know? Was she assaulted in other ways?'

'No Mr Anderson – there's no evidence of that so far but the post-mortem should confirm this.' Little comfort but it always seemed important for the husband to hear.

'Daddy...' We turned to the top of the stairs where Alice was standing bleary-eyed. 'Is that mummy crying? Have you had another row?'

TWO

A Long Day

I attempted to shake off the melancholy that crept up on me on my return from The Anderson's. The prospect of a motherless childhood for the kids left behind, never failed to trigger something in me. I threw the wrapper from my recent Milky Way addiction into the bin and hoped the sugar rush would lift my mood.

Josh had not wasted any time in setting up a new evidence board and the room buzzed around me as I digested the events of the day. 'The Press are going to lap this up,' I kicked off. 'This well-heeled-mother-of-two-murder is going to cause ripples. If the husband continues complaining about the Police not taking him seriously when he reported her missing, Spatchcock is going to get twitchy.'

'And it's also only a matter of time before our beloved local M.P. pops up on the news, to turn it into a race issue,' Josh thought aloud.

'Well, she'll be stretched this time as the recent unsolved murders are Eastern Europeans gangs – but she never let the truth get in the way of a good camera angle. Luckily it's too cold for the riot season...' I stared at the board... 'Let's see if we can find the jewellery...'

'Already on it...' Josh was pinning pictures of the missing jewellery that Darren Anderson had sent through. 'We're going to pull in the specialist Fences this afternoon when you're at the post-mortem.'

'Did Anderson send the purchase receipts?' I asked.

'Yeah... All from Hatton Garden.'

'Then get someone down there as well. That engagement ring might come full circle and be offered back to them but start low-level at the Pawn Brokers. Also pull her car in. You owe me a tenner by the way... a Range Rover Evoque.'

'So, what does that say about her status?' he asked with

an undisguised hint of sarcasm.

'Plenty of it... It was sitting next to his new Range Rover Sport.' I spun around to the desk behind me and picked up a picture of Darren Anderson and pinned it up. Josh used the black marker in his hand and wrote the inevitable: *The Husband?*

I turned around to direct the team who knew to hush and grab their nearest notepad and pen. At the front, Angela Jackson: the smartest. Smart enough to know that she would have to work twice as hard as her male colleagues to achieve the career trajectory she was destined for. She needed to lighten up and not be so perceptibly intense. In contrast, John Cuthbert sat tucked away at the back; an old-timer, seeing his last few years out before retirement: still smart and dapper, despite his loss of interest in the job. When handled properly, proved useful and at times, even productive but was becoming increasingly unreliable. Michael James, our tech expert, sitting not far from Angela. A healthy rivalry developed between them – good for both – which I invariably encouraged. His Jamaican roots presenting him with his own set of stumbling blocks on his way to the top. Susie Tam, the baby of the group was where she preferred to be – out on the streets.

'What do we know? What should we know? Angela... back to basics: was her life insured? What is the pay out? Does he have any financial issues? John... go interview his bosses… work mates… any gossip? A bit on the side...? Josh... tell Susie to coordinate the uniform's door to door and ask Anderson for a DNA sample under the guise of elimination.'

'Not sensing it's a mugging?' Josh asked.

'Doesn't feel right... Even the most hapless mugger would turn up with a knife which would be enough for her to hand over the goods. The purse would be one of the first things to nab. Why bury her and position her body with such care? Was her phone in the bag?'

'No...' Josh confirmed. 'Forensics are still looking around the area.'

'Pull the report from Woodford Police on this other mum she travelled with. Interview her yourself if you think there are any holes in any of it.'

I stared at a picture of Fiona's face. Artificial youthfulness... 'Find out where she has her face fixed and her gym. See how loose-lipped she was about her life.' I could hear the earnestness in Josh's note scribbling. 'Have you started on the CCTV in the area yet?'

'Yes Boss,' Michael raised his arm. 'I've some uniform seconded and trawling through them now although I'm not sure how helpful they'll be for the particular spots we need – but we'll see.'

'Then don't look for the obvious... I'm off...'

I stood behind a glass viewing-platform and popped a handful of chewing gum pieces into my mouth – my instant stomach-settler – as Doctor Monroe made his first cut. Josh covered our P.M.s but I sensed that I needed to be closer to the source of information on this one, especially as he had a habit of rubbing Monroe up the wrong way. I refocused my eyes to avoid the sight of my reflection screaming at me to get some sleep and have my roots done.

'Are you ok up there Josephine?'

'Yes, thank you Ewan. Do your worst.' He looked more like a butcher approaching a carcass which belied the delicate tenderness with which he worked on the victim. His tech-team were as ghosts, floating in and out around the body. I followed his sing-song flow of narrative as he worked efficiently through the body, looking to pick up any anomalies amongst the expected, and there it was...

'She was pregnant...'

'How far gone?' I asked.

'From the foetus measurements... around 2 months...'

'We're requesting a DNA swab from the husband so if you could match up with the foetus ASAP, it would be helpful.' I said, confident that he was more efficient than most.

'We aim to please...'

I observed the Doctor and his team work respectfully through the body for over an hour. Taking precious swabs for microorganisms that would later reveal their tales. He worked through the organs with precision. 'A fit woman for her age with some obvious assistance... Some wear and tear of the liver – too much bubbly perhaps? We'll confirm stomach contents later.'

He arrived at the telling wound at the back of her head. Here I waited for some more instant facts. Thankfully, Monroe never felt the need to show off his prowess with convoluted, medical jargon and I was always assured of laymen's no-nonsense-speak.

'The blow to the head was fatal and from the angle, we can confirm that the attacker was left-handed and around the same height as the victim.'

'How tall is the victim Ewan?'

'173 centimetres or five foot seven in old money. We'll extend our calculations on the impact on the wound, i.e., the strength of the attacker which may contribute to the presumptions of build.'

'That would be helpful.'

'The wound suggests multiple blows – a frenzied attack I would say. The lack of defensive wounds suggests that she never saw the attack coming.'

'What about the weapon? What can you tell me?' I asked, hopeful that his thoroughness usually yielded results.

'The fragments already retrieved from the wound are a match for those in the immediate vicinity. We have an impression of an indentation in the soil that we believe could be where the rock was originally embedded. Using dimensions from the impression, the wound and typical formations found in the area, we're creating a replica of the rock. If the attacker has taken it with him, it could be his undoing.'

This seemed eccentric but in keeping with Monroe's pet projects.

I arranged to meet Josh back at Victoria Park the next morning. The crisp autumn air was a welcome contrast to the blood and guts of the previous afternoon. A decent night's sleep had alleviated my mood which notably changed Josh's strategy for managing me. Joggers, of varying expertise and serious attire, trotted past, inter-dispersed with reluctant and enthusiastic dog-walkers. The former, wearing their winter coat over some type of 'loungewear,' aka pyjamas, smoking a cheeky fag; the latter, all Barboured and Huntered up, waving a doggy-poop bag.

Back at the gate, now identified as the point of entry, Josh studied the plan of Fiona's route, established by forensics and tried to fathom: 'the park would've closed not long after she came in. Wouldn't she have known that?'

I stood at the pathway's junction, looking either way. 'That would be the most probable conclusion. So – she's not using it as a cut through to anywhere as the other gates would be locked by the time she reached them. She's not frightened to enter a park, even though it's about to turn dark. Then she must have entered with someone she knew or arranged to meet someone in here.'

'But she wasn't dressed for a quickie under the oak tree.'

'No... perhaps met a lover... told him about the baby... turns into an argument... she goes to walk away and, in a rage, he smashes a rock into the back of her head. It would also account for the degree of care taken with burying the body.'

We reached the rose garden where the incident tent had been removed but police-tape and the inner cordon were still in evidence as a lone Forensic assistant crouched down amongst the roses.

'What's your lot's fascination with flora and fauna?'

'Oh... hello Ma'am…' He stood up as he placed some indistinguishable bits of plants into numerous tubes. 'Doctor Monroe wants a thorough documentation of all the vegetation on the site. It greatly increases our chances of providing physical evidence, pertaining to this exact spot. Nature's helping hand you might say.'

Josh was fascinated and stayed chatting with the assistant. The difference between a graduate officer and one who had grafted through the ranks and not much love lost between the two.

I made my way down to the Stage School. What was the probability that anyone would have seen them? Michael had been right; no cameras were evident along the route but the school run would have been in full swing. The Stage School owner had arranged to meet me at The Community Hall she rented on Well Street Common, opposite the park. A lone, cream VW Beetle convertible sat in the small car park. The doors to the hall were open and I realised it was as bitterly cold inside as out. A woman stepped out from a side kitchen: platinum blonde highlights poked out from a top to toe, pink faux-fur coat.

She introduced herself coquettishly which was my cue to gush over this popular soap star – which I declined. I accepted her extended hand and limp handshake. 'Detective Chief Inspector Connelly... Thank you for agreeing to meet me.'

'My pleasure... Anything I can do to help. I heard about it on the news. I was telling everyone on set yesterday.' Another cue to be ignored, 'it's so horrific. Doesn't bear thinking about...'

Her chatter was high-pitched and excitable. I wondered what she had taken. I smiled as expected. 'Can you take me back to the last time you saw Fiona Anderson.'

'Well... I don't know what to say about that last time because there's not much to report. She dropped off Alice as always. She seemed in a bit of a rush but she did sometimes... think she popped off for a massage or something. She used to have that other little mousey mum with her – gosh... sorry... I can't even remember her name. But we often had a natter if she had time.'

'What did you normally natter about?'

'Oh, this and that... We had *so* much in common. She loved me on T.V.,' another prompt left hanging. 'We both loved fashion... eating in the best restaurants... partying in the trendiest bars... You know what it's like.'

'But you never met up socially?' I asked, easily imagining them as social buddies.

'Oh no... We got on well but I'm not looking for any more friends. Can't cope with the ones I've got.' The contrived levity was ruined by an unintentional snort.

'Did she ever have anyone with her apart from the... mousey mum?'

She gave her best T.V. pondering face, hampered by an over-botoxed forehead and a suspect, coke-habit reconstructed nose. 'Um... well... she had lots of friends so I wouldn't be surprised if she dashed off to meet one of them. I mean she'd have to hang around for a couple of hours and why not? Can't see her spending that amount of time every week with Mousey Mum?'

'Did you notice her meeting anyone?'

Pondering face attempted once more. 'No... No... Don't think so but then of course I'm so engrossed with my students I wouldn't notice much else I'm afraid.'

'And she didn't mention any names?'

'Nope...'

She stretched her neck trying to catch a glance at my notebook, presumably trying to figure out what was taking me so long to write, 'nope...' I looked up and gave her a not-so-reassuring smile. 'Can you tell me what happened at the end of the class that day?'

'Oh... erm... well... everyone was picked up as usual apart from Alice. Fiona was never that late and Alice thought that her mum was picking her up. I'd arrangements for that evening so couldn't hang around so rang her husband and I think he got Mousey Mum to pick her up.'

'You think?' I asked, accusingly.

'Well, I didn't see her exactly. Her daughter popped in to fetch Alice, so I presumed...'

'And did Mrs Anderson seem herself?'

'Oh yes... full of it she was. Buzzing... you know...'

'And what were your movements after that?'

'What do you mean? I went home of course. Oh my God... Am I a suspect? I better tell my agent...'

I thought she meant her lawyer before realising her priorities. 'No... You're simply helping us with our enquiries.'

'Is that what I tell The Papers?'

Good God was she for real? 'We'd take a dim view of any conversations with The Papers that could undermine this investigation.' I cut her off before she could protest. 'Were you in the hall for the whole duration of the classes that evening?'

She seemed affronted by the implication and the dumb-blonde act slipped momentarily, 'these parents pay for my personal expertise and that's what they get.' And the ditzy mask effortlessly reassembled itself.

I handed her my business card. 'Please call me if anything else comes to mind and if you could send through a list of any of the restaurants or bars that she mentioned – that would be helpful.'

'Is that it? Oh... don't you need me to come down to the station?'

'No, not at the moment but we'll keep in touch.' That seemed enough to keep her vanity on track and off she flounced.

'How was she?'

I was unsurprised but disappointed in Josh's interest as I liked to presume that a guy with his level of intelligence was above gossip-mag celebrities, but seemingly not. 'Blond, plastic and vacuous – defo your type...'

'Well as long as you're being impartial. Did she have anything of note to say?'

'Nope... merely confirmed that Fiona liked the good life. She should be sending some info on the bars and restaurants that Fiona mentioned. Get them checked out and see who she was there with.'

'Sounds like you're going with the lover theory.'

'Don't know yet,' I replied, 'but in the meantime take some statements from the other helpers there and see if Little Miss Soap Star was ever absent from the classes. Also, if you found the name of the other mum from the Woodford statements, see if her view of Fiona is the same.' Josh started flipping through his notebook. 'In fact – pull her in this afternoon.'

'You've got the Press Conference this afternoon,' he reminded me, knowing I'd do my best to dodge.

'Oh shit... yeah... Then you'll have to see her. We'll regroup tomorrow morning. I want as much info back from the team as you can, so kick some arse this afternoon.'

'Do you want a lift back to the station?' he offered.

'No thanks... I have my car with me. I need to run a personal errand.'

THREE
Useful Gossip

I watched my adult-sized child – now two inches taller than me – bound out of the school gates towards my car. 'Quick... drive!' She ordered.

'Do you have to be so evidently ashamed of me?' I asked, only half joking.

'I'm not ashamed Mum... you're a celebrity. They're all talking about *The Rose Garden Murder.*'

'Is that what they're calling it? How do your lot know about it? They don't strike me as avid news watchers.'

'It's all on Facebook... not that we look at that but Instagram... Snapchat… you know…' she replied, rolling her eyes which was her too frequent way of telling me to – catch up with the 21st century Mum.

My conflict with my youngest was that she was so much like me and raising a generation of irreverent children meant that there was no fear in telling me so.

'Look... everyone seems to know someone… who knows someone… who knows her or her kids… In fact, my mate Chloe Wimpole... her younger brother goes to football with the son of the murdered woman... In fact…' Emilia turned fully in her seat towards me. 'Oh my God...Why don't I see what I can find out about the family? Of course. What a brilliant idea!'

No…! It was not a brilliant idea. 'As much as I love your enthusiasm, any information you provided would be inadmissible in court. Conflict of interest and all that...' I didn't know how much of this drivel she believed – she was a bright cookie – but if I gave her an absolute no, it would only spur her on. 'Also... if my boss found out, they'd take me off the case. Emilia... Stop...!' I didn't think she was listening at all at this point as her fingers flew over the screen on her phone.

As I sat in the Orthodontics waiting room, pretending to

read a year old copy of *Hello*, I thought about what she said. I had often chatted about my work with Emilia – mostly the process of detection and working evidence. She had a sharp, inquisitive mind but burdened by a sixteen year old's attention span. I had no doubt that armed with a notepad and pen, she could produce more relevant evidence in a day then we could for the whole case.

I sent a few texts before Emilia returned from her check-up with a tight-lipped smile which she had adopted since the fixing of her brace. 'All good...?'

'Yep... he said no problems with cleaning.'

'Liar...'

We chatted all the way back, where, with little encouragement, she gabbled about titbits she already gathered on the family, seemingly gleaned from responses to the texts she'd frantically fired off as I was telling her the opposite. With her chin on her chest, she remained glued to the phone, continuing her unfiltered commentary: 'he doesn't post as much as the sister but that's not news as he probably spends more time on FIFA with his mates. Wow... they weren't kidding about the mum. Seems a bit desperate – sorry... know she's dead and all but it's a bit embarrassing the amount of her kid's postings she's in. Wouldn't surprise me if she posted them herself. Some mums are like that... not you of course. Ha... the thought...'

'Thank you... I think...'

'Looks like he didn't get on with his mum,' she informed me, very matter-of-factly.

'And how'd you figure that one out?'

Her fingers flicked across the screen, 'some nice postings of him and his dad... none with her. Doesn't take a genius...'

Note to paranoid self: check Emilia's phone.

'Oh My God... you'll have to check out her profile page. No wonder they didn't get on... what a show. I take it all back mum... you're never going on social media.'

'What are you looking at? I thought profile pages were private.'

'Only if you want them to be and she clearly didn't. What a state...'

Pulling up outside the school, she decided she couldn't get out straight away and began some nonsensical conversation while laughing in a manic fashion. 'Emilia... what are you doing? One minute it's – drive off at high speed, then it's – time for a natter. As flattered as I am that you want to stay here chatting, I have to shoot off back to work.'

'For God's sake Mum, weren't you ever young? Tony Jarvis is outside again and I can't make him think that I've seen him, otherwise he'll think I'm into him.'

'Er... okay...'

'Okay... right... bye Mum... Love you...'

'Remember to pick up your EpiPen prescription from the chemist on your way home,' I shouted after her in vain. I waited a while and watched her in my rear-view mirror. Did he just give her something...?

I observed the media scrum from an obscure spot at the back of the room. Darren Anderson sat between the PR officer and Spatchcock, like a bereaved groom on the top table. Ever a willing performer, Spatchcock pleaded for information on behalf of the family. Time-old soundbites followed: killer still out there... someone must have seen something... police doing all they can... The hacks looked bored and were scratching away writing up their own interpretation of what they were *not* being told. Neither side were to blame. We were not yet ready to say anything but our hands were being forced and working in a void would escalate the newspapers spin and hamper the investigation.

He continued hamming it to the max. 'She was a loving wife and devoted mother and the family are devastated by her loss.'

When my name was mentioned as the lead on the case, my usual journalist contact spun around to find me. Eventually making eye contact, I gave an imperceptible nod of acknowledgement which she knew to mean that I would find her, when it was mutually beneficial.

I hung around until the end, mainly to watch Spatchcock squirm with the challenges from The Press which – if the look he gave the press officer was anything to go by – he was not expecting.

'You've been accused of finding resources for this murder while The Nesbit House Estate stabbings of young black men from the summer, remain unsolved. Are the streets of Hackney safe under your watch Chief Superintendent?' An aggressive challenge made by a new face in the pack – desperate to make his mark.

'I can assure the people of Hackney that our highly trained officers treat every case with equal diligence. The investigation into The Nesbit House murders is progressing at a steady pace and is not short of resources.' What a big fat fib but not his first – or last.

The other journalists smelt blood at his uneasiness and some of the veterans perked up at the sport, 'with gang warfare in London Fields last month and now a murder in Vicky Park, are Hackney's parks the new, no-go areas?'

My journalist contact took her own, close-to-the-knuckle bite. 'Are the recent spates of gang-related stabbings eating into your diminishing resources? Are the cut-backs making the streets of Hackney unsafe?'

The press officer knew she would receive the brunt of his displeasure if this continued and jumped to his defence. 'I'm sure you'll all appreciate that in fairness to the tragedy suffered by The Anderson family, today's focus should be a request to the public for their help and diligence to apprehend the killer.'

Darren Anderson sat amongst all this, in a comatose state. Most in the room were untouched by this performance, instead, were beavering away at their contacts to find all the dirt they could on him. Praying he would deliver into their hands the perfect headline. I needed to stay ahead of their game.

Emilia was full-on at the dinner table that evening and I begged her to leave me eat my lasagne in peace but she was affronted that I wasn't the one giving the press conference, after all – it was my case. Peter knew that I never placed the family at risk by putting my face out there so ended the line of questioning in a stern, 'don't push it…'

Emilia took the hint with a sneaky, 'good job… that blouse was totally ageing.'

Cocooned in bed that night, Peter cuddled around me. His big arms and hands held me in a firm grasp – his way of overcompensating for the hopelessness he felt for not being able to protect me in my job. Whenever, I'd either been attacked or found myself in dangerous situations, he would raise the subject of retiring from the job. He never pushed it, knowing that it would only happen when I was ready but letting me know he was ready. I relaxed into his embrace. After suppressing the guilty recollections of what I put him through, I allowed his radiating warmth to lull me to sleep.

FOUR
The Husband

I arrived at the station the next morning to find that Josh had been in beyond a reasonable hour, reworking the board with new evidence, acquired since we last regrouped. Regardless, he stood by me in front of the board, sharp and smart. The signature wave in his hair, newly curtailed with a grade two, buzz-cut. Various members of the team sat at their desks, working diligently, or giving the appearance of diligence, only interrupted by the odd phone ringing through. I scanned the room, never failing to remember my time as an eager pup, desperate to impress but slapped down mercilessly by the ancient, misogynistic arseholes from another century. Then slavishly replicated by another cock-sure pack, eager to pick up the baton. It was only in the last five years that I relaxed my guard – with the rank and file at least. It would take another generation for those arseholes to clear out from the top. Well at least I was looking at a room, a quarter filled with women – that was a start I suppose.

'Morning All... I'm hoping in my absence you've pushed on, hell for leather, in the direction Sergeant Hughes has sent you and someone will come up with something useful. Josh... Can you start with forensics please?'

He walked around to the other side of the board and commanded the attention of the room, 'so far they've been able to tell us that the attacker wasn't that much taller than the victim, anything from 5 foot 6 to 5 foot 9 and the husband is 5 foot 9. Although there were repeated blows – reinforced by the blood splatters – the force behind them doesn't indicate a powerful build and we can see that the husband has a slight build. Shoe prints have been cross matched with the drunken youths and the remaining unidentified prints are these three...' He pointed to print-outs on the board: 'Size twelve Asics trainers, size eight

Campers and size eight Nike trainers. The husband is a size eight. Fingerprints from the gates have not matched with anyone yet known to the victim although there was a match on a local, petit drug-dealer – currently on parole, but his alibi checks out as CCTV places him in a petrol station in Mile End at the time of the murder.'

'Well... as Josh is getting all his forensic evidence to point to the husband – can anyone place him at the scene of give me a motive?' I put out to the room.

Angela stood up from her desk with her notebook in her hand. Josh gave her an encouraging nod to continue before she looked at me. 'I've interviewed his co-workers at his firm and they fall into two camps: those who seem to be reciting from the same script – happy couple... lovely family... devoted to each other and those who were easily persuaded to deviate. It was noted that his wife turned up at the office a few times and they were seen arguing. The latest was last month and they also mentioned that he'd commented a few times on the wife and the son not getting on.'

I could see that Josh was keen to interrupt with undeniably another damming piece of evidence. 'His secretary confirmed that although he was at work at the time of the attack, he was in fact offsite, returning to the office from an appointment in the city. Going via the park wouldn't have taken him too far off course and the timings are workable.'

I gave Angela the nod to continue her findings: 'it seems he was a self-made man having worked his way up through the Trading Floor. There were a few financial mishaps on the way, but notably rode through the 2009 crash and we haven't yet found any evidence that there were any financial issues with his current business status. We discovered that he enjoyed a game of Poker, so I'll be pursuing his contact to find out what level – or depth – of company he kept. His wife did have Life Insurance cover with an 800k pay out due, taken out over ten years ago so we're keeping this fact on the table.'

'Are we going through all of their social media? I'm told she was a prolific poster,' I said, sharing the fruit of Emilia's hidden talents.

'I'm going through that next Boss,' Michael piped up from his desk with an addict's eye to his screen.

'Susie – how did we do with door to door?'

Street-savvy, Susie Tam would have picked out the most interesting of the statements and revisited the witnesses. Dressed in torn jeans and tracksuit jacket, I allowed her more leeway to dress-down when out and about. Coupled with her mixed-race, oriental features and slim build, she seemed to disarm many a witness who felt like they were innocently chatting to their teenage daughter. Any poor sod who tried to take advantage, however, was soon treated to some unorthodox moves – not strictly in the training manual – that I was also happy to overlook.

'Unsurprisingly, most residents claimed not to have seen anything, whether it be The Users in a squat or the self-absorbed Mumsnet squad. So, it boiled down to an elderly lady, living close to the entrance who used to see Fiona Anderson regularly pass her window as she always noticed her, "lovely clobber." She says, she didn't see her pass last week which means she couldn't have gone far beyond the park gates.

'And a young bloke living in the flats opposite the community hall – who might have some budding, stalker-like tendencies – seemed to have a keen interest in Sammie Evans. He kept an eye out on the comings and goings while the class was on – eager to see Ms Evans – so was familiar with some of the other groupies. He recognised a photograph of Fiona Anderson and from what he could recall, thought she left in the direction of the park but couldn't remember if she was on her own as others left at the same time. He confirmed that a few of the parents would leave their cars parked in the hall car park, during the duration of the class – wander off on foot and return for pick up. Neither witness recognised a photo of Darren Anderson.'

'Good work Susie... Find the other parents who parked up and see what they know. Josh... How did you get on with the mother?'

I knew Josh would be the best person to get the mother on side. He played his posh roots well when it suited him.

'Although not an unbiased witness...' he began, 'in her babbling grief, she did disclose a few unedited home-truths. Fiona and Darren were childhood sweethearts, journeying together from Stepney Green to Woodford Green. They'd shown generosity with family members along the way which, in some instances, created more resentment than gratitude. The mum admitted that Fiona enjoyed a lively social life – in fact, seemed exceedingly proud as a measure of her popularity. She reckoned that socially, they stayed local with their local friends – either as couples or on boys or girls' nights out. The West End, upmarket restaurants and bars were the domain of Darren's business colleagues.'

'Where's John?' I asked, not missing his presence from any meaningful contribution he might have made – those days were long gone – but to limit his piss-taking ways, influencing the younger members of the team.

'On his way to Hatton Garden,' Josh confirmed.

'And at a leisurely pace knowing John. Right, you lot... apart from Fiona Anderson being a grade A bitch – what credible motive have we found for Darren Anderson to follow his wife into the park and smash a rock into her skull? Okay everyone, we'll spend the rest of the day trawling through Darren Anderson's life. Those Anderson kids have lost their mum so it's a massive responsibility taking that leap to accuse him – if unjustly – because the accusation will cling forever. Now get on and find me that motive.'

Wiping the remaining croissant crumbs from around my mouth, I finished my second coffee of the morning. The perfect combination to this duo would have been a quick drag on a Benson and Hedges but the cherry flavoured Vape in my bag did not have the same appeal.

Having spent the evening with Josh, suffering his – you're micro-managing me – huffs, we reviewed CCTV tapes from Fiona's previous trips to the Victoria Park area; painstaking scrolling through to see if she met anyone or at a stretch – was followed. Nothing...

I scrutinised Darren Anderson through the glass. His deteriorating appearance nicely fitted the part of the grieving husband: generally unkempt and his expensive shirt, crumpled. Was he a ruthless killer or were we a load of shits putting a grieving man through more pain and agony? Unfortunately, it had to be done. The stats were too highly loaded against the husband.

He looked up wearily as I entered the room. 'Afternoon Mr Anderson. Thank you for coming in.' He grunted compliantly. 'Can we get you anything?' He shook his head. I settled into my chair and placed a file on the table. 'I know it can seem heartless Mr Anderson, asking intrusive questions at such a difficult time but it is necessary to eliminate all possibilities at an early stage.'

'I understand...' His head was elsewhere and not in the room. Leaving me hoping that his guard was down.

'As you know, our forensic team are going through your wife's car,' I advised him, 'so after this interview, one of the team will be coming in to take a DNA swab to eliminate you from any found. Are you okay with this?'

'Yes... whatever...' he replied, picking absently at his thumbnail.

'The day of your wife's murder Mr Anderson... where would you have been when she dropped your daughter off?'

'Work... I'm always at work around that time.'

'On that particular day, was it in your office or out at a

meeting?'

He seemed affronted by the challenge and made a show of thinking back. 'Out I think – but why are you asking me this? What are you suggesting?'

'I'm not suggesting anything. These are all routine questions that need to be covered Mr Anderson so the sooner we get through them the sooner you can go home.'

I ploughed through and around his tetchiness which peaked when I probed his relationship with his wife. 'Normal...' was his initial, automated response. After allowing his defensiveness to hang, he mumbled about arguing, 'no more than any other couple.' The shutters came down when I mentioned the son. An understandable, protective reaction and a glimpse of a genuine emotion – presuming the previous were contrived.

I poked a little more: 'do you think that maybe your son's behaviour towards your wife caused her to be distracted enough to walk through the park on her own without a care for her own safety?' He shook his head vigorously as though to rid himself of the thought. 'Maybe he pushed her too far? Maybe he was proving too much to handle?'

There it was... the rage... I thought he was going to throw the table across the room. Josh must have been observing because within seconds, he barged in and pinned him down until he succumbed. A guttural sob accompanied his submission as Josh pressed his head down against the table. I nodded at Josh to let him go – which he did – but instead of leaving the room, occupied a place behind me.

We waited tolerantly. He raised his head slowly and I felt Josh take a step forward.

'Are you ready to answer some more questions Mr Anderson?' I asked. He nodded impassively. 'I have a list here of some bars and restaurants. Can you confirm if you, or to your knowledge, your wife, have ever been to any of these?' I read through and he responded mechanically:

'No... No... No...'

'Did your wife socialise often without you?'

'Sometimes... yes with her mates.'

'Can you name any of these mates Mr Anderson?'

'No... I don't know... They were mums at the school, I think. Ask Sue… she'll know…' He swallowed a sob and his eyes turned to liquid. I perpetuated a pause. His breathing regulated and he leant back in his chair.

'Was your wife popular?'

He flipped his head back and with his eyes scanning the ceiling, he sighed, 'she liked to think so. It was... important to her to be seen to have the best. As our circumstances improved – it was her thing. Some lapped it up but others...' he sat up and returned Josh's scowl, 'let's say others may have found her manner – irritating.'

'Did she have any enemies?' I asked.

'Enough to want to see her dead...? No... I've tried to rack my brain who it could be. I can't see any other reason for this other than a mugging or worse...'

'Can you think of any reason she'd walk through the park?'

'No... I don't know what she was playing at going through there in the dark. In bloody Hackney for Christ's sake!'

'Maybe she was forced...' Josh piped up, now standing at the back of the room.

'If you'd met my wife, you'd know she wouldn't go anywhere she didn't want to, without kicking and screaming. Someone would've heard.'

He submitted to a DNA swab with no resistance and left, under the illusion that we were done.

Josh looked more than smug as Darren Anderson played straight into his violent husband theory. 'And he didn't recognise any of the places that Fiona was supposed to have been to... There's no way that baby's his.'

'Either way... doesn't prove anything and we still haven't spotted him on the CCTV so remain objective or we'll miss something. Pull together the interviews from those bars and restaurants and remind Doctor Monroe that the DNA results are urgent. When we pull him in again, it'll have to be under caution.'

FIVE
Not Convinced

I sat opposite Chief Superintendent Spatchcock in his soulless office with the day's newspapers spread accusatory, across his Victorian reproduction desk. I didn't have to look down as the same display greeted me on my desk – courtesy of Josh – as I walked into the office this morning: *Rose Garden Killer held... Husband Suspect in Rose Garden Murder... The Husband Did It...*

'How did they get hold of this information?'

We both knew the answer... it only took a small percentage of the 31,000 officers, devoid of a conscience, to pocket a few hundred quid to pass on some, 'harmless' information to their friendly journalist. But I needed to go through the motions to escape from this office as speedily as I could and get on with some actual meaningful work. The Chief Super. however, must have had a free diary.

'Have you charged him yet?'

Knowing that he was already in possession of this information, we played on. 'No Sir... I feel for now, he's the obvious candidate but I want to make sure we're not blinded by our need for a quick arrest by making the evidence fit the suspect.'

'But isn't that your job?'

'Only if we believe he's – without doubt – the only suspect and I am not yet convinced.'

'*You're* not convinced?' He repeated. 'So, what do we need to do to convince you? After all, we'd hate to rush you. We can ignore the fact that this case is now spread over all the front pages of our national press.'

'I need to follow other strands of the evidence Sir and not just those leading to the husband. I've spoken with the C.P.S. and they're of the same mind. And if you wouldn't mind handling all the media intrusion Sir – I'll make sure you're fully appraised.'

And then the pre insult pause, building up to: 'do you feel capable of dealing with this complicated case?'

'I've recently closed two cases Sir which I believe would be considered far more complicated than this one. Obviously, I appreciate the heightened media interest in this case which I defer to your expertise and support you in taking the lead.'

Knowing he was being played but powerless to resist, he proved over-generous in his support on this matter. With his ego satisfied, I was dismissed.

'The D.N.A. results are back and the baby's definitely his,' Josh said, pushing his theory. 'Why are you so convinced that he didn't do it?' He asked for the hundredth time.

'I'm not... I don't yet feel we've covered everything.'

'You sure it's not because you don't like your cases too tidy?'

Maybe he was right? Maybe it was because I believed the husband? I'd seen enough fabricated grief to have an instinct about the difference and the evidence against him was staring to wear thin. 'So far, the statements from the bars and restaurants in the City and West End she claimed to frequent, collaborated that she was only ever there with her husband and his business crowd. We as yet, have no evidence that she knew she was pregnant but Darren Anderson seemed crushed when we told him.'

Josh was not buying it, 'maybe he didn't want it.'

'So, he kills her? No... From what his son told us this afternoon, there's no doubt he lived for his children.'

We managed to interview the son, Nathan, by himself. His Dad – distracted by the news he'd received – consented to allow the family solicitor to act as the appropriate adult. We were provided with a unique view of their domestic life; intensely affected by the death of his mother, despite the strained relationship. Years of therapy beckoned…

He was candid about the strife with his mum, as only children could, expressing it in his limited way: 'she got on my nerves... never interested in how well I was doing at school or football... she was an embarrassment in front of my mates… trying to act young and trendy when they all knew she was botoxed up to the eyeballs...'

Fortunately, not much prompting was needed as we would have been cut dead by the solicitor if we probed. It was as though he needed to get it off his chest and maybe with strangers, he didn't feel judged? We let his outpouring flow: 'we argued a lot... we argued all the time. She was trying to make me something I wasn't. Trying to dress me up in poncey clothes when I wanted to hang out in my trackies. She didn't like my mates and kept organising play dates like I was a baby so I'd be mates with her friend's kids. Well, I didn't want to... I didn't like them and they didn't like me.'

I couldn't imagine he had much trouble being sought out by the popular groupies; a naturally handsome lad whose fight against looking 'poncey,' only added to his appeal.

Darren Anderson offered the stability in the home and in contrast, had nothing bad to say about him. 'Dad knew... he tried to tell her but she wouldn't have it. Then they'd argue and it would be like shit. Alice was asleep, but I heard. Anything he did... anything he gave her... wasn't enough. But I didn't want her dead. I wanted her to be like a normal mum – like Jack's. But he's gone as well. Maybe it's my fault... It's too late now.'

He broke down sobbing with his head buried in his arms on the table. The Solicitor wrapped her arms around him and we nodded in agreement that it was enough. I reached over and squeezed his hand. 'Thank you, Nathan. You've been very brave. We'll take you to your dad now, okay?'

He nodded with his head, still tightly hidden.

Josh was enticed away from my office by the smell of freshly delivered pizza as I settled down to listen to an audio tape of his interview with the mousey mum. I guess I was as much scrutinising the performance of my team member as the suspect.

Josh sounded like a bank manager about to arrange a loan as he settled this woman into the interview: 'Thank you for coming. Please take a seat.'

'No problem. Anything I can do to help,' she replied, with a middle-class, London accent which seemed to determine the tone of response from Josh.

'I'd like you to go through the details of when you last saw Mrs Anderson and anything out of the ordinary about her behaviour or manner.'

'Well... I'm not sure how helpful I can be. I drove both her and Alice – along with my daughter – to the S.E. school.'

'The actress from EastEnders?'

'Yes... that's her. She personally manages the classes every week.'

'What's she like?'

'Oh, very nice... down to earth... She has a great relationship with all the children.' She sounded like she was reading from a script. So far, I was not feeling any sincerity.

'What did Mrs Anderson chat about on her way in the car?'

'That's hard to recall, to be honest. It was the usual chit chat… you know… how the kids were doing at school... friendship groups... upcoming exams at the Theatre School... stuff like that.'

'Did she talk about her personal life?'

'Well, we had the girls in the car so it wasn't appropriate to talk about her love life.'

'Did she ever talk about her love life?'

A fabricated pause followed before a pseudo-reluctance: 'I don't think it's my place to say.'

'Then I must insist. It may be important.'

Another heavy pause left hanging, before: 'I suppose you're right Sergeant. I didn't think of it like that but again, I don't know if any of it is helpful.'

I could picture Josh's encouraging nod to go on from her feigned hesitancy. 'She had problems... at home with her son. Everybody knew about it as she was quite vocal. I think... I think it caused a few problems at home between her and Darren – particularly if he didn't take her side.'

'Did she talk about them in the car that evening?' Josh asked.

'No... Come to think of it... she didn't. She seemed in an unusually cheerful frame of mind. We arrived at the hall, next to Victoria Park and dropped the girls off. She said that she'd be taking a cab home so not to wait and off she went for her massage in her usual direction. I had no reason to doubt it.'

'Where did you go?'

'I'd promised my daughter a tuna-roll for the journey home so popped my head into the local Gastro Pub and then a few shops to see if I could find one.'

'Any luck?'

'Sadly no...'

I could hear Josh scribbling away. 'What was Mrs Anderson wearing that night – none of her family would've seen.'

'Err... Let me see... She had a black tuxedo style jacket over a bright purple silky blouse. Black trousers I think and over-the-knee black boots.'

'No coat?'

'No... Not that I recall.'

'A bit cold without one, wouldn't you think?'

'Well, it certainly was for me,' she replied with a loaded tone.

'I'm not well up on women's fashion... but doesn't that all sound a bit dressy for a massage?' He pressed her further. 'Did her hair and make-up suggest she was going for a massage?'

'I couldn't say...'

'I'm afraid you must...'

I smiled at Josh's formal, firm but encouraging tone, in contrast to the brutal inferences he had to use to get a fence to talk yesterday.

'She was heavily made-up and her hair was styled as though... as though she were going out.'

'Did she tend to be this dressed up when she claimed she was going for a massage?'

'Sometimes...'

'Had she ever spoken to you about seeing someone else?' He asked.

'No... We didn't have that type of relationship.' She could not take the insult out of her voice.

Josh picked up on it as well and pressed: 'what type of relationship did you have?'

'We knew each other through our sons and our daughters both wanted to go to the theatre school so we agreed to take turns in car sharing. We didn't see each other outside that.'

'Did you get on?'

'Yes generally.' She kept this response light-hearted. 'If you let Fiona chatter on, she'll get on with most people. I'm one of life's listeners Sergeant – so I was happy to do so.'

'Did you like her?'

Too long a pause to expect an honest answer. 'She was pleasant enough company which is all that matters as our acquaintance never went deeper than these weekly trips.' Sounded like a well-rehearsed response.

'In your opinion, from what you've seen on these weekly trips: her manner, how she was dressed, did it seem possible that she was going to meet someone?'

'It could be possible...'

With enough seeds of doubt planted without soiling her

hands with any straightforward accusations, I imagined she thought she had done enough. I made out a final – scarcely audible – scratching of scribbling of the names of any known friends that Josh asked her for before she left.

Despite the cringe-worthy, transparent attempts to politely paint a dismal picture of Fiona Anderson – it was not an unreasonable view. Who would want to be locked up in an enclosed space with her on a weekly basis?

As I switched off the tape, Josh tapped on my door and stuck his head through. 'The phone's been found.'

SIX
The Lover

I glugged back 2 Nurofen with the dregs of a warm diet coke after an enforced detour and a less than harmonious meeting with Spatchcock – predictably obsessed with tabloid headlines.

'What a cock...'

'Alright Josh... save it for the locker room – he's still The Boss. Okay Michael... you said you needed to see me.' Josh followed me to Michael's desk.

'We've been through her phone...' He picked up his notes: 'Argumentative, text exchanges between Fiona and Darren, confirmed that not all was well in The Anderson household. It seemed she had a penchant for storming out of the house after heated arguments to, "go for a drive to clear my head." Vehement texts followed with pretty colourful language on her part.'

'Anything from him?'

'Plenty Boss... some unsympathetic, "we'd be better off without you..." or "do us all a favour and drive off a bridge..." I've been able to track some of these storm-outs with visits to bars in the trendier areas of Hoxton or Shoreditch. Susie and John have been down there, interviewing bar staff.'

'Anything on CCTV to back it up?' Josh asked as I dialled Susie's number.

'Yes Boss... She seems friendly with one bar owner.' He handed us a print-out of a still of Fiona Anderson, in an embrace with a tall, dark-haired man. 'Although there are three possibilities... I've pulled info on all of them.' He handed Josh a file.

'Susie...? Michael's filled us in. What've you got?' I asked.

'I've pinned her down to one bar in particular: The Cocktail Factory. Owner – one Lucca Manchini.'

'Lucca Manchini...' I repeated as Josh rummaged

through the files before nodding that he had his details.

'When I'm told, seen, "snogging the face off each other," for the umpteenth time,' she continued, 'not much of a stretch to presume he's the lover. No sightings of the husband down here though. Also, Manchini's staff confirmed that he was in the bar on the day of the killing from 2pm until 1am. I've checked his local nick and there's been no trouble with his bar: a young, affluent crowd coming down from The City. They suspect a bit of coke activity but nothing to suggest any heavy-duty, drug dealing or anything that would warrant their attention. Interestingly, the staff seemed to think that she was keener than him and that she didn't know about the other women he was seeing.'

'Where's he now?'

'He's due in at three. Is it alright if I go back to the park Boss? I want to drill a few more of the shopkeepers on the opposite side.'

'Sounds like a plan Susie. Good work. By the way... Where's John?'

'Dunno Boss... Said he had to see a man about a dog.'

We banged on the door of The Cocktail Factory: a clichéd converted warehouse, down a clichéd rejuvenated alleyway in Shoreditch. Josh shoved his warrant card in the face of an Eastern European, tattooed bouncer, more used to dishing out the menace than being on the receiving end. We followed him up stone steps to a first-floor office, lined with pictures of Manchini and Reality TV celebs.

Lucca Manchini was casually but expensively dressed. Every piece of clothing flashed a designer label: Prada this... Versace that... Oily and flashy. I had lulled myself into expecting a heavy Italian accent so was taken aback when I entered the room to be abused by a strong Glaswegian blast, 'what the fuck are you doing pestering me again? I have rights...' A pungent aroma of the ciggie he must have consumed earlier, mixed with his heady, musk cologne, wafted around the room.

'Good afternoon Mr Manchini.' I sat down in the chair on the opposite side of his desk. Josh positioned himself against the wall behind him.

'What's he for? Intimidation? Doesnay work with me Lovey... I want my phone call...'

Josh could not resist, 'you've been watching too much American TV Mr Manchini. We don't go in for phone calls in good old Blighty. And drop the "Lovey..." Detective Chief Inspector to you...'

With those little details cleared up, I continued: 'you seem agitated Mr Manchini. You're not under arrest – we would like your help with our enquiries.' He settled reluctantly but continued to look over his shoulder at Josh as though anticipating a smack. 'I'll cut to the chase Mr Manchini... We have evidence to suggest that you were in a relationship with Mrs Fiona Anderson. Can you confirm this?'

'Aye... of sorts. We'd fun... It was nay state secret – except to her husband of course...' A smug smile crept across his face. 'He didna understand her and she found me irresistible – what can I say?'

Josh rolled his eyes and as he shuffled his position, Manchini jumped nervously in his seat.

'What do you know about her death?' I asked.

'Jesus Christ... I didna kill her! Is that why you're here? I donnay know anything about it and I've got an alibi. Check... I was in me bar. Regulars saw me as well as me staff.'

'We're going through the CCTV from you bar as well as interviewing your staff. You were a hard man to find. Were you hiding? Why didn't you come forward after the Police Appeals?'

He twitched his neck as though adjusting his shirt collar and folded his arms in defence, 'I didnay think I could help and I didnay want any bad publicity for the bar.'

'Isn't any publicity, good publicity?' I opened the file in front of me, 'or is it because you've already served time for two counts of A.B.H. in Glasgow before you came down to London to seek your fortune?'

As fast as he attempted to lever himself out of his chair, Josh had pushed him back down. 'I've been straight for ten years now – you can check. I've built a successful business – legit.' An agitated leg twitched beneath the desk.

'Was Mrs Anderson on her way to see you that afternoon?' I asked, maintaining my good-cop civility to Josh's menace.

'Yeah... yeah... We snuck the odd hour while her sprog was dancing or the like. Then she'd get a cab to the bar.'

'Weren't you worried when she didn't turn up?'

'Nay... she could be a bit like... fickle... yeah that's the word – fickle,' he said, as though he'd solved a Countdown Conundrum. 'She was also a bit moanie lately. Going on about the husband and son, blah... blah... blah...' emphasised with a hand flick.

'Did you know she was pregnant?'

He shrugged his shoulders, 'yeah – nay mine... had the snip. Donnay wanna be forking out for frigging sprogs running round that I didnay ask for.'

'How was she feeling about the pregnancy?' I asked, not expecting an empathetic response – but worth a go…

'Pissed off... Her and her husband weren't at it much – so she reckoned. So, she couldnay believe it. She was getting rid. Think she had an appointment at some clinic the following week.'

'Any idea where?'

'Some posh place uptown. Where she had her kids, I think.' He looked at his watch before taking another sneaky glance sidewards, to check if Josh was still hovering.

'How long were you in a relationship with her?' I asked.

'Err... about two years,' he replied. 'Yeah – we met when she was at one of hubbie's Christmas dos in The Shard. She snuck out for a fag and the rest is history...'

His slime-ball smugness was wearing thin. Josh must have thought the same because he plonked himself down beside me. Manchini shuffled in his seat – unsure if he was at any safer a distance if Josh got handy. Josh fixed him a smile before asking, 'what did she have to say about her relationship with her husband?'

'Nay much... a bit of a passion killer if you know what I mean... She'd rant about him if they'd had a row.' He fumbled around in his coat pocket and pulled out a packet of cigarettes and fiddled with them anxiously.

'What did they row about?'

'Something about the son kicking off and some shite about making nay effort in the marriage.'

'Do you think he knew about her affair with you?' Josh continued at pace.

'Donnay know... Donnay care... But he's got to have his head up his arse nay to notice.'

'You must have been worried he'd find out. Ever seen him? His in pretty good shape... he'd have sorted you out in no time.'

He straightened up in his seat, 'I can take care of meself.'

Josh had him on touchy ground and intended keeping him there. 'Did she ever discuss leaving her husband for you?'

'Fuck no! We both knew what we were getting inta. Just a bit of mutual fun…' he said, laughing off the suggestion.

'And as you were firing blanks – no risk...'

'Fuck you...' No… he didn't like that.

I pulled out a photo of the corpse of Fiona Anderson and pushed it in front of him. He winced and pushed it away. 'For Christ's sake... there's nay need for that...'

'It's the only reaction you've shown to her death Mr Manchini. Didn't you have any feelings for her or about her death?' I challenged this now squeamish suspect.

His head remained turned to the side. 'I did... I'm nay a complete bastard.'

'Was there anything she said about their rows that would lead you to believe that her husband was capable of this?'

He relaxed at the implication, 'she said he had a temper. He used to do some mixed-martial arts bollocks so I'd say he'd be perfectly fucking capable.'

Josh leaned across, 'a bit poncey compared to what you'd seen when you were doing time in Barlinnie, I guess. I bet them guys knew how to punch.'

'Aye...'

'Not like these soft southern shites...'

'Aye...' He chuckled.

'Keep in touch with them since you've been down Lucca? You know... the ones who watched your back inside. I bet they'd be impressed with your business empire.' Josh edged closer.

Puffed up now to bursting, Manchini couldn't resist, 'aye...' he said. 'Helped a few of them. It's the least I could do.'

'Always handy if you need to call in a few favours.'

'Aye...' And pop... he saw he was being played. 'Nay... nay favours... nay need in my business.'

We were losing him. 'Tell me Lucca,' I asked, 'where did you take Fiona for your little liaisons – a fancy hotel?'

'Nay need... I have a flat above the bar.'

'A flat... nice... She must have seen the behind the scenes action of your business. You know... witness the dealings that make you so successful.' He was not biting. 'She was a good-looking woman. Can't have hurt your image to be seen with such pleasing eye-candy?'

'Aye... she was a class act.' He looked to one side as though recalling a memory.

'You must have been one of the few people who didn't find her irritating or maybe she didn't talk as much with you?'

'Fuck… she talked alright. Didnay need anyone to listen neither.'

'Have you ever hit a woman Lucca?' Josh jabbed the question at him.

The rising flush on his face and pulsating jaw muscles, contained his fury. He tapped his fingers on the desk to occupy his hands which at that moment he probably imagined around Josh's throat. 'Nay... I donnay hit women.'

Angela called as Josh and I settled back into the car and I put her on speaker. She sounded uncharacteristically animated.

'I've been going through Darren Anderson's phone records and bank statements and he's lately been dealing with a Private Investigator. Contact and payments ceased before her death. He's based in the city not far from where you are now and I've taken the liberty to check he's in.'

'Okay... sounds interesting… Text me his details and let him know we're coming and Angela... get a warrant to check Manchini's flat and a list of known associates from his time in Barlinnie. And check again on any history of violence from Darren Anderson. Make sure he wasn't practicing any kind of Kung Fu shit outside the classroom.'

'Will do... Also, Boss...We've found one of the rings... Not what we're expecting I'm afraid. A local vet called in to say it was removed from a boxer. I've spoken to the owner and he walked the dog somewhere in front of The Rose Gardens in Vicky Park.'

'I don't suppose they found the other ring or Rolex in there as well?'

'No Boss... no sign yet but we'll keep on top of our sources.'

I joined Josh in a deep sigh as we pulled into the street. 'Not a mugging?'

'Nope... unless he dropped it while running away.'

'What about the Italian Stallion?' he couldn't resist.

'He has an alibi but we can't rule out that he had enough dodgy connections to get someone to do his dirty work for him. But where's the motive?'

Josh was chomping with his view: 'she sees something she shouldn't... gets all mouthy about it, especially if he's not paying her enough attention. He gets one of his chums who owe him a favour to sort her out. Could be that he was supposed to frighten her but it went too far.'

'Maybe...'

SEVEN
The Investigator

'Bloody Hell...' Josh expressed my exact sentiments as we stood in front of a glass monolith of an office block. 'Not what I expected... thought we'd be looking for some dump above a chip shop.'

We swished up in the lift to the 20th floor and were ushered into a meeting room by a pert, heavily made-up, bottle-blonde receptionist.

'Thank you for seeing us Mr Beckett,' I began.

'Not at all – please take a seat. You're lucky to catch me. I've just returned from Shanghai.'

We sat in our slippery, black leather chairs, angled with precision. 'Nice offices,' I said as I re-angled my chair to face him more head on. 'I must confess it's not what I expected from a Private Investigator.'

He never reacted to the slight. 'We're used predominantly by corporate companies in the city: part of due diligence etc. The work I did for Mr Anderson was... more as a favour. I appreciate that it could be perceived as seedy.'

There was nothing seedy about his crisp-cut, pinstripe suit, manicured nails and flawlessly veneered teeth. Salt and pepper strands, flecked through his chestnut hair and a hint of crows-feet around the eyes, suspiciously engineered to invite trust. A concerted effort to blend in perhaps or sticking two fingers up at the preconceived view of his profession. 'Business good Mr Beckett?'

He returned a practiced smile – polite but evasive. 'How can I help you Detective Chief Inspector?'

'As I mentioned on the phone, as part of our investigation into the death of Fiona Anderson, we've checked the phone records of all family and friends and your number – including texts – appeared in Darren Anderson's logs.'

'Do you suspect him?' He asked with an even tone.

'We're following all lines of enquiry, enabling us to paint a picture of her final days. Being followed by a Private Investigator may play a part of this.'

'There wasn't much following I'm afraid – more investigating.' He held eye contact in case we had any doubts about having his full attention.

'Can you tell me when Mr Anderson first approached you about this job and what was his brief?'

'As I said, we were friendly through our work association and after a boozy lunch one Friday – about a year ago – he asked for my help. All a bit of a textbook scenario I'm afraid. He believed his wife was having an affair and wanted confirmation.' He seemed non-judgemental.

'Did you find any evidence of an affair?' I asked.

'Yes... fairly quickly. It seemed... well… let's say she didn't take many precautions to hide it. He could've found out himself soon enough. We did a lot of background checking on the boyfriend. Apart from a criminal record ten years ago – he'd kept himself clean although he'd remortgaged his flat to plough more money into his business.'

'How did Mr Anderson react when you showed him the evidence?'

'He remained composed and only showed signs of being shaken when I told him that she was pregnant.' He looked down at some papers on his desk as though to remind us he was a busy man.

'He knew?'

'Yes... yes, I believe I told him about a month prior. We found out that she was scheduled for an appointment at The Princess Alice Hospital in Kensington where she had her children. The good news was that the baby was his. We found medical records confirming that Mr Manchini had a vasectomy. The bad news was that she was booked in for a termination. And before you ask… all our information is obtained by legal means. Like you, I've built up a network of resources.'

I remained poker-faced. No need to make him feel too comfortable. 'How did he react to all this information?'

'There was a lot to digest and a roller coaster of facts. He was affected to begin with but I would say, swiftly built a wall of composure.'

'What would you say his objective was when he found out about the affair? Was he building a case for a divorce?'

'As her infidelity was discovered quite promptly, he wanted us to continue our surveillance to establish if it ended... if it was a one-off fling... that sort of thing. I believe he was also concerned that she'd been targeted for either their wealth or someone who wanted to affect him in business–'

Josh jumped in, 'he was only a Trader. They were more likely all at it, so marital affairs wouldn't hold much weight.'

'Oh... he was more than that. He was involved in some high-financed International deal – lots of zeros if you know what I mean.'

His delusions of grandeur were beginning to grate. 'What were Mr Anderson's instructions to you after he found out about the pregnancy and planned termination?'

'None... Not long after, his wife was murdered.' He shuffled awkwardly at the implication and we left him hanging uncomfortably. 'Well, I feel I've told you all I know, so if you'll excuse me, I'm due at another meeting.'

'One more thing Mr Beckett...' I said as he rose to his feet. 'What type of man was Mr Anderson?'

No longer attempting to hide his impatience, he walked round to our side of the desk. 'If you're looking for me to say that he was a violent megalomaniac, I'm afraid you'll be disappointed. He always presented to me as a rational, even-tempered family man. Even when fundamentally organising for his wife to be spied on, there were never any vindictive undertones. It was almost like he was more concerned about her safety. Believe me... I have dealt with the dregs of life and on a scale of authenticity, he rated highly.'

Josh did not want to leave it there. 'We have a variety of evidence which shows a capability of violence. Are you saying that you had no cause to investigate him, either in a professional capacity or before taking on his case which may have uncovered this?'

He looked at his watch in case we were not taking the hint, 'no... as I said... nothing to indicate a propensity for violence. I'm sorry I must get on.' The door opened and the bottle-blonde walked in with a large parcel. 'I've taken the liberty of copying all the information we've gathered on Mrs Anderson's case.'

We left the glass tower and Josh was grateful to the receptionist for agreeing to courier the parcel to the station. We stopped for a late lunch at a nearby Italian sandwich bar and a popped trouser button, did not deter me from devouring a toasted panini while Josh moaned about what a prick Beckett was, before woofing down his veal escalope ciabatta. I sipped my coffee and reserved my questioning until he swallowed his last crumb.

'Any final pieces of evidence we can scrape together before we arrest Darren Anderson?' I asked.

'Forensics should be finished with his car today so that report should be on your desk when we get back.' He took a swig of his American black. 'It doesn't matter how reasonable he appeared to Beckett, there's enough evidence now to convict. He lied to us about knowing about the pregnancy and the affair, and the abortion would reasonably send any man over the edge.'

'What are your thoughts on Manchini?' I asked.

'Our theory is possible but more of a stretch compared to the credibility of Anderson's motive. I'll follow up all the action points though so nothing comes back to bite us on the bum.'

I knew Josh's view was still blinded by his surety that Anderson was guilty but I had to agree. 'I don't think Manchini cared enough to take notice even if she'd pushed him to the edge and although I'm sure he liked his punters to think he was Mr Mad MacMafia, there's not a gangster I know who'd give him the time of day.'

'Then we need to pick up Anderson.'

EIGHT
The Only Suspect

Angela pulled out the last of the reports from Forensics, 'so plenty of forensic evidence that she'd been to the flat but he already admitted that. No other signs of her staying there: no toothbrush, no love letters...'

'Not surprising,' I said, with Manchini's cock-sure attitude in mind.

'I can't find anything in the statements or CCTV that contradicts his alibi and he's not been in contact with any credible players – just some low-level pond life from his time in Barlinnie,' she read from her notes.

'Boss...' Josh stuck his head around the door. 'We're ready...'

I watched Anderson through the glass as he sat motionless in his chair. Dressed impeccably for the day in the office, his sallow pallor and dark-ringed eyes, betrayed the strain. His equally dapper lawyer was alert, like a squirrel in his grey suit, whispering strategy into his ear. Only Darren did not seem to be listening, his vacant stare, fixed onto the wall opposite.

'His kids were with the mum when we got there. He didn't cause a fuss,' Angela informed me as another indicator of his detachment to what was going on around him.

I would be straining at the bit at this point of an investigation: a suspect under caution with evidence stacked against him, but I still found myself waiting for a reason to explain it all away. Doubting myself or the case?

I followed Josh into the room. The lawyer flexed his shoulders back, ready for the fight as I went through the preliminary, procedural introduction. He remained motionless throughout.

'Mr Anderson... would you like a drink before we start?'

He shook his head dismissively.

'Mr Anderson... are you yet able to provide any proof of your whereabouts at the time of your wife's murder? This is the one piece of evidence that has eluded us. Do you understand that the burden of proof falls on you to produce an alibi which you have failed to do so far?'

'My client has repeatedly told you of his whereabouts...'

'There is CCTV evidence from a petrol station near the A12, making it feasible for you to be in the Victoria Park area.'

'No... I have no evidence.' His deflated demeanour was unmoved.

I pressed on: 'Why did you have your wife followed Mr Anderson?'

His lawyer began to object but he held up his hand to stop him before speaking for himself. 'I believed she was having an affair.'

'And how did you feel when you were told that she was having an affair and in fact was pregnant.'

He looked up for the first time, 'it wasn't his... it was mine.'

'And you discovered that she was going to have an abortion.'

'She wouldn't have...'

'She had an appointment booked. What made you think she wouldn't go through with it?' I asked.

'Did you argue Darren?' Josh prodded. 'Did she laugh in your face?'

'No...'

'We've heard how cruel she could be. Did she tell you where to go? That she was going to get rid of your baby, then get rid of you?'

'No... No...' he gripped the edge of the table.

'Did she tell you how she preferred the Italian and your years together meant nothing?' Josh leant forward, invading his space.

It felt as though everyone jumped out of their seats simultaneously as Darren screamed, 'NO!' at Josh and reached out to throw a punch. His lawyer's chair fell backwards as he attempted to restrain Darren and I pushed back to prevent Josh falling on me.

The lawyer pulled Darren back into his chair, where he collapsed into a sobbing heap.

I stood up – my arms spread-eagled: 'okay... everyone... let's all calm down.'

The lawyer straightened his suit. 'That was unnecessary provocation and if you pull another stunt like that, I shall end this interview and submit a formal complaint.'

Darren had stopped sobbing and the lawyer passed him a tissue to wipe his face. Josh sat unrepentant back in his seat. I picked up the file that had fallen onto the floor before asking: 'did you argue Mr Anderson? Did you confront her about her affair and the abortion?'

'We did argue, but not about the affair. I didn't tell her that I knew although I'm sure she wanted me to know. That was the point you see... she wanted more of my attention... anyone's and everyone's attention.'

'You didn't mind her having the affair?' I asked.

'Of course, I did!' He screamed and Josh twitched, ready for action but Anderson seemed to deflate like a balloon. 'I loved her...' he continued. 'But I didn't know what to do. What she needed to do was get some help but she wouldn't have it. I had her followed to make sure she was safe. I knew it would come to a head and if I wouldn't play the game and confront her, she'd tell me about it anyway.'

'But there was a confrontation. The baby... When did this happen?'

'A couple of weeks before, she–' he trailed off, strain on his face as he tried to contain his emotions. 'I told her I found out about the pregnancy because the hospital rang me by mistake. I don't know if she believed it but she found the excuse to vent her fury. She did threaten to have an abortion...' He looked up squarely at me for the first time.

'And you thought she was lying?'

'I don't believe she would've gone through with it. I believe she said it to get back at me in the only way she knew how. To get back at me for thinking that I didn't care enough to notice that she'd been having an affair.'

'But she'd made an appointment for the termination,' I said.

'I know, she told me but I let her rant. If it helped her to get her fury out of her system, I was happy to take it.'

Josh leant forward. 'You're expecting us to believe that a woman in her forties, who's vain enough to spend all that money looking good and with the world and his wife knowing how she couldn't cope with her children – would be happy having another baby?'

He fronted up to Josh. 'Yes I am. Her problems, her insecurities and loneliness only began once the kids didn't need her as much. Babies she loved. Even if you look at the lowest common denominator – she'd be needed unconditionally, placing her smack in the centre of all the attention.'

'Sounds a stretch Mr Anderson. We've seen you've a temper when you don't hear what you want. You have her followed because you're a control freak… she's screaming at you... you don't get the answer you want and in a blind fury – smash her head in.' I allowed Josh the space to push and noted the lawyer placing a restraining hand on Anderson's arm. 'What man would put up with another man shagging his wife as a form of therapy? Maybe you didn't know that The Italian was firing blanks and that's what made you flip.'

'I wouldn't divorce her – let alone murder her. I don't want my children growing up without a mother.' The anger seemed to have diminished and his eyes were brimming.

'Maybe you'd had enough of her griping and bitching and had a bit on the side yourself? We interviewed some of your colleagues – quite a beauty pageant at your office. Not hard to find a sympathetic shoulder to cry on.'

He seemed to switch off from Josh's baiting although the lawyer shuffled uncomfortably and attempted to catch Josh's eye so he could give him one of his £500 an hour, glares. Josh did not oblige but sat back in his chair which was code for me to pick up.

I opened the file in front of me and pulled out a sheet. 'We've some forensic evidence that you'll need to explain: a footprint of a Nike trainer was found at the scene of the murder. The same trainer and size was retrieved from your house – freshly cleaned.'

'I run ...' he mumbled, 'three, four times a week. My trainers get muddy – they get washed weekly.'

I maintained the pace. 'Soil samples collected from the foot-well of your car were matched to the samples collected from the scene. How could that be Mr Anderson?'

Panic creased his face. He looked across at his lawyer. 'That can't be... I've never been there.'

The lawyer took over. 'Have these samples been cross-referenced with the parks and areas Mr Anderson runs in?'

'The combination is unique,' I confirmed.

'I haven't been there... I didn't kill her... That must have been planted...'

Josh jumped back in: 'your mistake was lying about the baby. Why should we or a jury believe anything you say?'

He slumped against the table with his head in his hands, 'I didn't kill her.'

'Mr Anderson,' I coaxed, 'who would plant evidence against you?' He shook his head with his fingers now gripping his hair.

As we left the interview room, I was confronted by D.I. Golding, making no attempt to hide the fact that he'd been observing the interview.

'Hi ya Josie.'

'Dave...'

'You don't mind, do you?'

'Josh... You go ahead. I'll catch up.' I turned to Golding. 'No... Not at all... Always happy to contribute to a colleague's learning process.'

'The Chief Super. told me to keep abreast of developments in case I need to step in.'

Ten years this arsehole had been in my orbit, rattling my cage – never quite getting over a lost promotion that I picked up. 'Yes... he told me but as I told him – I don't think there'll be a need.'

'Hard to say.' He kept his gaze on Anderson through the glass. 'These disciplinaries have unpredictable outcomes. You can't go off-piste like that and not expect some consequences.'

I placed my hand lightly on his arm. 'Thanks Dave. Your concern is touching. But... got to go... busy, busy, busy...'

I refocused and caught up with Josh in the corridor, 'that expensive lawyer will throw a team at this and crawl over every single speck of evidence so make sure everything is water-tight.' I instructed. 'Follow up on the challenge of the soil being planted in the car.'

'You're not serious…' he said.

'If he's raised it, you can bank on the lawyer being all over it. If their investigative team find something that we haven't, it could tip the case. Find out who else had access to his car.'

We reached my office and I collapsed into my chair, failing to keep mental exhaustion at bay.

'Are you still not convinced Boss?' Josh asked with no attempt to hide his frustration.

'We're about to take a father away from two children who have just lost their mother. I want our evidence to be absolute and not neglect anything else that comes to light.' A consequence that I just couldn't shake. 'They'll need to deflect the guilt away from Anderson and the prospective candidate will be The Lover. Get him in again and see if there are any holes in his story. Get forensics back in the Anderson house to see if we can find the rock that was used. I don't care if they have to dig up the whole garden.'

'Doctor Monroe will be pleased...'

The phone on my desk rang as Josh left the office. I stared at it, willing it to shut up – anticipating another summons to upstairs. Finally succumbing, 'Connelly...'

Although I met only silence, I was convinced I could hear a faint sound of breathing. 'Detective Chief Inspector Connelly. Can I help you?'

'You got it wrong at the press conference. She wasn't a loving mother.'

NINE
Amy's Story

I could hardly believe she was already Year 4 and the first term was nearly at an end. I looked over to the Reception kids, dwarfed by their oversized coats, bought for extended wear but hardly believable that they would grow to twice their size. They were still babies. *She* was still a baby… my baby... No longer needing to give me that over the shoulder glance for reassurance, too soon replaced by a confident dismissal as she chattered exuberantly with her mates.

An icy stare from the Head Mistress was enough to silence us parents during prayers in the freezing cold playground as we were transported back to our conditioned youth of catholic subservience. There was something strangely comforting about the collective chanting from a shared culture as my self-soothing rocking, followed the sway of the prayer. Conjuring up an image of American Indians huddled in a similar fashion, reciting their stories of ancestors long gone but determinedly unforgotten. The obligatory *Hail Mary* was followed by a request to pray for some family or another, suffering tragic circumstances.

'Jaysus... Sure I swear she's got a fecking hotline to A&E!' My friend Bernadette whispered, not quite soft enough and further egged on by the sanctimonious looks from the church groupies. 'Yeah… you can feck off as well...' Her Irish lilt distinguishable through her threatening – less audible – mumblings. I lowered my head in mock reverence to hide my smile. 'Right… I'm off...' She tugged at my coat sleeve to join her.

I resisted a while, to steal one last glance at Clara as her line snaked through the school doors, hoping to catch her sneaky – *I love you.* Yes... there it was. Now I was ready for whatever the day had to throw at me or pulverise me would be more accurate, if the last year was anything to go by.

Well at least today was a lingering day. My next deadline was not until Friday and I did not have to go into town for a meeting until Thursday. Today, I felt smugly gratified, knowing that her final peek would confirm that her mum was like the others: hanging around for a chat, maybe off for a coffee or organising a longed-for sleepover.

I tuned out as Bernadette began her morning rant, confident that I would get the gist of it by the final throes. I looked around at the other friends from my mum-gang, finishing up in their respective huddles. The necessity of playing the game with the mums from their other kid's classes, pre-empting the melt-down of an ostracised child. Furtive glances in my direction, confirming that they would be over soon.

An overwhelming stab of guilt pierced my thoughts as I watched turban-clad Fiona Lancing, manoeuvre her way cautiously through the exiting throng. What had I to feel sorry about when she was struggling through chemo with two children under ten to look after? But guilt had been my constant companion throughout my life. My Catholic guilt driven by... well just about anything and everything. Guilt, from leaving my mum behind in her self-inflicted, unhappy marriage; guilt from being more successful than my Alpha-male husband and now – my all-consuming guilt about Clara. A bundle of guilt handed to me to accompany my bundle of joy.

Did I have a guilt-free day since she was born? I guess not... And even now, when I transformed my life so that I could be around most of the time, it was under such crap circumstances and I was still so crap at organising our lives, that the guilt found no reason to evacuate its accommodating residence.

'Amy...'

I turned to face Paula Wagstaff as she gently touched my arm. 'Hi Paula... how did the run go?'

'Great thanks... we raised over £2000. I wanted to check

if the cake sale was still on after school tomorrow?'

Shit... 'Yeah… still all good. Drop your cakes off in the morning as usual.'

'Fab... I don't know how you do it? Working... running a home... chairing the fund-raising...'

'Badly – that's how...' She did not seem to appreciate my honesty and smiled sweetly before walking off. Maybe she wanted me to be as perfect a mum as I did?

'Oiy...' I dug Bernadette in the ribs as she engaged our other friend, Stella, with her rant. 'Why didn't you remind me that I'd organised a cake-sale for tomorrow?'

'Christ... not another bloody one. Haven't we raised enough for that blood-sucking, frustrated nun? They could build ten more playgrounds with what we've give them?'

Stella joined me on my free side. 'Don't worry, we'll help you out – won't we Bernie? Make sure you take an extra dose of HRT so you don't punch anyone.'

On cue, the tap... tap... tapping of Miss Sinclair's ring against her office window was our signal to depart her kingdom.

'Come on... let's grab a bite in The Green Turtle...' Bernadette suggested, while surreptitiously sticking up two fingers at the window.

I had a moment's hesitation as the cake sale had thrown my shaky schedule. Fuck it. 'Yeah... come on...'

Anna Rosso, the final member of our gang, jogged from the school reception out onto the road to catch up, waving a new school tie in the air which meant that her daughter Maria, must now be onto her sixth.

We settled down at our regular table in the cafe, positioned so we could see if anyone else from the school was encroaching on our sanctum but secluded enough to ensure that they were unable to hear us slating them.

I could only see Jazz Hands – AKA Bianca Rainer – and her clique today. So labelled, because she was clever enough to keep out of sight when any real graft needed doing, but up there, front of stage, to lap up the applause and plaudits. School discos, funerals, you name it... her timing was a thing to behold. We exchanged shallow smiles of acknowledgement before turning to our preferred companions.

'The bitch that said it, is over there...' Anna kicked off, pulling back her mop of dark Mediterranean curls into a ponytail. Not having a clue what she was talking about, I made the appropriate noises for her to go on.

'She called Stella, "Stella the Fella." That little poison dwarf... shuffling around with those kids attached to her apron strings like Mother Theresa with her butter-wouldn't-melt smirk. All the while, shit-stirring behind everyone's back.'

Regardless of the fact that we were all a bit guilty of the same, I pulled a suitable disgusted face, knowing that Stella could undeniably stick up for herself. Beautiful and exotic, her mixed-race colouring and athletic build, brought out the worst in Elaine – otherwise referred to as the 'poison dwarf.' I was certain of the day that sparked Elaine's spite: Stella, strolling into the playground in her running shorts. A crime in Elaine's book at any age, let alone for a 49 year old woman, despite a testament to Stella's recently relinquished army career.

On a drunken night out, when we wore down Stella with questions about her numerous tours in the Middle East, we were stunned in our inebriated stupors as she confided that she had in fact killed on many occasions and even at times with her bare hands. Our own shared stories of bastard exs or petulant kids, left behind as insignificant trivia. The irony lost on Elaine that Stella was the last person you would want to pick a fight with.

'Go on Stella...' Anna egged her on, 'fight...! Fight...! Fight...!'

Stella stood up and pushed back her chair, 'I'm popping

to the loo...' she smiled sweetly. Jazz Hands' gang shuffled uncertainly as Stella passed their table. She offered them a well-practised wave. They returned duplicitous smiles, punctuated with cowardly hope that she had not heard their snipes.

'It's pointless baiting her,' I said to Anna as I spied shamelessly on Jazz Hands' clique. 'If the Taliban couldn't get a rise out of her – I'm sure you won't.'

Bernadette picked up her vibrating phone to half-look at a message coming through as Stella returned to her seat and our food was served. I had already cut through my beautifully poached egg and was pushing the crushed avocado onto the same fork when Bernadette's lack of background chatter and/or cursing, proved too much of a distraction. 'What's up?' I asked, my brunch-laden fork suspended before my mouth. She did not answer, her face scrunched up as though she were trying to focus on a photo. 'Come on Bernie,' I persevered before devouring my first forkful.

'It's from Sarah... She says Miss Scott isn't off sick as we all thought. She's been reported missing...'

There was an inaudible buzzing in the playground for the rest of that week as busy worker bees, gathered information and returned to the hive of their clique. Bernadette's friend Sarah was a Teaching Assistant in the school and not a known gossip so fed back a sensible view, albeit little information to report. Miss Scott – the well-respected Deputy Head – had simply not turned up for work on the previous Friday. The Teaching Staff were interviewed by The Police and drilled along the same lines, 'when had they last seen her...? Was she depressed...? Did she talk about her private life...?'

I stood behind the trestle-table, stacked with sticky, sickly sweet cakes, numbly repeating my sales mantra to the grabbing little hands in front of me: '50p... 50p... 50p...'

Bernadette and Stella, deftly dealt with the masses while Paula Wagstaff, silently and efficiently, replenished the tables.

I was in a bit of a daze after hearing the news about Miss Scott – Catherine to me, since she had supported us so sincerely through our domestic upheavals, minimising the impact on Clara at school. She oozed such a genuine interest in the children, in contrast to the Head's unashamed focus on her power base. She was so intertwined with our history – a touchstone. My concern for her safety was enveloped in my panic at her loss.

The Previous Year

Separation

We sat opposite each other at the dining table in our newly refurbished, top-of-the-range kitchen. Since over-taking me in earning power (to my relief), Marc assumed command of the house renovations and filled it with all the latest gizmos to reinforce his financial status to both himself and any invited or uninvited guest. As it seemed to replicate every kitchen I had visited in West Essex, it was hard to recall which (drunken) conversations I had and where, because it was another fucking white kitchen... And I sat, staring past his shoulders at one of the three integral ovens I would never use and up to the floating steel structure, masquerading as an oven-hood.

He'd finished telling me that he'd been offered an unbelievable job opportunity in Dubai. The silence which now hung between us, confirmation that I neither wanted to go and he did not want to stay. Why didn't I make it easier for him and say it and wrap up the end of our relationship in a neat little bow? I was the one most capable of articulating such things. But I didn't feel like making it that easy. I had spent eight of the last ten years playing down my role as the main bread winner and not even asking him to take his fair share of the child-rearing duties for fear of implying that he could be a house husband. And when his earnings kicked in enough for us to materialistically live the life he wanted, and for me to move to flexible contract work and the life I wanted with Clara, I spent the last two years as penance, praising his masterful ability as hunter-gatherer. Finally realising that I no longer loved or liked the person he had become.

We were practically living separate lives and even our family time together was so cemented by Clara's presence that when she was quiet – we had nothing to say.

He was not much good at this game. I could sit in silence, staring at him forever. He didn't have the emotional maturity to take the lead so I let him mumble his mumblings. 'Er... obviously I'll miss Clara – but we could FaceTime...'

'You don't want us to go as a family?' He did love Clara so I knew it was a low blow. He picked at a ragged cuticle, a well-worn tell that he wanted to avoid eye contact. His curly fringe flopped down over his eyes, regardless of his absence, a mannerism I would see replicated daily by Clara.

'For fuck sake Amy! Why are you making this so hard?'

'Because I don't know what, "this" is exactly...' Untrue of course but it would be in my interest to play the wounded party. 'Is there someone else?' asking but not caring.

'No... No...'

I believed him as I knew every little nuance of his attempts at fibbing, preferring to tell the blunt, unadulterated truth with no empathy for the consequences – except with Clara.

He wouldn't have thought through the hurt he inflicted if he'd told the truth of an affair. No... Like me, he'd realised in his own dumb way that it was the end of our life together, although I had no intention of admitting that to him anytime soon. He was embarking on his steep career trajectory and all the excitement and pressure that came with it and I was utterly burnt-out by mine. We were at different places in our lives and truthfully, needed different people to share it with.

'Nothing will change for you financially. This job ensures that I can finance both lives and Clara will still want for nothing.'

'Except a dad...' Low, low blow...

His face crumpled for a moment, transporting me back to when we used to work together, fancied each other like hell but unable to do anything about it until I left the company. The pent-up chemistry resulted in the most explosive honeymoon-period of any relationship I'd ever had and most likely ever will.

'So we're clear Marc... you let Clara down once – with a missed FaceTime or a visit – I will find you and kill you.' I meant it. 'And you can pay to change this fucking kitchen before you go.'

We did our best to explain to Clara that Daddy would be working in another country but there was no getting away from the heart-breaking moment when she broke down sobbing. I thought that Marc might even change his mind as he was so affected by her reaction. It seemed to be his first realisation of what he was losing. My anger at him was my anger at myself for accepting the collapse of our relationship. I didn't want for my child to come from a broken home and I contributed majorly to the situation.

'I'll speak to you every day and I'll be back to see you... and you can come over to see me.' He blubbered. But she was inconsolable.

And so, he left... There was no talk of divorce or even the reality that we were separating but an unspoken acceptance that the distance should do the job.

Sitting outside Miss Scott's office, I was overwhelmed with new sensations: shame... admitting out loud the failure of my marriage and the presumption that we would be judged at this religious school. Then panic that Clara would be treated differently or how would they cope with her if she started misbehaving in class as a reaction to her father's absence?

I could not have been more wrong. My meeting with Miss Scott was a one-stop therapy session. She was like some mystical Empath. I couldn't help myself. I cried... I spluttered... I revealed my fears for Clara and yes... my guilt.

She listened with enduring patience and comforted me. She responded like she had all the time in the world. After my emotional outpouring, she took me through some practical coping mechanisms for Clara and reassured me that the most anybody need know was that Clara's father was working abroad and she was adapting to his absence.

I left her office, my head filled with admiration for the life-affecting skills of this remarkable woman and realising with gratitude that it was a welcome distraction from my own woes. Although Miss Scott left for a school field trip the following day, I felt better grounded to support Clara and reassured on her return as she kept a motherly eye on us both and called me in frequently to see how we were doing. I valued these sessions alone with her. No convoluted stories made-up to put off nosy-parkers or pretence of coping – which was my default position with my well-meaning, mum-gang.

Making a decision

'I can't just do nothing...' We were back in The Green Turtle Cafe, going through all the worse-case scenarios of Catherine's disappearance because there could only be worse-case scenarios. Responsibility ran through her veins. She was the least likely person to leave, let alone, leave without word.

'She could simply have had an accident and is lying in a ditch somewhere. Nothing sinister,' Bernadette bluntly offered.

'Bernie!' Anna was close to tears.

'I don't necessarily mean that she's dead. She could be unconscious in a hospital somewhere. I mean it can't be anything else. It's not like she has any enemies.'

'The hospitals are the first place they'll check.'

Stella was right but so was Bernadette. How could Catherine have any enemies? 'Maybe I should talk to the boyfriend?' I suggested.

'How do you know she had a boyfriend? I heard she's a lesbian.'

'No Anna – that's Miss Sinclair.'

Anna raised her eyebrows to confirm that she was not surprised and asked: 'how come you feel the need to get so involved Amy? I didn't realise you knew her that well.'

I was not in the mood to explain my relationship with Catherine, also knowing that they wouldn't be able to help themselves but feel affronted by the fact that I hadn't confided in them. If I was to be any use in finding Catherine, I would have to do it without their help.

Stella reacted to my lack of response and came to my aid, 'I hear they've already pulled in the boyfriend. He's a Maths teacher up at All Saints Comp. Very studious and not a typical candidate for foul play.'

'The quiet ones are the worst,' Bernadette decided. 'But The Police know what they're doing so I'm sure they'll get to the bottom of it and there's not much we can do.'

The best thing I could do was to think... think... think... about everything she ever told me and go to The Police. 'I'm off... catch you later...' I left a £20 note by my plate, grabbed my coat and headed for the door, not even stopping for a knowing smirk for Jazz Hands.

'No... I've already told you... it was totally out of character.' I was straining hard to contain myself but Jesus Christ I was ready to punch this arsehole in the face. How could I convey a sense of urgency without seeming hysterical to this twelve year old Police Constable, devoid of any sensibilities?

'Look... I don't know how much Miss Sinclair has already told you but as *I've* been trying to tell you, I knew something of her private life. Here... I made some notes...' He recoiled as though I'd pulled out a machete. Maybe I was appearing more manic than I thought. An uncomfortable shuffling in his seat followed as he resettled and I flipped through my notebook.

He seemed keen to put me back in my box. 'You know something of her private life but you've never been to her house, met her family or boyfriends and don't know who her other friends are...'

'I know... it sounds disjointed... but that's how she lived her life. I'm not sure any one person knew her entirely but it doesn't mean what I have to say isn't valid. Please... please take this seriously.'

Pissed off was now written all over his face so bang went any goodwill. 'If you'd like to go through any further salient points from your notes Mrs Whitehead, I'll pass them onto Missing Persons who can add them to her file.'

I left after providing my, 'salient points' which he jotted down with a well-practiced deadpan expression, presumably saved for humouring crazies. I could only hope that they would take some action as others came forward – like her family. I mean… where the hell were they?

By bedtime, this hope had evaporated. I tossed and turned imagining the worst, spurred on by incessant web-searches of murders in the area in the last couple of years and with Epping Forest up the road – an urban myth, perpetuated by The Krays legend– as the resting place for countless victims. I felt that in the morning, I needed to go back and show him real crazy. Maybe that would put a bomb up his arse.

But morning came too soon and was overrun with work deadlines and another one of Marc's inconvenient calls. I threw him a filthy look over Clara's shoulder as he knew FaceTiming before she went to school, wrecked her for the rest of the day. It seemed that as she became more resilient to the situation, he became needier. We had to get out of the door in twenty minutes for me to make a meeting in town. How to break this up without ending up as the bad guy? I sent him a shitty text while coaxing Clara. He looked down at his phone so I knew he received it.

'Come on darling... let's see if we can get in on time to pick up your Golden Certificate and you can show Daddy when you get home.'

'Well done sweetie... what did you get that for?' he asked.

Are you fucking kidding me? This prompted a five minute explanation from Clara but we could have made it in time if the traffic was not against us. And of course, it was... I pulled up – double parked across the road from the school gates. Lugging her book bag, P.E. bag and lunch pack, we sprinted across the road and inside the gates. After a hasty kiss and a gentle nudge towards the line and with a cacophony of car horns tooting my obstruction, I darted back to the car.

The next few seconds were dreamlike... I heard her unique, distinguishable call of – 'Mummy...!' Spinning around to the sound of a thud, followed by piercing screams. I threw myself back over the road, pushed hysterical children out of the way to get to the limp body of my only child.

A primitive scream rose from within me. I couldn't

breathe. I wanted to scoop her up in my arms but I could see blood seeping from her head and was subconsciously wired not to move her. Paula was by her side in an instant, checking she was breathing. I rambled on about keeping her head still. She was telling me she was alive but I couldn't focus. Paula used to be a nurse or something so I felt safe... safe for Clara... safe for me... I held Clara's hand and stroked her face, vaguely aware that the crowds around us were being pushed back until I only felt the presence of adults. Someone was shouting that an ambulance was on its way.

'Amy... Amy...'

Paula was trying to speak to me... reassure me I presume... I didn't know... I desperately wanted them to get here. 'Hurry...!' I screamed.

The paramedics worked around her like a swarm – moving as one. I was gently nudged back but clutched hold of her hand once more in the ambulance. The enormity of losing her overwhelmed me as the fragile thread of life dared to snap. Chanting like a shaman for her to be okay... to wake up... to smile…

I sat in the waiting area alone. Paula had tried to stay but I insisted she left. Bernadette, Anna and Stella were likewise turned away. I needed to be alone... I deserved to be alone... This was my fault.

'God... if you're there... if you're listening... please, please don't take my baby yet. Let her live a life. I'll take any punishment in return... anything...'

'Mrs Whitehead... Mrs Whitehead...' I looked up at the nurse or doctor. I wasn't sure. They were all wearing the same green scrubs. 'I'm Doctor Addis. Clara's back in her room if you'd like to come with me...'

I tried to focus as he reeled off her progress: a hairline skull fracture that should heal on its own; the MRI scan showed no damage or clots; a clean break in her right arm. I left him trailing as I entered the room and ran to her bed.

She looked like a broken doll. Her little arm plastered up, a bandage around her head and hooked up to various drips and machines. I sat on the bed beside her and held her hand. 'Is she asleep?'

Doctor Addis returned to my side. 'She hasn't come around yet, but that's usual. It's the brain's way of protecting itself.'

'*I* should have protected her.'

'Is there anyone we should call Mrs Whitehead?'

'No... I'm fine thank you.' I knew I needed to call Marc but I wasn't ready for the accompanying angst. I wanted this time alone with Clara, watching her breathing. I would never stop watching her breathing.

Memories played tricks with my mind as I was transported back to times spent in this hospital with her as a baby. Our first visit with bronchiolitis, gasping for air or the time she swallowed a plastic gem from her Disney Princess crown. She loved the attention and I was worried she would do it again so she could return. I felt a sharp pain in my neck and I was suddenly aware of the bleeping of one of the machines. I realised I had fallen asleep.

'Mummy... I feel sick...'

I jolted up. Not sure if I was dreaming. No... she was awake. 'Alright Princess...' I hit the call button and a nurse was instantly at my side.

'I feel sick...' she repeated.

The nurse held a small cardboard bowl to her mouth as I tenderly rubbed her back, blubbering nonsense as I tried to hold myself together. I marvelled at the colour that had returned to her corpse-like body. The flash of blue of her eyes; a flush rising in her cheeks and the deep plum, pumping through her lips, even her wonky little pearl teeth, flashing as she tried to smile. The nurse was brilliant, joking with her when she finished and making us both feel instantly at ease. Clara giggled at her Jamaican accent and asked her to repeat some words that she thought sounded funny. The nurse got her back and made Clara repeat some of her own words with her Essex twang and they were soon laughing together. I knew *she* would not have left her child run under the wheels of a car.

The doctor arrived and joined in the banter. I couldn't put it off any longer. It was time to call Marc so I popped out as the doctor examined Clara. Maybe I was too tired to break it to him gently or maybe I was too angry that he was living on the other side of the world without any responsibilities and that he should bear part of the blame. If he hadn't called this morning... no I didn't mean that... the blame was all mine...

Regardless, I launched a poison dagger straight at him: the blow – blunt and brutal. I knew I was hurting him but inflicting pain did not ease my own. When silence was followed by a gentle sob, I felt no pity amongst my swirling rage and I told him to 'get a fucking grip...' and to call back in half an hour to FaceTime Clara.

Hunger followed her sickness so by the time Marc managed to FaceTime she was stuffing a chocolate croissant into her mouth and flashing her cast which the nurse and doctor had already signed. I could hear him say that he would be home soon.

Feeling a presence at the door I turned around to see Paula: walking, breathing dependability. We worked closely together for the school's fund-raising activities and went for the odd brunch but never crossed into the realms of friendship. But what was friendship if not all that she had done for us today? Ironically, I responded to my close friend's texts of concern and kept them at bay. I hadn't thought of Paula and here she was.

For a fleeting moment, I unreasonably thought that she was judging me but it was another manifestation of my self-loathing, deflecting off others. I felt a worthless bitch when she unloaded a sports bag with everything Clara would need for her stay, even an iPad donated by the school for the duration. As she pulled out a pink pair of Princess Pyjamas, I crumbled. I couldn't help myself. I ran to the toilets, far away from Clara's earshot. Locking myself in a cubicle, I could feel the bile rise in my stomach and I retched down the pan. I heaved and sobbed until there was nothing left.

Losing sense of time, crashed there in a heap, the events of the last year merged into one. Marc leaving... Catherine disappearing... and now Clara, a near fatal accident... all nearly lost to me in some form. I dragged myself up and after splashing my face with cold water, returned to Clara's room, where Paula had joined in entertaining and offered me a reassuring smile, almost setting me off again. Another nurse arrived with balloons, cards and presents which were greeted with shrieks of delight.

Paula remained invaluable. The lack of a close friendship made it easier as boundaries were maintained and it kept in check the threat of my emotional breakdown. She volunteered to fetch some clean clothes and other stuff for me so I gave her a list, alongside the keys to my house. And true to her word, she returned within a couple of hours. As the sun dipped, Clara and I were left on our own, apart from the regular checks by the nurse. Clara was clutching her Golden Certificate which Paula had dropped in with her gifts. She pulled her sad face, 'I'm sorry Mummy...'

I squeezed her hand and swallowed back a sob, 'don't be a silly sausage... you've nothing to be sorry for. Mummy should have made sure you were in your line properly.'

'I know I should've stayed in the playground. Miss Sinclair says we should. I wanted us to get my certificate. I thought you'd forgotten.'

'Well, you have it now and it's fantastic. Well done darling, I'm so proud of you and you've been so brave.'

She allowed herself a brief smile before her dimples disappeared once more with a serious frown: 'will you get into trouble Mummy or the man who ran me over?'

'No darling. It was an accident. Nobody's fault...' But it

was... it was *my* fault. I had already been contacted by the police, a much different encounter than a couple of days ago. They offered support and said they were questioning the driver. I didn't want him to take the blame away from me with the mere technicality that he was driving the car.

My phone buzzed and I could see it was Marc trying to FaceTime Clara. I handed the phone over and felt grateful for his one redeeming quality: his ability to make Clara giggle and squeal.

In the same spot, less than twenty-four hours later, he walked into her room clutching an oversized Tigger.

'Daddy!'

I could see he was floored by the sight of his precious baby lying there, bashed-up and bandaged. I wasn't sure how or if he would have coped seeing her unconscious.

Her contagious enthusiasm, a joyous distraction, could not mask the physical signs that he was close to breaking down. After greeting me with an affectionate kiss on the cheek and an awkward pause, to confirm that I was not going to fall into his arms, he bounded over to Clara and gave her as much of a squeeze as her wrappings and wires would allow. She squeezed back and reserved as big a one for Tigger.

We were grateful that she was back at home after a week. The cast on her arm still proudly present and a gauze over the superficial wound, covering a hairline fracture in her skull. Headaches from her bruised brain were subsiding; visits from her friends, negating the need to remain still.

Marc took up residence in the spare room, smartly furnished so far from a hardship. He remained vague about his return to Dubai, working remotely in the meantime. I defiantly ignored his overtures of reconciliation – not trusting myself when I felt so vulnerable. Clara was thrilled to have him home and bounced and squealed, 'we're a family again.' He bounced and squealed back, forcing me to walk away as though I hadn't heard.

We rubbed along during Clara's recovery and he never once reproached me for the accident happening while Clara was in my care. I was sure his presumption would have been that I would have kicked off royally with an aggressive defence – how wrong he would have been.

Another young Policeman came to visit in that time and took a statement of my version of events. There was an issue with the driver – with witnesses corroborating erratic driving – so the officer was clearly disappointed when I confirmed that I had not seen the accident and was further thrown when I insisted it was my fault.

We sat in an uncomfortable silence as the last details of the statement were written up, sealing the document with my signature. The officer took a final swig of his coffee and I dared to ask what had crept back into my thoughts as we sat ill at ease together, 'is there any news of Catherine Scott?'

In search of Catherine

Stella sat opposite me at the island in her tolerable oak kitchen. She looked like a professional athlete after her gym workout while I looked like a heap of body fluids. I gulped down the orange juice on offer.

'I don't know Amy... Don't you think we should leave it to the police? Our meddling might get in the way. Why do you want to take this on anyway? Haven't you got enough on your plate with Clara and the return of the Prodigal Husband?'

'It's because of Clara. Catherine was such an amazing support when Marc left – to both of us. I feel like I've abandoned her if I don't help. Wouldn't you want your friends looking for you if you were in danger?' I realised I was shouting. 'Sorry... look... you're the most experienced out of any of us–'

'I was in the army – not the police for Christ's sake.'

'I know... but you know what I mean. You'll have a more logical approach to investigating and if we do get into a bit of bother... I'm not saying we'll go looking for it... but if we do... I know who I'd rather have my back.'

She stared at me in frustration. As I saw her discretely slip out of Catherine Scott's office on a couple of occasions, I hoped she was benefitting from the same support that I'd received. 'Don't you want to help find Catherine?'

'I'm going to pretend you never said that…'

'I'm sorry... Please Stella… I'd been doing the same if it was you.'

'I know you fool.' She held her head in her hands as I goaded her and eventually looked up. 'They'll have to be rules... this is not a game. If I say stop – we stop. If we get in the way of the police investigation – we stop. If we're in physical danger and I say we need to go – we go. I also don't want the others to know. I could do without a running commentary and if we get ourselves into sticky situations, I don't want them dragged into it. Agreed...?'

'Yes... Agreed...'

'Where do you want to start?' She asked.

I retrieved my sports rucksack from under the island. 'I spent quite a bit of time talking with Catherine after Marc left and as we discussed my troubles, she reciprocated and told me some of the things that had happened in her life.' I pulled out my notebook and pen. 'Before I went to my useless interview with the police, I made notes of anything that I thought might be useful.'

Stella had her own ideas: 'why don't we start at her flat?'

'Do ya think? Won't the police be all over it?'

'She's still only technically a Missing Person. I'm not sure she'll warrant that much resource yet.'

We agreed to meet there after lunch. Stella needed to fetch something before meeting up and when standing conspicuously behind the block of flats where Catherine lived, I discovered what. 'Where did you get them?' She was holding the keys to Catherine's flat.

'Remember, I used to do a couple of hours on a Friday morning in the school reception. I found out that some of the teachers kept spare keys to their homes in the school's key cupboard in case they were caught out. I remembered Catherine's family crest, key ring.'

We waited out of sight near the communal front door which was security locked. As a young professional left the building, she jumped forward and caught the door before it closed.

We climbed the two flights of stairs to her floor, keeping our heads down in anticipation of twitching curtains.

'Are you alright there, Sweetie?' Stella was through the front door as I turned around towards the direction of the voice. I smiled vacantly – panic rendering me stupid. 'Was that one of Catherine's friends I saw go into her flat? Are you with her?'

'Er... yes...' She looked harmless enough, only sticking her head out to show off her fresh shampoo and set. Smart in her M&S classics, she was visibly a few social levels away from reliance on a winter fuel allowance but a nosy neighbour all the same.

'Is Catherine back? It's that I've taken in a few parcels for her. I've tried knocking a few times... Wasn't that her, I heard go in?'

'No... Sorry... only us...' I returned down the few steps to her landing. 'We had a spare set of her keys. We haven't heard from her either and we were checking she wasn't ill.' My phone pinged with an impatient text from Stella, comprising of question and exclamation marks. I replied as I smiled reassuring: *You go ahead and I'll deal with the neighbour...*

'Oh no Sweetie... I think that lot from the school had checked already and maybe your friend there or maybe I saw her at the school? Catherine takes me to the school events you know. She's good like that. Do you know where she's gone?'

What to say? Should I have bolted because the plan was to try and sneak in and out unseen? Too late for that.

'Sorry... we don't know yet.' I moved closer. She smelt of lavender and toast. 'Did she say anything to you before you last saw her? You know... maybe mention that she might be going away or somewhere she'd been that she enjoyed.'

'Well... I know she loved China,' she said. 'But those kinds of trips she planned well in advance. Isn't one to dash off on impulse, our Catherine. She comes in quite late sometimes. I don't sleep right through so have my radio on but I hear her when she comes home.'

'Has anyone been to the flat while she's been away?'

'Well yes... as I said... them lot from school but no one since.' She placed her hand on mine, 'you don't think something's happened to her do you Sweetie? You hear such dreadful things.'

Her eyes were brimming as I placed my hand on hers, 'we'll do our best to find her Mrs...'

'Wilbur... Call me Dottie, Sweetie.'

'I'm Amy. Have you got a pen Dottie? I'll leave you my number in case you hear anything. Is that alright?'

'Oh... okay...'

Shit... I couldn't leave her in that state. 'Come on... let me see you back in...'

My phone continued to ping manically as Stella sent through a shed load of pictures from the flat. Taking a sneaky look as I shared a pot of tea with Dottie, I was relieved to see it was of the flat's layout and no dead bodies. I kept Dottie chatting before tearing myself away as I heard Stella tap on the door. We left separately with a plan to regroup in our local greasy spoon.

Stella had set herself up on a small table tucked at the back of the cafe. A mug of tea awaited my arrival and I slipped into the creaky, orange plastic chair opposite.

'From what I can tell from the pics,' I said, 'we haven't come away with anything apart from the obvious that she hasn't suddenly, taken off. Please tell me you've found something.'

'How she lived... Expensive minimalism and slavishly OCD... even the contents of her wardrobe and cupboards.' She turned her phone to face me and continued swiping. 'Her office was locked but I had a key to that and her filing cabinet. Her whole life was in that filing cabinet,' she began, all reluctance at investigating, now forgotten. 'One of the files I found was on adoption. She was already approved as a prospective adopter so there's no way she would cut and run on that.'

'Oh God... That makes it worse. She'd make a great mum,' I said.

'If I hadn't thought it already, this solidified my resolve that there was no way she disappeared on a jolly,' Stella confirmed. 'She hasn't always been a teacher. She was up until a few years ago, a banker and she still trades. I knew she was comfortable and had extra income from elsewhere but from what I can tell – she's worth a tidy sum.'

'It doesn't make sense,' I said. 'Her flat's pretty swanky inside but it's still a non-descript block and she drives a Ford Fiesta.'

'I think she's playing down her wealth in line with the part of an under-paid deputy head,' she said. 'I found deeds to six other properties that she rents out. She has trust funds set up for her nephews and nieces and donates considerable sums to charities. There was a recent letter from The Meningitis Trust thanking her for a £100,000 donation and she's been making anonymous donations to the school. She's also paying for her mum to stay in an expensive care home in Epping.'

All making me realise that I didn't know her at all. 'What's with the pictures of the kids?' I asked, squinting at her phone. 'I think I recognise one of the boys from school but not the other or the baby.'

'I don't know. I found them in her bedside drawer.'

'Do you think we should visit her mum to check the last time she's seen her?' I asked.

'We could, but I flicked through some photo albums on the bookcase and she's been on a few holidays with Maria Dalton. You know... the maths head at All Saints Comp. In the absence of any evidence of any other friends, I think we should start there.'

The crack of light through the curtain confirmed that I had been awake all night. We'd met up with her friend Maria and the last boyfriend, both agreeing that she wouldn't take off without letting someone know. We were all as clueless as when we started.

I rolled over as my bedroom door creaked open painfully, seemingly of its own accord until Clara's soft brunette curls popped into view. 'Mummy... Voldemort's in my room.'

'Come here Babycakes.' I pulled her in with me and wrapped the duvet snugly around her as I held her close. 'Who's been telling you about Voldemort?'

'James O'Brien... He said that if you read Harry Potter, he'll come alive in your room at night.'

'Well, we know what James O'Brien is don't we? A big fat fibber.' I inhaled the scent of the coconut shampoo from her hair and we both slipped into the security of our dreams before the alarm screeched at 7.30am.

I dropped Clara off at school. Now paranoid enough after her accident to stay put until I witnessed her go through the main doors and rooted to the spot for an additional ten minutes in case she ran out again. I also managed to squeeze in enough time to whisper in James O'Brien's ear that if he told Clara any more Voldemort stories, I would send the Death Eaters after him. We seemed to understand each other.

As the last of the line of excited kids snaked through the main doors, I had a clear view of Reception. I could make out two Police Officers talking to someone with their back to me. I stopped one of the mums as she shot out of the door. 'What's going on?'

'From what I could make out... some news about Miss Scott I think.'

TEN
Into The Woods

'You're late. The Cock's looking for you...'

I couldn't be bothered to pick up Josh this morning for his insubordination towards our bemoaned Chief Super. as I was at my limit with the number of times, he was dragging me in for an 'update.'

'I had to see a teacher at Emilia's school.' No reason to let him know that I was at one of my Spatchcock-enforced counselling sessions for wayward officers. 'How long's he been looking?'

'All morning – so you're out of excuses.'

Defeated, I made my way up to his ivory tower. 'Sir...' He indicated to the chair in front of his desk for me to sit as he made a meal of reading something in his embossed leather file. I sat and went through my shopping list in my head to make use of the next wasted ten minutes.

'Thank you for taking the time to come and see me D.C.I. Connelly.'

'I came up as soon as I received your message, Sir.'

He showed no sign of believing or caring as he continued. 'I've had a call this morning from The Chief Constable of Essex. A body was found yesterday by a horse-trekker in Epping Forest.' I waited through his theatrical pause. 'Preliminary forensics summary has concluded that the mode of operandi and the weapon of choice are similar to our Victoria Park murder.'

The pause this time was filled with silent contemplation from both parties on the prospects of the fall out if this was confirmed as the same perpetrator.

'The dots have been joined by Doctor Monroe who is very pally with his Essex equivalent,' he continued. 'He's already sent over his replica rock for match with the wound, along with other relevant evidence from our case.'

'So, I presume they'll keep us informed and we'll review

how to progress with our case.' My head was already filled with evidence to revisit.

'A bit more than that Josephine...' Oh dear... he moved onto first name terms. 'They've requested that with our Murder Investigation Team expertise, we could pick this one up, if it's now pointing to a serial killer. Although that is not officially what we are pursuing.' And here was the deciding factor. 'The Commissioner's Office has already agreed.'

So, I was to lose my case...

'The Commander believes that you are the best person to head the investigation with your involvement already and your local knowledge. And I, of course, was only too willing to support this endorsement.'

Neither one of us would have seen that one coming. 'Thank you, Sir, for your vote of confidence.' A complete fabrication.

Spatchcock had made it clear to me since my return that he was more than pissed off at being handed the responsibility of supervising my cases until the powers-that-be were confident that I behaved in a more stable and conforming manner. I had no doubts that the 'endorsement' conversation had an attached caveat: 'of course Sir… but if she messes up again, I'm afraid we should cut our losses...' His strategy of how to extricate himself from all responsibility on this case was predictably already drafted.

'I've told The Essex Chief Constable that you'll make your way there pronto,' he informed me.

'Yes Sir... and what about Darren Anderson?' I asked.

'Until you can prove that these murders are the same killer then he stays put.' Holding his *get out of jail* card close to his chest, he would have taken it as a personal slight that one of his neatly wrapped up cases was unravelling.

'Grab your coat,' I barked at Josh as I retrieved my

own. A quick text to Peter to say I would be late – again... and I jumped into the passenger seat of an unmarked police car with Josh soon joining me at the wheel.

'You seem animated or agitated – I can't make out which.'

'A bit of both... Destination – Epping Forest before you ask.' I punched a number into my phone as I continued. 'A body's been found with the same M.O. as the Anderson murder. They've asked us to manage both – been cleared by all involved.' Josh jumped out of the car as I made my call.

'Hello Ewan... It's Josephine...'

He seemed unsurprised by my call: 'I wondered how soon I'd be hearing from you. Told them lot to get you in and get on with it,' he said.

'Thank you – I think... Anything left up there for me to see?'

'Yes… plenty... I've been commandeered as well so I'm here as we speak and have maintained the body in situ. Don't know how long I can break that procedure so get here sharpish please. I'll send the location.'

Josh returned, throwing our wellies onto the backseat. He didn't need much persuasion to put his foot down.

Once driving down the track roads into the forest, the real sense of seclusion and the threat of nature loomed. The *beware deer* signs were generally ignored until a freaked-out buck rammed into the side of your car, and you carried the guilt of killing Rudolph for the rest of your life.

I lost the signal on my personal phone which I had anticipated – having driven frequently through the main road cutting through the forest on my way to the M25. I'd already taken a photo-shot of the map Monroe had sent me as back up as well as ensuring we had a good old fashioned, police radio.

'How much further...?' Josh sounded impatient.

'A bit... Not too familiar with this deep into the forest but there should be a small car park up on the left.

Slowdown in case we miss it.'

We did indeed closely miss it and were only alerted to its existence as we swerved, almost hitting a police car attempting to turn around. As Josh and his not-so-friendly colleague, exchanged cop-specific expletives, I caught sight of Monroe on the opposite side at the back of his mud-splattered Land Rover.

'Ah… good timing Josephine,' he strolled over purposefully before bellowing at Josh, 'don't park there... we're working on tyre tracks.' Josh obliged and nudged further up the road. 'Follow me... it's not an obvious site to get to.'

We pulled on our boots and followed him along deserted pathways and over a picturesque brook. 'I've visited the forest many times over the years and don't recognise this part at all,' I told him.

'It's a bit too far out for the nearest towns to bother with so is a hidden gem for the lucky few,' he replied. 'Also, the proximity to the biker's cafe down the road acts as a deterrent to the faint-hearted. This way...'

We trailed behind, away from the path in through the silver birches until we reached the police tape in a dense patch of ferns. Before entering the white pitched tent, I slipped on the obligatory, protective gear. The density of ferns inside made it feel more like a cannabis factory. In the centre was a small clearing where the grave had been discovered. The latest victim was laid out as though in a Chapel of Rest, similar to the body of Fiona Anderson.

'Not a very deep hole this time,' I commented, peering down at the battered face of the latest victim.

'No... Between the loose soft soil, the prolific amount of dead leaves and the secluded spot, not much heavy work would've been involved.'

'Who is she?' I asked.

The tent rustled behind me and I turned around to Josh zipping up his protective suit. 'Catherine Scott... I've been filled in by the first officer at the scene.' He pulled out his notebook. 'She was a deputy head mistress at The Immaculate Heart of Mary Primary School in Woodford. She was reported missing over 2 weeks ago. Considering her age and lack of dependents, it wasn't escalated as a priority.'

'Because deputy heads are known for upping and leaving during mid-term...'

'They did take statements from friends and colleagues with the general consensus being that it was totally out of character. They've handed me the file so we can go through on the way back.'

'Thanks Josh. Well Ewan, over to you...'

'Preliminarily...'

'Yes, I know... to be confirmed...'

'Yes indeed... There are three wounds to the head: the one on the forehead as you can see; one on the top of the head and one on the back. The damage caused by the one on the top suggests that it was administered at a great height. There are defensive wounds, along with the injury to the forehead, suggesting that she turned at some point to face the assailant.' He took a couple of steps away from the body. 'The murder occurred here and you can see from the tracks that she was dragged into this natural dip and positioned as so.'

'She was out jogging but they'd be no reason not to stay on the path,' I said. 'She must have run away from the murderer or knew them and followed them into the woods.'

'We haven't found any broken foliage leading to the murder sight or corresponding marks on the body to suggest she was running. There's no evidence yet to prove a struggle anywhere else apart from this spot.' His tone remained neutral, always scrupulous in avoiding swaying conclusions.

'There's also a clearing not far from here with a log, big enough to sit on. The team have swabbed as much as they can. Not sure how much luck they'll have with tyre tracks or footprints as there's been quite a lot of rain since it happened but the soil samples from her trainers should give a history of where she's been.'

I returned to the body which was in a worst state than our first victim, her face unrecognisable from the blow to the forehead. I could make out auburn hair through her mud and blood-encrusted skull and a toned body beneath her running gear. 'I can't distinguish the degree of composition and what are wounds or possible animal bites. Any view of how long she's been dead?'

'Around two weeks...' he said.

Josh stepped up beside the grave, 'which coincides with the date of her disappearance.' He joined me in scrutinising the body. 'The violence shown does seem at odds with the laying out of her body. Does it show regret? But again, that doesn't sit with the likelihood that this was premeditated.'

I looked down at her pulverised features. 'Why would a deputy head warrant more aggression than the Essex mum?'

'I'm ready to move the body and get on with the P.M. Are you finished here?'

'Yes, thank you Ewan.' I needed to get out of the tent. The density of the foliage created a claustrophobic, almost tropical micro-climate, heightening the pungency of decay.

Josh followed me out into the woods. We made our way down to the clearing Monroe had referred to and stepped over the surrounding police-tape where he sat down on the log. 'You've got to be a pretty confident person to come jogging in such a secluded space.'

'What does it say in there about the victim?' I left him to rummage through the file as I circled the clearing.

'She wasn't always a teacher... in fact she used to be in banking in The City. Unmarried... no kids... an on-off boyfriend... some statements from friends and colleagues...' He paused a while as he skimmed through them. 'They all agree that she's a nice person... Only known her to help and support others... An inspirational teacher... Unthinkable that she'd have enemies...'

'So, the opposite to Fiona Anderson...'

Josh closed the file. 'Not much in here – standard misperp stuff.'

'If the evidence shows that they were in this clearing, was it a chance meeting or did they plan to meet each other? Arrange for us to re interview all those who've given statements. Get Angela to attend the P.M. and we'll catch up on the results later. Find out when the bikers hang-out at The Cafe and send Susie down to ask around.'

We walked back together on the main path, scrutinising every inch for signs of any random evidence while he was on his phone, delegating tasks until we reached the brook. Josh picked up a stick and hurled it in and we watched it bob amongst the froth as I continued my brain dump: 'bring the evidence of the cases together so we can begin to tick off the similarities between the two. It goes without saying that the comparisons in forensics will prove a major part of the case so let's ensure that we're on top of this as it comes in, before our time is bogged down with the human element.'

We were momentarily mesmerised by a young doe navigating its way over the water, further down the brook until Josh spoke aloud our shared thought, 'Darren Anderson was in custody at the time of this murder.'

'I know... but let's not get a head of ourselves.'

'What about a copycat?'

'Can't be discounted... Let's see what Monroe can prove and follow the evidence before getting carried away with the serial killer frenzy.'

After a heart-breaking visit to the care home to inform Catherine Scott's elderly mother of her death, we arrived back in time for our meeting with Monroe. He'd completed the post-mortem and had made some inroads into the comparison between the cases. We were shown into a meeting room where pictures of the deceased and the scene were already up on a screen. Josh helped himself to the coffee on the table while I scrutinised the cleaned face of the victim. 'Why were there so many blows to the head this time?'

'She was trying to get away...' Monroe strode into the room laden down with boxes which he proceeded to unpack as he spoke. 'Sorry to keep you waiting but the sister turned up unexpectedly to ID the body.'

'I thought she wasn't due until late this week,' I said, annoyed that she could have been with the mother when she was given the news.

'I know... it seems she managed to get away sooner and flew overnight.' He pushed a card towards me. 'She's staying here and presumes you'll want to speak to her. I've given her your details.'

He pulled his reading glasses down from his head as he rummaged around in one of his boxes. I stood, scrutinising the picture of the victim.

'As I was saying – the first blow wasn't fatal.' He picked up his replica rock from the first murder. 'The wounds and dust particles collected, match the murder weapon from Victoria Park and the direction of the blows – again a left-hander as with Victoria Park. In conjunction with the drag-marks, footprints and blood splatters, I would suggest the sequence of events: she was struck at the back of the head – presumably from behind – and staggered a few steps; she turned to face her assailant and was struck on the forehead; she fell into the ferns, managed to turn around and dragged herself forward and received the fatal blow on the top of her head. Good old blunt force trauma is once again the culprit and as with the first victim – no signs of sexual assault.'

'Not such a clean kill as the first. Any forensics in the

clearing?' I asked.

'Yes. Fabric fibres found in both areas match as well as footprints.' He pushed forward casts made of the footprints from the scene. 'Treads match those of Adidas and Asics trainers – both size eight. A size eight footprint was found at the Victoria Park scene although not of either brand. We can establish with further analysis if the wearer from both sites is the same. We've isolated the fibres that don't match the victim's clothes and will complete further analysis on their origin.'

I picked up the cast and ran my fingers through the treads. 'I know Darren Anderson is size eight but it's still a pretty small shoe size for a man. Anything to suggest that this couldn't be a woman...?'

Monroe pulled a non-plussed face, 'nothing forensically... just the low stats on women with size eight feet and female murders or at least those working alone. But that's over to you to interpret.'

Josh searched for a space to put down his coffee cup as he asked, 'anything to suggest there was a third person present?'

'There were other footprints in the clearing but nothing in the murder site,' Monroe confirmed.

'Josh has a point... If there was an accomplice, they could've waited in the clearing so make sure you record anything collected from there.'

'Well... enough about tracks and trails – you'll need to know about the victim.' He did not wait for a response, 'as previously mentioned, the only other marks on her body were related to the attack. She was incredibly healthy, apart from removal of her ovaries although there is evidence that she has been pregnant at some point. We're waiting for her medical records to confirm the cause which there seems to be some issue in tracking down.'

'Anything else you have that might be helpful at this stage?' I asked.

'Only to confirm, that the DNA results prove that the two victims were in no way related.'

Josh and I attempted to digest the range of evidence as we drove to our next stop. 'A woman...?'
Josh had been so wholly committed to Anderson's guilt that everything else was sounding fanciful.

'I'm not saying it is but if the murders are connected, we have to approach them with a fresh perspective, including presumptions on gender.' He snorted his disbelief as I flicked through the file that he had left on the seat. 'Explain to me the connection of this witness to Catherine Scott.' I asked.

'She's a friend and a one-stop shop for info. She, with another friend, wouldn't accept that Catherine had gone missing and decided to start their own investigations.'

'Could be interesting although I hope for their sake, they haven't stumbled on something and contaminated our process.'

ELEVEN
Nobody Listened

Amy Whitehead opened the front door to her large semi-detached Victorian house. She ushered us in but it was clear that her actions were almost robotic. She looked like she was in shock. 'Thank you for seeing us.'

She offered us a seat. 'It'll be all too little too late, won't it? If you lot hadn't been so dismissive, she'd still be alive.'

She was right but it was no good pitching the reality of the amount of Missing Persons cases that came through our doors that we could not escalate to foul play because of the lack of evidence. 'I know... but there's still a murderer out there Mrs Whitehead and we don't know why they're killing and if they'll kill again. Anything you can tell us... anything... could help us stop this.'

She stared out of the French windows into the garden as if she wanted us gone. I could see Josh in my peripheral vision, doing a sneaky sweep of the room. 'Her sister arrived from New York. Would you like us to give her your details? I'm sure she'd like to speak to those who knew her.'

'No!' She screamed but the anger caught in her throat and ended as a sob. 'No... How could I face her when we failed Catherine so badly?'

'You didn't–'

'I did! I let that fucking P.C. Plod dismiss me when I should have created merry hell to get him to do something... anything...' She threw her hands to her face as she attempted to control her sobbing.

We left her until she had calmed down a little and Josh offered to fetch a glass of water. As he left the room, I attempted to engage her once more. 'Please tell us what you know Mrs Whitehead.'

'Stop bloody calling me that. It makes me sound like some senile old biddy you're humouring. My name is Amy.'

'What do you know Amy?'

She took the glass of water from Josh and after a few sips and wiping her face, settled back into her armchair and tucked her legs under her body. She wrapped her arms around herself as though she was fending off an Arctic wind while Josh and I were sweltering in the artificial heat.

'When you talk to anyone who knew her,' she began, 'they'll all tell you the same – that she wasn't the type to go off without telling anyone. She had too much of a sense of responsibility.'

We remained still and silent, giving her the space to continue her story. She returned to her view of the garden. 'When your lot wouldn't do anything, I asked my friend Stella if she would help me to find out where she'd gone. We talked about the worst that could've happened but not believing that these things happen to people you know. We managed to get hold of the keys to her flat... don't ask me how because I won't tell you.' She threw another accusatory look but this time, Josh's way. 'I got side-tracked by an elderly, concerned neighbour – Dottie…' she continued. 'And Stella went in. She covered her shoes and wore gloves so as not to mess things up for your lot and sent me pics of the flat as she went through.'

'That's helpful Amy and although we'll find the same things that you found, I'd be interested in your perspective – knowing her better and all.'

'You'll see that she wasn't some old fusty spinster: minimalist loft style... what you'd expect I suppose from someone in the city. You'll find most of the information you want from the files in her office. They'll confirm her financial status: secretly fairly well off and generous with it. The paper trail for her adoption process is there.'

She looked at us pleadingly even though it was too late to save her. 'Everything in that flat screamed that she hadn't abandoned her life. A full wardrobe... a full fridge... suitcases untouched...'

'Any evidence of a personal life...?' I asked.

She slumped back in her chair and pulled her legs in tighter, 'Stella found some pictures in her bedside cabinet. I believe one of them is of a boy she was looking to adopt. We also recognised a woman from some holiday photos she found and went to see her: Maria Dalton... another teacher but works up at All Saints High School. They regularly went on adventure holidays together. She said that she'd come forward.'

She retrieved her phone from the coffee table. 'What's your number? I'll send you her contact details.' I pushed my card towards her on the table. She picked it up and continued tapping. 'I'll also send you her ex-boyfriend's details, although I think he's already been interviewed.'

'Damian Murphy,' Josh read from his notes.

'Yes – that's him. He seemed a nice enough bloke.'

'You met him?' I asked.

'Yeah... Maria knew him and text him to meet us. Much younger than Catherine... a bit of an intellectual scruff but I suppose opposites attract.'

'You said he was her ex...'

'It didn't sound too serious. A bit on and off when it suited either of them. I believe it was currently off because she was focusing on adopting and he was planning to move on – although he did seem genuinely upset at her disappearance.'

'Do you think he could've had anything to do with it?'

She looked back into the garden as though searching for an answer. 'I didn't think so at the time but... I don't know what I think. Maria might know more.'

'So, what was your friendship about Amy?' I asked as tactfully as my mood allowed.

'She helped me out during a difficult patch, seeing me during school hours as well as the odd drink in the evening. There're a lot of people she helped the same. She was selfless like that,' she whispered, as though to herself. 'She was there for us when we needed her but we couldn't manage to do the same.'

'If you don't mind me asking Amy, what troubles did she help you through?' I asked.

'I can't see the relevance,' she said, more frustrated than defensive, 'but my husband and I split for a time. I went to her to ensure that my daughter didn't suffer in school and she intuitively seemed to see that I also needed a bit of support...'

'Did she ever talk about her personal life?'

'The most she ever went into detail was about an ex-boyfriend who stalked her. Hold on...' She uncurled from the chair and left the room. We could hear her rummaging around in the kitchen before she returned with what looked like a folder. She sat down with the folder in her lap and flicked through the pages before retrieving a dog-eared page with scribbles in red ink. 'Before going to the police, I sat down and racked my brain for all the details of her life that we would've discussed.' She handed over the page which was scrawled with: *The Stalker*. I scanned down her notes. 'There's his name and the area they lived in. The dates I think she was referring to for their relationship and when he stalked her and when he left for the Far East. I don't even think your lot took notes when I went through this.'

'This is all good stuff, Amy,' I said, conscious of keeping her on side. 'Would you mind if we took the folder with us?' She sat back in her seat and wrapped her arms around the file as though protecting a child. 'We'll take copies and return it to you by tomorrow. I promise,' I assured her. She looked suspiciously from me to Josh before reluctantly releasing her grip and handing it over.

She picked up her phone once more. 'I'll send you the photo's Stella took of the flat. I don't know if they'll be helpful because you'll see the same but anyway...' My phone pinged as an endless succession of picture texts came through. 'Stella went through her files so she'll know more about that.'

'Thank you, Amy... You've provided so much information already but as you seem to be the one person who has attempted to connect anything Catherine told you to her disappearance – can I ask you one last thing? Can you try to remember anyone else that either she mentioned or you knew about, who would have come to her for help or support as you did? And would any of these people have a reason to hurt her?'

She looked up from her phone, 'I can't think about that now... Could I come back to you?'

'Of course. We'll leave it there for now. Don't get up... we'll let ourselves out. Thank you again Amy.'

She nodded in acknowledgement but the contempt from our inaction never left her eyes. Josh turned around as we were leaving the room. 'Sorry... I forgot to ask... Did you know Fiona Anderson?'

She returned his gaze, 'no... Wasn't she the woman murdered over in Hackney? Is it connected?'

'We wanted to rule out any coincidences or cross over. Thank you, Amy.'

'You alright...?'

'What...? Yes...' I lied as Josh came out to meet me in the station car park. A morning of innocently putting Emilia's washing away had uncovered a box of nitrous oxide canisters, stashed at the back of her drawers.

What to do...? Tell Peter...? No... Let Emilia know that I know...? I could write the ensuing argument word for word: 'invading my privacy... not illegal... you can talk – you were an underage drinker.' All true – but kids were dying with this hippie crack. I could only think of one option – deal with the source.

'How'd it go?' he asked.

'What...?'

'The meeting with Catherine Scott's sister...' he said to my blank expression.

'Oh... her...Well... She's undoubtedly cut from the same cloth. Another high achiever… working as a successful lawyer in a large corporate firm in New York. Maintained a dignified composure, even in her grief. She offered her assistance, if needed, to any of Catherine's friends. All together – very Zen but a helpful insight into her sister's personality.'

I must have reeled that off too robotically because he asked once more, 'you sure you're alright?'

'Yeah... a bit of trouble with my manipulative daughter.'

Josh was grinning away to himself, 'manipulation... at such a tender age?'

'You've no idea... Teenage girls are a whole different species. Boys are like soppy puppies in comparison: smelly, hungry, bumbling... Whereas girls... they're like cats – making you feel like they're doing you a favour. There's always an agenda.' Josh looked like I was trying to explain the laws of Quantum Physics.

'If this murderer does turn out to be a woman... Well... I've not dealt with a female murderer before.' He sounded like he was having a wobble.

'Let's not run off at a tangent. I'd prefer you keep an open mind otherwise you'll miss what's under your nose. But feel free to recap on whatever course you attended on the subject.'

'I think I did. I'm sure there's a textbook or two I could dig out on the psychology of the female murderer. Any tips in the meantime?' Josh liked nothing better than a slice of academia to back up any new process or experience.

'The usual clichés apply. Women are natural carers and nurturers, so there must be a tipping point to push them into taking a life. But when that's reached... none of this testosterone, on the spur of the moment, gory-rage; they'll plot and plan and wait...'

'Is "gory-rage" what we're seeing with these murders?' He asked, ever keen to classify.

'I don't know but it's not typical of a woman to use such violence although this is at odds with the care taken in arranging the bodies before they were buried.'

Josh's pursed lips meant that he was computing the possibilities of a scenario outside his comfort zone. I used the remainder of the journey to scroll through the pictures of the flat that Amy Whitehead had forwarded which turned out to be mainly of the contents of cupboards, documents, even the inside of the fridge. 'Take a left here...'

We pulled up to the non-descript, purpose-built block and made our way to the communal entrance. Josh pushed the neighbouring buttons on the intercom until some law-abiding citizen allowed us access. 'What time will Forensics be here?' He asked.

'About an hour I think – unless we find another pile of dead bodies.'

Duly following procedure, we put on our gloves and shoe protectors. We used a key obtained from Catherine's sister to enter the flat and as Amy Whitehead had described, were at first sight, taken aback by the sophistication of the interior.

'Swanky...'

'Couldn't think of a better word myself...' I headed for the kitchen while Josh focused on the lounge and as if at home, I sub consciously opened the fridge: empty shelves. Where was the bin? I found it under the sink – empty. The kitchen cupboard was ajar and I opened it further as I returned to the photos on my phone.

Josh joined me in the kitchen, 'not much in there – some family pics.'

I showed Josh the photo of the full fridge and opened the empty one, 'and there's nothing in the bin.' I scrolled to the photo of the cupboard. 'Confirm that there is a set of suitcases in this photo but none in there.'

He nodded, made his way into the hall and I followed. We entered the bedroom. I headed for the wardrobes and he opened the drawers. All her clothes had gone. Again, I put the corresponding photos on my phone screen for both of us to confirm the original presence of a full set of clothes. 'So, what do we think?' He asked. 'Her things are cleared out to give the impression that she's packed up and left – over-confident that her body won't be found?'

'Why would you do it if you knew the body was discovered? Where's the office?'

We returned to the hall and as Josh fumbled with keys to find one to the door next to the bedroom, I popped over to the bathroom to confirm the same scenario. I dialled a number from my contacts...

'Hello Amy... D.C.I. Connelly here... Hi... sorry to disturb you but a quick question... where did you manage to get the keys to Catherine's flat from? Don't worry, they'll be no comeback but it's vital in relation to further developments. Okay... thank you… So, your understanding is that anyone in that reception office could do this? Right... Okay… thanks again. Goodbye...'

Josh managed to open the door, behind which was Catherine Scott's inner sanctum. I dialled another number and called Angela to send her down to the school to pick up the keys and interview the reception staff and called Forensics to come to the flat A.S.A.P.

Josh turned on her computer and I opened the filing cabinet.

'A spare set of her keys were kept in the school reception. That's how Amy's friend, Stella, got hold of them and I suppose whoever cleared out the flat.'

'This is password protected so I'm not going to waste my time trying to crack it. I'll take it with us and give it to Michael,' he said, unplugging the computer.

I scrolled through Amy's pictures with Josh one more time on my phone, looking for any of the office and its contents. 'From what we can tell, nothing in here has been touched.'

'Agreed... Although I can't see the logic,' he said, sounding as bemused as I felt.

'Ran out of time perhaps? Regardless... you can start by digging around in that cabinet. It's all filed in meticulous order so begin with the finances.' I turned to investigate the contents of the bookcase and had to concentrate to see past the display by colour and height, to notice the details of the books. 'I can imagine your flat, organised like this.'

'You'd be disappointed.'

Among the classic novels were self-help books and a selection on child-development and traumatised children. It called to mind the photos Amy had mentioned and I rushed to the bedroom and the bedside table. I opened the drawer. Gone... Josh looked up as I returned to the office as though anticipating my gloom. 'The photos of the boys are missing.'

'I suppose they could've got lucky and found them or they already knew the layout of the flat. Her disappearance wouldn't be as believable if she'd left behind something so personal,' he suggested.

I fired off a text to Amy: *'did you tell anyone about coming to the flat and what you saw?'* I returned my attention to the bookcase as I awaited her reply and pulled out a book from a shiny black selection to discover they were photo albums; an artistically arranged catalogue of her life. I moved swiftly from her family to the holiday snaps mentioned, although these too were of a quality that seemed like she had a professional photographer follow her around on location. The scenery from the far-flung places was as extreme as it was exotic and all jarred with the pedestrian life she would have lived as a primary school teacher. I removed a selection to take with me.

'Is that you?' Josh asked.

'What?' He was right. It was my phone pinging. I read the text and updated Josh, 'Amy and Stella didn't tell anyone they came here.'

'That may have saved their lives. We'll have to tell her to keep it that way.'

I kept my return text to Amy, blunt and to the point. 'I reckon the killer will be pretty jumpy when he or she finds out that the body has been discovered and if we're lucky – make a mistake.'

'Could be a double bluff to try and make us think along those lines,' Josh suggested. 'I'd be interested in hearing Stella's story. We're seeing her in the morning.' He's thought process had seemingly shifted.

'Sounds like you're already convinced it's a woman.'

'You mean like I was convinced it was Darren Anderson?'

'I never said that...' Not what I thought but he was beating himself up about it.

'You didn't have to...'

'I'm not ruling out a copycat theory yet and I suggest you keep an open mind. Darren Anderson may yet be involved.' Josh grunted his disbelief. 'What are these?' I bent down to the bottom shelf of the bookcase, to a thin navy selection with gold embossed writing on the spine: '2015, 2016, 2017... Diaries... Okay... let's see... This year and last year...' I pulled out the two volumes and flicked through the pages. 'No Dear Diary... some appointments and a few notes.'

'Any names you recognise?'

'Maria... Damian... Amy's here – quite a bit...Then there's Stella which I presume is the same Stella?'

'Stella Winchester?' Josh put down the bank statements he was scrutinising and flicked through his notebook. 'Yeah... that's her.' He returned to the bank statements. 'There's a monthly payment for 500 quid from her bank account with that reference.'

'Do we know anything about her?'

'No... Not yet... I'll get Angela to pull a file together before we see her tomorrow.'

‘Hello...’ A noisy commotion disturbed the calm in the flat as I walked in on the Forensics team swarming into the lounge. ‘Hello Boss... Is it okay to get started?’

‘Of course... We think the perpetrator could have cleared out the flat so look beyond the obvious. Also try and find where the communal rubbish is kept and have a rummage around as a whole week’s worth of food shopping has been disposed of. We’re finishing up in the office, we’ll be out of your way soon.’

When I returned to Josh, he had created two neat piles of documents and was packing up the computer. ‘If you could take those and I’ll lug this to the car.’

Back at the office, Michael deftly over-rode the password and was sifting through files and emails with an over-eager Josh at his shoulder. As most of my team were still out gathering statements, I began to compile a list from her diaries of those she had seen, either professionally or personally and the frequency of these meetings. I slipped the list to Josh to find their contact details from Catherine Scott’s computer and any corresponding emails. One reoccurring name stared back at me on the same date each year: *Daniel.* I wrote it in my notes and underlined it until the nib tore through the paper.

I knew I would be at my worst during this period with a killer at large: impatient with the gathering of evidence; questions not asked that I think would be obvious; connections not made from one piece of evidence to another. Any further murders... on me. I would be screaming in my head, ‘do I have to do it all my fucking self!’ I jumped out of my seat and stuck my head around the door, ‘Josh! Bring me in what you’ve got...’

He knew the look.

TWELVE
The Female of The Species

'Didn't you sleep well?'

Peter rolled over and struggled to curl his pliable body around my ramrod posture, a telling sign of my sleepless night. 'Some old haunting memories...'

He managed to melt my body enough to wrap his powerful legs around mine. 'Don't tell me... The Alexander case...'

I snuggled my face into the top of his head with his thick wavy hair tickling my nose. 'Was I talking in my sleep?'

'No... But the moment you told me that it could be a female serial killer, it wasn't much of a stretch to know that you'd be thinking of the one that got away.'

'Is that supposed to make me feel good?'

He squeezed a little bit harder, 'you should feel good because you did your best but if after everything you've been through, you still haven't exorcised that demon, I reckon you're panicking that it might cloud your judgement in this case.'

'Go back to sleep clever clogs... it's still early.' There was no reason for us both to start the day feeling shattered. I felt his breathing deepen and the odd twitch confirm that it hadn't taken his body much to comply. He radiated heat like a hibernating grizzly and I relaxed into his warmth. My mind returned to my old case; two years had not lessened the sting of the failure. The expectation haunted me from every case of mine since, to wake to a headline: 'cop from the failed Alexander case...' Thankfully it never had but this time I felt I was riding my luck. Once out there, the comparisons would be too great to not recall the original case. I closed my eyes, not with the hope of sleep but to improve my mind's eye as I reran events, more frequently than I would ever admit.

Was I carried away with being one of the youngest promotions? Sure... I had a chip on my shoulder at the misogynistic world I had to battle through. The dicks from my early years chanting, 'slag' or 'lesbo,' when I failed to succumb to their oily charms, were long forgotten. Not so much the line-managers, who struggled to find it in themselves to support a female promotion over a male colleague. Their mantra from earlier years ringing in my ears: 'are you seriously coming back after that second baby?'

Was I too inexperienced to head the case? No... I scrutinised the evidence and uncovered early on, the nurse who murdered seven women in three different hospitals. But was I too concerned with the views of those above me to move swiftly enough to stop her in her tracks? Yes... giving her time to claim an eighth victim and abscond to some back water in The Balkans.

The alarm stirred me from my thoughts and Peter released me from his grip as he rolled over. I slipped out of bed and checked to hear Emilia's deep breathing as I passed her room. No, 'hello mum...' this morning as she would undoubtedly still be in a strop from last night, after both of us arrived to pick her up from her party, 'like some Disney Princess.'

'Oh... put that away will you,' I begged Josh as my stomach turned at the smell of the bacon sandwich he was waving about.

'Not like you... hang-over?'

'No, I bloody haven't, you cheeky sod...' I replied, snatching my mug of tea from his grip. I blew on the tea as he opened the newly created file on Stella Winchester.

'An interesting lady…' he began. 'Ten years in the British Army rising to the rank of Captain: tours in Iraq and Afghanistan. What we can find out – and I'm sure there's loads we can't – a competent officer, well liked and from the honours awarded, can without question, look after herself. She left to focus on her children but tragedy followed with her son falling ill and dying – no suspicious circumstances. A surviving daughter... Medical records for this child don't indicate anything out of the ordinary.

'She now works as a personal trainer and is active in charity work for Army Veterans. I checked through the diaries: a concentration of meetings with Catherine Scott around the time her son died and on-off until now but with more regularity over the last 6 months.'

'Any financial issues that would account for the payments from Catherine Scott?' I asked.

'We won't be able to get at her bank details until this afternoon but we'll see what she has to say this morning. She's arranged to meet us at the gym she uses to work with her clients.'

'Seemingly wanting to steer us away from her home.' I suggested. 'We'll go along for now.'

Having agreed to meet in the canteen, I headed for a table in the most secluded spot while Josh joined a queue for coffee and strolled uncomfortably back towards me with his tray. 'What's wrong with you?'

'Nothing...'

Then I looked around at all the body-beautifuls at the other tables and realised that his awkwardness was his attempt to pump himself up to his full height and hold in his hardly-there stomach. 'I never knew you were so shallow.' Before he could respond, a slim, mixed-race woman, more covered-up than most in the room, stood behind him.

'Hi – You must be D.C.I. Connelly,' she said. The eloquence of her managerial training, evident. I half expected a salute.

'Yes... hello and this is Sergeant Hughes. Thank you for taking the time to see us today Mrs Winchester–'

'Please call me Stella...'

She sat down in the spare chair next to Josh who attempted to check out her footwear before her long legs disappeared under the table. 'I appreciate that Miss Scott was a friend and this must all be upsetting.'

'It is... everything about it is… well... out of the ordinary and inexplicable.' She remained calm and somewhat emotionless. Hard to read... She held herself ramrod with her hands in her lap: defensiveness or good posture?

'I'm sure you've seen worse in conflict,' I said. She raised her eyes in acknowledgement but with no intention of engaging. 'Can you tell us a little of your relationship with Catherine Scott?'

'We got to know each other through the school and when my son passed away, she was supportive; a genuine, authentic person.'

I had to swallow my own threatening wave before continuing. 'Sorry... I know this must be difficult but I believe your son died of a congenital heart disease?'

'Yes... we tried to give him as normal a life as possible but his death was... well... expected. None the less... no less painful.'

'Did you see her out of school? Would you say your relationship developed into a friendship?' I asked.

'Yes... I saw her for the odd drink. We were friendly and I'd like to consider us friends but it never stepped into the realms of intimacy – of knowing everything about each other's lives and secrets. The kind of relationship I have with other friends. She never opened up and I never pushed. There was always an element of professional restraint. I don't know... maybe that was all she was capable of and wasn't intimate with anyone.'

'You have an air of professional restraint yourself Stella,' I commented, keeping it light.

'Do I?' She smiled and seemed to self-consciously relax a fraction. 'I guess it's my army conditioning I'm afraid and as a woman, when every visible emotion is spun as female hysteria. You soon learn to mask your feelings. I guess that was what was so remarkable about Catherine, she saw through it and seemed to almost stealth-like, get you to open up.' Her tone, nevertheless, remained officious as though reporting an incident.

'Did you ever kill anyone Stella? In the line of duty of course...' I asked without judgement.

There was the first sign of discomfort and a glimmer of emotion. She looked across at me. Amber flecks splattered throughout her hazel eyes, softening an otherwise hardened stare. 'Yes, I have... and does that mean that I would find it easier to kill someone in my civilian life? No, it doesn't. Because I know that even in conditions where the world justifies and excuses taking a life – it never leaves you. You live with that horror every day.' She held my gaze as though a challenge. I paused, allowing her time to resettle before resuming the flow of the interview.

Josh flicked to his notebook: 'we've picked up from her bank statements that she made a monthly payment to your account for £500. Can you explain what that was for?'

'Yes... I'm involved with a variety of charities for ex-army veterans. Catherine's dad had been in the Armed Forces so kindly made a monthly donation to our work. She made the payment directly to me as I would distribute it to the various causes. I've kept my own accounts to validate this – which I will happily provide.'

'Weren't you curious how she could afford such a large monthly donation?' he continued.

'To a degree,' she shrugged her shoulders, 'but I suppose I made the presumption that she could credible afford it if she didn't have any dependents and she never seemed to live life excessively. Obviously, we were surprised to find the extent of her wealth when we went through her files,' she said, without a hint of awkwardness at having broken into Scott's flat.

'Knowing her as you did, was there anything you found

that struck you as odd?' I asked.

'Only that we didn't know her that well. We knew nothing of the extent of her wealth... about the friends she holidayed with... her hopes to adopt... Although anything we did find, cemented what we did know about her: her generosity, her capacity to care and think about others. I reflected on why we didn't know more and I'm ashamed of the realisation that we were so busy talking about our own problems and what we wanted from her, we took little time to ask her about her life.' She appeared genuine in her sentiment.

'You cared enough not to accept that she'd gone missing,' I said, which didn't seem to affect her look of regret.

'I did... but Amy drove the whole – taking some action. She was determined. She seemed more convinced than me that something serious had happened to her. But she was right...'

'Is there a Mr Winchester?' I asked.

'There was – we divorced...' She seemed comfortable enough on the subject. 'We remain good friends and he's still in our lives.'

'He helps you out financially?'

'He pays his share...' a slight prickle slipped into her tone. 'But I'm financially secure regardless, thank you.'

'Can you think of anyone in Catherine's life – whether you knew them or not – that would want to harm her in this way?'

'You'll know about the boyfriends already but we only met the recent one, who seemed harmless enough. We all seem to know only a bit about her life but not enough to rule anyone out.'

'Even you?'

She turned to Josh with his allegation. 'I know you're doing your job… so yes… even me.'

'What about the keys to her flat?' I asked. 'I believe you

acquired them from the school reception. Were they hard to steal?'

She visibly winced at the word and considered this second allegation before responding. 'Yes, I did steal them and I've returned them since and no – they weren't hard to remove without anyone noticing. The reception area is always full of parent-volunteers, popping in and out and if you catch it at a busy time, you can quite easily slide in and out unnoticed.'

'We believe you focused on Catherine's office when you searched the flat. Did you find anything interesting apart from what you've discussed already?' I asked.

'Her finances in the main and a file on the adoption process. I didn't hang around too long to be honest.'

'Whose idea was it to search the flat?'

She raised her head and hesitated – an acknowledgement of the implication as she answered. 'It was my idea...'

'Amy Whitehead didn't end up going into the flat.'

'No... But the original plan was that she would so we wouldn't have known beforehand that she'd be side-tracked by a neighbour.'

Josh torpedoed a parting question, 'did she ever mention Fiona Anderson?'

'Yes... she did.'

THIRTEEN
Concluding Evidence

'Boss...' The Desk Sergeant hollered as I sprinted towards the main doors, already late for a rare family gathering.

'Not now George...'

'I think you'll want this one Boss.'

I froze with my hand on the door. 'Shit George... You really know how to push my buttons. It better be good,' I warned him as I approached the counter.

'That young lady...' he nodded towards the far end of the reception area, 'claims to have information proving the innocence of Darren Anderson.'

Perched self-consciously on one of the chairs was a chain-store-smartly-dressed young woman, clutching possessively onto a large tote handbag on her lap. My interest was piqued.

By the way...' George went on, 'I've had no luck finding out who that crack phone call was from. Although it would be helpful if you could determine if it was a man or a woman.'

'Sorry George... I couldn't tell.'

'Alright... but I'll screen your direct line calls for a while and see what that delivers.'

Settled with a glass of water in Interview Room Two, I encouraged the young lady to begin her story. 'My name is Karen Blakely and I was the holiday cover for Darren Anderson's P.A.' A slight nervousness tinged her secretarial efficiency. She had made the effort to dress as impeccably as a day at the office, perhaps in an effort to be taken seriously. 'I've been on maternity leave,' she added, 'and what with managing a new baby and all, completely missed the drama about Mrs Anderson's murder. It's only when work colleagues stared to pop in to see the baby that they filled me in.'

She paused – possibly waiting for a reprimand. 'Go on...'

'I was pretty sure that the dates for the murder coincided with the period I worked for Mr Anderson so I did some digging.' She pulled out a manila file from her bag and placed various documents on the desk. 'Friends at work helped me out with these but I don't want to get them into trouble.'

'They won't…'

She pointed to the first document. 'There's an optional tracking facility on the company cars. I like to use it to give honest answers to any enquiries to when – whichever boss I'm working for at the time – will return to the office. This is a print-out of his whereabouts on that day when he left the office. I highlighted the time I believe, from what I've read, that the murder occurred.'

She was right. He was ten miles away. 'Why didn't his current P.A. show us this?'

'She doesn't use it so wouldn't think to look. Permanent P.A.s can sometimes have a...'

'Misguided sense of loyalty,' I finished for her.

She smiled, 'yes... I guess. They'd see it as spying. This... I believe should be the clincher.' She pulled out a copy of a penalty charge for entering a boxed junction and a timed photo. 'You can see from the date and time that he was nowhere near the area at the time of the murder.'

'And he didn't know about this because...?'

'They never do. The P.A.'s deal with all these low-level issues and never bother their bosses.'

Containing my seething rage at the stupidity of his current P.A. who had misdirected us, presumably, believing she was covering for him only to land him in the shit, I sought to find out more: 'Karen... you seem a decent sort. Coming forward like this when you didn't have to, will make the difference in exonerating Darren. But there could be something you came across in his everyday working life that might help us find whoever killed his wife.'

She looked down at the documents on the table as though contemplating her next move and sorted them into a tidy pile. Laying her hand on the top of the file she raised her head. 'There was one bit of gossip – if you like – that I noticed wasn't mentioned in the newspapers. Again, I'm sure not mentioned out of loyalty but it was firmly believed he had at one point – or maybe regularly – played away.'

Maybe his usual P.A. was an ex-lover trying to land him in it after all? I called John down to take her full statement and the evidence and I bombed it home.

I kissed Jude and his new girlfriend goodbye as we left the restaurant. They were staying at her sister's flat in Brixton which was far cooler than hanging out in your childhood bedroom at Mum and Dad's. Although the - no sleeping with girlfriends while Emilia's at home – rule, swung the decision. His cool was sorely tested as Emilia teased and baited him throughout the meal. We pulled her into check when it looked like he was going to swing for her. Regurgitating his exs was enough to break the most virtuous – which Jude was not.

We strolled home, full of pizza and a good Barolo, content, that considering what was going on, I managed to attend this family event. The restaurants along our high street were packed and I savoured being amongst this normality for one rare evening.

'Why were you so late Mum?' Emilia noted my raised eyebrow. 'Come on... I was good... I stuck to your – no business at dinner – rule. It's time to spill the beans.'

Another rule coming back to bite me... 'You want me to tell you the details of the case?'

I linked Emilia's arm with Peter on the other side: the one the picture of the other. If I had been the father, her parentage could be in doubt but Emilia had grown up all her life with the running commentary that she was 'the image of her dad'. It used to upset her at times, needing reassurance that it didn't mean that she looked like a man but that her button nose was a lady-size version of his and her thick wavy hair was the envy of her mates and their menopausal mums.

'As impressed as I am at your interest in my work, if I told you – I'd have to shoot you.'

'But I'm one of your best informants.' She tugged away at my arm.

'True... You've provided me with some valuable intel. but I wouldn't go around telling your mates that or you'll be known as a Supergrass and you'll be socially shunned and end up under my feet even more than usual.'

'You're never in to be under your feet,' she shot back.

'Touché...'

Peter scowled across, 'that's out of order young lady. Your mum's in enough, to feed, clothe and pick up after you.'

I gave him an affectionate squeeze, 'I didn't know you noticed.' He leant down and delivered a welcoming kiss.

'Eeee... get a room. I thought after your twentieth anniversary you'd stop being so gross.' Emilia pulled away, at which point, Peter, determined to embarrass her even further, spun me around and dipped me tangoesque. She stuck her finger in her mouth to faux vomit.

'Don't do that!' I squealed. 'You've just eaten.'

Curled up on the sofa that evening with Peter, listening to an old Portishead album, I was more inclined – as Emilia put it – to spill the beans. The only person allowed to witness my vulnerabilities and in return I appreciated how hard it was for him at times, to continue to support me in a job I loved, knowing how often it put me in harm's way. Unlike any other husband conditioned to protect his wife – and physically he was more than able – he had to suck it up and not retaliate. The Alexander case had driven me close to a breakdown and he had uncomplainingly seen me through, even when it took me away from the family. I was blind to the strain it had placed on our relationship and was forever thankful that he had the strength to hold it together for the both of us.

'What was the unscheduled interview about?' he asked, saving the most burning question until last.

I fought against the weight of the consequences of the new evidence, crushing my rare and precious moments of intimacy. But as the impact on my home life would be immediate, I had no choice but to keep Peter well informed. He slipped his arm around my neck and I lay my head on his chest and recounted the interview.

'Have you told Spatchcock?' He was restrained in his tone, considering what he knew about my superior's conduct during the Alexander case and his condescending treatment towards me since my return. I had heard through the grapevine that Peter had confronted him and maybe gifted Spatchcock a bloody nose. Neither mentioned it, so I played dumb while secretly hoping it were true.

'I couldn't get hold of him, so I've left a voicemail. His peace will be disturbed soon enough.'

And before I knew it, I was sitting in front of Spatchcock, having divulged the latest information and concluded that we would have to release Darren Anderson without charge. Spatchcock was pondering... I watched the cogs whirling, knowing that he was predictably calculating ways to distance himself from the decision-making process of arresting Anderson.

'Then I presume you'll prioritise linking the evidence from the Scott case to the Anderson case?'

He had been generally unsupportive of this, pursuing his own personal agenda, trying to save face with the arrest of the wrong man. 'Yes Sir. We're following the evidence...'

The cogs continued to whirl. 'So… I can confidently

announce that although we've had to release him, we've made great headway in identifying that we are looking for the same man for both murders.'

'Or woman Sir...'

'I'm not going to throw them that titbit. They'll be enough hysteria with the pack screaming – Serial Killer... I'll make a press statement this afternoon so if you can collate the points of information requests for the public A.S.A.P please.'

I got out of the lift on my floor and glanced through the glass doors towards the stairwell as something caught my eye. Josh... Josh was climbing those stairs as if he were wearing lead boots. There would be no other reason to go up there, unless to see or be summoned by Spatchcock.

He never mentioned anything all that afternoon and now we were sitting watching Spatchcock in his favourite place – on the box at prime time. Typically overdressed for the occasion, the only item missing were his white gloves and I could imagine him standing in front of the mirror, trying out the overall effect. Substituting serial killer for, 'linked murders,' in his statement, would not deter the press headlines from the most sensational. However, if we solved the case, Spatchcock would encourage his association with the term.

'A Spatchcock shit-sandwich...' adeptly assessed by Josh. 'One more thing,' he added, 'the families are okay with us publishing information to the press to gather further evidence – even Darren Anderson, who had every right to tell us where to go.'

'He'll have no choice. The suspicion he's under won't go away until his wife's killer is caught.'

The victim's pictures flashed on the screen; full of life and youth and no inkling of what lay ahead. The press would find their own narrative of a male serial killer and fill in any gaps from the statement and feverishly declare a sexual predator on the loose. It handed us a breather. Spatchcock only took a few questions from a couple of journalists, clearly favoured, primed and not very challenging. He flounced back up the steps at the front of the station, like Cinderella escaping the ball.

FOURTEEN
Friends

'You can't do that...'

'Oh yes I can you little shit. See this badge...' I shoved my warrant card a millimetre way from his spotty face. 'This means I'm a law unto myself and if I hear about one single dose of that gas showing up at any of those parties or you even breathe the same air as Emilia – I'll be coming for you.'

Swallowing back his tears, he sprinted to pick up the bike I'd kicked from beneath him. Flung his school rucksack over his back and shot off.

'Where did you disappear to?' Josh asked as I slotted beside him. 'We had to bear the brunt of Spatchcock's post-press briefing displeasure.'

'A little errand I needed to run at Emilia's school.' I looked up at the evidence board, now organised with precision by Josh with the two murders side by side and the links, both evidence-based and circumstantial. Boyfriends of both the geekish and stalkerish variety, discounted from The Scott case, unmuddied the waters.

'We've got to find the connection Josh, otherwise we won't know if this is a personal vendetta that's over or we actually do have a serial-killer.' I tapped on the picture of Stella Winchester: 'where are we with this one?'

'We should get her in and push her more on her relationship with Fiona Anderson and alibis for both murders. Angela is digging further into her finances and I've got a meet with her old Commanding Officer. But why would she clear out Catherine Scott's apartment knowing that they had photographic evidence to prove the opposite?' He asked.

'For the exact reason you've raised – casting doubt on her involvement. We already know that she knew how to gain access to the flat and credibly there was something amongst Catherine Scott's stuff which incriminated her. By taking everything, she can hide what she needed to conceal. Remember she searched the flat on her own. We've got to find out what connects the two victims and for now, she's the only person who knew both.'

I sipped my tea as Josh pointed at the picture of Darren Anderson which he insisted on remaining on the board until all suspicion in his mind was ruled out – which clearly was not yet. 'There are still the traces of soil evidence found in the foot-well of his car so if it's not him, someone must have framed him. How did they get access to his car? Would they have known where he worked or where he lived? Did he know them? We're going to have to reinterview him.'

'I know – and by all accounts he's making it known that he wants to do all he can to find his wife's killer so shouldn't be too awkward.' I stared once more at the picture of Stella before turning to the team. 'Does anyone have anything on the rest of Amy and Stella's friends? There's bound to be a group of them.'

'I do Boss...' Susie Tam joined us at the board. 'I found out that there are two other women they're close to.' She referred to her notebook: 'the first – Anna Rosso. I managed to track down yesterday to the Italian restaurant she runs with her husband in Woodford Green: a mother of three, the youngest aged ten – which is how she knows the others. She didn't seem to know that Amy and Stella had been off looking for Catherine Scott although she understood because they considered themselves closer to her.'

'And she didn't consider herself close?' I asked.

'She knew her... she liked her... but only mixed with her at school events. I was more interested in probing her view on her mates under the guise of finding out more about Catherine. I didn't have the impression that she was aware we were questioning Stella, otherwise I think she would've been more defensive.'

'Did she reveal anything interesting?' I asked.

'She commented that she felt the other mums in the playground were bitchy about Stella because she was...' Susie looked down at her notes to retrieve the quote: '"fit and gorgeous..." She said it never raised a reaction from her and she never seemed bothered. She knew that Stella had been supported by Catherine Scott but hadn't pushed her on it as she thought she'd tell her if she wanted but believed that she saw her up until her disappearance.'

'Did she give a hint of anything suspicious about Stella?'

'Well without being too obvious, I joked about Stella being able to take out any one of those mums. She agreed that she wouldn't want to get on the wrong side of her but when pushed, she'd never seen her lose her temper.' She returned to her notes once more. 'I asked if Catherine Scott helped anyone financially and she wasn't aware that she had and said that both Amy and Stella wouldn't need any help – as far as she was aware, they were both comfortably off. She did however know Fiona Anderson.'

'How well?'

'She used to eat in her restaurant with her family. She said that she'd pick at the food as though the whole place was beneath her but that the husband, mum and kids were nice. Sometimes she noticed that she left halfway during the meal, leaving her family behind and that she could see that the husband was pissed off.'

'So, she confirmed what we already know,' Josh added, 'that Fiona Anderson was a real bitch and that her husband had enough of her.' He held up his hands, 'don't worry I'm not going back there.'

'And no account of aggressive behaviour from Stella? What about the other friend? Did she give the same story?'

'The other friend – Bernadette Connor – heard that I'd seen Anna Rosso and has left a message that she wants to talk to us. Apparently, she's a bit of a handful...'

'You won't mind if we pick this one up?' Josh held his hand out for her details and made his way to the door.

Everything about Bernadette Connor screamed that she was wound up for a fight. A picture of truculence from her red hair and ruddy complexion to her bolt upright posture, punctuated with clenched fists.

'Thank you for seeing us today Mrs Connor, although–'

'Well... I was beginning to feel left out. After all, you've practically accused all my friends of murder.' She sat upright in her floral armchair with the menacing presence of framed family members, visible over her shoulder. Her hardened Dublin accent, exaggerated to heighten her threatening tone and a statement she needed to get off her chest. I sensed it was not her last.

'Your friends are merely helping us with our enquiries. Nobody has been accused of anything.'

'Sure... not even Stella?' She asked, accusingly.

'Why would you think we'd suspect Stella Winchester of these murders?'

She hesitated as though she didn't want that seed to germinate but decided to proceed regardless. 'She won't tell me much – probably doesn't want to worry me – but I know that you've dragged her in a number of times.' I left the accusation hang for a bit. She looked up a Josh, 'what are you staring at like an eijit? Are you supposed to be intimidating me? Because I tell you what lad – it's not working.'

'I wouldn't dream of intimidating you Mrs Connor, in fact I shouldn't think anyone would dare.' He returned to scribbling his notes, avoiding eye contact with the Staffordshire terrier settled by his feet.

'Too fecking right...' She shuffled around in her chair. At one point I thought she was going to kick us out.

'What do you want to tell us?' I asked encouragingly, in a

feeble attempt to diffuse her defensiveness.

She looked between us before choosing her words. 'As I said... I thought you'd want to speak to me but I can't think why it's taken you so long?'

'Amy Whitehead and Stella had valuable information to share concerning Catherine Scott and were proactive in wanting to help us. In contrast Mrs Connor, you seem to be more interested in hurling abuse.' She stared back hard with piercing green eyes, presumably re-evaluating her next move so I pushed on. 'If you have any information that you feel may be pertinent to the case – no matter how trivial – we'd be grateful to hear about what you know.'

She seemed to relax more into her chair and unfolded her arms from her ample breast as she began to speak: 'I came across Catherine Scott at an event at another school before she came to The Immaculate Heart.' She paused but I did not fill the gap. 'A bunch of us went to a fund-raising dinner and dance and Catherine was there so were The Andersons. It was there I saw how pally Catherine was with them. More with the husband if I'm honest, but that was the norm for most people they knew – Fiona was too busy having a love affair with herself to bother engaging with anyone else. I got chatting to Catherine at another do and from then on, we always seemed to end up in deep conversation when we bumped into each other. I think it made a change for her to do the talking with someone else listening. She had a queue of people always making demands on her time with their problems. She couldn't say no you see.'

'You're aware that your friends were amongst the people, "making demands" on her.' I suggested.

'I know...' she replied with little patience for interruption, 'but I don't mean them or those with genuine problems. I mean the likes of Fiona Anderson who would've spent her time going on about me... me... me...'

'Did she discuss any of their problems?'

She shook her head vigorously before confirming: 'no... no... nothing like that... If I was ever nosy and asked, she proved repeatedly that whatever was said to her in confidence, stayed as a confidence. No... We generally talked about her and her life. She seemed comfortable and it worked because I never needed anything from her. As I said – I'm a good listener.'

It was a stretch to believe – but I went with it. 'You sound like you became quite close. How come your friends never mentioned this to us?'

'Simply because I never mentioned it to them... I didn't want to make them feel awkward in case they thought Catherine was telling me about their problems and I didn't want Catherine to feel that I was tittle-tattling back to them. I reassured her that I wouldn't let on.'

'Are you prepared to tell us anything of relevance that she may have told you Mrs Connor or do you believe that you need to keep her confidence?'

'She's gone now...' The words seemed to catch in her throat as saying them aloud made it real for the first time. She recovered and continued. 'She was one for keeping up appearances, and in that circle the gossips didn't need much encouragement. I believe I was one of the few – if maybe only person, that she confided in about her personal life which despite her appearance – was pretty colourful.'

I felt Josh fidgeting around with frustration. I tapped his foot to settle down. I didn't want him setting her off again. 'Go on Mrs Connor...'

'Well... You should already know that she originally worked in the city and was fairly successful.'

Josh – quiet too long for his liking – interjected. 'Yes, we've seen the evidence.'

She looked at him ready to play her trump card, 'did you know that when she worked there, she worked alongside Darren Anderson?'

'They knew each other?'

She swung back to me, 'more than that... They were lovers for about three years.'

I tapped Josh on the foot again as I felt his body jerk. 'Was he married at the time?' I asked.

'Yes... and she was also going out with another Trader who found out and went ballistic. He threatened to tell Fiona but Catherine managed to calm him down. They split up, although I think he pestered her for a while.'

Josh looked up from his note-taking to ask, 'did she continue her affair with Darren Anderson?'

'No... That's when she walked away from him and that world.'

'How did they seem to interact when you saw them together at these school events? Did they seem awkward or maybe intimate?'

She pursed up her lips in contemplation, 'before knowing about the affair – I presumed they were pally. After knowing, I watched them together. She seemed at pains to come across business-like with him. I did ask her if she was seeing him again but she denied it.'

'Did you believe her?' I asked.

'Yes... You see... something else happened... something that greatly affected her.' She sat back in her chair and sighed. 'She fell pregnant... It was Darren's but I'm not sure he knew. Anyways, the most tragic, demented thing happened after she gave birth – the baby was snatched from the hospital and never recovered.' I looked across at Josh, a shared realisation of our incompetence at not having discovered this vital piece of information.

'And to push her to the limits of human endurance, she had medical issues later and although I didn't pry into the gory details, I believe it affected her ability to have any more children.'

Josh and I sat there in uniformed silence, attempting to disentangle the intricate web of relationships. I could hear Josh scratching away frantically in his notebook, a familiar sign that he was in the process of a brain dump before the gossamer threads of thought evaporated. I nudged her on, 'the victims clearly have a connection. You're a woman with strong opinions Mrs Connor – do you have a view of who could've killed these women?'

'Darren Anderson of course...' She folded her arms once more, underlining the accusation. 'That's why I couldn't wait any longer for you to come and see me. When I heard you'd let him go, I knew I had to tell you what's been going on.'

Josh leaned forward across the table. 'What's his motive? And why now?'

'I don't know... that's your job. But they're linked and you can't ignore that.'

She looked towards me for support but it didn't add up. 'Darren Anderson has an alibi for the time his wife was killed and he was in custody when Catherine Scott was murdered.'

'I don't care. He's connected somehow.' She was steadfast in her view.

'Is there anything else you'd like to tell us Mrs Connor?' I asked, mindful of the fact, that despite her demeanour, she was a mine of information.

Having exhausted her story-telling, she sat tight-lipped before wrapping up the interview in her own way, 'sure wasn't that enough? Have I to solve the fecking case for you an' all...?'

We finished up and returned to my office. Josh flicked through his notebook.

'Jesus Christ... you couldn't make this up. She's right – it should be Darren Anderson but it can't be and I don't know where the hell to start.'

'Were all the details of his alibi checked?' I asked, pointlessly.

'Yeah... as you can imagine I did it myself.' He used his

fingers to tick off his checklist: 'all the tracking data checked out – I even cross-referenced it at source. As we now had a fixed point to reference for his route, I followed a trail of CCTV along the route from where he got the ticket. The P.A. had no reason to cover or lie for him. I revisited some of the staff to root out any office gossip – none... Other departments she'd worked for confirmed that she used the procedures she claimed to use with Anderson and again, I cross-referenced at source to see if she had dealt with tickets for other managers and she had. I checked out her references with the previous companies she'd worked with to confirm her reliability – all sound. Anything I've missed?'

I responded with what I knew already, 'no... nothing... It's time to re interview Anderson I think.'

'I thought we were going to give him some breathing space,' Josh said.

'With this new evidence we need to dive back in. Call him and see what you can arrange. Maybe suggest meeting him on neutral ground somewhere if it makes him feel more comfortable. Get one of the team to start tracking down some of the other parents who would've been at these events and know both parties and see what their view was of the relationship between The Andersons and Catherine Scott. Also, anyone who noticed the closeness of Mrs Connor and Catherine.'

'Why...? In case she's got a dose of – Single White Female?' He punctuated with air-quotation marks and he knew I hated air-quotation marks.

'Not unheard of... And for Christ's sake – dig out everything we can about this supposed baby abduction. I can't recall anything like that in the last ten years.'

FIFTEEN
A Useful Journalist

'A coffee Josie...? Are you on the wagon?'

'Gotta keep a straight head on me Becky – a long evening awaits...'

She drank her lager straight from the bottle while eyeing me up – a noted habit amongst her predominantly male, journo colleagues. 'So… what are you after...? Are you going to pump me for information or are you going to give me something I can use?'

'Put the violin down... you've done well enough from me so far,' I reminded her – not that she needed it.

She leant forward earnestly, 'yes – but never any real dirt, only the occasional heads up.'

'Still don't dish dirt I'm afraid but you're not kidding anyone – we both know who your sources are for that.' She flopped back on her chair, smiling in defeat. I needed to keep her onside. I knew what the Press Office were about to reveal on the case so I could trade a day's notice for her paper to steal a march on the competition to get what I wanted. 'Do you remember a baby-snatching case from about 12 years ago from The Homerton Hospital? A boy named Daniel Scott. He was only days old when he was taken.' I took a swig of my coffee in desperate need of a caffeine kick.

She held her head in her hands and rolled her eyes to the ceiling, searching for the corresponding headline to the memory so I continued churning out what I knew: 'the mum was a city type... no father mentioned... the baby was never found...'

She sat up, animated, 'got it... *100k reward. What price for a life?*

'She offered a reward?'

'Yeah... I think it kept going up. She was desperate. Understandably...' She picked up her phone – her fingers almost a blur as they flew over the screen. 'But it was twelve years ago so I'm a bit foggy until I revisit some of the interviews.'

'You interviewed her...?'

'Yeah... I was the lead reporter on the-' She froze and looked from her screen to me. 'Holy fuck! It's Catherine Scott. The second murdered woman.'

'You can have the exclusive on the connection but only when I know all there is to know so feel free to start sharing,' I warned.

Her head fell into a rhythmical nod as she speed-read her old work. 'Okay... worked in the city as you said... hired her own investigation team when Police failed to come up with any leads. She thought it was someone at the hospital but no evidence.'

'Forward me the details of the investigators,' I said, unsure if she was listening.

'God… I remember now... she was a hard one to read. Not exactly emotionless but very controlled. At one point I thought she did it herself.'

'You're kidding?'

'I know... I know... sounds fucked up. But it's a fucked-up world out there. Do you think there's some connection between her murder and the snatching?' she asked, her journalistic senses tingling.

I raised an eyebrow.

She took another swig of her beer, eyeing me suspiciously before her challenge, 'it's pretty obvious to me why you've had to come to some old hack for your info.'

I tilted my head with feigned ignorance.

'You lot cocked up,' she continued as she leaned in across the table. 'D.I. Foster was on the case… coming up for retirement… already demob happy from what I can recall. Never took Catherine Scott seriously and pounced on the theory that the baby was already out of the country. I bet the paper trail is practically non-existent.'

She wasn't far off from the truth. The files we'd managed to pull weren't worth reading. I was embarrassed for whoever thought that passed for policework – presuming they had some integrity about the job…

'No… there are files,' I said, in the grey area of truth. 'But I'm interested in what's not there. I need as much background info as I can on her. Didn't you follow through some of the leads?' I asked, in an attempt to swerve her away from finding something before we did.

I could tell she wasn't buying it as she rolled on the back-legs of her chair. 'Yeah...' she confirmed. 'I door-stepped a few relatives and friends on her side but they were all loyal with nothing much to say. I followed through on some hearsay reports of, "weird acting" staff. Thought it might lead to some paedo baby-snatching groups. Did uncover some paedos but no baby-snatchers.' She rolled her beer bottle between her palms. 'I came to the same conclusion though as the mother – that it was someone in the hospital. They closed ranks and were generally unhelpful. As I said… one theory was that the baby would be well out of the country and on the continent. I know from a police source that Interpol had been involved. There was nothing on CCTV except staff coming and going – all recognised and accounted for… apparently...'

'But you didn't believe it...? I asked.

'Nah... Someone knew something. But it would look bad on them. So, the months went by and police resources were needed elsewhere and headlines changed. I don't think I heard about it since.'

'Weren't you curious?'

'Sure...' she sounded regretful – for a second. 'But news moves on and keeps coming at ya.'

SIXTEEN
Contact

The office was buzzing so was my head. I couldn't hear myself think. I vaguely made out the chant of 'Boss,' and lifted my head. It was George at the door with his finger and thumb against his face like a phone. 'Is it them?' I mouthed. He nodded.

'Right, everyone... shut up!' I hollered. The team looked around as though I'd lost it. 'Michael... try and trace this... George put it through to his extension.' Josh gave me his – what the… – look. I indicated to the phone on his desk to listen in on the call. I waited for Michael's nod before picking up. 'Hello D.C.I. Connelly. Can I help you?'

'Hello Josephine...' The synthetic voice was genderless.

'Hello... who am I speaking to?'

'Fiona Anderson won't be missed...'

I controlled my breathing and tried to keep the urgency from my voice. 'I think her family will miss her. Two kids growing up without a mum isn't good in anyone's book.'

'You're not fooling anyone Josephine. You'll know enough about her now to know she was a crap mother and those kids will be better off without her.'

'Sorry... do you have some information about her murder? Can you give me your name?'

'Some information...?' A deep chuckle followed. 'Well… I was disappointed that she wasn't breathing when I buried her. She would have deserved that.'

I frantically looked across at Michael but he shook his head. 'Are you saying that you killed Fiona Anderson?'

'She wouldn't shut up.'

A pause... and all I could hear was my own blood pumping in my head. 'Why not tell me about it. We could meet…'

'Have you found the Rolex yet?' The phone clicked as they hung up.

'Shit...!'

Josh held the phone away from his ear looking stunned.

'Not long enough...' Michael confirmed, shaking his head vigorously.

'Josh... Come on snap out of it... Do you know if we released details of the jewellery?'

'No... No...'

'Right... Susie... Track down Stella Winchester. Find out where she was at the time of the call and stick to her Susie... Don't let her out of your sight for a minute. And remember... she's ex-army so stealth-mode please.'

The tail end of, 'yes Boss...' was heard as she shot out the door.

I turned to Michael, 'I want you and all your techie mates from the basement to come up with some creative solutions to analysing that voice pattern and look for a match.'

Josh followed me into my office, 'we haven't got Stella Winchester on tape.'

'I know... Get her in...'

'What are you thinking Boss...?'

'This changes the game... She knew my name.'

'She...? You think it's Stella...?'

'Maybe... maybe not. But I do think it's a woman. No sexual activity... the tidiness of the burial... reference to motherhood...'

'We've been told of the availability of a profiler if you think it'll help?'

'No... They'll clutter up my thinking... Angela...!' I yelled. She bolted into the room. 'Find me a connection... Look into all the schools mentioned – cross reference everyone. Shake the tree and see who falls out.'

Susie returned after a long day's surveillance. 'It would've been around the school run,' she said, looking tired but wired. 'Usual domestic toing and froing since...

Odds are, a pay-as-you-go was used but that'll be long gone and no trips to purchase any more and no home deliveries that I witnessed since.'

'I'll see her on my own,' I told Josh. 'You observe. I don't want to spook her and Susie… keep out of sight.'

'Okay Boss... by the way,' she said, looking sheepish, 'as I followed her here, I noticed she was carrying a large sports bag so I called ahead and asked the Desk Sergeant to tell her to check it in for security purposes – thought I'd have a rummage. If she mentions it...'

'I'll pretend I never heard that, now bog off.'

Stella Winchester was dressed in gym gear once again and looked generally relaxed. I needed to keep her that way. 'Thank you so much for coming in. I hope we didn't drag you from work?'

'No problem – I got the Overground straight here from my last client.'

'Good... good... well I'll try not to keep you long, it's just... as you've probably heard on the news, we're working on the theory that the Catherine Scott and Fiona Anderson cases are linked. We're revisiting anyone who knew them both to see if they can help us with a connection.'

'As I told you the last time, I didn't know Fiona Anderson too well. She was one of those pushy mothers I saw at a theatre school our children attended but she left in a huff to join another one I believe.'

'Yes, I remember... but I'm interested in anyone else she was friendly with there. Did she have any friends? Did you know anyone who knew her there?'

'She wasn't the type to have friends – more of an entourage I'd say. She'd collect people... manipulate them for her own gain...'

She maintained the same dispassionate detachment I experienced in our last interview. Hard to crack. 'And you saw all that from drop-off at the theatre school?' I asked.

'Do you have children?' she asked.

'I do...'

'Then you'll know that the school gate, even a theatre one such as this, is a microcosm of life played out for all to see.'

I smiled encouragingly. 'Was there anyone in her entourage that you knew or were pally with?'

'Do we look like we'd have any friends in common?' She managed to say, without seeming patronising.

She continued making little effort to engage and managed to control any tone in her responses. It suddenly dawned on me that she would have been trained in interrogation and we were amateurs in comparison. I was feeling uncomfortably self-conscious but ploughed on: 'Oh I don't know... sometimes opposites attract.'

She gave a frustrated sigh, 'well not in this case.'

'What did you think of her as a parent?'

'I told you... I didn't know her well enough,' she replied, maintaining her even tone.

'I know... but indulge me... tell me what you observed in that, "microcosm of life," at the gate.'

She folded her arms as she leant back on her chair, scanning the room as though it was something she had to dig deep to think about. I let her ponder... 'What did I see...?' she began. 'Well… the daughter looked like she wanted for nothing but surprisingly, never showed any brattish tendencies when Fiona kicked off about anything to do with her classes. The daughter always looked embarrassed and asked her to stop. She acted the doting mother in front of everyone although I didn't witness any spontaneous acts of affection towards each other.'

'Did you see the son or the husband?' I prodded.

'Yes... the son was a grumpy teenager towards her but seemed more relaxed if he ever turned up with the dad. As did the daughter... a much more genuine dynamic I'd say between the three of them.'

'What did you think of her as a mother Stella?'

She readjusted herself in her chair and sat taller. 'I think that is a more loaded question. How can any of us mothers judge each other, unless we know what's going on in the home.'

Well played, I thought, before broaching another line of enquiry. 'Is there anything you know about the connection between Fiona Anderson and Catherine Scott?' I asked.

'As I mentioned in my last interview, I saw Catherine one day when I was out in Belsit for lunch. I popped over to say hello and she introduced me to the woman she was lunching with and it was Fiona Anderson. The next time I saw Catherine, I innocently asked about Fiona because I recognised her – although not surprisingly she didn't recognise me. She told me – in confidence, so I didn't give the information up lightly – that she'd helped Fiona when she was a teacher at her previous school. Fiona's son was playing up at school and she was called in to discuss it with Catherine. And as is... was... Catherine's way, she realised that there was more to it and tried to help where possible. She said that Fiona was a difficult woman to help but she persevered for the sake of her son, feeling that she didn't have time for him.'

'It seems to chime with the agreed perception from everyone we spoke to, that she was a – right bitch...'

'As I said… I didn't know her well enough to make that assumption.' She was not biting.

'Did Catherine Scott ever bring her up again?'

'No... never...'

'Or mention the husband?'

'Never...'

'Does anything about how she speaks resemble your caller?' Josh asked as we watched the tape of the interview for the second time.

'No... We're not going to pick it up by ear. We're going

to have to see what Michael and his geekies can match.'

'And she never let your baiting about Fiona get to her. Her lack of response was almost worthy of a politician.'

'I know...' I agreed, 'too controlled for my liking. Her alibi's still not water-tight enough to rule her out. She also claims not to know Darren Anderson – let's see if he knows her?'

SEVENTEEN
Revisiting An Old Suspect

We parked up by the club house at The Essex Golf Club beside a row of Range Rover Sports, punctuated by the odd Bentley, Hummer and Porsche Cayenne. I finished my call with Susie as we climbed out of the car. Josh strolled off along the rows of cars, peaking through the tinted windows before moving onto the next. I caught up. 'Anything interesting?'

'The interior of the Maserati isn't as nice as the Cayenne.'

I pulled a face, 'and yet I am unmoved...'

'Did Susie find anything from Stella's gym bag?' He asked as he slipped on his suit jacket.

'She says, the shoe size matches and she's taken photos of the trainer-treads to give to forensics and a sports bra seems to have fallen out "by accident," when Stella handed in the bag – which is being returned to the owner via forensics.' Josh pulled a face. 'I know... nothing we can use and don't tell Monroe how we obtained it but it will give us a steer whether to continue pursuing her or not.'

He followed me onto the gravel path up to the club house. The Victorian Gothic building's exterior was sympathetically replicated inside as dark wood panelling and crimson red plush carpets, paved our way to the bar. Josh couldn't hide his annoyance. 'Is this the neutral ground he needed to meet us on to feel comfortable? Or is he trying to rub our noses in it?'

'Stop being so paranoid. He's never once played the flash Cockney Trader.'

He grunted something I chose to ignore as I scoured the bar for Anderson. The room was practically empty. I presumed most would have been out on the green this late in the afternoon and pots of tea seemed to be the beverage of choice. I spotted a high-winged chair, angled to face the wall in an alcove at the back which fitted the bill.

Josh fell in behind me as I approached. I stepped in front of the chair. 'Mr Anderson...'

He looked up from his newspaper. 'D.C.I. Connelly…'

'Do you mind?' I indicated to the chair in front of him as Josh dragged across another, like a dead body from a crime scene. He nodded noncommittally, returning to his paper. Josh was now settled beside me.

I allowed him his moment of disdain and sat in silence as he continued to ignore us. Succumbing to the inevitable, he folded his newspaper and placed it on the table before looking up.

'Thank you for seeing us today Mr Anderson.'

'Did I have a choice?' he replied, expressionless.

'I presume you'll want to do all you can to help catch your wife's killer and as we now believe they may have killed more than once.'

'And what...? You'll try to connect them to me?'

'No Mr Anderson but there are questions that need answering from new information brought to our attention.' He pulled a – so what – face, so I continued: 'as I'm sure you already know, Catherine Scott – the Deputy Head of The Immaculate Heart primary school – was murdered while you were on remand.' I searched for a speck of acknowledgement. Nothing... I was not disposed to continue offering him polite courtesies so I changed my tone. 'Can you explain to us why you never disclosed your relationship with Catherine Scott?'

Now the face changed. From frozen with a glimmer of panic, landing on incredulity. 'It was a long time ago and irrelevant to my wife's murder.'

'That's for us to decide Mr Anderson. As you can imagine, although you're not being accused of Miss Scott's death–'

'Because I was locked up at the time...'

'The connection cannot be ignored and will require

further investigation. Because if you didn't do it Mr Anderson – someone who knew both women did and there's a strong possibility that you'll know who this person is. Now in your own words do you want to tell us about your relationship with Catherine Scott?'

'What do you know?' he asked, reluctantly.

'Presume we know everything but now want to hear it from your point of view.'

He took his time in fixing both of us a determined look of distrust before he decided to begin: 'I loved my wife… always have... always will... But she was a complex woman with constant demands. She didn't have mood swings... she had personality swings. The thread of a craving for constant attention, running through both.' The weight of accusation now lifted, seemingly freed him from the fear of self-incrimination as he continued. 'When her behaviour started to impact on the children, together with her mum, we managed to convince her to get some help. She was diagnosed as Bipolar.'

'There was no indication of medication from the P.M. toxicology report.' Josh was right. This was the first we'd heard of it.

'There wouldn't be... a discreet, private doctor saw to that. It was a constant battle to get her to take her tablets. She felt it was a conspiracy to control her. I can give you the details of her private doctors.'

With-holding evidence... How much more did we miss?

'As I said... I loved her. I somehow held onto the hope that she would get better. That she didn't mean the vicious things she said or did. Even when I found out about the affairs, I knew her intent was to get a reaction from me but if I went there... the marriage would be over. I never acknowledged her infidelities but I ensured she was safe.'

'And what about your own infidelities...? What was your intent when having an affair with Catherine Scott?'

'A semblance of a normal relationship, I guess. I lived in

parallel worlds. Both dysfunctional in their own way but ironically, work provided the normality to help me cope with the insanity of my home life. Catherine Scott and I were work colleagues. We had a lot in common. We got on and... we became close. Neither of us was looking for a relationship so it worked. In fact, on her part, I believe it wasn't mutually exclusive.'

He reeled his account off as though a common occurrence – leading me to ask: 'Did you love her?'

'No... But that doesn't mean that I didn't care for her.'

'How did you feel when she told you she was pregnant?'

'I was pleased for her,' he didn't hesitate in saying. 'She told me it wasn't mine and that she was going to keep it. She'd made a shit load of money and I knew she was tired of the lifestyle. It made sense when she walked away from it all. Until... well... you know about her baby being taken?'

'Yes… we do. Did you have any contact with her at that time?'

'No... We agreed not to contact each other when she left – part of her desire for a clean break. I attempted to contact her when it happened. She didn't return any of my calls and I didn't want to add to her anx. I let her know that I was there if she needed any help but I presumed she involved the father.'

Josh referred to his notes before posing the next question: 'the files on the case state that Catherine Scott wouldn't reveal the name of the father as he didn't know but she told a close friend that it was you. Didn't you at least suspect when she told you?'

'Me... No... I... I'm sure we used protection, otherwise I would have questioned it.'

'Why would she say it was yours?'

'I don't know… Catherine would want to get on with it herself. If it was... is... mine... I'd do all I could...'

He looked away, distracted. An essential attribute for men who have affairs, is that they need to be good liars. It was hard to trust any of his reactions. I pushed on. 'When did you come across her again?' I asked.

'What...? Err... many years later at some school function, I think. I surprised myself at how pleased I was to see her. She seemed full of life and plans for the future. It was infectious. In fact, Catherine ended up teaching at the school our kids attended for a while before moving on. Ironically during that time, Fiona went to see Catherine for help with our son. Well... not for him. It turned into the usual need for Fiona to manipulate someone onto her side. Catherine let me know, giving me the opportunity to say no. But I thought… if my son could benefit indirectly – I was all for it.'

The waiter had been hovering for a while before taking the plunge. 'Can I get you or your guests anything Mr Anderson?'

'I'll have a mug of breakfast tea please.'

Josh took my lead and shook his head politely as I continued, 'your wife didn't suspect?'

'Fiona wouldn't have had any reason to suspect. She deemed Catherine no more than an old work colleague and she didn't match Fiona's photofit of what a threat would look like. In fact, she referred to her as – The Ice Maiden.'

'And that suited your cover?'

'I wasn't looking for a cover Sergeant,' he batted back at Josh. 'My wife was too preoccupied with her world of self-obsession to notice anyone else.'

I wanted to tone down the accusations. 'How often did you come across her? Did you ever meet up separately?'

'No... I bumped into her three or four times at the most. She told me about her new life in teaching and that she was hoping to adopt. She seemed happy. I was pleased for her.'

'And how did you feel when you heard about her death?' I asked.

'Shocked, more than anything,' he smiled his thanks at the waiter who delivered the tea. 'Shocked that she was murdered... She was a decent person. Even in the pressure cooker that is the city, she was one of the few authentic people.'

'Apart from when she was having affairs with married men...?'

Okay Josh – stop going there. Not helping... I nudged his leg.

Anderson took a sip of his tea before taking his time to place it back on the table. 'I was the only one. It broke her code. I think that was part of her walking away from everything in the city. Including me. She was becoming something she couldn't live with.'

'Didn't you question the connection when you heard about her death?'

'If you recall… I was in custody with everything stacked against me. I was preoccupied with the prospect of my children living a life without either parent. I didn't think about her death beyond what I've told you.'

I allowed him that shot. He could have fired it earlier in the interview but I had to give him his due – he remained restrained, considering how much he could have kicked off with his wrongful arrest. 'And now Mr Anderson...? Have you thought of the connection since your release?'

'No... Selfishly I haven't. I've been focusing on helping my family through their grief after being robbed of this opportunity after my wife's death.'

Shot two... Still justified although I suspect Josh was at the end of his spectrum of tolerance.

'The vital piece of forensic evidence held against you was the soil sample in the foot-well of your car,' Josh began, 'matching the soil in the park. Are you still holding fast that there is no explanation for the soil getting there?'

'On the contrary... The explanation is that it was planted.'

He was missing the point, so I laid it out: 'then Mr Anderson... with your wife murdered and your ex-lover murdered and someone trying to frame you, I suggest that you think long and hard if there is anyone in your professional or private life who could have a grudge against you?'

'No... No... No one would do this!'

'Do you owe money to anyone? Got into a financial deal that went wrong?' Josh prodded, reverting to his tactic of pushing him to the edge which I preferred he avoided in front an audience.

'No... Some deals do go bad but there's no Russian heavy or African warlord behind any of them or anyone out to get me. If that were the case, they'd be after something and I would've been contacted by now?'

'Maybe one of Catherine Scott's ex-lovers wanted to get their own back?' I suggested.

'What with murder...? No... no... it's too far-fetched.'

'We've been interviewing some of the mums from the school, who could have a connection with both women,' I began as I pulled out a photograph of Stella Winchester. 'Have you ever met this woman?'

He took the photo from me and scrutinised it, 'she looks familiar but I can't place her...'

'Does the name Stella Winchester mean anything?'

He shook his head. 'No... No... Never heard of her.'

'She was one of the mums at the theatre school from a couple of years ago,' I prompted.

He looked back at the photo, 'I may have met her... but I couldn't be sure... Why...? Has she got something to do with it? Is she a suspect?'

The last thing I needed was him mouthing off to the press. 'No... We're eliminating anyone who knew both women but she was never a friend of your wife. Look... this murderer is still out there. I suggest you get thinking about a possible cause for the safety of your family.' He sat ashen-faced and stared at the wall. I could see the waiter approaching again in my peripheral vision and signalled for him to go away. 'I think a starting point might be if you could list all the people who could've known both Fiona and Catherine. Our belief is that they both knew their murderer. Can you do that?' Remaining fixated on the wall, he nodded his agreement. 'We'll need the list as soon as possible.'

He nodded once more before asking, 'did they find him? Did they find the baby?'

'I'm sorry no...' Josh told him. 'The case is still open.'

We left him in his comatose state. All eyes on us in the now full bar, as the waiter darted back to Darren Anderson with a whiskey-laden tray. A sea of garish lemon and salmon pink V-necks stretched out before us; the Pringle trend of my youth flashing before my eyes.

We escaped to the car park. I strapped in as Josh started the engine while making an unconnected observation, 'was that Charlie Wright in there holding court? I didn't know he was out,' he said.

'Me neither. Send someone to his old haunts down the Hackney Road. I could do without that kicking off again – at least until we've this case sorted.'

Josh asked his burning question: 'what do you think of Darren Anderson? Still think he's innocent?'

'Well… he hasn't been straight with us but yes… I do... In fact, now that he's been exonerated, he could be a potential victim. If someone took the trouble to set him up, they're not going to be too happy at the moment.'

EIGHTEEN
The Silent Witness

'Where've you been?'

Josh flopped down into the chair in front of my desk, 'to the Twilight Zone… well Interview Room 2.'

'Not in the mood Josh. Spit it out or get out.' Knowing the boundaries of my tolerance after a meeting with Spatchcock, he shaped up. 'A priest has come in. He mentioned the murders but won't say anything else.' Wavering between intrigue and annoyance I looked up as he continued. 'That's it... We went around and around in circles. I asked a bucket load of questions relating to the murders to provoke some kind of response but he remained stony silent.'

'And where is he now?' I asked, doing nothing to hide my impatience.

'He's still in there. It's too weird not to be of some importance. Do you want a go? I thought – being one of your lot – you might fare better.'

'My lot... Really Josh? Sod it... why not. This day can't get any weirder.' A spot of spiritual guidance might be what I needed. I grabbed a file and my coffee from my desk. 'Angela... with me...'

Angela followed me into the interview room and sat down in the left-hand chair, already knowing my preference.

The priest rose to his feet and held out his hand. 'Good afternoon. My name is Father Michael. I'm from Our Lady of Lourdes in Wanstead.'

I grasped his hand and was taken aback by its roughness, a hand covered in calluses more reminiscent of a navvy than a pampered priest from an urban parish. A face blighted by rosacea and yellowing bloodshot eyes, betrayed his drinking preferences. His skin was leathery as though too much sun exposure, hard to reconcile with sun-deprived London so it was difficult to age him: somewhere between 50 and 65 at a guess.

'Nice to see you Father. I'm D.C.I. Connelly. Can I offer you a drink?'

'No thank you...'

'I'm up the road at St Anne's but I do attend your fetes. Can't recall having seen you there though...'

He sat back down as though exhausted after a day's labour. 'I tend to keep to myself I'm afraid. Not one for meet and greet.'

'I thought it was part of the job Father although if you don't mind me saying, you don't look like a typical priest from a city parish. A bit of a fish out of water I'd say.'

'No... I don't...' He seemed to relax – ever so slightly. 'I was a missionary in Africa – Uganda to be precise.'

'Missionary...' Angela looked across at me, 'do they still have them?'

'I know it sounds an old fashioned concept,' he continued, 'but it's not about the white man imposing his religion onto the savages. We're there to help the most vulnerable living in desperate conditions, in whatever humble way we can.'

'I'm aware of some of this work Father. Our school fund-raises for the missions. We hear terrible reports: nuns kidnapped... shootings... Not for the faint-hearted. What brought you back to Wanstead?'

He looked down at his worn-out hands; a tell-tale tremor inducing him to slip them down onto his lap. 'I was recalled on medical grounds.'

I suddenly felt a wave of shame. He didn't deserve to feel humiliated. He looked like he'd suffered enough. 'I understand Father... I believe that you've come in today enquiring about some of our murder cases. Is that right?' His head remained bowed. The first stumbling block... 'Can you confirm the cases you're referring to?'

He looked up, 'Fiona Anderson and Catherine Scott.'

I took a breath as I mulled over where to go with this. 'And did you know the victims?' I began.

'No...'

'Did they attend your church Father?'

'No...'

He looked at me with eyes pleading for me to ask the right questions. I felt like a doctor trying to communicate with a coma victim: blink once for yes, twice for no... 'Did you know any of the victim's family or friends?'

'No...'

'Have you seen something relating to the murders?'

'No...'

'Why can't you tell us what you know Father?' Angela said with undisguised annoyance.

He ignored her desperate question and I continued, 'has someone told you something in confidence that you are reluctant to betray.' He remained fixed on me. 'Father... has someone told you something in The Confessional, relating to these murders?'

He held my gaze; his rheumy eyes, masking any true emotional reaction. I could feel Angela holding her breath. 'Has the murderer confessed to you Father?' I knew what I was asking. I knew that there was no way he would break the seal of the confessional. I knew that if the answer was no – he would have responded with firm conviction. He did not.

I rested my face on my hands in front of me, formed as though in prayer. How to continue...? The question had been such a long shot. I was genuinely shocked by the outcome. We had a real chance of catching this killer through the cooperative priest who was prohibited in his ability to cooperate.

'I'm not insensitive to what it must have taken for you to come here today Father. Please accept my thanks because what you've revealed is not insignificant and could save lives.'

He swallowed hard and seemed to need to take a deep inhalation of breath. As he unlocked eye contact with me, his head fell to his chest and his gaze dropped to his lap.

'I know you've gone out on a limb coming here. I've met enough of the Bishops to know none of them would stick their neck out.' A vision of Spatchcock in Bishopric finery popped into my head. 'And undeniably don't know what you're doing but I need to ask you a few general questions if that's okay?' He nodded slowly. 'If someone wanted to go to confession at your church, would they have to keep to the allotted time or would you see them as they demanded?'

He paused with the weight of a response. 'The latter...'

'And was the voice in the confessional one that you'd ever heard before?' I asked.

'No...'

I opened the file and pulled out six photographs and lined them out in front of him. 'Do you recognise any of these people Father?'

He looked down and, in his defence, gave them due consideration. He pulled aside the pictures of Catherine Scott, Fiona and Darren Anderson. 'I think these are the two women who were murdered and the husband who was accused.'

'Have you seen any of them in your church?'

'No... But neither do I see anyone who has been in the confessional.'

I pushed the photo of Darren Anderson forward, 'have you ever seen or met this man in any circumstances or engaged in conversation with him?'

He scrutinised the photo once more and looked back up at me, 'no...'

I picked out the picture of Stella Winchester, 'and what about this woman?'

'The same...'

I was not expecting an answer from my next question

but it had to be asked. 'Father.... Was the person in your confessional a woman?' I searched his face for the slightest twitch or flick of an eye that I could translate as a confirmation. Nothing... and no denial... 'You see I believe it is a woman Father so I'm going to cut out the fannying around and talk about her openly.' He gave away an unconscious slight nod. 'You see Father, she's been in touch...' He stared across with a look of disbelief. 'She's admitted that the first wasn't planned but seems to have justified it to herself. Not only is there a complete lack of remorse, I believe that she now feels she has a mission. We need to discover the belief that drives her Father to prevent any further deaths.'

'Yes... I understand that...'

'Did she reveal to you what has happened in her life to trigger this killing spree?'

Once again, he took his time before nodding, 'yes...'

I noticed that he was beginning to sweat, punctuated with a sweetly stale odour, it was easy to recognise alcohol sweats. 'Angela... could you get Father Michael some water please?'

Suddenly self-conscious, he took a greying handkerchief from his pocket and dabbed his brow. 'Would you like a break Father?'

'No... I'm fine.'

Angela returned with the water which he gulped greedily.

'What do you feel you can tell me about the cause of her compulsion to kill?'

'She prays to Our Lady...' he said with firm affirmation. As much as he could tell us. What the hell did it mean?

Angela blurted an intolerant, 'what...?' to which she received a nifty kick under the table.

'Father... do you think she will kill again?' I asked.

'Yes...' he replied, slumping back as though the Holy Spirit himself had left his body. 'I firmly believe...'

'And will she return to you?'

'I think so...'

I knew he was unable to tell me anymore and pushing him further might dissuade him from assisting us later. 'Thank you, Father. One final question... Have you been concerned for your own safety?'

His expression seemed to relax, released from the straight jacket of our constrained exchange. 'That's difficult to answer as I have long past caring.'

I believed him and presumed he cared even less if The Bishop got hold of him. 'We'll take it from here, Father. Continue doing what you've been doing, business as usual but do not put yourself in the way of danger. That's what we're here for and besides... my mother would kill me if I was responsible for the death of a priest.' He smiled and for a moment I saw a glimpse of the man he once was. 'Here's my card Father. Please call me any time – immediately if there's something I need to know.'

I was back in my office with Josh and Angela standing in front of my desk. 'You got all of that out of him although he said nothing?' Josh was not convinced.

'It was like some weird voodoo magic...'

'Yes, thank you Angela – that'll do. I want to make it clear to both of you that I don't want it to be known outside this office that the priest was in here today. We'll say we're working on a tip off. Now Angela, go and see if there's CCTV set up near the church.'

'Yes Boss.'

'What's the plan?' I could see that Josh wanted to fly out of the door as well and do something meaningful. 'This could be the break we need.'

'If there's CCTV down that road, I want it scoured for any known faces and if any of them live in that area. If there's none, I want one set up straightaway with a live feed to this office. I won't get clearance for surveillance as it's all too vague for Spatchcock.'

'Do you think Father Michael will contact you if they do?'

'I believe he will. He's come this far. If the murderer has seen him more than once, we can presume Father Michael is now part of their process.'

'So, he forgives them – giving them licence to go and kill again?' His accusatory tone, in-keeping with his agnostic views.

'No... It doesn't work like that.' I tried not to sound defensive, my own view of the man-made practice not far from his. 'They've got to be penitent to receive absolution and they'll know that.'

'Then they're going to torment Father Michael or God?'

'Perhaps... But it does tell us that they are or were Catholic. So far, everyone involved is associated with the Catholic schools within a four mile radius from the church.'

'Couldn't he have given some clue to who we're after? I mean, what's supposed to happen? You don't believe in all that fire and brimstone rubbish, do you? Can't his superiors make him talk?'

'It's not the armed forces Josh. If he breaks The Seal of Confession, he'll get the ecclesiastical boot and as he's given us the best lead that we've had in the case so far, I don't want to bring that down on his head. He's risked much by coming here.'

'Even though he sat there saying nothing?'

Our religious debate was interrupted by Angela tapping on my door, 'Boss... We've a camera down that road. May I...?' She walked around to my side of the desk and logged onto my P.C. – deftly navigating her way through The Met's programmes until the live feed popped up on the screen. 'Good view of the bank but not of the church entrance.'

'Josh – can you arrange for a camera opposite the church please.'

'I can do that... Sorry...' The colour flushed Angela's

cheek with self-awareness of her boldness. 'It's just that I went to Uni. with someone in the department who'll push it through for me.'

'Great Angela... Go to it... Josh, create the paperwork and pass it on. Do you think you can get it organised by the morning?' She smiled back and left the office which was enough for me. I turned to Josh, 'get someone down there with a camera until the CCTV is up. Knowing our bloody luck, it'll all kick-off tonight.'

Josh headed for the door and stopped, 'if we think she goes to confess after one of their services, we should see if anyone recognises any of the suspects?'

'No... I don't want you to scare her off. Focus on the CCTV first and see who pops up. I'm worried about Father Michael though. There's no guarantee that he won't say something that doesn't agree with the killer's script. He's already shown that he wants to stop her by risking so much coming here. He might be stupid enough to take her on so that camera is also for his protection.'

'Boss...!' Michael shouted from his desk. 'It's her...'

NINETEEN
Mary

'Should I get Spatchcock to listen in?' Josh asked as we headed for Michael's desk, now set up with extra hardware.

'Don't you dare.' I looked around the room. 'All ready?' And with a returned collective nod, I picked up the receiver. 'D.C.I. Connelly speaking...'

'Hello Josephine...' The synthetic voice remained.

'Hello... Ready to tell me your name yet?' Static filled the pause. 'No...? Why don't I give you a name then? The Press love something to hang their headlines onto. Do you know what...? I think I'll call you Mary. How does that sound?' Still no response... shit... more static...

'I see you've been to the woods Josephine; scrabbling around in the ferns for rodents.'

'What did Catherine Scott do to you Mary?'

'Mary... Holy Mary, Mother of God... I like that...'

'Why did you kill Catherine?'

'She knew why... She was still scratching around in the dirt even after I hit her hard so I took the time to tell her. To remind her. She hadn't made the connection silly bitch and when I told her, do you know what she did?' I held my breath not wanting any utterances to stop her flow. 'She cried... she cried for the loss... but it wasn't her loss… it was mine.'

'What did you lose?'

'Have you ever killed anyone Josephine?'

None of her business… but… why not…? 'Yes…'

'Then you'll understand. That moment... that moment of exhilaration... euphoria... it takes away the pain. Did you find that?'

'No... No… I didn't.'

'It's only temporary of course which is why it's so addictive. But you'll know that...'

'No... I don't...'

'There are so many of them you know... so many of them who shouldn't be allowed near children. I see that now. You will too...'

'What do you mean...? Mary...? Mary...?'

'She's gone Boss but we've got her,' Michael blurted out. 'The Laundry Cafe, Cambridge Heath Road...'

Josh drove full pelt through the congested London roads while I tried to get hold of Susie. After numerous rings, she answered. 'Have you sight of Stella, Susie?'

'No Boss... I'm down by the church...'

'What the hell are you doing there?'

'John told me that Sarge said I was to hang around and see what I could find out.'

I looked across at Josh, 'Susie... Listen to me carefully – you're to stick to Stella Winchester until I tell you different are you clear? Now go and try and find out where she's been for the last hour.'

'Yes Boss.'

'You took Susie off Stella Winchester to cover the church...?' I launched at Josh.

'No...' he batted back. 'I put John on the church.'

'I want that arsehole off the team...' I ranted as we pulled up outside the cafe.

Uniform came out to meet us. 'Nobody there...'

'CCTV...?'

'Not in the cafe...'

'Shit... shit... shit...' I did a full 360 degree turn… taking in the street... looking into the faces of the crowd gathered outside and those going about their everyday business. Was she here...? Was she watching...?

Josh came up beside me, 'we found the phone in the loo but Michael's not hopeful. The cafe owner's some middle-class anarchist – talking about police states, blah... blah… Claims he didn't notice anyone...'

'It figures...' The gawping crowd grew. I needed to get away. 'Drop me off at Our Lady of Lourdes on the way back will you.'

I entered the church as a service finished. The elderly congregation smiling at me as though recognising one of their own. My nostrils filled with the scents of the burning rituals of the mass, each provoking my own memories of family, both as a child and with my own. I dipped my hand into the font and made the sign of the cross. As wavering as my faith was, there was still something spiritually enlightening about a catholic church. Once you removed the sanctimonious clergy with their self-profiteering rules, you were left bearing your soul to a greater being – whoever that may be. I liked to think it was a place where I didn't have to explain myself: who I was or what was happening to me. He or she – just knew......

I was drawn to the altar of Our Lady. Looking up at the statue, I remembered the gothic religious images dotted around my childhood home with eyes that followed me to bed. Did she pray to Our Lady here? Looking into the same eyes that stared back at me now?

My Convent School brainwashing, kicked in and I lit a candle and began my school prayer:

'O Blessed Virgin Mary, never was it known that anyone who fled to your protection, implored your help or sought your intercession was left unaided. Inspired by this confidence, we turn to you, O Virgin of Virgins, Our Mother. To you do we come-'

'Chief Inspector...'

'before you do we stand, sinful and sorrowful...'

'Chief Inspector...'

I turned towards the interruption. 'Father... sorry... I was miles away.'

He smiled knowingly. 'Were you looking for me Chief Inspector?'

'Josephine please... and no… not really. Trying to get a

feel...'

'Has something happened?' He led me by the arm towards the pews. On auto pilot, I performed a little bob of genuflection towards the altar and settled into a familiarly uncomfortable pew as we both gazed at the altar.

'We'd a chance at catching her this afternoon,' I began, 'but we blew it.'

'I don't think she's going to be that easy to catch.'

'She...? Are you admitting she's a woman Father?'

'I'm sorry... I want to help but I'm getting no guidance here. I went to see the Bishop before I came to you.'

'And how did that go?'

He smiled, 'he couldn't get out of the room quick enough but luckily passed it onto an old friend of mine – Father Pablo: an envoy from The Vatican dealing with other weighty matters. He's been advising me. I spoke to him after our interview.'

'Did she know you... did she seek you out?' I asked.

'No... I haven't done well connecting with the Parishioners I'm afraid. I've been somewhat resentful about my return to this...' He waved his hand around.

'God's own waiting room...' I finished for him.

'Yes... but when she told me what she'd done, I felt I'd a purpose again.' He rubbed his palms together as though drying off sweat. 'I was prepared to give it all up to tell what I know – a small sacrifice I felt to save a life – but Pablo persuaded me otherwise. He reminded me that I could be ex communicated even as laity and I would do untold damage to the trust placed in a priest in the confessional.'

I was torn between my need to know and his spiritual conscience. 'Now you've had further advice Father, what more are you comfortable with telling me?'

He began as though he already thought through what he could share. 'Those who attend confession are regulars; I didn't recognise her voice and I think she's not one of our parishioners. She had little regard for me as a priest – and spoke to me like an annoyance she must tolerate to connect with God. She's strong in her conviction that she has his approval. I believe she will continue killing...'

'You mentioned that she prayed to Our Lady... When she called and wouldn't say her name, I gave her one… Mary...'

'You were baiting her...' he said.

'Maybe... partly yes... but she said, "holy Mary Mother of God." She's targeting mothers isn't she Father? Those that she thinks are bad mothers. Fiona Anderson treated her son poorly; Catherine Scott had her child snatched.' He sat still with his hands in his lap. I could feel him willing me on. 'She talked about loss… eaten away with the pain of grief and has found some sort of temporary relief when she kills.' He remained in his meditative pose which is all the confirmation I needed.

'She talked about both victims like she knew them. Did she mention them to you Father? Any idea of who she might go for next?'

'No... Nothing... But she is becoming more self-assured each time she kills and she will return here, I'm sure of it.'

We sat staring at the towering carving of a crucified Jesus on the altar. 'I've often wondered why, a religion, supposedly rooted in love and compassion, should have such cruelty at its heart. I mean – look at that – what a violent image to shove into people's faces.'

'I've long given up the imagery forced upon us – not much call for it in the make-shift churches in Africa.' He tilted his head as he searched my soul, 'can I presume you're struggling with doubts with your faith Josephine?'

'No struggle Father... My doubts won long ago. I think we should live our good intentions, not create a cult like the Catholic Church where it all becomes... well… warped. Wow... did I say that? Very profound...' He never interrupted but smiled. 'Oh, don't get me wrong – I'm also a complete hypocrite. I returned to mass so I could get my kids into the local Catholic school.'

'And how did you feel during the mass?'

'Strangely spiritually connected Father...' I laughed. 'So, he got me in the end.'

'He gets us all in the end. But you don't need a church to validate your moral compass Josephine,' he looked around. 'These are mere trappings... rules and regulations that bind us to earthly regimes.'

'Steady on Father. You're sounding positively subversive.'

'Then we are not so different I sense.'

'Except it's a lot more difficult for me to get confessions out of people.' We returned our gaze to the cross.

'It must be a strain...' he began. 'The contrast between family life and this – it must take its toll.'

How to explain, as I sat there mulling over the next strategic steps to catch a serial killer while making a note-to-self to return Emilia's permission slip for a trip to see Macbeth and to sneak in a quick online shop as I noticed Pete's pants were looking a bit threadbare in the last wash.

'It's like a flip switch,' was what I visualised, 'flipping from one world to the other with as little cross contamination as possible – although I'd be lying if I said that hasn't happened more than once.'

'And yet you survived...'

'By the skin of my teeth Father...'

'Survivors both Josephine...'

TWENTY
The Disciplinary

'It's a unique situation Josephine.'

'I appreciate that Sir...'

'But regardless... it showed an unprofessional disregard for protocol and brought the reputation of The Metropolitan Police Force into disrepute.'

I stopped myself from my utterances of apologies after every statement – sure that it was getting on their nerves as much as mine. I avoided looking at Spatchcock at the far end of the table if I was to hold it together, knowing he was revelling in my discomfort and thinking of the next humiliating detail of my jaunt to rub in my face.

The Commander continued: 'we've heard the facts around this case Josephine but we are prepared to listen to your personal statement if you would like to proceed please.'

I looked down at the statement I'd prepared with the guidance of my Rep which ticked all the contrition boxes necessary to get me out of this mess. But I knew the more I practiced this piece of fiction, the more I stumbled over it – as it was simply not my voice. I folded over the piece of paper in my lap and felt my Federation Rep beside me, hold his breath.

'You say it is a unique situation Sir and on one hand you're right but there's nothing unique for a Police Officer to have a visceral need to put an end to a murderer on a killing spree. Nurse Alexander murdered eight people. Holding a position of trust that would leave vulnerable people exposed to her time and time again. Whether it was our mistake or fate which allowed her to abscond to the Balkans, is debatable and I will take any disciplinary action that accompanies this judgement. But I could not stand by, knowing that there was a possibility, no matter how small, that I could do more.

'Yes... I became somewhat obsessed and travelled through these countries for three months at a risk to my position here and my family relationships but I did it from a genuine intent to make things right and not to consciously act in an insubordinate manner to the detriment of The Met.'

Recounting it aloud yet again was like dredging up one of those nightmares where you find yourself out on the street naked: gripped by the pain of shame and vulnerability as four pairs of accusing eyes from across the room, bore into me. The Commander seemed to conduct himself in a genuine enough way during this interrogation but my other colleagues could all have old scores to settle.

I left the room with focused dignity with my sole supporter, my Federation Rep. 'Well done, Josephine...' he dared to say as we left the building, both behaving as though the corridors were bugged. 'There's little precedent for this so if those with knives out have their way, we'll tie them up in knots.'

I made my way back to the station, far from reassured.

The lift door opened onto my floor and I was confronted head on by D.I. Dave Golding. 'Josie... fancy meeting you here.'

'Not really Dave... I'm sure you've been hovering around for this exact moment.'

He fixed a knowing smirk. 'I was checking your team were okay in your absence. Not too taxing a morning I hope?'

'Piss off Dave... some of us have real work to do...'

I ignored his comeback as I brushed passed on my way to my department, accidentally scraping my three inch heel against his shin as I went. I faintly heard the remnants of a parting farewell of 'bitch' in my wake.

Josh followed me into my office, 'very unnerving seeing you in uniform Boss.'

I pulled off my killer heels and slipped into my loafers. 'Thank you, Sergeant, – and if you've got nothing more interesting to note then bog off.' He remained hesitant in front of my desk. I looked up, 'well...? Spit it out...'

'Where you've been is your business Boss but the whole station is saying that you were called over to get the chop.'

'And yet… here I am...'

Josh waited for some elaboration and when there was none, jogged on. 'Well, seeing as you're looking so officious today, shall we get him in?'

D.C. John Cuthbert sat opposite me with Josh standing to the side. His peacock, pristine appearance as irritating as his smug demeanour. We both knew he was untouchable, having gathered enough dirt on the cronies I'd been up in front of, to guarantee a smooth ride until his – not so far off – retirement. We also both knew that he was the source of the gossip that Josh mentioned. As his parting gift from my section, I would make sure everyone knew he was the cause of the fuck-up.

'Yesterday I told you to peruse the area of the church to see what you could find out and with the slim chance that our killer may return,' Josh kicked off.

John kept his eyes defiantly on me and replied, 'yes Sarge...'

'Susie seems to think that you told her that I had ordered her to go to the church and you were passing the message on.'

'I can't think why she presumed that Sarge. I made it clear that I was caught up with Victoria Park statements so I needed her help.'

'Let's cut the crap shall we John?' I interjected as I wanted him gone. 'You were on one of your jolly jaunts that you're so famous for and deceived another officer to cover for you and not for the first time. The problem is John, that this time you took an officer off a surveillance that would have established if this suspect was the killer or not. And now we don't know... so at best it's going to cost scarce resources to find out and at worst, in the meantime, they could kill again. And that John, lands firmly at your door.'

'Well – I don't see it like that Ma'am...'

'Well – I don't give a shit John. You're being transferred with immediate effect to Newham CID, where a man of your talents will find plenty to occupy your remaining time. Now get out of my sight and don't ever show your face around here again.'

'Ma'am...' he responded with a mocking nod of the head as he laconically rose from his chair and sauntered out of my office, like John Wayne riding off into the sunset.

'You sure you don't want to go down a disciplinary route with him?' Josh asked. 'It's what he deserves.'

'It's a waste of everyone's time. He'd only run rings around them and one of his mates would cover his arse. Also, I don't want to give him any more oxygen. Now tell me where we are with finding Stella's whereabouts at the time of the call.'

'A solid alibi I'm afraid,' he began. 'She was taking a class down her gym so we can't prove it was her.'

'Not even with her phone?' My eye was drawn to my vibrating phone on my desk with *no caller ID* on the screen.

'Michael thinks it's possible – but at a stretch.'

I held my finger up to Josh as I picked up the phone, 'Hello D.C.I. Connelly.'

'Is that the police...? She had your card on her desk... I don't know who to call...'

'It's okay Sir... calm down and tell me slowly what's happened.'

'My name... my name's Marc Whitehead. My wife... Amy... she's missing...'

TWENTY ONE
Another grieving family

We pulled up outside Amy's house and I had no sooner swung the car door shut, then the front door flew open. A dishevelled Marc Whitehead stumbled down their steps. 'Have you found her? Is she alright?'

'Come Mr Whitehead... let's step inside.'

He brushed my arm away as he followed me up the steps. 'Don't try and manage me. Answer my question. Is she dead?'

We steered him into the hallway. 'We don't know any more than you which is why we're here. Please Mr Whitehead... I need you to calm down and focus so that we can do the best for your wife.' He led the way into the lounge and sat on a sofa in the window bay while Josh and I sat opposite in coordinated armchairs. His head in his hands, he ran his fingers through his hair, tugging as he went. 'You have a daughter – Clara – is that right?'

'Yeah, that's right... Clara...'

'Where is she Mr Whitehead? Is she safe?'

'Of course, she's safe. Stella's taken her to her house. She'll be safe there.'

I could feel Josh looking across at me as I asked my next question. 'When did Stella pick her up?'

He looked up, 'she's just left. Why are you asking about Stella?'

'It may be better that a family member has her, we may need to interview Mrs Winchester as a close friend of your wife.'

'Er... okay... I see...' He looked disorientated as though he were in a stranger's house before picking up his phone from the oak coffee table and texting. 'Amy has a cousin who babysits sometimes...' He finished his texting with corresponding pings confirming responses. 'There... That's sorted. Now please help me to find my wife,' he pleaded.

'When did you last see her?'

'This morning at breakfast but her routine would have been to take Clara to school and today I think she was working from home.'

'Did she have any other plans? Would she have met up with a friend for lunch?'

'I don't know... we... she doesn't tell me what she gets up to in the day.'

'I'm sorry to ask... but is everything okay between you and your wife?'

He rocked to and fro on the sofa with his head once again in his hands. 'Yes... No... We had some difficult times but since Clara's accident... we're working on it. I was away with a new job which didn't help but now I'm back, we're a family again.'

'Does your wife see it like that?'

'What...? Yes... maybe... it's complicated. But when we came close to losing Clara, we've both tried hard. Why are you asking these questions? Why aren't you out looking for her?'

Then the unwelcomed question, 'do you think maybe your wife was seeing someone else?'

'No!' He flipped and jumped up from the sofa. 'You're barking up the wrong tree and wasting time. Even if things aren't as they should be between us, she'd always put Clara first which... which was one of our issues I guess but I was too stupid to realise what I had.'

'She hasn't been missing that long Mr Whitehead,' I reasoned calmly. 'It's not unthinkable that she's caught up somewhere, her phone has run out of charge and she'd know that the school would contact you to pick up Clara. You are beyond frantic. What do you think has happened to her?'

He remained standing and expectantly looked out of his front windows. 'It's these murders. She was getting herself too involved in them.' He spun around to face me. 'I saw the folder she'd collated. I don't know what she was up to because she wouldn't talk to me about it. I went up to her office to see if there were any clues to where she could be. Her desk is swamped with notes and names of people I don't recognise.'

'Could we have a look at this office? It may help.'

'Yes... yes... follow me...'

We climbed two flights of stairs into what would have been a loft conversion. The light, bleached-wood décor, followed throughout the house. Three wooden doors lined the corridor and he led us into the only open door. He was right... the desk was a mess. 'Does she always work like this?'

'There'll be an element of organised chaos but not like this...'

The desk was strewn with the contents of the folder that she'd entrusted to us for a couple of days. Any of the leads had already been discounted, Scott's ex boyfriends and all, but we needed her help to piece together scraps from her thought process.

Josh picked up a few of the notes from the desk. 'Whatever she was going through, she may have come across something. It looks like she abandoned this lot and left in a hurry.'

Marc Whitehead remained by the door, paralysed with a bag of raging emotions. 'Those other women were killed on the spot, not followed or taken. If the same killer was after her, the likelihood is that she's dead already – isn't it?'

'That's a big leap Mr Whitehead,' I attempted to reassure him. 'We need to stay focused on finding out where she went.'

Josh had been strolling around the room looking through the bookcases at files and reading matter before asking, 'do you mind if I use your loo?'

Whitehead pointed to a door down the hall as we heard the doorbell ring. He became agitated again, not wanting to move.

'Go answer it – it may be important,' I said.

He reluctantly left the room. At one point I thought he was going to come straight back in. The uncarpeted oak stairs echoed his urgent pace. I sat at the desk and gathered the notes in front of me as I half-listened to the conversation at the front door – only making out a female voice.

Josh returned to the room. 'Looks like he's banished to the attic and he sleeps in the room at the back. And there's all his stuff in the bathroom. Do we think he's got anything to do with it?'

'All I'm feeling right now is the more information we have, the less we know. What's his connection? Remember we did some digging after we spoke to Amy Whitehead. I think he worked abroad until his daughter's accident so he wasn't here for Fiona Anderson's murder. He was still travelling after that so let's cover ourselves and check if he was around for Catherine Scott's murder. However, I agree with what you said, she found something here and ran.'

I handed Josh some of the notes I scooped up but we were soon interrupted by Marc Whitehead and his guest. He seemed breathless after his climb in comparison to her stillness.

'Hello Mrs Winchester.'

'Hello D.C.I. Connelly... Clara's been picked up so I thought I'd come and help where I could and before you ask...' she seemed to turn towards Josh at this point, 'I was at an army reunion lunch today and I've plenty of witnesses.' She handed a list of names and telephone numbers to Josh. He left the room where I knew he would chase up every last one.

'Why would you say that?' Marc Whitehead asked Stella before turning to me. 'Why does she feel the need to give you an alibi?'

'I believe I've been a person of interest but please

Marc... It's okay... Let's focus on finding Amy.' She laid a hand on his arm as he seemed to want to persist. 'What can I do to help?'

I met her gaze, 'do you think something has happened to her?'

Without hesitation, she answered straight, 'I do...' She pulled out her phone and played a voicemail on speaker.

Amy Whitehead's voice was instantly recognisable: 'Hi Stell... it's me. I know you think I'm nuts but I'm not going to let them pin this one on you.' With a raised eyebrow, Stella looked across at me. If she was trying to make me feel uncomfortable, she would have to try harder. 'I've had a brainwave about someone who knows both women and might know something. I'll let you know how I get on. See you later...'

'What time was that?' I asked.

'Before eleven.'

'And you've no idea who that could've been?'

'No... None...'

'Then we believe she was going through these notes before she left. Do any of these names mean anything to you?' I handed her the largest piece of paper on which Amy had written names and some notes beside them.

She skimmed the list, 'well they're self-explanatory. This family are known as a handful – but I can't see the link to the other murders. Fiona Anderson wouldn't wipe the crap off her shoe with him but they could've been one of Catherine's lost causes. This bloke...' she pointed to another name, 'as her note said, for a while we thought he was quite close to Catherine but he's remarried since. The group of women on the list would have known both victims through the fund-raising. A load of bitches but I don't think any would have enough of a grudge to turn them into a serial killer.'

Josh nodded his confirmation of his checks as he rejoined us. Stella picked up on it. 'Hopefully that'll put your mind at rest,' she directed at me.

I felt my phone vibrate in my pocket: Angela's name once more reliably flashing on the screen. She fired out her information, knowing the urgency for every scrap, 'we've found her car Boss.'

'Where...?'

'Near the school but they've been clever and avoided every CCTV camera.'

'Any idea how long it's been there?'

'One of the mums, who knew Amy hadn't turned up, called it in around 4.15pm. Hold on... I've been given some info on earlier CCTV.' I heard the shuffling of papers before she continued. 'A camera on the Charlie Brown's roundabout caught her car at midday.'

'Keep at the CCTV Angela and get back to me with what you know. Are forensics down with the car?'

'Yes – they'll do some preliminaries on site and transfer it to the pound to continue.'

I could see Whitehead ready to pounce. 'Let me know as the info comes in.'

'What is it?' He looked close to breaking down.

'We've found her car near the school.'

'Then something has happened to her... My God...' He slumped down on the floor. Josh caught him before he collapsed. Stella crouched down and together they helped him up onto one of the office chairs. He held his hand up to his face. Stella rubbed his shoulder. 'I'm sorry...' he mumbled.

'It's alright Marc...' Stella said. 'But there's no need to give up so soon. Amy isn't stupid or naive. She'll have her wits about her if she thinks she's in danger.'

I couldn't blame her for trying to make him and herself feel better. Josh and I exchanged looks, knowing the diminishing odds. 'Her car was seen at The Charlie Brown's roundabout at around midday. Can either of you think of where she would be going?'

Whitehead was still too choked to speak so Stella continued. 'That could take her anywhere: Chigwell, Woodford, South Woodford... Any of these places have shops or cafes she's been to.'

'What about the rest of the names on these lists? Do they live in any of these areas?' I asked.

She took the list from me. 'Yes – they all do but I don't believe any of them are credible suspects.'

Josh pulled out the stack of notes I handed to him when we first came in. 'Do you want to cast your eye over these?' He passed them to Stella. She flicked through the multi-coloured notes, considering each one, desperately looking for an answer.

I returned to Amy's desk. The pandemonium of her work reminded me of Emilia's room. I had to stop myself organising her stuff into neat piles. A pin board leant against the wall with a splatter-gun display, echoing the chaos on her desk although any notes or pictures pinned up, seemed to be more of a personal or domestic nature.

I followed the trail of post-it-notes appointments. One caught my eye and I pulled it off the board and showed it to Josh, 'haven't we seen her?'

TWENTY TWO
Amy's Hunch

She responded to my text, saying she was home if I wanted to pop over. As I was already on the move, I found myself in no time, standing on her front step, having second thoughts and losing my nerve. We never got to where I could say we were close and we hadn't seen each other in a while so there was only so much of the – popping in for a quick catch up – I could push.

My hesitation was denied me as the front door swung open. 'I thought I heard you. Lovely to see you...' We exchanged a clumsy hug but rather than invite me in, she joined me on the step and purposely closed her front door. 'I hate to be a pain but I've got to pick something up from The Post Office and thought we could have a spot of lunch near The Queen Elizabeth Hunting Lodge.'

She deftly rail-roaded me towards her car, already conveniently parked on the roadside, pre-empting any chance of my car blocking her in. Pulling away, she switched off the radio.

'It was nice to hear from you. We haven't seen each other so much since Clara's accident.'

'No, you're right. That's why I thought it would be good to catch up.' I wouldn't believe me – would she?

'But why so urgent? Why today?'

'To be honest...' or not... 'I've been meaning to catch up for a while. You know how it is... Catherine Scott's death affected me more than I thought. I suppose it's made me realise how short life is and I'm now feeling quite impetuous.'

'Well, it's nice to see you anyway. How's Clara?' She asked. 'I get a fleeting glimpse of her at the school gate nowadays.'

'She's faring well. You know how kids are... pretty resilient compared to us. I'm a nervous wreck every time she goes near a road but luckily, she's oblivious.'

She remained fixed on the road ahead – stony-faced. 'And you and Marc? I see he's moved back in.'

This was a weird conversation to be having with her. I never confided the details of my home-life to anyone apart from my closest friends. What did she know? I suppose it wasn't too much of a stretch to believe that playground gossip was rampant on the subject and she could have picked up on it there.

'Oh… you know... Doing the best we can. I do feel in a way that the accident has brought us closer together,' I half-lied.

'That's good.'

I didn't want to over-think it so got straight to the point, 'I suppose you went through something similar when Jack... sorry... I didn't mean...'

'It's okay... I like to talk about him. Most people feel uncomfortable mentioning him and tiptoe around the subject. But that's like acting as though he didn't exist which is more hurtful.'

I could have cut my tongue out but she was right. I witnessed a few of those toe-curling incidents: parents talking excitedly about what their sons were up to in front of her then mid-sentence, a realisation dawned of a screaming lack of tact and they clamped up and fumbled to change the subject. She generally pretended not to notice.

'To answer your question... we did struggle although I think a mother feels it more acutely than a father, don't you think?'

'In some respects, yes...' I agreed. 'But you had Jack before you were married – is that right? Sorry... I sound so nosy, don't I?'

'No... It makes a change for someone to show any interest. Yes, you're right. We got together when Jack was three. I wasn't interested in letting the father know so Tom's been his real dad in every way. Oh... here we are... I won't be a tick...'

She jumped out of the car and popped into The Post Office and I was unsure where I was going with this. She seemed different or was I imagining it? She was typically... compliant, I would say but I felt like today she was in every sense in the driving seat and it felt uncomfortable.

She returned with a parcel in her hand which she threw into the boot before slipping back in front of the wheel. 'Okay... let's go... I'm glad you contacted me today,' she began in a contrived way. 'We never did talk about Clara's accident and what happened that day.'

Why did she presume I would talk to her about it? 'You were good the way you remained calm and tended to her for which I'll be forever thankful.'

'Do you know one of the biggest issues for me to reconcile about Jack's death?' I didn't feel she was waiting for a response. 'It was that I wasn't there with him when he died. He was left with strangers.'

I had no words...

'I blamed myself at first for leaving him in the care of such incompetent adults. But I realised where the blame lay – with those who should have acted sooner... those who should have contacted me sooner so my beautiful boy didn't die afraid, without his loved ones.' She remained dispassionate and almost detached from the statements she was making. Perhaps containment was her way of coping?

'I can't imagine your pain. It must be something you live with always...'

'Yes... yes... you're right... you understand… You see a smiling face and a willingness to participate and become involved but I'm not there – not in that way. I've created a kind of avatar that I control to keep the world at bay. The only person I'm open and honest with is Esme.' She became animated as she mentioned her daughter's name.

'The councillor advised that children sense an artificial facade and if you're not honest, they'll fill in the gaps in their own head which could be even worse. We have a little cry together and every so often, we talk about our grief. I think it helps both of us as Tom is burying his deep. It will catch up with him one day but he won't accept any help.'

I felt a bitch for being there with such a ruthless agenda but she did know the murder victims and if I could establish her relationship with both and any link, it would give me some peace of mind. 'You said you blamed those in charge on the trip. Wasn't one of them Catherine Scott?'

'Yes, she was. But she was much more than – one of them. Let me give her, her full due: she was the one in charge; the one who made the decisions. It was down to her that Jack never got to the hospital in time and down to her that we weren't contacted in time to see him before he died.'

Okay... so I wasn't going to get a balanced view on this topic. 'You were quite close before that though, weren't you?'

'I supported her in some of her work and saw her regularly after Jack died – when I was trying to make sense of what had happened. That was before I came to realise that she was the cause. After that of course – I couldn't face her.'

'Did she know you felt that way?' I asked.

'No... I never said. I avoided a confrontation for Esme's sake.'

'Did you reconcile before she died?'

I thought I saw a hint of a smile cross her lips as she confirmed, 'yes... we were reconciled.'

I looked back up at the road in front of us and realised that I didn't know where we were. We seemed to have taken a turn down one of the side roads. 'Shouldn't we be heading in the direction of The Hunting Lodge? We seem to have driven a bit further out.'

'Sorry... I was on automatic pilot. I like to park up on this side of the forest and take a walk through. You don't mind, do you?'

I did. And I was seriously beginning to feel like I was being manoeuvred but if it afforded me some more time to try and reveal what she knew, I would play along. 'No probs. Seems a nice day for a walk.'

We parked in a small clearing, designated for cars but currently deserted. Well past dog-walker's rush hour. I had no idea of our location and doubted we were the short distance she claimed to our lunch venue. It must have shown on my face.

'You okay? You seem a bit bewildered,' she asked innocently.

'Well, I am...' I confessed, trying to keep the note of suspicion from my voice. 'I didn't realise that there was so much of the forest I haven't seen before.'

'I know.' She looked longingly into the trees. 'I only discovered it myself since Jack passed. I took up running as a form of therapy, I guess. The woods are a perfect place to focus my mind and have a breakdown in solitude when the need arose. I wasn't looking where I was running most of the time and found myself lost on many occasions. And you know what it's like out here – no phone signal – so I couldn't even use my map. But finding my way out each time became part of the challenge that I relished. I'm almost disappointed that I now know this area so well.'

I understood her need for the solitude offered by the woods when she was deranged with grief. I couldn't imagine what, if anything, would console me. Clara's accident had proved that. But one thing I did know, I was very, very uncomfortable not knowing where I was so was keen to get on with the hike until I recognised something.

She got out of the car and threw a lightweight rucksack on her back and smiled across at me reassuringly. We followed a pathway, wide enough for us to walk side by side. Despite the overnight rain, the trail had not turned into one of those impassable bogs, I frequently failed to negotiate. Trying to discount my unease, I settled into an appreciation of the surroundings and seized on the opportunity to continue my questioning. 'You've lately had your fair share of dealing with tragedy. I don't know how you coped so well. Fiona Anderson was a friend of yours as well, wasn't she?' I winced at how contrived I sounded.

She pulled a leaf from a passing bush and picked away at it as she spoke. 'I don't think Fiona had… friends. Our sons were friends although it wasn't something she encouraged.'

'Why's that?'

'Jack didn't wear the right clothes… we didn't hang out with the right families… Her son was upset by her interference. They never got on. She wasn't a good mother.'

'Is it right that you were the last person to see her alive?'

'I'm not sure...' She wasn't as enthusiastic talking about this one but I left her enough space until she continued, 'we used to car-share our girls to the theatre school. Not my choice but she did have a habit of bamboozling you.'

'She sounded a piece of work.'

'She was... It's an awful thing to say but the family are better off without her.'

I took a breath before responding because it could easily tip into a disagreement and the conversation would be over. 'Isn't that a bit harsh? The children would have been devastated.'

'Oh... I've helped the family. Darren is particularly appreciative.' She smiled a self-satisfying smile.

'But wasn't he the main suspect?'

'Yes, I believe he was. Well... I could understand why he'd do it. She used to treat him terribly. She'd taunt and humiliate him at every turn. I never understood why he stayed with her for so long.'

Was she accusing him? 'But he was released recently,' I said, trying to keep the pushiness from my voice. 'Evidently he did have an alibi for the time of the murder and someone came forward with evidence that he was elsewhere.'

Having cut across a well-tended clearing, the path was now taking us into a densely wooded area. Weathered silver birch stood to attention, daring us to pass.
I wanted to heed their warning as I continued to feel disorientated.

'You mean the evidence the P.A. provided? Rather convenient...'

'Are you saying that you think he's guilty?' I asked.

'On no... That's not for me to say.' But her intonation remained loaded with implication. 'Personally, I think he's a lovely man who has already suffered so much. I'm simply saying it would be understandable if he did do it and any jury hearing his circumstances would be sympathetic. He would've got off with manslaughter and even a suspended sentence.'

I couldn't help but think that it sounded like a well thought through scenario. 'I'm not sure it works like that. But I heard they suspect the two murders are linked so what would his motive be for killing Catherine Scott?'

That seemed to throw her into deep thought and she walked ahead as the path narrowed. I checked my phone for the time and confirmation for my own peace of mind that there was no signal. None... I would never get back in time to pick up Clara from school at this rate so decided that I would call a cab when we arrived at the cafe.

She joined me once again as the path widened and she'd picked up a sturdy but gnarled branch that she used as a walking stick. 'We were talking about Clara's accident before we got side-lined by other events.'

I decided to let her continue as I now felt a rising urgency to get to wherever she was taking me so I could attempt to return home.

'I saw you that morning as you dropped her off', she persisted. 'You were in your usual distracted state. The poor child was hardly through the gate before you rushed off.'

Did I detect a tone? Was she turning on me? 'You're right. I live with that guilt every minute of every day which is why I've made changes to our lives to ensure she's never exposed to similar dangers – ever again.' I didn't feel like I needed to justify myself.

'I don't suppose you realise that in that respect you're not that different from Catherine or Fiona.'

This was turning into something creepy and I was beginning to feel vulnerable. I held my tongue as I wanted to escape from the fucking forest that I felt sure she had led me deeper into. 'Look... can we get out of here otherwise I'll be late for Clara.'

'No problem... Straight ahead... After you...'

TWENTY THREE
Closing In…

'*Call Paula Wagstaff Easter fete...*' The handwriting on the note was more considered and although from the same hand, not the manic scrawl scattered across the desk.

'She's the Mousey Mum,' Josh called to mind. 'We interviewed her over Fiona Anderson's murder. You gave her quite a tough time and weren't convinced that she was telling all she knows.'

'I remember...' I began, dialling Angela's number.

'Boss...?'

'Paula Wagstaff.... where did she say she was at the time of the Anderson murder?' I asked.

'Trying to find somewhere to buy her daughter a sandwich.'

'Was it ever corroborated?'

A telling pause before she answered, 'I'm not sure... In part maybe...? I'll get straight onto it.'

I hung up and turned to Stella, 'do you feel she's somehow connected?'

The distrust for this change of tact towards her – never left her eyes. 'That's for you to say not me. I would say that she was involved with both victims and more importantly – Amy.'

'How...?'

'Well, you'll know more than me about her friendship with Fiona Anderson. Catherine Scott on the other hand was one of the teachers on the school trip that Paula's son died on. She did see her for a while afterwards, so I can't confirm if she bore a grudge. And lately she was supportive towards Amy when Clara had her accident.' She looked down again at the note. 'I'm not saying that I think she had anything to do with it – just... possibly... Amy might have rightly or wrongly come to that conclusion.'

'A woman...' Marc Whitehead took the note from Stella.

'Killing two women... that's not likely. You're wasting time. You must have leads from the other murders. What about the husband...? Didn't you arrest him at one point? Shouldn't you get him back in?'

I needed to calm his hysteria, 'the husband was cleared and this name could be a credible lead. Believe me Mr Whitehead – a female suspect is highly likely.' I turned to Josh, 'let's get down and see what they've found on the car.'

'I'll come...'

'No Mr Whitehead. Stay here in case she returns or tries to contact you.'

I ushered Josh from the room before Marc Whitehead could persist. Josh's phone pinged as we left. 'Angela wants to know if you have your laptop with you.'

'Yes... why?'

A text exchange delivered the answer. 'She says – can you log on and open the CCTV files from the night of the murder at Victoria Park and call her when you're ready.'

I grabbed the laptop from the boot and logged on. I remembered asking for these files with the full intention of once more, scrutinising every frame, until events over-took good intentions.

My phone rang impatiently, 'sorry Boss... eager to get on.'

'Okay Angela what am I looking at?'

'Open the folder labelled *Cadogan Gate*, then the file named *DD News* and forward the tape to 6.45pm. This footage was only recently received from the convenience store opposite the park.'

I followed her instructions and as Josh turned the ignition in the car, my phone flipped to Bluetooth and hands-free.

'As you're doing that Boss, I can confirm that Susie's latest feedback from interviews is that there's no evidence that she visited the shops she claimed she went into that evening.'

'Okay... that's a start.' I isolated the frozen frame on the CCTV which showed a figure by the locked gate. I clicked forward frame by frame. The figure made at least three attempts to climb over the railings before succeeding.

'Boss... if you open your email, I've sent you two images.' I flipped over to my email and continued to follow Angela's instructions and opened the images. 'One is an enhanced image of the person at the gate. The second is of Paula Wagstaff.'

I scrutinised both, desperately trying not to fall into the trap of seeing what I needed to see. I knew what I thought but handed it over to Josh for his opinion.

'It's her...'

My body morphed into a ticking clock. Every nerve and sinew wound up; every stream of thought synchronised to grasp the dissolving fibres of events that could save Amy's life. The familiar knot of apprehension reached my chest.

'I agree Angela. Go and pick her up – and Angela... is the car at The Pound?'

'Yes Boss...'

'Then Josh and I will go there to pick up any info before coming back to the station to question her. Get a DNA swab as quickly as possible and get it to Doctor Monroe. Play it down Angela. I don't want to spook her. We haven't got a body yet so if there's a slim chance that Amy is alive, we need to work her to find out where she is.'

'Yes Boss.'

'Also, send someone from forensics down to the Whitehead's house to pick up D.N.A. swabs and prints from there and anything belonging to Amy for the same.'

Under a blue light, we sped to The Car Pound. John Mitcham – a senior forensics officer – met us. 'Anything...?' I snapped.

'Follow me...' he responded, entirely business-like and devoid of any civilities and led us into the garage where two other members of the forensic team were diligently working on the car. He marched purposefully over to a workbench and picked up a clear plastic bag the size of a bin bag, full of what looked like recycling: crisp bags, empty bottles of water and comics.

'Firstly, we had a bit of a clear-up: plenty of prints and fibres but no blood or guts. No sign of a struggle or violent activity in the car.'

Josh made his way over to the car and kicked the wheels. 'Any evidence of where the car has been?'

'Nothing more exciting than typical urban driving but we've picked off any bits of vegetation stuck in the tyre tread, air-con or roof which might narrow down the areas.'

'Can you cross reference any of it with Paula Wagstaff's house or road please?'

He followed Josh over to the open boot. 'Compared to the car interior, this was relevantly clean. Not scrupulous – as in, not a post-incident clean-up – just not used as a dumping ground.'

I joined them as Josh remained fixated on the boot interior as though expecting to find something missed by the experts. John ignored the implication and turned to me as I spoke, 'I know you're always being pushed for everything yesterday,' at which, he rolled his eyes, 'but this time it counts. There is a chance this woman is still alive John and I haven't a clue where to start so I'm in desperate need of anything you can find.' He nodded his acknowledgement and with that last plea, Josh and I headed back to the station.

Angela was engrossed in her screen as we walked across the office. I stood behind her for a while until she realised I was there. She was frozen in concentration. The only visible movement was the infinitesimal flutter of a forefinger, tapping on the pad of her laptop to progress the CCTV frames on her screen. Feeling the weight of my presence, she turned around. 'Boss...'

'No... It's okay...' I said, 'tell me what you've found.'

She returned to the screen, 'I've been looking at the roads close to the church before we put up the camera. There's no recent sign of her visiting yet, by the way. However, in the absence of any specific details from Father Michael, I'm using the dates of the previous murders to see what it flushes out.'

'Did forensics get down there?' Josh asked her from the opposite side of the desk. He looked up to explain this piece of unexpected information. 'I didn't think it would hurt to sweep the confessional box. Don't worry – they agreed with Father Michael to go in the dead of the night.'

'Yes Sarge – they've been.' Angela spun around in her chair to face me. 'I've put Paula Wagstaff in Interview two. I've pulled a file together on all we have on her and her interviews. It's on your desk.'

'How was she when you picked her up?' I asked.

'I think she was disarmed because I'm a junior officer. I implied that her information is invaluable because she knew all the victims.'

I made my way to the ante room while Josh fetched the file. Looking through the two-way mirror into the interview room at a composed Paula Wagstaff, I had a feeling she knew she was being watched. She sipped at the tea she was served in a Metropolitan Police crested mug.

A tan, leather Belstaff jacket, neatly hung on the back of her chair. A silver, Tiffany chain, circled her throat which she fiddled with coquettishly between sips. Josh entered the room and stood beside me, absorbing the scene, 'she doesn't look capable of such visceral attacks. If it's her, she seems more of... a poisoner.'

'What do we have?' I asked.

Josh produced what looked like a timeline, undoubtedly a piece of Angela's work. He handed it over. A clear one-page summary of key pieces of information from the file, including, 'lived and worked in Hackney.'

'What did she do?'

'We won't know that until this afternoon but it does say that she left work due to stress... Not long after she had her son Jack. Addresses are all in Woodford from then on.... She married four years later – Thomas Wagstaff. She had a girl – Esme, not long after marrying. Nothing much after that... Then the death of her son.' Josh pulled out another sheet of paper: 'he was on a school trip when he contracted meningitis and by the time they managed to get him to a hospital, he was too far gone to save. There were some questions over the handling of the situation by the teachers in charge. As Stella already mentioned, Catherine Scott held overall responsibility.'

'It wouldn't be unreasonable to conclude that she never forgave,' I said. 'It was the stuff of nightmares every time Jude or Emilia left the house. Jude needed a meningitis jab before he went to Uni – at the time it was rife there.'

'I thought it only affected babies,' Josh stated the typically held view. 'Would it be enough to turn her into a murderer?'

'Yes...' I confirmed without a breath of hesitation as I looked upon the controlled composure of Paula Wagstaff. 'I would be raging. But if this were a premeditated murder then what was her motive for killing Fiona Anderson?'

'The manner of it seemed to suggest that it could have been an unplanned explosion of fury.' He reeled off his list: 'the whole set up left her exposed to discovery; she's cited as the last person to see Fiona alive; the odds of getting Fiona into the park – willingly; the site of the murder... would you have picked The Rose Garden?'

'No... I would've chosen one of the rarely visited, far-flung corners of the park. In fact, I wouldn't have chosen the park at all because one thing Hackney isn't short of – is potential murder sites.'

Josh continued to shuffle through the papers, 'according

to her statement it's obvious that she didn't need much prodding to reveal her thinly-veiled dislike of Fiona.'

'I remember that but she never went further than an implication. What about Amy? Another hopeless mother in her eyes after Clara's accident?'

'Maybe...' He pulled out another note from his file, 'here's a summary of her activities during the murders. Let's see... Fiona Anderson... We know she was in the area and we now know her alibi of shopping for a sandwich is not corroborated. Catherine Scott... Angela spoke to Paula's husband when she was trying to track her down and he mentioned if she wasn't out doing some chores, she might be on a run in the forest. The more remote – the better. She claimed it helped to clear her head.'

'And Amy?'

'So far she's commented to Angela that she was out and about. She mentioned The Post Office in Chingford – Angela's waiting for confirmation on that. I've got my iPad so she'll send through anything additional while we're in there.'

'Okay... follow my lead and remember – our primary aim is to find out where Amy is – if she's still alive.'

TWENTY FOUR
Third Time Lucky

I could see that Josh was struggling with the contrast between the smashed in skulls and the fragrant stillness of the woman in front of him. His Cambridge-educated chivalry not quite having transcended to urban reality – no matter how neatly packaged.

She smiled credible innocence at us both; flashbacks of Nurse Alexander, too easily accessed in my mind. I had enough self-awareness to know that I shouldn't allow that to taint my judgement but neither was I going to let another murdering bitch get off.

'Thank you for coming in today Mrs Wagstaff.'

'Paula, please... Your nice young officer was so convincing that I could be of some help and as I managed to contact my husband's secretary to pick up my daughter... well… I'm all yours...' She smiled once more but notably at Josh, perhaps sensing his inner battle. He sat up straighter in his chair and attempted to fix an impartial expression.

'Firstly, I'd like to go over some of the details in your previous statements taken for the Fiona Anderson enquiries.' Not a hint of disquiet troubled her face. 'You implied that she was not your type of person...'

'I think you'll find that she wasn't anyone's type.'

'You're right... We did find that. There was a consistent theme from those we interviewed that she was self-obsessed and not very pleasant to her son. How well did you know her son Nathan?'

'Very well... He was one of my son's best friends and we used to see him regularly until–'

'Until your son died.'

Like an untreated tick, she winced at the comment, exposing a raw nerve. 'You know of my son's...'

I helped her with her struggle, 'death... Yes Mrs Wagstaff. I'm sorry for your loss.'

She recalibrated, 'yes… I knew Nathan well. In fact, I would say we were close. He could talk to me about his problems at home. I guess we had the mother and son relationship so patently absent from his life.'

I tried not to become too distracted by Josh who was flicking through papers and fiddling with his iPad, devouring every piece of evidence that Angela was undoubtedly firing at him.

'It must have been difficult for you when she criticised him? Which I presume she did as it seems she took every opportunity, even with those she hardly knew.'

'Oh yes... every opportunity. The professional victim...' She looked beyond us to the doorway as she elaborated, 'at best, he was merely a disappointment: refusing to wear the expensive clothes she lavished on him; being obstructive towards her attempts to engineer friendships with preferred families. At worst – she claimed that he had some kind of disorder and tried to organise sessions with a child psychologist.'

'I take it she wasn't happy that he mixed with your son?'

She was in the moment, reliving the rebuff. 'Evidently... But I was very proud of him. He stood his ground and remained his own person.'

'You encouraged it?'

'Definitely...' Satisfaction crossed her face not spite. 'I think we gave him the strength he needed.'

'It sounds like you treated him as a second son,' I suggested. She took this as a compliment, glowing with the idea. 'But now, with your own son's passing, there was no reason to visit?'

'We're still close. He misses Jack terribly.' She visibly wobbled, swallowing the knot of grief which threatened to constrict her airways. 'I couldn't turn him away as she seemed to become more erratic.'

'Why put yourself through the torture of being cooped up in a car with her every week while she implicitly criticised your son for not being good enough? And her lack of tact... thoughtlessly tearing her own son apart without a single nod to the fact that you lost your own and would do anything to have him there. Hearing that week after week after week... She sounds quite a bitch.'

Too readily she responded, 'oh she was...'

'Is that why you snapped?'

'Sorry...?'

'One trip too may? One, slagging-off session too many? A mother nobody would miss?'

Her posture stiffened at the realisation of the accusation. 'Don't be–'

'I wouldn't judge your anger. There she was – a hopeless mother with a son she didn't deserve and you... a caring, nurturing, natural mother... and your son taken in such cruel circumstances. That can't be right, can it?'

She flicked from Josh to me and back again as though waiting for the punchline before returning to her defiant composure. 'I didn't come here to have ridiculous allegations thrown at me. I've come here in good faith… voluntarily... to help you…'

'We could charge you now if you like,' Josh offered as he placed a series of photos across the desk. He continued with the evidence: 'she made one sarcastic comment too many and you flipped. You picked up a nearby rock and smashed it into her head.' He tapped on the close-up of the back of Fiona Anderson's head, congealed, blackened blood, clinging onto a matted honey-blonde mess. He moved his accusatory finger onto a photo of her post-mortem face. The artificial pallor of a corpse: mottled blue with a waxy skin. 'You certainly shut her up.'

She jumped up from her seat. 'I made it clear that the last time I saw her was leaving the hall. I don't know how you've come to these ridiculous conclusions but I would like to leave now.' Devoid of anger, her voice, the right level of indignation, no higher than being picked up for not paying the school dinner money on time.

'Sit down Mrs Wagstaff please,' I offered firmly. 'You will be interested in what we have to say.'

'Do I need to call my solicitor?' She threatened.

'Do you need one?'

She threw Josh a look of betrayal which he seemed comfortable with this time. He turned over another photograph as she hesitantly returned to her seat. 'This…' he tapped at the close-up shot, 'is you... which has also been confirmed by face recognition.'

'You've been following me?'

'No...' He turned over the second photograph, showing her attempt to climb over the park railings. 'You were picked up on CCTV.'

A rap on the door was followed by Angela assertively entering, 'Boss...' I stood up and left the room. 'The husband's called and he's on his way with a solicitor.'

'Okay... When they get here, stall the bloody solicitor as long as you can. I could do without this turning into a – "no comment" saga.

Before I returned to my seat, she began her rebuttal, 'that is not me and I was not there. I don't care what you claim has verified this. You're mistaken...' Pitch-perfect for the falsely accused.

I pulled up my chair and returned her glare, 'where were you?'

'I told you in my previous interviews, I popped into a few shops to find my daughter a tuna baguette.'

'Yet... there isn't a single scrap of evidence or CCTV to show that you visited any of these establishments. But let's move on... Catherine Scott...'

'Good God!' The first crack in the veneer. 'Am I being accused of her murder as well?'

'She was in charge of the school trip when your son died. Did you ever find out what happened?'

She seemed as though she was resisting but the urge to

put the record straight was too compelling. Her tone had shifted, 'I did find out,' she said. 'To cut a long story short – like his own precious life was cut short – there was no course of action taken when he presented with the initial symptoms and we weren't informed. Only when it was too late did they take him to hospital and again, delayed informing us. By the time we got there, he'd died. Died alone... frightened... with strangers...'

'Do you know I can't find a single person who has anything bad to say about Catherine Scott? She seemed to dedicate her life to helping others. Guilt maybe...? Guilt about losing someone on her watch...? What do you think?' I prodded.

'Guilt won't bring my son back. My question to *you* is that maybe she was liable for manslaughter? What do *you* think?'

'Is that why you killed her?' She didn't flinch. 'I mean... not only did she not pay a price for the death of your son, everyone else thought she was a saint. And he didn't die alone, did he? He had Catherine by his side and by all accounts, they were close. That would have been a comfort.'

'I am his mother!' Her hand slapped down on the table. Josh recoiled, correcting his natural reflex to pin down an aggressor. 'Every effort should have been made to get us there.' The rage percolated more than erupted. Her emotions remained at a reasonable point for a grieving mother instead of a calculating killer.

'But she did everything she could,' I offered. 'She was a decent, selfless woman. How lucky for Jack that she was there...?' Her jaw tensed as she tactically decided to abstain from reacting. 'You saw her for a while after. She must have been a great help. I believe she instinctively knew when to reach out and help others.'

'I saw her a few times, yes... But to make sense of his final hours. I brought him into this world and I needed to know every last detail – however distressing – on how he left. She owed me that.'

'What else did she owe you? Her life...?'

'What proof do you have to start throwing around these allegations?' She looked back and forth between me and Josh – not as self- assured.

He picked up the point with relish, 'we have a substantial amount of forensic evidence from both murders.'

A stretch, but we paused, waiting for the expected protestations of innocence. None came. She seemed to be fixing her face into a neutral zone. I suddenly felt self-conscious taking my first steps into approaching the disappearance of Amy. Did she know what was coming?

'Here's something we need your help with... Amy Whitehead. It seems you were supportive of her when her daughter Clara had an unfortunate road accident.'

She looked between us both once more as though sensing a trick or a change of tactics. 'I was glad to help – it was the least I could do. Everyone else around was becoming hysterical, including Amy.'

'You visited her in hospital as well. You seemed to do more for her than any of her friends.' I looked up from the statement I read from, 'and that's a quote from one of her close friends.'

'Again, I think it was because I offered practical help. With her husband away, it looked like that was exactly what she needed, not someone blubbering and breaking down in front of her.'

'But it must have been hard for you? Memories of a sick child... Both blameless mothers...'

A twitch of her mouth betrayed her thoughts so I perpetuated a pause until: 'not quite blameless... She rushed her out of the car at drop-off and didn't ensure she was safe inside. She was distracted most mornings, so it was an accident waiting to happen.'

'Not such a good mother either?'

She fixed me a look. 'I'm sure she did her best under the circumstances but she took on too much you see, when her focus should have been Clara.'

'Did you see her as another orphan to take under your wing?'

'I beg your pardon?' Her response was weary.

'Now that Amy's gone missing, you could step right in – like you have with Fiona Anderson's children.'

'I have no idea what you're talking about.'

I held it together for the next question but I was screaming in my head, 'Amy Whitehead has gone missing. Do you know where she is Paula?'

'This is now too farcical to even respond to. I would like to call my solicitor.'

'He's on his way,' Josh responded and turned his iPad towards her with newly forwarded evidence from Angela. 'This is you in Chingford High Street Post Office...'

'I don't deny I was there. I picked up a parcel.'

He swiped the screen, 'and this is you at the traffic lights on Station Road.' He swiped once more, 'and this is a close-up of your passenger – Amy Whitehead.'

'I'm saying no more until my solicitor arrives.'

'Then let me say it for you.' She turned her head away as I began. 'We believe that you've murdered Fiona Anderson and Catherine Scott. You will spend the remainder of your life in prison. And what will your daughter think of you? What legacy will you leave in Jack's name?' Her face had turned to stone.

'I can understand that Fiona's murder may have been in rage. She was an unpleasant woman and would have provoked a saint. Catherine Scott's killing was premeditated but I can see you convinced yourself in your grief that she was responsible for Jack's death. Jurors will understand all of that. But Amy...? What did she do? Nothing more than most of us imperfect mothers...' I struggled to keep the fury from my voice. 'I lost my daughter in Marks and Spencer's when she was four – would I be next on your list for your type of vigilantism? Don't we all make mistakes as mothers at some point or another?'

Every facial muscle remained paralysed.

'Esme will be the one who'll have to live with the fact that you cold-heartedly killed Amy especially if she becomes a mother herself one day. Can you imagine the headlines she'll have to endure? Yummy Mummy Triple-Killer…'

Her eyes were glassy and lifeless as though in a trance. It was time to beg. 'Amy is different to the others. Maybe you thought twice about killing her? If she's alive Paula... let us know. You can't undo what's been done but you can stop and minimise the impact on Esme's life.' She had disconnected. 'Shall we pray for her Mary? Will Holy Mary Mother of God, hear us?'

She turned her head slowly and met my gaze.

TWENTY FIVE
X Marks The Spot

The whole team was assembled, listening to my latest time-check as time ran short for Amy. An abundance of espresso coffees, the only evidence of an average of four hours sleep since the last shift. Eager to make their contributions, phones pinged as information continued to flow. Favours returned... deadlines pushed through...

'Josh is in with the husband now, hoping to pin down some of Paula's haunts and possible sites of where she could be keeping Amy – if she's still alive. In the meantime, The Essex Police are currently carrying out a search of Epping Forest, based on the fact that she runs there regularly. An expensive solicitor has arrived,' I continued. 'A different league to their original family solicitor so expect every scrap of evidence to potentially be torn to bits. On every point – ask yourself – how could she wiggle out of this one? Now let's see what we have: Angela... I believe all the forensic results are being channelled through you, so fire away please.' Welcomed news as I knew Angela would have already assessed, sorted and categorised.

'Consistencies with both the murders,' she began. 'Paula Wagstaff is a size eight shoe and she's left-handed. She matches the height profile for the angle of attack. Trainer brands found at both sites have been discovered at her house although they look new so it rules out any distinguishable marks on the tread. There's no match to any of the soil samples from Fiona Anderson's murder, in fact her clothes are spotless – too spotless. She would have dumped anything she used. Forensics are currently working on the clothes she came in with today and I'm also waiting on the results of a sweep of the foot-well of her car.'

She took a quick breath before continuing – all without glancing at any notes. 'A hair identified as Fiona Anderson's was found on a jacket but this could be explained away from the contact when they were car sharing.'

'We need the bloody murder weapon,' I said as a statement out of frustration, not stating the bloody obvious to my highly experienced team. 'The elusive rock left behind fragments in both murders and it's not something she could just slip into a handbag – did anyone see her carrying a rucksack? What about forensics specific to Catherine Scott?'

'Fibres and footprints found in the clearing were identified as Catherine Scott's,' Angela continued, 'and one other and again a size eight, Nike trainer. The tread did match to one of the footprints from the Fiona Anderson murder but no proof that they're Paula's.'

'We can link the murderer to both killings but apart from the CCTV, we can't forensically link the killings to Paula Wagstaff. Okay,' I said, 'let's move on from forensics. Where is she disposing all her stuff? Have we found anything from the clear out of Catherine Scott's flat?'

'No,' Susie stepped up. 'We've visited every local charity shop and recycling bank. Rubbish is only collected every two weeks so we've checked rubbish tips from the last run. There's also no evidence in the garden that she's been burning anything.'

'Then she can only be stashing it somewhere. Do a sweep on the local lock-ups. Check CCTV for any regular routes and follow that trail.'

'Well, what we've checked so far,' she went on, 'and there was a lot... mainly shows her toing and froing in the direction of The Forest. I'll continue to check elsewhere but I think that's our best bet.'

'Then direct resources to any buildings, out-buildings, barns, new and old throughout The Forest and follow through on local lock-ups.'

'On my way...' and she was gone...

'Boss...'

'Yes Angela?'

'There're old ordinance survey maps of The Forest that might throw up any disused buildings.'

'Great... get onto it...' I urged.

'He's a cool one.' Josh joined me by the board. 'He's been well briefed by the fancy lawyer who luckily went straight into Paula.'

'What did you say?'

'I implied that his attempts to be evasive would lead to an implication that his wife was guilty of something. His pre-planned strategy soon wobbled as he wasn't yet aware on what grounds we were holding his wife but it did allow me to probe on her whereabouts at the time of the Catherine Scott murder.'

'And...?'

'Unfortunately, he can't pin-point the exact date but confirmed what we already know... that she liked to run so not a stretch to be in The Forest.'

I could see Angela out of the corner of my eye, mumbling into her phone as I continued to listen to Josh.

'I went through the circumstances of his son's death and how his wife had coped since. He said that they'd different ways of dealing with it: he threw himself into work, she got involved in charity work for The Meningitis Society and he seemed to think that the running also helped. He didn't pretend that things were easy and he was honest that he didn't know how it would work out. He described it as trying to hold it together for the sake of their daughter.'

'What about her relationship with the victims?' I asked.

'He thought she had the same view as everyone else – that Fiona Anderson was a bitch. He seemed uncomfortable when I asked him about the relationship with The Anderson boy. When pushed, he intimated that he felt his wife was interfering too much. Although he agreed Fiona was a crap mother, he knew the boy wasn't neglected and the dad was a stable influence.

'He thought that they were taking over his life too much and it was beginning to feel like she was looking for a substitute for their son Jack,' he said.

'Was he concerned about her behaviour?'

'He made one comment that there was no, "normal" behaviour since their son died.'

'Did he mention his view of Catherine Scott? Any indication that he blamed her for his son's death?'

'No... He referred to it as a tragic accident and that pointing fingers wouldn't bring his son back.'

'Very reasonable... Maybe too reasonable? Giving some personal answers to deflect. What do you think?' I asked. 'Maybe he's in on it with her?'

Josh did not look so sure. 'He still wasn't clear why she was in here. He wasn't defensive about questions he should've been if prepped, although he said enough to give the impression that he was cooperating. Could've been a strategy from the solicitor?'

'If he didn't know why she was here, why rush in with a solicitor in tow?'

He checked his notes, 'a neighbour called him to say that she'd seen Paula being carted away in a police car.'

Angela finished her call and joined us in front of the evidence board. 'We may not be able to track the soil evidence from those involved but the cars have proven more fruitful.'

'Go on...'

Angela was not one for bigging up her part.

'The remnants of flora and fauna found on the exterior of Amy's car, match the tree outside Paula Wagstaff's house.'

'Got her...' Josh clapped and rubbed his hands together.

I was not as confident. 'Only if we can prove that she hadn't been there before. We need to find out when her car was last cleaned.'

'Noted...' Josh replied and literally did so.

Angela had more to tell: 'the samples collected from Amy's tyre treads were, as we know, consistent with urban driving but Paula's had a multitude of samples matching fauna from the forest. In fact, Doctor Monroe has cross-checked and ruled out a number of sites and car parks where he's already collected control samples.'

She joined a Civvy who had been waiting patiently by the door for her and returned with a large folder. 'The archives are now computerised so they've printed off a cross section of maps.'

We gathered around one of the larger desks at the back of the office, promptly cleared by the occupier as we approached, where Angela spread out one of the maps. Reading from her iPad held in one hand and a red marker poised in her other, she set about the task with characteristic diligence. 'It's weird. I mean… there're pockets of it everywhere.'

'I know...' I replied as she seemed to be filling up a substantial proportion of the map. 'But to start, we'll concentrate on the bulk from Chingford to Epping and we'll have to presume that Paula Wagstaff knows every nook and cranny.'

She came to a purposeful stop and placed her iPad carefully on the table behind. 'The areas with crosses are ruled out. The remaining areas are all possibilities and as you can see – pretty remote.'

A collective mumbling of agreement rose from the team. All, at some time in their lives having trekked around Epping Forest – the nearest our part of London could call countryside. So, I checked, 'has anyone visited any of these areas?'

A few responded with a definitive, 'no.' Others scrutinised the map further, identifying their Sunday cycling routes or their daughter's horse-riding stables, before offering the same negative response.

Angela had clambered up onto a chair and the team

made way as she attempted to take a picture of the map on her phone. 'I'll send it to Susie so she can coordinate the troops.' She jumped down and began circling areas on the map. 'These are buildings within the forest – used or unused.' She picked up another map from the pile on the floor, printed onto tracing paper and laid it on top of the existing map. 'It's from 1960 and should show any other buildings that may've been missed.'

I swung around to the door as I heard the desk Sergeant calling my name and after waving my arm around, saw him approach with a uniformed visitor, 'Head Forest Keeper, Adrian Lewis, Boss.'

A portly man of around fifty, dressed in utility khaki, stretched out his hand. 'Thanks Sergeant. Hello Mr Lewis, thank you for coming in,' a rough, powerful grip and an authentic smile left me in no doubt of his credentials.

'Pleased to meet you D.C.I. Connelly... I was supposed to meet D.C. Tam but it seems we've crossed paths and she's now down at the forest.'

'Yes... But we could do with your help here if you don't mind hanging on for a bit?' He looked over at the maps and joined us at the table. 'We've officers from both police forces traipsing blindly all over your forest. We believe the third victim of the park killer is in the forest and if we're lucky, she's still alive but we don't have much time.' He looked through the maps as I spoke. I joined him by his side. 'If you were going to hide someone in the forest, where would you do it?' He lined up the older map and bending over, scrutinised them together. He looked like a General in a War Room, plotting battles. A collective silence fell over the room until he tapped his finger: 'there... You won't see it on the new maps but it's ideal.'

'Josh... Get that to Susie now and tell her we're on our way.'

I grabbed my coat and marched through the door only to bump into an unusually flustered George, 'she's gone...'

'George I'm on my way out... can't it wait?'
'No... Will you listen... Paula Wagstaff...'
'What George...? Spit it out...'
'She's done a runner...'

TWENTY SIX
Finding Amy

'For Christ's sake George...!' I stared into the interview room – last known sighting of Paula Wagstaff.

'She asked to go to the loo on the way back to the cells,' he reported, without a hint of defensiveness. 'The attending P.C. stood on guard but was drawn into a punch up as the two suspects from the moped gang came out–'

'Enough... I can't bear it. How much time has she got on us?'

'15 minutes...'

'Where's the husband?' I snapped.

'He's been gone half an hour.'

'The solicitor?'

'He tried to slip out when it all kicked off but I've invited him to wait for you in Interview Three.'

It was no good having a pop at him – he was experienced above and beyond and as Duty Sergeant that shift, knew he would have more than the book thrown at him. Regardless, he remained focused and walked away purposefully as I left with Josh.

'Go to the forest and coordinate the search – I'll follow shortly.'

'Angela's checking CCTV now and we've uniform out there,' he reported.

'I'll be in with the solicitor...'

I rammed the door open into the interview room and the solicitor recoiled as though expecting a punch. I wished... 'If I find you knew anything about this – let alone being involved – I'll have no hesitation to do you as an accessory.'

'I'd be careful throwing around such allegations.' His bravado could not hide his alarm.

'I think you're the one who'll need to be careful if she goes out there and kills again.'

'You have no-'

'Cut the crap... Is the husband in on it?'

'There is no – it – he snapped, before inhaling a calming breath. 'Any business conducted with my clients indicated nothing out of the ordinary.' He fiddled agitatedly with his cuffs.

'Do you know where she's going or what she's going to do next?'

The facade dissolved and as beads of panic formed on his brow, he struggled to look at me. Staring down at his files, he shook his head.

'Then you're of no use to me.'

I returned to Angela in the office, who was sitting by Michael. 'I doubled back as soon as I heard,' he said. 'Here watch this...'

The recording from the reception desk was running on one of his screens. Wagstaff walked through the security door behind another officer. Wearing a baseball cap, with her head down, she slipped out. 'What is she wearing?'

'Police combats, jumper and cap. The women's lockers are right next to the loos.'

'Go back...' I asked, 'before she leaves... there... freeze it...' She looked straight into the camera.

'Cheeky bitch...' Angela said, with a mixture of anger and admiration.

'So, she's not hiding it anymore. That makes her even more dangerous.' I stared at her face until my focus lost, rendered a pixelated blur.

'Boss...'

I dragged myself away from her taunting face to another one of Michael's screens.

'This is as far as I can track her,' he said. 'She goes down the alley beside that Chicken shop and I haven't been able to pick her up again but I'll keep at it.'

'See if you can track the husband as well.'

'I've already checked the car park cameras. He seems to

have come on foot,' Angela added. 'Don't you think that's weird?'

'Yes, I do... Unless he had a car parked nearby that he was trying to keep from view. See if their family cars pop up anywhere and eliminate them first. And get Air Support over the Forest in case she heads there,' I barked at Angela as I ran to my office to answer an insistent phone. 'Connelly...'

'Josie... It's Ewan.'

'Oh... Hi...'

I must have sounded more despondent than I realised as he asked, 'anything wrong?'

'Sorry... yes... Our main suspect has absconded from the station.'

'Not good... That'll play right into the hands of your fan club.'

'You're telling me...'

'Who is it?' he asked.

'The suspect...? Paula Wagstaff.'

'Then I have some relevant news. We've had a DNA hit on the system that matches Catherine Scott.'

'Sorry Ewan... Catherine Scott...? I didn't know we'd asked for one.'

'You didn't...' he confirmed. 'But it's one of the automatic programmes run when we loaded her DNA onto the system. Anyway... it matched a sample already loaded from another case.'

'An old murder...?' I asked, my mind already reaching for probabilities.

'No... Jack Wagstaff's death… his mother pushed for suspicious circumstances so some overeager bod must have ordered a DNA test. It matches Catherine Scott. She is Jack Wagstaff's biological mother...'

I was at risk of losing the precious connections of focus as my brain whirled and synapses fizzled, trying to connect this random new data. I knew I had to drive it from my mind. As we headed for Epping Forest, the temptation was too great for Angela and with her filter button flipped off, she rambled on.

'It would explain the motivation behind Catherine Scott's murder at least but it would be a hell of a coincidence for her to run into Catherine, years after snatching her baby. Maybe she was stalking her? Do you think Catherine knew he was her child? Do mothers know their children regardless of passing years?'

All the questions I was failing to keep from invading my own thought process. 'Pull over...' Angela responded like a child about to be scolded and obeyed without the usual barrage of questions. I allayed her concerns. 'I can drive while you fire off your emails to your contacts.' She took this as the compliment it was intended. 'Track down the case files on the missing baby case. Then Paula Wagstaff's work-history for the last fifteen years – in fact, further back so we can have a better understanding for her possible motives.'

We pulled over and exchanged seats and with Angela now preoccupied, I was left to my own thoughts. What was the chance that Amy was still alive? Pretty slim... If she was not where The Ranger was taking us, I was out of ideas. Paula's rushed attempts at burying her victims, lead to their easy discovery. With the manpower already down there – we would know soon enough.

We parked up in the clearing next to Josh's car but he was nowhere in sight. The Ranger however had arrived and was waiting beside his truck. Angela was on the phone issuing out instructions. I motioned for her to stay in the car and carry on, before joining The Ranger. 'How far from here?'

'Quite deep in the forest,' he replied. 'I've sent Sergeant Hughes and some of your men ahead but it's not an obvious find so they'll have to wait until we get there.'

I jogged to keep up with his strides as he avoided any predetermined pathways and as far as I could see, was heading straight into the dense foliage. Only on approach did the forest's own secret trails become visible and The Ranger seemed to know them instinctively. All my childhood fairy-tale images spun before me, as the apprehension of the real possibility of being lost in these woods took hold. I was entirely disorientated as I followed in his wake.

My sensible – but not forest-worthy shoes – were beginning to leak, not helped by the impossible to navigate, mud-puddles, camouflaged by decomposing leaves.

I was about to turn into my five year old self and plead, 'are we there yet?' when we passed through a regiment of sturdy oak onto a gravelled road. I never suffered from claustrophobia but empathised with the relief as I stepped out into open space and was not quite sure if my breathlessness and damp body was due to the physical exertion or dread of a probable outcome. Across the road, into a less dense part of the forest, I spied a cluster of police-emblazoned uniforms and other First Responders shuffling around rudderless. 'I think they're waiting for you.'

'Yeah... They're in the wrong spot.' He raised his fingers to his lips and released a high-pitched shrill. The team turned their heads collectively, like meerkats on an African plain and waving his arm westwards – beckoned them on. I jogged once more to keep up with his pace as we progressed along the main road with the pack of police, moving parallel to our route. Completing a sharp right-turn, we once more entered a wooded area.

The Pack stood silent, awaiting the arrival of The Ranger as I straggled behind. 'Not far...' he reassured me, a nod to my struggle with the terrain. The Pack followed behind obediently. A mulch-carpeted path fell away as a natural plateau developed and a wall of earth rose to our left, exposing gnarled, ancient roots of the towering oaks.

The Ranger stopped in front of a mound of grass on the plateau and began scrutinising the wall in front of him. He beckoned me over as he snapped on his latex gloves. I followed suit as did the approaching team.

'This has been disturbed,' he said, as he pulled across a curtain of creepers to reveal an iron-riveted door with rusting bolts. 'A World War Two bunker with a twenty first century lock,' he added, as he fiddled with a shiny silver padlock. 'Cutters...' he barked down the line, eliciting an immediate response.

As the padlock was removed and bagged, The Ranger stepped back, allowing me to take the lead, only offering assistance as we pushed in the aged door. The air was damp but not putrid as expected.

'Amy!' I called out as I stepped into a dark tunnel. I spun around to The Ranger, 'what's the layout?'

'Follow this straight ahead and you'll come to another door to the actual bunker.' He handed me a small torchlight.

'Amy!' I cried out in vain as I flicked the torch around the tunnel, secretly praying for the absence of rats, regretting devouring the James Herbert novels of my teens. 'Amy!' I swung the light back behind me as a panic attack threatened at a scurrying noise. 'Josh...'

'Sorry...' he sounded out of breath, 'been talking to Doctor Monroe. He's not far behind.'

'He's here...? Not with a body bag I hope.'

'Do you want me to go first?'

'No... it's okay. But stay close.'

Reassured by his physical presence, we soon reached the inner door which was locked with a simple bolt. I held the torch as Josh wiggled it free. We entered the bunker, proving as dark as the tunnel and fumbled around for a source of light. 'Hold on... there's a wire here,' Josh's voice, guiding in the gloom.

'Amy... Amy...' I felt desperate in the silent room as my words bounced back at me. There was no further comfort when Josh connected the lights, illuminating the absence of Amy. 'Shit...'

'What is all this stuff?' Josh stood amongst a pile of black bin bags at one end of the bunker and began ripping through the plastic. 'Clothes...' He pushed some of the bags aside and stretched forward to grab something at the back, hauling into the air what looked like a suitcase. 'Hold on...' He fumbled in his pockets before retrieving his phone and I watched him speed-swipe over his screen. 'Here...' he held the screen towards me, 'this is Catherine Scott's stuff.'

I looked at the picture on his phone and down at the suitcase, 'yes... they're the same.' It was hard to know where to start. The amount of stuff was overwhelming and we had no time if we were to find Amy alive.

'What is this place? It's like a hippie hang-out.'

He was right. What should have been a dank, confining space was painted bright white with humidifiers set throughout, masking the damp atmosphere. In fact, I could detect a whiff of jasmine. The opposite end to where the bags were stored was laid out like a Shoreditch Coffee Shop: a mound of floor cushions next to a large beanbag sofa and brightly coloured rugs, swamped the floors.

Josh continued to rummage like a scavenger amongst the bags and boxes, grunting with exertion as he went and I headed towards the sofa, discovering a splattering of photographs pinned to the wall. I stood up onto the sofa to get a better look at the family portraits. I had yet to see a photo of the son so the handsome, young man, staring back from his family hug, filled me for a moment with a sense of the rage at her loss. I looked across at another group of photographs, partly obscured by the pile of floor cushions. 'Jesus... Josh!'

Josh sprinted across with the same speed that I pounced on the cushions. Stuck behind them, face down, was a body. 'Careful... careful...' I needlessly instructed as Josh gently lifted the body and laid her on the floor like a cut-down marionette. 'It's her... Is she alive?'

He checked her neck and wrists for a pulse and placed his ear against her lips. 'Yes... barely...' he replied before grabbing his police radio and instructing the paramedics to be sent in and telling everyone else to stay out.

'Have you got anything to get these off?'

Josh handed me his penknife and I gnawed away at the plastic restraint at her wrists and ankles as he held out an evidence bag for me to drop them into. 'Amy... Amy...' I stroked her head, willing her to consciousness, adjusting to the stench of soil and decaying leaves clinging to her clothes as though some mystical wood imp.

With no response, I frantically checked her body for injuries. 'There's only blood coming from a head injury but from what I can see, it's fairly deep.'

Her face was caked in a blood and mud concoction. A swollen, split lip rendered her unrecognisable. Angry purple welts had formed around her wrists from the restraints. Her breathing was so shallow that the lack of any significant rise or fall of her chest made me doubt she was alive until her eyes began to flicker. 'Amy... Amy...,' I urged. 'Amy... Can you hear me?'

Only managing to pry her eyes half-open, a tear trickled down, streaking through the mud as it travelled over her cheek. A rasping sound, spluttered as a whisper through her battered lips. She was trying to speak. 'Who did this Amy? Who did this to you?' I held my head close to her mouth, desperate to decipher the sounds into recognisable words.

I strained to hear her saying, 'Clara...'

'She's okay Amy... She's safe... Who did this to you Amy?'

With finality, her eyes closed fully as a team of Paramedics burst in. I knew better than to get in their way if she had any chance of surviving. I stood by helplessly with

Josh as they set to work on her, only contributing with a précis on the condition we found her in and that she was fleetingly conscious.

Needles and drugs were pushed in with efficient urgency but when the defibrillator was powered up, we knew that we could be looking at the third murder victim. It was as though she held out until she knew her daughter was safe. Josh and I were transfixed as they fought to save her life. Her slim frame looked like it would snap as she jerked violently with the force of the electric current. The rough physicality needed to save her life, was necessary but it seemed heartless after all she must have endured. I could feel Josh willing her on beside me as I played out scenarios in my head of informing her already traumatised husband of her death, knowing, well enough, the life-changing effects this would have on her daughter.

How many more jolts before they gave up?

TWENTY SEVEN
Paula's Rebirth

The wave of nausea returned as I entered that toilet cubicle and relived the pain and horror from last year, when – as if in slow motion – I witnessed my longed-for baby, miscarry into his porcelain grave. Any sensibilities from my midwife's training, discarded with the hope that this premature collection of bloody cells could develop full-term.

The desire was only stimulated after conception. An on-off boyfriend didn't arouse any maternal instincts in me. I couldn't have been farther from an urge to settle down and nest. Yet, once my son was in me, growing, I alarmed myself at the transformation. The boyfriend disposed of... plans were made. A future mapped out and played on repeat in my head. And then he was gone.

Ignoring all advice, I threw myself back into work; self-medicated by caring for others and their babies. But it soon became evident that this masochistic decision, altered me once more. Things could never be the same. The compassionate strand of my DNA which had guided me to midwifery – dissolved, replaced by a vicious prejudice of these contemptible mothers, giving birth to sons that I deserved. I hid behind a mask of civility to such an extent that my superiors had all but forgotten about my trauma. But I had not.

My resentment solidified into a rational process of judgement on each mother, scrutinising her background and motives. How many children did she already have? Too many? Would she have enough time for the new baby? Was it a feckless mother, giving birth to a season-ticket to the welfare state? Or was it a career mum about to dispense her responsibilities to a series of nannies and tick off, 'having a baby,' from her – to do – list? I had categorised them all.

My own personal purgatory fuelled when I was sent to help on the – unofficially titled – abortion ward. Patients, through their own shame, were not inclined to complain about a miserable nurse so I was less disposed to hide my disdain for these women, intent on throwing away something so precious.

I left the cubicle and gazed into the mirror as I robotically washed my hands, another shift over. The frenetic pace of the delivery suite ensured that my head was filled with the moment and not the past. I knew I'd stroll onto the ward under the pretence of carrying out baby-checks before leaving. Like a drunk, with no recollection of getting home, I was there, albeit with my coat already on, and the initial intention of heading home.

Exhausted mothers, comatose, still unused to the responsibility of the little life, bundled beside them. My mind ticked over once more with the possibilities of taking one of these babies as my own. I had planned a route: unseen and unchallenged. I even concocted a plausible reason not to return to work and everything in between before introducing him to the world as my own. Every day I ran through this but every opportunity missed by a pang of conscience or lack of nerve.

The night-time peace was broken by the guttural wailing of a baby in one of the private rooms. As I entered the room, I noticed the paraphernalia surrounding the mum – a tell-tale sign of a caesarean birth. A stray arm hung from the bed. I tucked it back before attending to the baby. A little boy: a month premature but not enough to require neonatal support. I scanned his chart… his last check not ten minutes since.

He instantly self-soothed as I held him securely in my arms as I whispered, 'hello little man.' I strolled from the room into the bottles prep-room, 'let's see what's on the menu.' He sucked greedily on his midnight feast as I inspected his identity bracelet: Daniel Scott.

Holding him high in my cradled arms so he could focus on my face, I caught sight of a windy smile that travelled to his chestnut eyes. I smiled back and felt a warmth flood through me as we connected. I wiped away the excess milk from his plump lips after he demolished the bottle, only for him to latch onto my finger and continue to suckle with all his might. A spontaneous giggle escaped from a lost place within me and I felt choked and overwhelmed by the realisation of the absence of such an emotion for so very long.

The downy skin between his eyebrows and on the bridge of his nose was begging to be stroked, until his eyelids drooped and he succumbed to his inevitable slumber. With his face close to mine, I brushed against his cheek and kissed his forehead. His scent was familiar as though I'd inhaled it all my life.

I knew he was the one but fought against the paralysing desire and returned to his room. The mum stirred as I entered and a crack of light from the corridor sliced across her bed. I saw her face for the first time. I knew her... I couldn't remember her name but yes... her face. Where...? Where...? The image reassembled in my brain as the faded memories were accessed. I reran a long, tiring, double shift on the abortion ward. I recalled her dispassionate demeanour to what should have been a traumatic event. She arrived, suited like a city banker, carrying a Mulberry holdall as though she was on her way from the office to the gym.

She also paid extra for one of the private rooms and although she didn't behave entitled, she remained detached, using her laptop as a barrier to any human contact. Even the box of 'thank you' chocolates she left the next day, seemed part of a corporate efficiency – doubtless bought by a well-oiled P.A.

She was one of those mums. What life did this little boy have mapped out for him? The best of everything materialistic, to substitute what every child needed: love, contact, time. How many of these children could I continue handing over? No more...

Gripping him tightly with one arm, I used the other to arrange the sheets in his cot into a body-form which would be enough to distract a stretched night-duty nurse. I popped back into the bottle-prep room and filled up my jacket pockets with ready made-up bottles from the fridge and made my way to the linen cupboard. Removing my coat, I used his blanket and a sheet from the shelf to wrap around my body, securing him soundly in his sleep to my chest.

Wrapping my coat around us, I zipped up, leaving his precious face visible to me but not to others. After a final check that his head was positioned at the right angle to breath, we made our getaway. My practiced route avoided every possible CCTV, except the inescapable exit from the maternity ward and the car park. Nods of farewell from the porters and night-duty staff – used to seeing me come and go – bolstered my confidence. My heart was bursting through my chest nevertheless. I froze at every stirring from my bundle until I was sure he had settled. Once in the car, I repositioned the driver's seat to allow myself the widest clearance from the steering wheel before tentatively driving my precious cargo home.

Inside the safety of my flat, my legs turned to jelly and I collapsed onto my sofa and breathed to control a wave of dizziness before unwrapping my boy, like a desperately longed-for Christmas present. I spent the next half an hour staring at him, absorbing the miracle of my son. He was mine. My first priority was to give him the name I'd always wanted for my son: Jack.

Our first night together was bliss. I'd never known such a connection... such love... I didn't sleep much but I felt exhilarated after settling Jack as he finished his morning feed and didn't hesitate in making the call to severe my commitment to my work. My carefully constructed back-story was woven around my inability to cope with the intensity of my job; a delayed reaction to my miscarriage – predictably lapped up.

The next few weeks, Jack and I were snugly cocooned in the flat. Everything ordered and delivered, negated the necessity of scrutiny from the outside world as we established our own routine together and we were beyond content. Consciously avoiding the T.V., radio and papers, so blissfully oblivious to if or how Jack's disappearance was reported. After a couple of weeks, I never even gave it a second thought but I needed to make plans for our future. We would need to move to somewhere where we weren't known. Somewhere to start afresh...

Soon I found a place, far enough away from my old life to ensure anonymity and a perfect area to raise my son. We moved within a month. I was able to register him official and I used the advantage of his premature birth to establish a new birth date as a month later and severing a significant tie from his previous life. Any awkward questions when I registered his birth, I waved away and they accepted once they discovered I was a midwife – the least disposed profession to raise suspicion. Dangerous, how trusting people can be...

In our new home, Jack and I rejoined the world, venturing out with gusto, visiting parks and coffee shops, joining toddler groups. I was as much enthralled with my role as a mum as I was with his physical presence.

News had moved on so I was rarely confronted with my actions and when I fell upon a sliver of information, I felt annoyance, not guilt. I imagined the woman (because she was never his mother), more inconvenienced than distraught as she would invariably return to life's shopping list: Chanel bag... perfect baby...

I knew, as I watched the rise and fall of his little chest every night as he slept, that I would never let him go.

I looked across to Josh. 'Do we know when this was recorded?'

'George said that Father Michael had been frantically trying to get hold of you. It seems she went to see him after she absconded from here. She didn't know that he'd been to us and he didn't know that we'd bugged the box.'

'I didn't know we'd bugged the box... the Confessional...'

'Yes... well... sorry about that but I thought you'd let your religious inhibitions cloud your better judgement and you'd say no so I manipulated Spatchcock for an authorisation.'

'How?'

'I told him that it was something you'd be dead set against.'

'You'll go far.'

'There's more...' He clicked the play key as I closed my eyes to visualise her kneeling in that place of sanctity before the priest. She seemed to be relishing in every detail of her memories whether the triumphant act of acquiring her new son or the condescension of her cause.

She listened to my story as she lay there gasping for her life. She was trying to speak, 'Daniel...' she cried. I didn't want to hear her ramblings. I wanted her to get my point so I told her, 'his name is Jack and I'm his mother and you took him from me. You took my precious boy. You failed him at the beginning and you failed him at the end.'

She mumbled her realisation that I had him all that time. Was she pretending to care? I bent down close to her face and told her that I doubted if she gave him a second thought. She rasped her response as blood spluttered from her mouth and claimed that she thought of him every day.

I jumped back and gripped the rock even more tightly. Would she have done more to save him if she'd known? I told her that there was a reason she couldn't have any more children. That she wasn't fit to be a mother. She looked like she was struggling to breathe. I could finish her off. To finish her off for Jack...

'We could've left you know…'. I told her. 'When I first recognised who you were, I was petrified that you'd recognise Jack – but how could you? You had no motherly bond with him as I did. And now I must live with that decision. If we'd gone away... away from you, he'd still be alive. Have you any idea of the pain you've caused? You left me paralysed with grief with no respite, until–'

But I had enough of the talking... I had nothing left to say to her. Remembering the care and time I'd taken to keep him away from her… to keep him safe… I now longed for the temporary relief, putting an end to her life would bring. I raised the rock above my head...

'A full confession of Catherine's Scott's murder but can we use it in court?' Josh asked.

'Seeing as we haven't yet caught her that's the least of our problems but it does confirm to us that she did it. Anything else worth hearing?'

He resumed play and we listened to Father Michael for the first time.

You carry a great burden taking a life. No matter how justified you feel – you will carry that pain forever. But what next? Is it over?

His voice sounded calmer and more considered. She took her time answering and his anxious breathing filled the void.

I feel no remorse if that's what you're looking for. If you want to know if I've killed again Father – well I might have. And will I go on to wipe out more selfish women? Most certainly...

We listened to the shuffling as she left the box and

Father Michael pleading after her to return.

'Is it me…?' I asked. 'Or does she sound like she wasn't only talking to the priest?'

'There's no way she knew she was bugged,' Josh replied, 'but maybe she hoped the priest would pass the message on.'

'I had better luck with the voice analysis on this sample than your anonymous phone calls,' Michael said. 'This is a match with the Paula Wagstaff interviews.'

'Has anyone been able to get hold of Father Michael since?' I asked.

'No... No one at the church has seen him for a while.'

Josh looked across at me. 'Shit...'

TWENTY EIGHT
A Final Confession

'Doctor Monroe is helping the team around the bunker looking for fresh graves.' A clear message from Josh that he believed the priest was the next victim.

'I can't comprehend that she could be so prolific in such a short time-frame.'

We parked on the busy high street in front of the church. I hopped out of the car and searched for the CCTV camera Angela would have accessed. 'Is that what you're looking for?' Josh pointed above a cluster of trees opposite the church. 'That's going to give a limited view. Plenty of other ways she could have snuck in.'

'Plenty...' I sighed as I spied the beginnings of a graveyard around the side. 'Angela spent hours on the tapes with no hits. I'll look for the rectory housekeeper – they're the eyes and ears of the parish – and you have a nosy around the grounds.'

We went our separate ways as we approached the church gate and I was soon in the company of (as opposed to being greeted by), the housekeeper. The martyr of the rectory: suitably hostile, territorial and laden with sanctimonious bitterness. She was flagrantly not a fan of Father Michael and did not disguise that she was more inconvenienced by having to report his disappearance than concerned. She had a fixed dedication to being as unhelpful as possible, rebuffing any questions on his possible whereabouts with remonstrations of: 'I'm not his keeper...' and seemed more put out by the fact that, 'Father Theodore had to cover Evening Prayers – and he's not a well man.' And in case we were not getting the message – confirmed: 'I only called you lot because Father Whitney – he's in charge – said that Father Michael was doing something with you lot so to keep an eye out for anything strange.'

'Has Father Michael proven to be unreliable?' I asked, a

sarcastic tone wasted on her.

'Well no... but sometimes he was in a state that... well... maybe he shouldn't have bothered – if you know what I mean...'

I was in no mood for her spite, 'no, I don't Mrs Rooney but if you wouldn't mind showing me to his room, I'll take it from there.'

With a disapproving grunt, she led me down a meandering hallway, heavy with the stale, musty odour of inertia, passing God's waiting room of cat-napping priests.

'This one...' She opened the door to a tiny room, scarcely able to accommodate a single bed, wardrobe and bedside cabinet. 'I'll leave you to it,' she snorted before attempting to shuffle off.

'Before you go Mrs Rooney... can you confirm where you've looked already?'

She maintained her disinterest and just about bothered to shout back as she departed, 'I've checked the whole house and the church. All the other buildings are locked from the outside.'

His room was a pitiful sight – soulless. For a man who lived his life in the missions, such lack of home comforts, I doubt would be missed. I opened the mahogany wardrobe, not expecting any more than I found: a couple of battered suits and black shirts. A rummage through the drawers, only delivered a few weary-worn garments; no furtively secreted black book, titled – *secrets of the confessional.* His bedside cabinet held the remnants of his previous life: dog-eared photographs and thank-you notes, all tucked under a half-drunk bottle of vodka. I took one last look under his mattress and bed before my phone began to vibrate in my pocket. 'Yes Josh...'

'I think I've found him. Come down to the church hall – I'm about to break in.'

I jumped over the busted padlock as I sprinted into the

deserted hall. 'Josh!'

'In here...'

Following his voice into the kitchen, I found him crouched on the floor besides an unconscious Father Michael, blood pooled around his head. 'He's alive and the ambulance is on its way.'

'I'm sorry... I'm so sorry...' I looked up and stood to one side was an elderly man – somewhere in his eighties: his head in his hands, rocking and shaking.

'That's Mr Jericho...' Josh explained. 'He was banging to get out. He witnessed some of it... I don't know how much.'

'Are you alright here?' I asked Josh. He replied with a nod – not taking his eyes off the priest.

'It's okay sir...' Jericho backed away as I approached. 'It's okay... I'm Detective Chief Inspector Connelly. Come... let's find somewhere to sit.' I shepherded him along, away into the main hall. Dragging out two chairs, I settled him in one and pulled up close. Lightly placing a hand on his heaving shoulders as he silently sobbed. The doors burst opened. The paramedics rushed through and Josh led them to the kitchen.

'Mr Jericho... do you think you can tell me what happened here?'

He inhaled as he tried to control the sobs. 'I was working in the storeroom,' he began, his head still bowed; silver, candy floss tufts of hair, hovering across a flaky scalp. 'Father Michael was in the kitchen.' He looked towards the kitchen as the chatter and clatter of the paramedics working, filled the hall.

'Was he alone?'

His attention drew back to me, 'yes... at first. I heard the door go so came out to see who it was but she was already in the kitchen talking to him.'

'Did you see her?' I asked.

'I watched them through the hatch.'

'In your own time Mr Jericho... recount what you heard.'

He rocked in his chair as he spoke. 'I heard her say, "aren't you going to offer me a cup of tea?" He looked anxious as she stepped towards the kitchen counter, you know as though he thought she was going to attack him but she pulled two mugs off a mug-tree and smiled at him as she made some tea. She sipped the tea and watched him... He asked her why she'd come? She said she wanted to confess and began, "Bless me Father–" He refused but she kept baiting him, "bless me Father..."'

He rubbed his cheeks as though washing his face: rough hands scratching over his patchy bristle before continuing.

'He said he didn't believe she was looking for absolution and that if she wanted to brag about her latest heinous crime, to go call a newspaper. She called him a stupid, ignorant man. She went for him, saying that she didn't need to brag... didn't need the endorsement of others. That what she was doing was right. These women wouldn't be missed and the children in their care would lead better lives. I don't know. I didn't understand what she was saying. It didn't make sense. Maybe I didn't hear right.' He ran his hands down the thighs of his creased chinos and continued his rocking.

'Go on Mr Jericho,' I urged.

'He still didn't seem at ease but he kept talking to her. He asked her what she wanted with God. Did she think he was giving her some kind of licence to continue this killing frenzy? "Bless me Father–" she kept saying, "bless me Father..." And... well... he snapped...'

He raised his hand to his face as though to hide his shame, 'I should've stepped in. I'd heard enough to know how evil she was.' Lowering his hand, he went on, 'you should've heard how she spoke to him... it was chilling.'

'If you had,' I reassured him, 'the paramedics would be working on two victims today. This is all helpful so please continue if you can.'

He looked sideways at the kitchen where the activity

continued. 'As I said... he seemed to snap. He challenged her to tell him about her latest killing. Not to hide under the guise of confession. To know about the family who'll have to mourn the senseless loss of their loved one. Or maybe she'd murdered a mother again, destroying the life of some poor innocent? I don't know if she heard him properly but she started going on about something like, if he'd ever thought why woman weren't allowed to be priests? She said if she were confessing to a female priest, a mother, she'd understand...' He hung for a moment as though suspended in his thought before continuing without a prompt.

'He asked about her daughter and if the pain of the children of the women she'd killed was any less than that of her own child? She wasn't interested. "Bless me Father..." she said again. He began to sound different. Defeated… He asked her name and told her his, but she said she already knew and again repeated, "bless me Father Michael for I have sinned." He turned his back on her and stared out of the kitchen window. He asked her what she needed to confess. But she toyed with him, saying it was... a dilemma... yes that was it – a dilemma, because she didn't feel like she'd sinned.

'She went on anyway saying something about another mother whose neglect nearly cost her child's life, someone who sought her out.' He rummaged around in his pockets and pulled out a pristinely pressed handkerchief and wiped around his face. He looked over to the kitchen.

'Did she say anything else about this woman?' I asked with slightly less urgency now that Amy was safe.

'He asked that – but I'm not sure... she said something like, "they'd not parted on good terms." He did push her to say where she was. She didn't like that and he said that he could go to the police. Give them enough clues without breaking The Seal of Confession for them to begin a search...'

I placed my hand on his shoulder as he raised his hand

to his face once more, 'it's okay Mr Jericho... go on... please...'

He continued through sobs, 'I could feel the clunk of the kettle against his skull. His chin hit the worktop where he fell and blood poured from his mouth. He was propelled backwards landing on his back and I thought... I thought he gave a final look of lament before ending up unconscious on the floor.'

'What happened after that?' I prompted a now sobbing Jericho. 'Did you see where she went?'

He blew his nose before continuing, 'I panicked... if I'd gone for the door, she would've seen me so I made my way back into the storeroom and hid. I hid until I heard someone rattling the door while Father Michael lay there...'

'If you hadn't, we wouldn't know what went on here today and it will help to put her away.'

We both looked up as Josh made his way out of the kitchen. Reluctant to make eye contact, he took a deep breath and shook his head.

TWENTY NINE
Something To Say

'Josephine... Are you with us...?'

'Sorry Ewan... yes... fire away.'

'You give this speech enough times to your team so it's time you listened to your own advice,' he began. 'There's nothing you could've done to save his life.'

'Father Michael... his name is Father Michael.' Saying his name as we both stood over his lifeless body, made me feel that if I shouted it loud enough, I could conjure up his life-form and return it to its empty husk. I looked around the room wondering... wondering where was his spirit...? His soul...? Entities that we were both conditioned to believe. Was he – like some article in a Sunday rag – on top of the cupboards looking down? Relieved that he didn't have to carry around the weight of his broken body: a testament to his mortal failings? Did he knowingly push her, believing that his death would ultimately lead to her capture?

'You weren't responsible,' he repeated the sentiment.

'No... But I feel I could've done more to protect him. We knew she sought him out and I was too worried that he'd get into trouble for coming to us. I should have spoken up... organised some protection. Something... anything... It's such a waste.'

'It'll only be a waste if you lose your focus and let this woman slip through your fingers.'

I knew he was right but this victim... I felt a connection and the fact that his whole existence had been solely to help others, made it seem even more perverse. I contemplated that she knew this. Possibly followed me...? Saw us together...? A sick twist in her killing spree.

'You know your every move is being scrutinised Josephine – don't hand it to them on a plate.'

'We've seen enough of them come and go Ewan to know they'll get me in the end. There's only so much they'll take of me not playing the game and I've no intention of changing now.'

'They're still some who know your worth and won't let that happen.'

'Perhaps...' I touched the outline of a military tattoo adorning Father Michael's upper arm: cold creping skin, once inhabited by youthful biceps. Part of me wanted to believe that this was his way of sticking two fingers up to his own sanctimonious cult.

'He would've been knocked out cold and not regained consciousness,' Monroe said, with a sense that I needed reassurance. But who was I to be reassured? 'The blunt force trauma resulting in a bleed out in the brain,' he added as he respectfully covered his broken body with a sheet; his own religious tendencies kicking in when handling the body of this cleric.

'The murder weapon this time, doesn't sound premeditated,' I suggested.

'No... But neither do the blows reflect a frenzied attack as with the first victim although the power behind the blow does indicate strength of purpose.'

We reconvened in the forensic meeting room with photographic evidence from the case already loaded onto the screen. 'How long do you think you can keep Amy Whitehead and Father Michael out of the news?' Monroe asked as he poured us both a coffee.

'If the predictable leaks don't happen – then until I catch her, I hope. More publicity will fuel her righteous cause. What have you got for me here?' I flicked through the report in front of me as he scrolled through pictures on the screen.

'Her DNA and in fact that of her family are all over the items in the bunker – even the deceased son so unless they're using it as their own personal version of Centre Parcs, I suggest the items are from the family home.'

'What about the items we think are from Catherine

Scott's flat?'

He pointed at the screen, 'images on the left are from the bunker and on the right, a corresponding image from the photos sent by Amy Whitehead. However, there's none of Paula Wagstaff's DNA on Catherine Scott's possessions or the bags used.'

'What about in the church?'

'Nothing in The Confessional and she's done a clean-up job in the kitchen. The cups of tea your witness spoke about... washed and put away. The kettle has disappeared but the wound on the head and force of impact would concur with the use of this object as the murder weapon. She seems to be forensically aware for a stay-at-home mum.'

'She's spent many years hiding in plain sight, crafting a new identity. I think covering her tracks would be second nature.' I looked up at the freshly loaded pictures of Father Michael's body. 'Could she have thought that he was dead when she left him?'

He followed my eye-line. 'To a layman, maybe... blood pouring from his head... shallow breathing... she could have made a presumption, particularly as she was distracted by covering her trail. But with her medical background, I would conclude that she would have instinctively checked and without leaving a trace.'

'So, she either wanted him alive or wanted him to suffer a long, lingering death.'

'Or was happy to leave it in the hands of the gods...'

'Or to put it back on me, knowing that I'd believe, if I'd got there sooner, he may have survived.'

Monroe looked across at me, 'is this personal Josephine?'

'She's making it...' Saying it aloud forced me to accept that it was now a reality, sending me back into a black hole until the shrill of the office phone pierced my thoughts.

Ewan picked up and looked across at me, 'yes she's

here... okay... I'll tell her...'

'What...?'

'Amy Whitehead has regained consciousness.'

THIRTY
A Survivor

As I drove to the hospital, I couldn't ignore the fact that here was another victim she had left half-dead. Was there a difference in these last two victims, compared to the others?

I had avoided thinking about Amy Whitehead in her coma as much as possible. Not out of lack of compassion or even the obligatory guilt at not having found her sooner but the thought of a consciousness, entombed in a paralysed body as the world moved on and progressed in your absence, was the stuff of nightmares for me.

I met Marc Whitehead in the hospital corridor, resembling part refugee, part lost boy. I reached out and touched his arm, 'good news Mr Whitehead. You must be so relieved.'

'What...?' He seemed disorientated... dazed. 'Yes... but no... She can't feel her legs. They don't know...'

I guided him to a seat. 'It's early...'

'I know... that's what they said. But I have to tell Clara.' Silent tears trickled over his unshaven cheeks. 'What will I say...?'

'As close to the truth as you can I always find best. We underestimate how resilient children are and if we spend our time sending them out of rooms while the adults talk – they'll make up their own truth which could be worse.'

He wiped his face with his crumpled Coldplay t-shirt, 'yes... yes... you're right. Clara's such a bright girl... she'll sense it.' He turned to face me, 'have you come to talk to Amy?'

'I'm sorry but yes. There's still someone out there doing this.'

'Is she in danger? Does she know she's alive?'

'We can't be certain but we'll keep an officer with her until she's caught,' I attempted to reassure him.

The officer at the door saw me coming and stood to

attention. The on-duty nurse was harder to negotiate, reluctantly allowing me fifteen minutes before her return. Although cleaned up, Amy's injuries were as violent as when we found her but she seemed to be more alert than I expected.

'Have you caught the bitch?' Her speech was thick and lispy through her swollen lip.

I pulled a chair close to her bed. 'Not yet... how are you?'

'Not bad for someone whose was left for dead and may not walk again,' she said with justifiable anger.

'Do you want to help me catch her?' I asked.

'Too fucking right...'

'Then tell me everything that happened but try and keep calm or your nurse will kick me out.' I looked out through the window to check she was not already on her way.

She rubbed her bandaged head, 'parts are foggy but I've been concentrating on piecing it together.'

'Start from the beginning and chronology sometimes helps the memories connect.'

'Pass me that bottle of water would you – my throat's killing me after they pulled out all those tubes.' I passed her the water and she took a few sips. 'I was going through a list like you asked, looking for connections – with the added incentive that you seemed intent on focusing on Stella as the suspect.'

'In fairness Amy, I wouldn't be doing my job if I didn't follow the evidence,' I said, trying not to sound defensive.

'I know... I know... and if I'm honest, I had a talk with myself when it was all proving so compelling against her but the fact that I knew her to be a genuinely decent person, won the day.' She swigged once more from her bottle. 'I was being literal in sifting through the list – looking for who was capable and missing the point of who could be linked to both women. When my post-it-note reminder with Paula's name, stared at me. I initially thought that she might know something about both women and help with some info.'

'What changed your mind?'

'How she was acting... You know she helped me when my daughter was knocked down outside school?'

I nodded not wanting to stop her flow, conscious of the sceptre of the returning nurse.

'Well… we never became what you would call close but she was efficient and supportive and always in an unassuming way. But this Paula was different: assertive, somewhat edgy and successful in manipulating me into the woods.'

'Where did you think you were going?'

'She said she had to run an errand and we could have lunch at The Queen Elizabeth Hunting Lodge but parked at the opposite part of the forest – supposedly by accident – persuading me that it was no problem to walk through.' She closed her eyes for a moment and rubbed her forehead.

'You alright to go on?'

'Yeah... I'm fine... a bit of a headache forming.' She opened her eyes, 'so we're in the forest – she seemed to know her way quite well, whereas I was beginning to feel a bit panicky. I tried to slip in my questions about her relationships with both women. She didn't take much prompting to let it be known how little she thought of them and even at that stage, the connection to her son's death – you know he died of meningitis?'

I nodded.

'Well... I began to realise that maybe that was what it was all about.' She seemed to drift off into her own thoughts before continuing. 'She went on to make a few pops at me, implying that Clara's accident was down to my neglect. Which I don't disagree with...'

'How did you end up in the bunker?'

'I don't know... One minute we're walking along... next thing – something crashes into the back of my head and... I come around in the bunker.'

'And she was there?'

'Yeah... by then in full-on psycho mode. It's like she wanted someone to listen to her rambling. I didn't take much in at first. So much of my body hurt. She must have dragged me along or something because I was covered in blood and mud and I didn't know if I could feel my legs. I remember panicking that she'd done something to Clara and called out her name. She said that she was alive and would be better off without me.' She closed her eyes as she said, 'I remember thinking that too and knowing she was safe, I remember accepting that I could go.' I could see the tears brimming around her closed lids before spilling in abundance down her face. She wiped them away and opened her eyes. 'Sorry... didn't expect that. I'm so consumed with rage I haven't processed what she did to me.'

'Don't be hard on yourself Amy. She's the one who caused this.' Amy replied with a slight, unconvincing tip of her head. 'Are you okay to go on?' I asked, a ticking clock reverberating in my head.

She took a deep invigorating breath and found a strong voice once again. 'She was reliving the death of her son,' she began, 'as told by Catherine Scott from what I could make out. I think she said that she made her retell it one last time before she killed her.'

'What happened to him?'

'It sounded a tragic accident – there for the grace of God and all that...' we both absorbed that thought. 'They were on a school trip, he reported feeling unwell. They gave him some Calpol but then he took a turn for the worse. They took him to the local hospital but they never called the parents in time for them to be there at the end.'

'"They…" being Catherine Scott.'

'Yes... and she was going on about stuff that I didn't understand so I'm not sure if I heard right... something about... she was right about protecting him from her... she was never his mother... I don't know – maybe I dreamt it.'

'No... You heard right. Catherine Scott was Jack Wagstaff's birth mother.'

'Fuck... no wonder she's pissed.'

I turned towards voices at the door and could see through the glass, the nurse in conversation with the Constable. Whatever was said, caused the nurse to high tail it back down the corridor. The Officer looked through the glass and gave me a thumbs-up. I accepted this stay of execution and pushed on. 'I'll fill you in later but in the meantime did she say anything about the Fiona Anderson murder?'

'Plenty... I think that's what whetted her appetite. She'd had enough of listening to her slag off her own son...'

'We know a lot about the details of her view towards Fiona so before I'm chucked out by your nurse – any details on the murder itself will be helpful.'

'Got it... right... She said she was leaving the hall and Fiona came up behind her and hijacked her to cut through the park together. Fiona thought it a laugh if they avoided the Park-keeper and were locked in and had to jump the gates. She said she acted like she was giddy... pissed... or on something. She kept on bitching about her son and from what I could make out, Paula snapped, called her a shit-mother...

'Fiona responded that Paula was a nobody who couldn't keep her son alive. Whatever Paula said back – Fiona whacked her around the face and she went flying. As she went to walk away, Paula picked up a rock and smashed it into her head.'

I pictured the scene from my visits as she recounted the story. 'Go on...'

'She talked about her reaction… her euphoria... the weight of grief temporarily lifted… That she made no attempt to resuscitate her and half wished she was alive when she buried her. Something about ripping off her gawdy bling and throwing it into the night. I lay there not moving a muscle. Praying that she'd forget I was there.'

'But she didn't...'

'For a while perhaps... She also said that she hid the weapon in the fund-raising box at school but from what I can make out it's a rock, so why do that?'

'Because it became her weapon of choice,' I explained. 'Was there anyone she spoke about when relating these murders that would make you think they could be the next victim?'

'We all fuck up somehow so I think anyone she meets is a potential.' She took another sip from her bottle before continuing. 'She spoke about you...'

'Excuse me...?'

'She seemed to know all about you. Mentioned seeing you on the TV appeals. Reckoned that she's spoken to you a few times – just to let you know she was there. She mentioned your husband... son and daughter.'

A wave of nausea threatened to rise. I breathed deeply. I never fronted those appeals – intentionally keeping nutters like this at bay. I would have been mentioned though so it wouldn't have taken much effort for someone with intent to track me down. 'What did she say?'

'She admired your tenacity to get on in a man's world but ultimately it would be your children who would pay the price for your ambition.' She began rubbing her head again. 'I think I lost consciousness... Look that's all I can remember for now. Is it okay...?'

As if on cue, her nurse burst in, 'good try on the wild goose chase. Time to go...'

'You've been brilliant Amy,' I said as rose from my seat. 'Look... I have to say, I thought that she didn't know you'd survived and as we kept this out of the news, unless she's gone back to the bunker – she shouldn't know. We'll still keep you guarded in case.'

‘Don’t worry... I’m not going anywhere. Plenty of time to plot my revenge. And by the way...’ She added as the nurse was not so subtlety pushing me through the door. ‘I don’t know how you figured it out – but thanks for finding me.’

‘Just another day at the office...’

THIRTY ONE
The Family

I sat in front of the husband and took my time to observe this man, who supposedly claimed he knew nothing about his wife's killing spree. Planning to disarm him by turning up at his doorstep at this late hour, rather than calling him into the station, where he would be over-prepped and over-defensive. The dimmed lights could not mask the sleep deprived pallor and crystal glass of whisky at his elbow – a hint to his self-medication.

'Where's your daughter Mr Wagstaff?'

He looked at me suspiciously. 'I've sent her away to my sister's in France. Away from this circus...'

Of his own making but I needed to keep him on side. 'Where does she think her mother has gone?' I asked.

'I'm not prepared to talk about any personal details concerning my daughter.' The anger never left his tone.

'But she must be distressed at not having her mum around and shipped off to another country with some distant relative?'

'As I said... my family relations have nothing to do with you.'

'Then let's talk about a family relation that does have something to do with me – your wife... We believe she's already killed three people. Doesn't that concern you Mr Wagstaff? Because I have to say, you're not looking as disturbed by this state of affairs as I would expect.'

'That's because I do not believe your accusations,' he replied wearily.

'We have witnesses now so there's no avoiding the inevitable.' His expression remained detached. 'Then why has she disappeared?'

'What do you expect? What would you do if you were falsely accused?'

I rummaged around in my coat pocket for my phone, set

up the recording and laid it on the table. The voice of his wife filled the room as she taunted Father Michael in the confessional. He could not disguise the flash of recognition. Each physical inference that he was about to get up and turn off the recording was countered by his compulsion to continue listening. I searched his face for tell-tale signs of his thoughts as he listened to her recount the abduction of her self-anointed son from Catherine. Detaching from the characters involved and knowing their fate, it was objectively an empathetic story of desperation and hope. Could he be hearing this for the first time?

Never meeting my gaze, his furrowed expression was tinged with confusion as he sat twisting his wedding band. The transformation as she described the last moments when she murdered Catherine Scott, exposed an unguarded, genuine moment of disgust. Only then did he interject, 'enough...!'

I remained still, allowing the revelations to sink in. He lifted his head as though straining against a gravitational pull. 'I didn't know.'

'Which bit?'

'All of it... Jack... I raised him as my own. Never thought, never considered him as anyone else's. She spoke as though he was a result of a one-night stand. Do you have proof that this isn't another story?'

'I'm afraid so... everything from witness statements to D.N.A. evidence,' I confirmed. 'And the murders...?' I went on. 'What do you know of them?'

'Nothing...'

The anger was gone but for me it was not conclusive enough to prove ignorance of all she had done. He needed a nudge. I pulled out a file from my bag and placed photographs of the dead bodies of both Fiona Anderson and Catherine Scott on the table. 'These are two women who crossed your wife.' I placed a photograph of Father Michael beside them. 'Let's not forget the priest who spent his life as a missionary, dedicated to others but was unfortunate enough to get in your wife's way.'

He looked away momentarily as though to steady himself before returning his gaze. He leant forward and picked up the photo of Catherine Scott and held it in front of his face. 'So, this was Jack's mother...'

'His name was Daniel.'

He continued to stare at the photo. 'Do you have children?'

'I do...' I replied.

'Then maybe you can appreciate when I say that I understand... I understand the rage... the grief that drove her to this. The cruel twist of fate that the neglect of this woman she'd been avoiding all Jack's life, may have caused his death.'

'And what about the grief that Catherine Scott lived with all her life? The torture of not knowing what happened to her only child. Never able to mourn... Not knowing if her child was still out there and to be tormented at the end. How understanding should we be to your wife's sick sense of justice Mr Wagstaff?'

He returned the photo to the table but I was not finished. I held up the picture of Fiona Anderson. 'We all know what an irritating cow she could be but irritating enough to have a rock smashed into her head? I don't think her family feel understanding – she left behind two children.'

He closed his eyes and regulated his breathing, twisting his ring once more before looking across to a family photograph on a sideboard. 'She's unwell... she needs help, not locking up.'

'Mr Wagstaff,' I said, sharp enough that he was in no doubt that I required his full attention. 'Your wife's state of mind has progressed from momentary lapses of sanity into full blown psychosis. The fleeting rush of euphoria she feels, releasing her from her crippling grief – has become addictive. She is now on some righteous mission against anyone she considers an unworthy mother. She WILL kill again.'

'She's not well...'

'Did you know she was going to abscond?'

'No...'

'Why didn't you drive in that day?'

He ran his fingers through unkempt hair. 'I did... she told me, through our solicitor, to park on the street.'

'You didn't think that suspicious?'

'I thought she was getting out and didn't want to be seen in your car park or the like...'

'What happened when she got out?' He looked back at the family portrait. 'Mr Wagstaff...?'

'I waited in the car... she found me and jumped in and told me to drive. I could see how she was dressed and put two and two together. She said that you wanted a conviction and were twisting the evidence to convict her. I believed her...'

'Where did you go?' I asked, trying to keep him focused.

'We came back here... she took enough stuff so as not to be noticeable when your lot came back and ripped the place apart.'

'And where is she now?'

'I don't know. Truthfully...' he said, looking into my doubting face. 'She said she'd be in contact and we could all be together again.'

'And has she been in contact?'

'No... not yet...' he replied, tinged with regret.

'Mr Wagstaff... does she know where your daughter is?'

He reached for his glass and downed the dregs of the whisky before answering, 'no...'

I held my breath as I tentatively turned the key in the lock, praying that Peter and Emilia would remain true to form and stay comatose, despite my night-time manoeuvrings. I dumped my coat and bag in the hall and after pouring a large glass of Chianti, flopped onto the sofa. After a medicinal glug of the soothing nectar, I put my feet up and closed my eyes. Despite my body protesting a leaden weight fatigue, the processing machine in my head would not comply.

'Hey You...'

I opened my eyes to find Peter looking down at me.

'Sorry... didn't mean to wake you.'

He sat down on the sofa, placing my outstretched legs onto his lap, 'don't worry... I was working in bed anyways and lost track of time.'

'The Steelman case…?' I asked as he began to massage my feet and I let out a soft groan.

'Yep... Closing arguments tomorrow. How about you? Catch the bitch yet?'

I smiled as I looked across at this big hulk of a man. His naturally curly hair, untamed and un-lawyer like at this time of night. 'You've been hanging out too much with that teenage daughter of ours,' I said, reaching across and tucked a wayward curl behind his ear.

'Well… we did have an interesting conversation this evening – whether her human rights were being violated by the tracking app we use on her phone. I had to let her down by telling her that I couldn't take up her case as she couldn't afford me.'

I adjusted my position as I succumbed to the anesthetising effects of the wine and massage. 'Has she decided on her work experience yet?'

'She still wants to go in with you.'

'Not a chance Pete. I want you to keep to your promise that you'll help me steer her away from a career in the police.'

He raised his hands in surrender, 'okay... but if you make it forbidden fruit, you'll entice her. I'll take her in with me and show her how boring Law is and that'll certainly make her mind up not to go into the police.'

'Then what do we do?' I asked, exasperated by this continual dilemma.

He resumed the massage, my toes curled up in gratitude. 'What about a bit of reverse psychology? Take her in with you. Attach her to something boring or shitty and let nature take its course.'

'Have you met our daughter...? She'd see through that in a second.'

He reached over for my glass of wine and took a hefty swig before asking, 'you still haven't answered if you've found Paula Wagstaff yet?'

I let my head flop back, 'no... The bitch is still out there and I've no idea where she is. The husband claims, he doesn't know where she could be either.'

'Do you believe him?' He asked.

'I don't know. He seemed taken aback when I played one of the confessional tapes and kept saying that she wasn't well.'

'Knowing she's guilty and willing to help you catch her are two different things.'

'I know...' I retrieved my wine from his outstretched hand. 'What would you do in his position?'

'I'd do all I could to protect you,' he said, without hesitation.

'Aw... thanks babe...'

'But I'd get you help and only give you up if you were a threat to our children. Is she a threat to their daughter?'

'I don't know yet,' I realised for the first time.

THIRTY TWO

The Hunt

We stepped out of the church into an irritating drizzle as Josh pretended not to notice me wiping my eyes.

'That was quite happy-clappy as far as funerals go,' he said, stumbling over his choice of words. 'The African choir was great and the stories about his time in Uganda were interesting. Sounded quite an adventurer in comparison–'

'To the burnt-out alcoholic who rocked up at the station?' I finished his thought process for him.

'Still a shame though... Who was that you were in a headlock with at the back of the church?'

'His friend, Father Pablo... he gave me this...' I held up the envelope I was clutching. 'From Father Michael... He knew she'd come for him so in case anything happened to him, he felt free to give us the details of her confessions.'

'Anything we don't know?'

'Not really… it adds to the weight of the evidence against her, although he does sign off with a plea for us to offer her some understanding and forgiveness.'

'That's a bit of a stretch,' he said, pulling his collar up against the damp wind as we made our way to the car. The senselessness, still on his mind as we drove off: 'it was a waste if he put himself in her line of fire, only to provide information we already had. That's going to be hard to live with.'

It was – and I was struggling to shake it from my mind as I stood at the head of the team, staring intently at the pictures on the board.

Josh had been withdrawn since the funeral and set upon reviewing the evidence of the case with a dogged determination. He walked around with some file or another permanently attached to his armpit as though every precious moment and detail counted.

'Fiona Anderson... The first...' he began, 'spent years wearing her down with her tactless drivel until she snaps. No premeditation... although a half-decent clear-up job.'

'And tries to stitch up the husband,' Angela adds.

'Finds she has a taste and a talent for it,' I continue, 'but then takes a different approach. Catherine Scott,' I move on. 'She selects her victim for her multiple sins: birth mother to her precious son and the cause, as she sees it, of his death. Plans meticulously to bump into her in the woods and even brings the talisman from the first murder: the rock used as the murder weapon. Susie… did you get it over to forensics?'

'Yes Boss,' she replied, standing at the back against the door, once again looking as though she was waiting for an excuse to leave.

'Good... Confident enough to hide it in plain sight. Knows the killing site well and poor luck that the body was discovered. She uses her time with her victim to tell her about the tragic irony of their son and torments her with it at the end. Again – as with Fiona – no remorse. Next… Amy Whitehead comes knocking. Sticks her nose in about the murders. Could stumble on something that threatens to expose Paula. Paula takes her back to her familiar killing site but uses her hide-away to prevent another body being found. Did she intend to kill her?'

'But...' Angela interrupted. 'She had no way of knowing that we'd find her bunker and get to Amy before she died.'

'Or planned to come back for her, unaware that she'd broken her back?' I suggest. 'And she moves on to Father Michael – her confessor. He had to go when there was the threat that he was going to the police.'

'And now...?' Josh asked.

'What's her next move?' I put out to the room. 'To disappear...? Or is she going to kill again and if so – who's her next victim? Let's start with the family. Josh what do you have for me?'

He stood beside me, as able to command the room, 'we've surveillance on the husband: both physical and technical. Nothing as of yet...'

'Does she still consider him an ally?' I asked. 'Has he done anything that she would consider a betrayal?'

'It depends if she thinks he's discovered her full story. But there's no way she knows that we know. I think she'll head for the daughter.' He pointed to the recent addition of her picture on the board.

'Do we have her location?'

'Yes... an address in Lyon.'

'Who here speaks French?' I asked, not truly expecting a response.

'I do Boss,' Susie piped up, unable to conceal the fact that she thought she'd hit the jackpot. 'Passable anyway...'

'That'll do. Get over there and follow her every move. Michael... give her any gizmo's that might help her surveillance.' He gave a detached nod of acknowledgement as his attention remained on the multiple screens now set up in his area. 'Josh... Get hold of our French equivalents to avoid baguettes at dawn and organise a French contact for Susie to have as back up should it get messy. I'll clear it with upstairs.'

'We've already notified them that there's a possibility she could be in the country.'

Susie followed Michael from the room, setting off to his techie mates in the basement.

'Right... so back to friends. Who has she pissed off?'

'I've been back to the school interviewing parents,' Angela began, sat in her usual spot at the front of the class. 'I couldn't find anyone who considered her a close friend or knew anyone who could be a possible candidate. They mentioned her involvement in some school committees like the fund-raising which all seemed to include Amy Whitehead and her friends.'

'We know that Stella Winchester lost a child. Find out

more about the circumstances of that death and if she falls into Paula's – unworthy mothers – radar,' I instructed.

'One of the teachers did mention a mum that still had children at the primary school but had an older lad now at secondary, who she thought was close to Paula when her son was alive.'

'Did you track her down?'

'Yes,' she responded as she flicked through her notebook. 'Anna Shelby. She was reluctant at first to engage – didn't want to say anything that would get Paula into any trouble. I managed to persuade her that we needed to stop her before she harmed her family or maybe children – at which she folded.'

'Were they close?'

'They hooked up as Anna Shelby's son hung out with Jack Wagstaff and Nathan Anderson. They seemed like-minded in their criticism of Fiona Anderson and she didn't show any sympathy for Fiona's fate. She painted a picture of Paula as a fun-loving, fully engaging mum... Up for a laugh on nights out and a great friend in times of need.'

'And after the son died?'

'They lost touch. She said she cut herself off. Refused offers of support or comfort. She was aware she saw Catherine Scott for a while and did try and reconnect after that but gave up. Letting her know she was there if she needed her. She still saw her in the playground as Esme attended the school but felt that she avoided her. She presumed it was too painful for her to engage with anyone who knew Jack. Seemed pretty understanding of her situation.'

'When was the last time she spoke to her?' I asked.

'She claims not for years.'

'Do you believe her?'

She flicked her pen against her notebook as she considered her answer. 'I'm not sure. She didn't at any point condemn what she did.'

'Anything she said give you cause to think she's on Paula's list?'

'No... Nothing...' she said after consideration. 'I warned her that she needed to tell us if Paula makes contact.'

'Josh... Add her to your list to keep an eye on.'

Michael returned to the room as the team dispersed with their action plans. Josh followed me to Michael's desk. 'Is she all set?' I asked.

'Yeah... You know Susie...' he commented, 'halfway out the door before you've even finished your sentence. I've included a tracking device on her for peace of mind although with that one, I'd like to chip her like my cat to know what she gets up to.'

'Think you're over-sharing Michael,' Josh said as Michael settled into his seat, like he was on the bridge of The Enterprise.

'Right… you two… need your thoughts,' I said, settling next to Michael. 'We've explored the possibilities that she could be on a mission with her killing spree. Now, let's look at it from another angle: say she isn't... Say she knows she can't go near her husband or child again without being caught and decides it's best from them if she walks away. Maybe with a dream that sometime in the future, she'll reconnect. How could she do that without being traced?'

'Well… she's shown how resourceful she is by coolly walking out of a police station,' Josh kicked off.

'What's her digital footprint since, Michael?'

We were glued to his screens as he recovered the evidence to back his findings: 'we lost her on CCTV when she slipped down a side road from the High Street.' He flicked through CCTV screens as he qualified, 'she must have changed somewhere along the way because I haven't picked her up on surrounding streets in that timeline. This is the nearest to the Wagstaff's road. The only cars or pedestrians are all accounted for so she was either in the boot of Mr Wagstaff's car – which went straight into their garage – or she waited until it was dark and snuck in over the gardens.'

'What about bank statements and use of her phone.'

'No activity...' digital copies of both filled the adjacent screens. 'Direct debits as usual but no ATM or credit card activity.'

'Not beyond the realms to have picked up cash or jewellery to sell from the house,' Josh offered. 'And the husband's not going to volunteer such info.'

'No phone transmissions since she was here but not hard to pick up a burner,' Michael added.

'What about border activity?' I asked.

'Not on her current passport and no car hire either.'

I stared at the screens, willing them to reveal something... anything we could use. 'And what does this tell us?'

'She's fucking cute and knows how to stay off the grid,' Michael concluded what we all knew.

'Yeah… but she's not some international spy for Christ's sake,' Josh added. A throbbing vein in his temple, a tell-tale indication of a soon to be lost temper.

'Or…' I began, 'someone's helping her to lie low until she figures out her next move.'

THIRTY THREE
Another Missing Person

We stood outside the Wagstaff's house, fully armed with a warrant, breaking down the back door. Angela joined me as we entered the kitchen, 'neighbours haven't seen him for days and no sightings of any visitors.'

The house looked pristine as though a cleaner had swept through. Josh was finishing up in the lounge as I climbed the stairs. Unnerved, I half-expected to trip over another body or have Paula bolt out of a room and push past me on the stairs. The bedroom doors were shut and Angela and I tried one each.

She disappeared into the room at the back, promptly followed by the scraping of cupboards and drawers opening. I was less inclined to touch anything in the bedroom I entered as it was undeniably a shrine to their dead son. A West Ham duvet, bore the indentations of a reclining body where either parent would have lain to immerse themselves in the memory. The musty smell of a teenage boy still lingered. My body tingled as I transposed reality and imagined the loss of my own son Jude, smothering this morbid thought before it took hold.

I forced myself to take a tentative peek inside the wardrobe although knowing, that she would not sully this sacred ground with any connections to her current path. Muddy football boots, sat beneath a rail of tracksuits and school uniform. A bashed-up rucksack, squashed to one-side. Schoolbooks and discarded pens, lay scattered and abandoned on a desk beneath the window, above which was a wonky timetable, hanging precariously by a blob of blue tac. Photos of Jack with various family members were thick around the room; realistically recent additions as no teenager I knew would allow such 'embarrassing' stuff on show. I closed the bedroom door with care, mindful not to disturb the ghosts.

'Master bedroom up here,' Josh shouted from the floor above, with Angela already in the bathroom.

'Any bodies?' I called out as I reached the top stair.

'No nothing.'

I followed the sound of his voice into a substantial bedroom, the full length of the house; flooded with light bouncing off pristine white walls and not a crinkle in the bed linen or a sock out of place. 'Looks like he's had an industrial clean after the forensics visit. Find anything of interest?'

'It tells us the same as when she disappeared – that they've so much stuff, we can't tell if anything's missing.'

'There's plenty missing from the daughter's bedroom,' Angela said, as she joined us, 'enough for a long trip.'

'Go try his work again. See if he's been in touch,' I told her as my phone screeched for attention, only feeling an eagerness to answer once I saw Susie's name on the screen. I flipped it onto speaker so Josh could listen in. 'Susie...?'

'Boss... She's been seen...'

'When...?'

'As recently as this morning... I've hooked up with my French liaison. He helped me cover local shops and the International School in the town and they've been several sightings. I got him to take the lead in interviewing the sister, Jane Wagstaff. Unmarried... no kids. I sat there playing the dumb cop. I don't want to alert them to the fact that we're over here.'

'So why did she think you were there?'

'He told her that they were informed of the family's troubles and wanted to check they're okay and to let them know that he was there if they needed him.'

She sounded a lot more alert than she should have, considering the amount of sleep deprivation she must have suffered. How I envied the adrenalin of youth. 'Is she staying with them?'

'Not that she's admitting. We asked to check the house

to ensure they were safe. Nothing to show she's there. But I did manage to leave a few of Michael's bugs which I kept to myself.'

'Did you see the daughter?' I asked.

'Yes... she seemed withdrawn. Held onto her aunt's arm all the time. Marcel – that's the French cop – he was good with her but she's bewildered and scared. She kept looking up at the windows as though expecting to see someone pop up. Claims she hasn't heard from her Dad in a couple of days.'

I looked over at Josh as I contemplated out next move. 'Okay Susie... Stay put and use your new cop friends to keep an eye out for her. She's hanging around for a reason so we're going to join you out there.' Josh pulled a face.

'Yes Boss.' She hung up before I did.

Josh continued his face-pulling. 'You think Spatchcock will okay that?'

I was confronted with more face-pulling at home as I packed a bag in our bedroom with Peter standing over me in a rare moment of reproach. 'It's for a couple of days,' I tried to reassure him. 'If nothing happens, I need to ensure that I can set up face to face contacts within the French Police. Get them on my side so they can give me a heads up if something kicks off.'

'Aren't you even aware that it all sounds familiar to what you said before disappearing to The Balkans for six months.'

I moved around to his side of the bed and held his face in my hands. 'There are similarities that I'm not even going to try to defend: yes, another crazed woman who managed to escape and yes... again made her way abroad. But that's where it ends. The difference this time is… me... I've changed Peter.' I held his hand as we sat on the edge of the bed. 'I'm not going to deny that I'd love to catch up with Alexander and ensure she gets her just-desserts but not to the exclusion of what is truly important to me. I know I cocked up Peter and we're only here because of your resilience.'

He went to speak but I put a finger to his lips. 'I won't risk that again. It's my job to assess the situation whether it's here or aboard but no longer my obsession.'

'Can I speak now?' he mumbled beneath my fingers and I let them drop. 'Don't tell me what you think I want to hear. I've no doubt of your good intentions but I know you won't be able to help yourself. Once you're in the thick of it and events start gaining their own momentum – you'll be sucked in.... dragged along. There's no escaping that. All I ask is that you keep yourself safe and sane.'

I don't know where it came from. That's a lie… It had been buried, weighted down with an unmovable stone, deep in the pit of my stomach. But Peter had moved that stone and it couldn't be contained. We spoke about it rarely – which had been my choice. It was too painful to touch on what I had put at risk. Only confronted with the possible outcomes in my dreams – so powerful that it would take me a minute after waking to realise that I was not alone. That Peter was beside me and my children were somewhere, tucked safely in bed.

A sob broke through the lump that had formed in my throat. Another sob and a wave of tears besieged me. Peter put his arm around my shoulders and my face fell into his chest. He held me tight as I released the pain from the failure of The Alexander case. The guilt for the families left behind with no resolution for their lost loved ones. The grief for the family I nearly lost... forgotten in my selfish endeavours. The facade I erected – there to front colleagues and superiors – crumbled.

And as they drained away and my body ceased its spasms, I could find only the most genuine sentiment to explain: 'I'm sorry...' I croaked into his chest.

'I know...' he replied with a gentle squeeze. I lifted my

head and he wiped my face. 'Now there is something I want you to do before you go. Go and speak to Emmie. She thought you were never coming back the last time. Remember the nightmares she had for months afterwards? Go and tell her the details – be honest...'

I washed my face and straightened myself up before heading for Emilia's room. I touched the door to Jude's as I passed, remembering the battles about the mess and the smell, now both conspicuous by their absence, and his. I gave a little tap on her door – an agreed compromise after a heated debated about 'respecting privacy.' I pushed the door open after no response.

She was sitting cross-legged on her bed with her headphones on and schoolbooks, spread out in front of her. She looked up as I found a spot on the bed to park my bum and she flipped off the headphones.

'Err... okay... what've I done?'

'Has it come to this, that a mother can't come in to see her beautiful, intelligent daughter without suspicion?'

'Err... yes...'

I spun myself around and lay lengthwise beside her, 'whatcha up to?'

'Physics revision for a test tomorrow... Wanna help?'

'I think we both know that's yours and Dad's "special thing." I wouldn't like to interfere.'

She rolled her eyes and lay back with me. 'So, what's the speech about?'

'Am I that transparent?'

'Maybe I'm a natural detective...?'

'Don't start that again.'

'I won't...' she said, too confidently, 'but I will wear you down…'

I had no doubt. 'Well as you've unearthed my cunning plan, I do need to tell you that I'm going on a work trip to France tomorrow.' She lay on her back and stared at the ceiling. 'It'll be two days max.' She continued her silence. I gently grabbed her chin and turned her face towards me. 'Two days Emmie. I promise.'

'How do I know that you'll keep your promise this time?'

'Because it's France and you know how much I hate the bloody French.' She cracked a faint smile – barely on the mouth but evident in her eyes. I wrapped my arms around her but she left hers defiantly by her side. 'I lost it the last time. There's no denying that darling. The weight of responsibility for her absconding was too much to bear. But it's a different case and I'm in a better place now so I'll never put us at risk again.' I could hear the fast pace of her young heart, her slight breath against my cheek. I squeezed harder as her arms encircled me and she squeezed back.

THIRTY FOUR
The Crossing

We picked up our hire car from the airport and drove as fast as we dared through the flat French countryside after receiving Susie's latest message. As we arrived at the small village on the outskirts of Lyon, we came to a halt at a no-messing Police cordon.

We parked up and with the aid of our warrant cards and limited French, managed to proceed on foot towards the house, surrounded by emergency vehicles and swarming with accompanying personnel. Susie came running towards us as we approached.

'What the fuck Susie…?' Josh met her head on.

'I know... I know...' She looked defeated as she beckoned over to someone near the house. 'Look... let me get Marcel involved in our conversation as he'll keep his lot off our back. He's already told them that you're coming so can act as our liaison.'

'Good idea...' I replied as I attempted to conceal my surprise as a crumpled, rotund Frenchman, waddled towards us.

'This is Inspecteur Bisset.'

'Marcel please...' he added, in a softer accent than his peasant-like appearance suggested.

'Pleased to meet you Marcel and my thanks for supporting Susie out here.'

He bowed his head in acceptance before continuing earnestly, 'you won't be allowed inside yet. I'm working on getting you some access but my boss thinks your presence will create confusion.'

'I understand,' I said, looking over his shoulder to the house, itching to get inside. 'Now can you both give us some idea of what happened?'

Marcel prompted Susie to take the lead. 'Jane Wagstaff ran out of the house this morning and I followed her to the

International school, Esme has been attending. I waited a while and got Marcel to ring the Head Teacher – again, initially under the guise that their details had been passed on by the British Police and he was checking that all was okay.

'The Head Mistress told him that there had been some confusion this morning when Esme's mum had come to pick her up: she had I.D. and Esme recognised her and she took Esme away. When the Head Mistress called Jane Wagstaff later to see if Esme would like some work sent home, Jane said she knew nothing about it and raced down to the school.'

'We don't have the depth of CCTV coverage you have in the U.K. but I've looked at the school security cameras and captured this...' Marcel showed us a still photo on his phone and a clear shot of a woman walking out of the school gates with a young girl. 'Is this the woman you seek?'

'Yes...' I replied with Josh echoing the same. 'Go on Susie...'

'She leaves and I follow her and Marcel sets about putting out an alert with police forces from here to the airport and ports. Jane spends the next two hours visiting various houses – I presume of friends – and a couple of hotels in the area and we end up at the airport. She goes to ticket desks; she checks flights to London and even searches all the loos. It's as she leaves that I approach her.'

'Why wait so long?' Josh asked.

'I wasn't yet convinced that she wasn't in on it and hoped she'd lead me to her.'

'What did she know?'

'Nothing... She was petrified that Paula had snatched her but also confused. Her brother had told her a couple of days ago that he was coming over but hadn't turned up. She couldn't get hold of him so at one point, thought that maybe he'd met up with Paula first. She seemed terrified at the prospect.'

'The sister-in-law from hell...'

Marcel excused himself and walked back towards the house as Susie continued. 'I left my car there and drove back to the house with her. I asked what she thought their plans were for the future: if he was coming out to stay and was she supposed to join them? She thought that Esme would only be over here while her brother figured out what to do. She believed that he genuinely didn't know where Paula was and she was surprised that he was coming over.'

'Where is she now?'

'They've got her sedated in one of the ambulances over there.'

She pointed beside the house as we noticed Marcel walking back towards us. 'I've convinced my boss to allow you in. He's seen enough so doesn't think you can mess anything up.'

We were led to a van where we changed into forensic suits. I nodded an acknowledgement of appreciation to Marcel's boss who was off to one side smoking, surrounded by his team. He returned his own begrudging nod. Marcel took the lead with the forensic team still in the house, where we were allowed upstairs. The team downstairs, worked in silence and the covers on our feet softened our approach. We should have bounded up but there was a collective hesitation.

Marcel stepped to one side to allow me in first. The room was orderly, no shambolic crime scene for Forensics to scavenge amongst or piece together. I stood at the end of the Provencal-style bed, looking down at the bodies laid side by side. Tom Wagstaff – clean shaven even at the end – was neat and tidy in his travelling clothes of jeans and an England Rugby fleece. His boots appeared hardly worn and it even looked like his hair was brushed. There was not a blemish on any visible flesh or a mark or tear on his clothing. His arms by his side, one hand encircled around the hand of the second body.

I could feel Susie beside me trying to control her

breathing, struggling to contain her body's impulsive reactions to the shock of seeing the second body. Esme Wagstaff lay motionless like a fallen angel. The room, now full with the four of us, was perpetually still. I whispered a little prayer and fought the instinct not to wrap her up tight or stroke her hand as I would with my own two.

It felt obscene that she lay there like a curiosity to all these adults, under the guise of doing their job, when she should have been protected and made safe. All too late...

'Is this how you found them?' I asked Susie.

'Yes...' she replied, after the first attempt stuck in her throat. 'I asked Jane to stay outside while I searched the house on our return. By the time I came up to this room, she was behind me so she saw... this...'

Esme was dressed smartly in her school uniform: a check skirt, brown blazer with the collar of a brilliant white shirt, peeping through. Even her loafers were pristinely polished. Her pallor in the dim light, deceptively tinged with the blush of life as though a gentle shake would awaken her for school.

We were all torturing ourselves.

I turned to Marcel, 'would you mind asking one of the Forensic team to fill us in on what they found?' He left without question. Josh strolled around the room scrutinising the contents, an unashamed alternative to confronting what lay before him.

'How was Jane when you found them?' I asked Susie.

'She went to pieces. I had to physically drag her out of here so she didn't harm herself or contaminate the scene. I checked for signs of life and Marcel arrived, thank God. I found it tough to hold it together...'

'You're not alone Susie...'

Josh walked over and stood between us, holding a photograph in his hand. 'I recognise this from the Wagstaff house. Remember the blown-up version they had in their lounge?'

I took the photo from his hands. The family grouping included their son: a treasured holiday, somewhere on a beach. 'A calling card or a farewell memory…?'

Marcel returned with one of the Forensic team. 'I've already questioned him on what they believe is the cause of death: their reasonable assertion, before a post-mortem, is that they were heavily sedated.' The Forensic officer approached the body of Tom Wagstaff and pushed up his sleeve for Marcel to continue, 'they've made a reasonable assumption before tests, that they were injected with an overdose of a barbiturate.'

'No other injuries?' I asked.

Marcel translated the officer's response of, 'nothing visible.'

'Where do they think she killed them?'

Marcel summarised a lengthy response, 'she must have lured them up into the bedroom either immediately after drugging them, or they drank their drinks in this room. There's no evidence of dragging the bodies up here unless she had an accomplice.'

'Jane...?' Susie questioned in a whisper.

'No... She works alone. This is her crusade,' I replied.

'The post-mortem is tomorrow if you're around?'

'Yes... I can stay one more day. Josh, you return and start checking if she's found a way of getting back into the country. Susie... Are you okay staying another day?'

As though shaking off an enchantment, she stood up straight before confirming, 'yes Boss...' Marcel gave a smile of approval.

After a defensive update over the phone with Spatchcock – left with the implication that I orchestrated these deaths on the continent for the sake of a jolly – I relaxed into the comfort of a FaceTime exchange with Peter and Emilia. They showed no hint of doubt after telling them that I'd be here a second day as I fed Emilia's interest in the process and procedures I needed to go through before returning. Peter steered away from details of Esme's death, hearing the wobble in my voice.

The morning brought a terse meeting with Marcel's boss who was pissed at his superiors having agreed with Scotland Yard that The Met would take the lead in the investigations. Nothing lost in translation on this occasion. He handed it over to Marcel as though it was a punishment but with his back to his boss, he seemed more than pleased.

The post-mortem was well underway when we arrived; perfectly engineered as none of us had the stomach to watch Esme Wagstaff in that state. Seeing father and daughter separated on their cold steel beds, made me want to push them close so they could be reunited once more.

I was introduced to the pathologist – Jean Bertrand; his physical similarity to Monroe, a welcome comfort, only surpassed by an incongruous, jolly countenance. 'I've already been contacted by Doctor Monroe,' he told us enthusiastically. 'He filled me in on his findings: a harrowing case.'

'Yes... and I'm afraid it goes on. Is there anything you can tell me so far Doctor?'

'The bodies were treated with great care. There wasn't a mark on them except for the needle puncture and even that was inserted with precision into the vein.'

'She used to be a midwife.'

'Ah...' He adjusted a sheet he'd already used to cover Esme. 'Our toxicology tests confirm an overdose of barbiturates: again... a precise measurement to do the job. They would have died peacefully which is little consolation when a child is murdered, I'm afraid.'

By this time, none of us could look at Esme's body and if anyone else was feeling the same as me – they would want to get out as quickly as they could.

'They were only dead around an hour before they were found and died in situ.' Sensing our unease, he added, 'the forensic department is down the corridor if you want to follow up on their findings. I will ensure all the reports are forwarded to Doctor Monroe as soon as possible.'

We were seen by the same young, Forensic officer we met at the house. Marcel spoke to him first and made notes so that he could recount and translate all the findings at once. He seemed to ask him a good number of questions as he rattled away. I was hopeful they would equal what was on our minds as Marcel was proving to be in sync with our thought process.

'The team have received DNA and fingerprint details from London for Paula Wagstaff but none of these were picked up in the house.'

'Surely she can't believe that she's not our main suspect?' Susie asked.

'We can only presume that she's creating – what you call – reasonable doubt. Would you agree Chief Inspector?'

'It's a reasonable presumption Marcel.'

'They did however find a small trace of the sedatives in the kitchen sink,' he continued. 'Fibres from a dishcloth matched 3 cups cleared away also with traces of the sedative but it tested as – what you would know as rohypnol, so didn't show up on the toxicology report. The barbiturates and syringe were found on the bedside table.'

He referred to his notes. 'There was no evidence of a struggle anywhere so she must have directed them to the bedroom.'

'Staging a suicide...?' Susie asked. 'She must be completely deluded.'

'It may be her reality,' I said, 'a way of detaching herself from the ultimate heinous crime. To kill what is most precious to her.'

'There was no note,' Marcel added, before calling something over to the Forensic officer who handed over an evidence bag to Marcel. 'The child was holding this is in her hand.' He pulled out a silver medal. I turned it over: on one side, The Virgin Mary with outstretched arms, surrounded by stars; on the reverse, an engraving: *To our darling Esme on your First Holy Communion.*

'Holy Mary...' I whispered to myself.

We reconvened at the local station as Jane Wagstaff had been brought in to be interviewed. An incident room was set up where external officers had arrived to support Marcel and they took us through their efforts to track Paula. Despite the intensity of their work ethic, the French team afforded themselves levity in their banter, but we were too emotionally shattered to engage.

'The camera coverage will mostly be on motorways I'm afraid,' Marcel explained. 'They've tracked a number of cars that left the area in that timeline and eight ended up at stations, ports and an airport.'

'Six were discounted,' a young officer called Francois jumped in, 'once we identified the driver and passenger. But this one I think is of interest...' We homed in on his multi-screen. 'We can't fully identify her face from any of these angles but I think she changed cars in Dijon.'

We scrutinised the grainy recordings. At every opportunity the woman in the shots kept her head down. 'I agree that it could be the same woman but are there any other clearer shots to confirm it's Paula Wagstaff?'

'None... and I've been through them all.'

'Where did she end up?' I asked.

He pulled up another recording on the screen. 'I lost her at this service station outside Calais.'

'Hitch-hiked Boss?' Susie suggested.

'I thought that...' Francois replied. 'We're now trying to see if any of the vehicles have passengers they didn't have before the stop.'

'Thank you, Francois. Could you send it on to the contact I gave you in London?'

I left the room with Marcel, leaving Susie to assist

Francois.

'That's brilliant work...' I told him, 'but it's all too slow for what we need.'

'I know... But once I report that we believe she's left the country, this resource will be gone and there will merely be me as liaison so we need to get as much out of them as we can.'

We moved on to the interview room where Jane Wagstaff was waiting for us. I was not sure if she was still sedated as she looked a tad comatose. 'Thank you for waiting.' She raised her head. 'Jane... what do you think happened?'

She looked at me but at the same time, through me. The resemblance to her brother was strong, but more unsettling, was that to her dead niece. With her cosy, country clothes and velvet, Home Counties accent, she would at least have provided Esme with some parental comfort in the absence of her own. Her unconditional dedication to the child was unquestionable. 'She did this didn't she?' the tremor in the voice, mirroring that in her hands.

'I think so... but it was set up to seem like a suicide. What can you tell me about your brother's mental state? Would he do this?'

She shook her head as though exorcising a demon, 'never... never... He adored his children.'

'The last time you spoke to him – what did he say?'

She smiled a broken smile and her eyes filled. 'He was trying to hold it together but I could tell. It tore his heart out being away from Esme – sending her here. She was suffering too...' The tears coated her face but whether from remarkable self-control or a grief-ridden emptiness, her body remained motionless.

'What did he tell you of Paula?'

She seemed to wince at the name but recovered and continued. 'She used to be okay... a bit obsessive over the children. Tom adored her. I think she loved him but there was always a part of her that was shut off... detached... which got even worse as the years went on.'

'Did he believe she'd committed the murders?'

'No... Not that he said. No... He didn't have to say it... he wouldn't believe she was capable. He said that the proof was all circumstantial. There was no physical evidence so they'd be able to prove her innocence. That was the reason he explained for her disappearance. She was supposed to return when the Police found the real murderer.'

'Why did he say he was coming over?'

She picked rhythmically at her cuff. 'He said to see Esme. He said he had good news...'

'She lured him here?'

'Probably...' She gazed out of the window as though searching for answers.

'Did she ever contact Esme?'

'Not that I was aware of. But... I don't know... Esme was jumpy at times. Looking around her expectantly... Sometimes she came out of school elated as though she didn't have a care in the world. Making me think that somehow she'd managed to get hold of her.'

Marcel opened the file he brought in and placed in front of her, a series of the photos Francois had printed off. 'Do you recognise any of these as Paula?'

She wiped her face and picked up each one in turn, holding them close. 'I don't know... They match her general description but the face is too blurry.'

He pushed forward the First Communion medal. 'Do you recognise this?'

She held it up on the side of The Virgin Mary and turned it tenderly in her hands. At the sight of the inscription, her hand flew to cover her mouth to contain her first audible sob.

I reached across to grab her free hand. 'It's okay... It's alright... I know it's hard.'

She nodded her head before lowering her hand, 'yes... I

recognise it. Esme wore it around her neck with a ribbon.'

'Jane... Do you think Paula committed these murders?'

She did not answer immediately. I could only imagine the weight of having to speak aloud something so alien. 'I do...' she admitted. 'From what I've observed over the years, she liked to control every situation... every detail of their lives, especially since Jack died. I think this was her way of controlling their end.'

'But why not join them? Why not take her own life?'

She stared down at the photographs as she answered, 'because I don't think she's finished.'

THIRTY FIVE
Home

Despite the exhaustion and tucked up securely in my own bed, I couldn't fall asleep that night. Peter and I had some time on our own after Emilia disappeared to her room. Unquestionably relieved that I had not been sucked into another crusade away from home, he held no punches voicing his concerns about the toll a similarly, 'out of control' case was having on me. I was not as defensive as I thought I would be. Keeping up with her, without a risk to more lives, seemed insurmountable.

The team were eerily silent as I walked through the office that morning. Josh was not far behind me as I slumped into my chair.

'You alright Boss...?' He asked.

'I've been better. What's with the sponsored silence out there?'

'They're all a bit shell-shocked. Didn't see it coming.... And the murder of a child... you know... They feel even more responsible.'

'Well, I need their heads back in the game and *now* Josh. Her family are gone so she has nothing to lose and now she's on the move and I have no idea where or why.'

'Michael might have some news on the where if you'd like to join us?' he offered.

'Sure...' I replied as my desk phone began to ring. 'Go on,' I said. 'I'll join you in a min.' He left the office as I picked up the phone to hear my summons to Spatchcock's office.

A reassuringly hostile tone was constant from Spatchcock, 'so, you have a body count of five and one near miss?'

It was unremarkable that this had become *my* body

count. I didn't have the energy. I stared back.

'Nothing to say?'

'Sorry Sir... was that a question?'

'I don't think you're in a position to be sarcastic Josephine.'

I needed to retreat before I said aloud what he already knew I thought of him. I turned around as someone else entered the room. A striking middle-aged man, silver haired and built like an ex-rugby player. The type of ageing you could only hope for in your own husband. Shit… 'Commander Lewis...'

'Josephine... please sit...' He pulled up a chair beside me. 'So how far have you got James? I don't want to stop your flow.'

Spatchcock could not hide his intimidation and had already transformed with practiced slickness. 'Actually... well timed Commander, Josephine was about to update me on the events in France.'

I wasn't so sure how transparent this was to Lewis. He had a reputation for not suffering fools and Spatchcock was the biggest one I knew. Spatchcock manifestly knew Lewis was coming and wanted to disarm me for his own warped agenda.

'Yes... The Assistant Commissioner had quite a job on her hands persuading the French to let you take the lead on this. Hopefully you reaped the benefits?'

'Yes Sir. We were lucky enough to have a supportive French officer on our side.'

It was not difficult to have more respect for him than Spatchcock and it was evident that Spatchcock envied him his effortless manner with the troops. He smiled what I wanted to believe was a smile of encouragement, 'please... proceed Josephine.'

'It was as my report stated Sir. I concluded from the set of circumstances and evidence presented that she arranged to meet her husband under the pretence that something positive was going to happen. His sister stated that he had, "good news." I would surmise that maybe she told him she had evidence to prove her innocence. Implying that they could be together again as a family. But there's also the possibility that he confronted her about the tapes and sealed his own fate.'

'Do we know how long she'd been over there?' he asked.

'I would think since her daughter moved there. His sister believes she may have been in contact with the daughter and we know her children were her life.'

He nodded his head rhythmically before asking, 'you report that she set this one up to seem like a suicide so her M.O. is adapting with each murder?'

'I think she is evolving as circumstances change which is why she's so hard to predict.'

He folded his arms and tapped his finger against his lips before asking, 'do we know if she's back in the country?'

'One of my officers was about to show me an update before I was called up here.'

'What do you think she'll do next?'

Spatchcock scrapped his chair in an attempt to remind us that he was there which was uniformly ignored.

'I don't think she would've killed her family without believing she'll join them soon,' I went on. 'Whatever her plan is, I believe it will be her grand finale.'

'Then we are on the home stretch Josephine would you say?' I nodded but felt he was building up to something. Spatchcock looked across at him with muted bewilderment. 'I therefore need you focused without any distractions, one of which is the conclusion of your disciplinary.' Spatchcock squirmed in his chair as Lewis continued. 'So, I can confirm that no further action will be taken and the details we'll leave for the final report.' And without taking a breath or acknowledgement that my future had spun on a sixpence, he continued: 'and for this final push, we'll give you all the resources you need.' He turned to Spatchcock. 'The Chief Superintendent has suggested that D.I. Golding could offer you support. Is that someone you need?'

I joined Lewis in his focus on Spatchcock. 'That's generous but we have plenty of management on this case – what we need are more boots on the ground.'

'Good... that's settled,' he said, leaving Spatchcock no room to manoeuvre. 'I'll be making a statement this afternoon. We've agreed with the French, a news blackout on the details on these murders but will have her face out there as a person of interest in case she's spotted. Anything else we haven't covered Josephine?'

'Not that I can think of at the moment Sir.'

'Then go get her.'

I was back doing something worthwhile as Michael showed Josh and me the footage picked up of a suspected Paula Wagstaff. 'This is the truck the French think she hitch-hiked on at Calais and here it is… on the A2… you can make out a passenger… a woman. Here it is... coming out of Canterbury… no passenger. Running a track on cars and lorries that completed a journey from Canterbury to London… I think this could be her... ending up in Hendon or this... in Wood Green.'

I stared at the blurred features, only sharpening in my mind's eye. 'It could be but...'

'I know,' Michael grunted, 'not clear enough.'

'Yes... but I do think it's highly likely, so keep searching. Anything from the bugs Susie placed in the house?' I asked hopefully.

'No... The main action was in the kitchen and Jane Wagstaff's bedroom, neither of which Susie managed to bug.'

'Figures...'

Josh was at my shoulder as I entered my office and took a seat before asking the question he held in for the past hour, 'how did it go?'

'Mixed,' I replied. 'The good news is that we're getting extra resources, the bad news is that the expectation is to close the case A.S.A.P.'

'Wow... Didn't expect Spatchcock to be so generous.'

'He wasn't. It was the in the gift of Commander Lewis.'

'And Spatchcock supported you?' he said as though he'd misheard.

'He did his usual and played both sides.'

He snorted a sarcastic laugh before unburdening, 'well he's blatantly trying to play me. He's had me in a few times.'

'I know...'

He looked like he was going to ask how, before slumping back in his chair. 'Then you'd have guessed he's been working me to be his little protégé and take my Inspector's exam early to slot me here, "if the need arises."'

'Well, it might...'

'No... No... No...' he shook his head like a defiant teenager, 'I'm not playing his game. I told him – in Spatchcock appropriate language – that I didn't believe the need would arise but thanked him for his confidence.'

'"Spatchcock appropriate..." I love it. You'll go far.' He looked unsure. 'Look... Don't worry. Do what you think is right. Don't feel you need to get in the middle of me and my nemesis. He knows as well as I do that I have too much dirt on him to go quietly. He's hoping I'll crack under the pressure and fade away. Which... for your information... I won't.'

I gave him the reassuring smile he needed before he sighed, a very loaded: 'Where to next? Who is there left for her to kill?'

'I don't think we need CCTV images to confirm what we know – that she's heading back to London. We can start by making sure Amy Whitehead is safe.'

'I'll keep Stella Winchester covered too in case she's considered another loose end,' he said, with an awareness that the list could get longer.

'Good idea... but I think we've got to accept the reality that if we can't track her down, we'll have to play a waiting game.'

Our attention was drawn to a commotion in the office before Angela came running in; her outer calmness failing to mask her contained panic.

'Paula Wagstaff's turned up at the front desk.'

THIRTY SIX
Accusations

A note to call Peter was shoved into my hand as I sprinted out of the office. I tucked it into my pocket before taking the stairs two at a time. Still not a long enough stride for Josh, who I could feel at my heels, only slowing our pace once we were told she was secured in an interview room with two of our burliest armed officers at the door.

We allowed ourselves a breather to regroup before launching in as we stood in mutual silence staring through the glass at Paula Wagstaff. She looked more drawn since the last time she sat there: no make-up and her clothes – clean but more like supermarket basics than her labelled classics. Everything about her appearance, I knew, would have been constructed for effect.

Her solicitor fixed at her side. I needed to let the anger subside. Part of me didn't want it to. I longed to burst into the room, smash her face down on the table until she confessed. Instead, I had to join in the dance.

'What's she said?' I asked.

I could feel Josh's controlled fury, threatening to erupt. 'Nothing... except that she'll only talk to you...'

Susie stood in the corner of the room behind Wagstaff. Her threatening stance, belying her size. Josh had followed my eye-line. 'Susie's in Rottweiler mode and won't be letting her out of her sight.'

'Sarge...' Josh turned towards the voice at the door. 'Mr Jericho's here.'

He looked at me and I nodded, 'bring him in.'

A nervous Mr Jericho shuffled through the door. I held out my hand and guided him to the window. He pulled back. 'It's okay... she can't see you. Come...' I stepped back to the spot he felt was as far as he dared. 'Take your time and have a good look at the woman sitting at the table.'

He raised his head and looked ahead. His breath

quickened and he swallowed a sob. 'Do you recognise this woman?' His hand was covering his mouth and he nodded. 'Would you mind saying it Mr Jericho? It's important there's no misunderstanding.'

Lowering a trembling hand, he managed, 'yes... it's the woman who attacked Father Michael.'

Josh and I were left alone once more and assumed our positions. As before, she had an awareness of being watched and held a pose. 'What's her game?' I said, more to myself.

'Maybe the killing spree's finished,' Josh offered.

'No...' I said, 'she cleared up after Father Michael and her family. She'll know little of the detail of what we witnessed in France. I think... she believes she can get away with it all. Look at her. Does she look like anyone we've had in here who's confessed or been caught?'

'I've lost the plot on this one,' he sounded bemused.

'She's come here because she's got something to say. Let's see what it is.' I decided not to attempt to compose myself before going in, an element of raw anger was what I needed to untangle her web.

The solicitor shuffled uncomfortably as we took our seats. I nodded to Susie an acknowledgement to leave the room, knowing she wouldn't be far. Wagstaff seemed unnecessarily relaxed and did not avert maintaining eye contact with me. We listened to the solicitor's diatribe.

'My client has returned here today of her own volition. During her last visit she felt unduly stressed at the unjustified accusations put to her and in a temporary moment of madness, left the premises.'

'Temporary insanity... is that what you're going for...? Are we also referring to the calm manner you dressed up as a police officer to abscond from this station or are you claiming temporary insanity for the murders you've committed?'

'I would also like to point out,' the solicitor jumped in,

'that my client has suffered a devastating personal tragedy with the loss of her family which was her motivation for coming here today in their memory.'

I studied her face for a hint of that devastation. 'You seem remarkably together considering your family has been murdered. Didn't you think to go and see them?'

'Murder...?' She turned to her solicitor. 'I was told it was suicide.' He played his part with a responding look of indignation.

'Why would they commit suicide Paula?'

'It's understandable. The intolerable pressure they were under by the false allegations aimed at me.'

'But Esme wouldn't have taken her own life, would she? This suicide pact would have involved your husband murdering his precious child. Did you turn your husband into a murderer Paula?'

She crafted her harangued posture and with it the atmosphere in the room, prompting the solicitor to gallantly step in. 'My client has come here voluntarily.'

She averted my gaze but not I felt as an act of avoidance but more to perpetuate her victimhood. 'Why are you here?' I asked.

'This incessant persecution has meant that I've lost everything. The only thing I've left is my name and to fight these lies you're spreading and prove my innocence. I did not commit these murders and there will therefore be no evidence to support these accusations.' She made little attempt to keep the smugness from her voice.

I scrutinised every nuance of her reaction that would expose the murderer within. 'We have DNA evidence that Catherine Scott was the biological mother of Jack Wagstaff.'

Not a moment's hesitation before her response: 'this is not true. I am Jack's mother.' Her comeback was strong and unwavering.

'There's no evidence in any hospital of you having given birth.'

She sat up straight and began to recite: 'I previously suffered a traumatic miscarriage so I had an unassisted home-delivery. At the time I didn't trust the birth to anyone but myself and although in hindsight, there was an element of risk, as I was a midwife, the risk was minimised. Jack's birth was registered at Walthamstow registration office – you can check…' A well-rehearsed account which would have lain dormant all these years for this very challenge.

'The timings of your departure from your job and your registration of a full-term baby with no physical evidence of a pregnancy – align with the supposition that you abducted Daniel Scott. It was all about your son, wasn't it? The unbearable burden of grief and guilt that maybe you could have prevented his death, eating away at you. Having to face Fiona Anderson each week, going on and on and on about her useless son – a son that she didn't deserve.'

'We've listened to this fabrication already...'

But I wasn't paying attention to the solicitor, 'was it a coincidence that you came across Jack's mother once more, or did you seek her out?'

'I am Jack's mother...' she repeated, now looking beyond me.

'Maybe she sought you out? Did she discover that you were the one who stole her baby and deprived her of all those precious years? Was there a confrontation that got out of hand?'

'I am Jack's mother...'

'At least he got to spend his last moment with his real mother. That must have been a comfort to them both.'

'So far this all sounds circumstantial.' The solicitor jumped in, sensing his client might snap.

'The evidence says otherwise but let's move on to Darren Anderson.' She looked at her solicitor but I pressed on.

'What did he ever do to you that you'd want to stitch him up for his wife's murder? Easy I suppose, considering what you'd already done to Fiona. A little soil sample in the foot-well of his car was enough to tip the balance of suspicion. What were your plans after depriving his children of both parents? Were you going to adopt them? Were you already planning to set up Marc Whitehead for Amy's murder?'

'I have no idea what you're talking about,' she didn't flinch in her delivery.

I maintained eye contact, 'You haven't asked about Amy yet? Don't you want to know if we found her?'

'Of course I do. I consider her a friend and only wish her well,' she said, with an unbelievably straight face. Did she know what was coming?

'We found Amy and your – not so little – hide-away. Do you want to tell your solicitor how much evidence we'll find in there Paula? How much of your other life you have stashed in the bunker in the woods?'

She held her default expression, masking any genuine reaction which should at least have been incredulity.

The solicitor hid his panic as best he could. 'I'd like to spend some time alone with my client.'

'Of course... *After* this interview because I'm sure your client will want to tell you about Amy. She's alive, Paula. Alive... so she'll be able to identify you and has already recalled your stories. Don't worry – you left her in an awful state. Was that the purpose this time?'

'My client will not be answering any more questions.'

'But she doesn't know what I'm going to ask yet, do you Paula? Like... have you moved on from straight forward murder to torture? Was that what you were going to do with Amy – starve her to death? Or let her endure a slow painful death from the injuries you inflicted? What would best suit this unworthy mother?'

She sat there and held my gaze, occasionally inhaling deeply as though she had forgotten to breathe.

I pressed on, 'quite an interesting hide-away and lock-up. What do you think our forensic teams found there Paula? We have a possible contender for the contents of Catherine Scott's flat. Coincidentally, Amy had already sent us pictures of everything in the flat so that's been easy enough to match up. What about your cosy little beanbag corner? What amount of DNA evidence did that yield?'

'As I said... I did not commit these acts so there will be no physical evidence.' The solicitor tried to interject as she repeated this, but she silenced him once more.

'You're a catholic aren't you, Paula?' I began on my new tact. 'A practising catholic...'

'Yes I am...' cautious in her response.

'I'm an on-off one myself. It's hard sometimes to keep to the values when you see so much evil in others – don't you think? How do you keep your catholic values Paula?'

Something switched. Something too inherent to turn off: the justification of the righteous. 'I do the best I can by being a good mother and helping others.'

'Helping others – that's nice... I hear you support The Meningitis Society, enter marathons and organise lots of cake sales. Is that what you discussed with Father Michael?'

'I don't know a Father Michael. My parish priest is Father Antony,' she responded bluntly.

'Well Father Michael knew you. Didn't he hear your confession?'

'No... And if you're a catholic you'll know that a priest cannot break the seal of confession.' A sneer on her face accompanied that in her tone.

'But he didn't. Father Michael and I had a code – very clever when you think about it,' I revealed. 'But he was so disturbed by what you told him that it was enough to bring him to my door. You picked the wrong priest there Paula.'

'Where is this leading to?' The solicitor's impatience contrasted with Paula Wagstaff's fixed edifice.

'Do you want to tell him Paula? No…? Well, let me enlighten you. This cake-baking, charity-raising, good catholic mother, lost her temper with a priest and smashed his skull in with a kettle.'

'She's already told you that she doesn't know this priest,' he protested unconvincingly.

'Why go to confession Paula?' I asked. 'Did you think God was on your side? Or was it to taunt him? To get him back for taking your son?'

'I pray to Our Lady...'

The solicitor looked across nervously, unsure of where she was going.

'I know... Father Michael told me as much. I'm sure you noticed Paula that I refer to Father Michael in the past tense because your blow did prove fatal. Now… I don't know what you were thinking when you cleared up after your nice cup of tea. Did you think he would live but unable to repeat anything you told him under an enforced seal of confession?' The table vibrated as her leg twitched beneath. 'Do you know why we have enough to charge you with Father Michael's murder Paula? You see my Sergeant here was a bit naughty. Unbeknownst to me and my catholic inhibitions – he bugged the confessional.'

'That will be inadmissible,' The solicitor sounded unsure.

'Well, the CPS, think not.... And do you know what else we have Paula? For all your attempts to clean the scene – we have a witness. Yes... someone was in the hall and saw everything that happened and has already identified you.'

The solicitor was about to offer another objection but she touched his arm and he refrained.

'Do you think Catherine Scott prayed for her loss when you stole her son?' Josh began and pulled out a photo of a baby. 'Do you think you prayed harder than Catherine when he died?'

Her body stiffened as she fought the physical signs of her rising grief. She swallowed hard but could not prevent the onslaught of tears welling up in her eyes which she wiped with a flick of a hand only to be outwitted by the next wave.

Grappling for those trigger points, I pushed, 'he was a beautiful baby... such a waste...'

She picked up the photograph and consciously steadied a spontaneous tremble in her hand as she held it closer to her face, 'beautiful...' she whispered.

'Is that definitely a picture of your son as a baby? There are so many.'

'Yes... it's Jack. A mother always knows her own.' She looked up at me as she possessively held onto the prized image. 'Where did you find it?'

I snatched the photograph from her hand, 'this is from the files for Catherine Scott's missing baby boy, Daniel Scott. The baby you stole.'

A flash of panic crossed her face as though we were snatching her baby from her breast, before correcting herself and eradicating any signs of vulnerability with a return of her steely facade. 'I am Jack's mother,' she repeated robotically.

Josh placed another photo on the table in front of her. 'You must have an iron stomach to put an end to a child's life. Was she worth so much less than Jack?'

'That's enough,' the solicitor cut in.

She turned her head purposefully to look at Josh. The tightening of her jaw, the only sign of a contained outburst. 'I've just lost my family – do you realise how sick your statement is?'

Josh held the photo up to her eye-line. 'Look at what you did. Look at how she lies beside her daddy, like an angel. Fathers are supposed to protect their daughters, aren't they? But he couldn't protect her from you.'

She looked away as the solicitor began another rant, 'this is ridiculous. You have no proof that she was even in France.'

'But we have...' I confirmed. That caught her attention.

'We had an officer there all the time and worked closely with the French Police. We have all the evidence we need to connect you to these murders as well as the other four.'

'Four...?' She asked, 'I thought Amy survived.'

'You're keeping count.'

'I did not commit these murders so I am confident that your evidence is thin at best.'

'Yes Paula... I'll give you that... you are extremely confident. I'll ask you one more time: why have you come here today?'

She made a performance out of drinking some water from the plastic beaker in front of her before placing it with precision on the table. 'So, Detective Chief Inspector...' she began. 'How's that lovely daughter of yours? Emilia, isn't it? I hear she has a severe nut allergy. Tricky...'

THIRTY SEVEN

Please God… No…

The next time I had any sense of my surroundings, I was stretched across the table with my hand around her throat and Josh was trying to pull me away. His words were ringing in my ears, 'no Boss... no...!'

'You fucking bitch!' I screamed: a voice alien to my ears. 'If you've laid a finger on her... I'll kill you myself.'

I had a vague awareness of being dragged out of the room by Josh and as terror gripped hold, I caught the odd word until reality came back into focus. We were outside the room. Josh had a firm grip on both my shoulders as he tried to steady me. I watched his lips moving until my brain connected enough to make out full sentences. 'Call Peter...' he kept on repeating. 'Call Peter...'

I ran to my office where my phone was charging. The note, that Peter had called – a dead weight in my pocket. My hands shook as I clicked on his name.

He picked up instantly. 'Thank God... I've been trying to get hold of you.'

My voice cracked as I asked, 'is she missing Pete?'

'Emilia...? Yes... I don't know. What's going on Josie? You sound weird.'

'Where is she?'

'I don't know – that's why I'm calling. The school called to say that she didn't return after lunch and wanted to check that she didn't have an appointment. Josie... What's happened?' He screamed my name once more as I scrambled to find the words.

'I think... I think Paula Wagstaff took her...'

'Jesus...'

I could hear his laboured breathing and his hopelessness. His mind would have been, as mine, actively running through the outcomes. Our different professions had a shared commonality of being exposed to the horrors, seemingly ordinary people commit. His desperation at not being able to protect his daughter would be tearing at his heart.

As the shock wore off, I sobered up. 'Pete... Pete...'

'Yes, I'm here...' His voice, broken.

'Do you trust me...?'

'Of course. For Christ's sake Josie...'

'Listen to me… Paula Wagstaff walked in today, supposedly to profess her innocence but we have enough evidence to convict her so I knew there would be one last closing act. When she started asking about Emilia – I knew what it would be. We're going to send out everyone we can looking for Emilia but to have a real chance, I'm going to have to play whatever sick game she has planned.'

'God... Oh God Josie... I can't...' He couldn't contain his howl and my heart broke again.

'I know... I know... Look... I may not be contactable but someone will keep you updated as much as possible.' Saying goodbye was hard, knowing what we might have to face the next time we spoke.

The office was now cleared when I walked through, except for Michael. I made my way into the Ladies and into a cubicle. With my head over the bowl, I retched up my heart and slumped to the floor with my hand over my mouth, stifling my sobs. I thought of Father Michael and prayed to... I didn't care... anyone up there who would listen and keep my girl alive.

After splashing my face in the sink, I made my way to find Josh. He was standing in the ante room, observing Wagstaff. 'You alright...?' I nodded unconvincingly. 'Angela overheard your conversation and has organised the first wave of troops. Michael is accessing all the CCTV from the school and its surrounds.'

'Does Spatchcock know?'

'No... He's away on that course. I think he'd take you off the case. Commander Lewis is around though.'

Not sure if that was good news. We continued staring into the room. She was waiting... waiting for our next move. I could not afford to be taken off this case or stand by. Trusting anyone else to find my child, was not an option but I badly wanted to go in there and tear her throat out.

'What's the strategy?' Josh asked, attempting to keep me in the here and now.

'Go in there first and charge her with the other murders and attempted murder. Go through all the evidence so both her and that solicitor are clear on the outcome. I'll check with Michael on what he's found and I'll come in.'

Michael had four screens on the go. I pulled a chair up beside him. He wasted no time: 'this is over the road from the school gates…'

Emilia appeared on the screen coming out of the school gate. I reached out to touch the screen and as my hand dropped, we watched her being approached by a female uniformed officer. Michael pulled out two photos: 'this is Wagstaff dressed as an officer when she absconded from here and this is the officer leading Emilia away. I would suggest it is the same person.'

'It would make sense,' I admitted. 'Emilia is far from naive but would've been more susceptible to believing something from a police officer.' My mind was racing. To do best by my Emmie, I needed to pull back and focus. 'Have you picked up where they went?'

'She turns down the road beside the school that leads to the golf course. We lose her here.'

I stared at the frozen image on the screen. 'Did she have help?' I asked, forcing myself into my process.

'From who...?'

'What about that truck driver who brought her back into the country... anything on him...?'

'Some...' Michael sounded hopeful.

'Track him down,' I instructed. 'See where he ended up and if they're still in contact.'

Michael answered his phone as I stared between the screen and the photographs. 'Yes... she's here...' he looked over to me. 'Okay... will do...' He replaced the receiver with an encouraging look that I was not going to shoot the messenger. 'Commander Lewis would like to see you now in Spatchcock's office. Look I'll get this information out to Susie – she's down by the school.'

I did not know what to expect from Lewis. Josh was right – Spatchcock had been looking for a reason to take me off the case and supplant me with his man, Golding. Maybe Spatchcock had been able to persuade him? I entered the office and sat down as instructed.

'How are you, Josephine?'

'I've been better Sir.' I sounded more defensive than I intended. It must have been the effect of Spatchcock's office and his piggy eyes, boring holes into me from the numerous vanity photographs dotted around the room. 'Sorry Sir... it's just...'

'There's no need to apologise. I'm not sure I'd even have the strength to still be here if I was in your shoes – but here you are...'

'Yes Sir...' If he would get on with it, I could make my plans. If I was to be kicked off, I would have to work unofficially through Josh. I knew he wouldn't have a problem with it and in fact I knew that Angela and Susie would be the same although I would rather not put them in that position.

'I've seen the interview tape: the attack on Wagstaff.' I did not respond. I could not, without landing myself in deeper. 'Your position as SIO on the case is compromised.' His tone was even, devoid of the sarcastic edge present in all Spatchcock's exchanges. Maybe he was being genuine?

'Yes, Sir I know...'

'Then we need to find a workable solution that doesn't involve also compromising the case with displays such as in that interview.' Keeping it zipped was still my best advice to myself. 'I suggest that you shadow the investigation but you have no further direct contact with Paula Wagstaff. D.S. Josh Hughes seems perfectly competent at conducting the face to face. You can give audio instructions in interviews if you feel the need.' He searched for a response. 'Can you work within these confines Josephine?'

I nodded as I digested the practicalities.

'I'm offering this compromise which could fall foul of a conflict of interest because as a parent, I believe you would otherwise go rogue on me Josephine and I would rather use your skills within the case than against. You are an intelligent officer so you know what actions could jeopardise the case – I am trusting you to steer clear. But if I see any further evidence of you losing it – I'll not hesitate to pull you off. I will deal with the aftermath of this decision so I just want you to focus on finding your daughter.'

'Thank you, Sir...' I replied feebly, knowing what he offered, broke every rule.

'I have seconded Chief Superintendent Spatchcock to the training division for an unspecified time so for the remainder of this case, I'd like you to report directly to me.'

I struggled to thank him this time as I could feel the prickling of tears behind my eyes and I was worried that whatever I had to say would end up as a sob. He seemed to sense as much and continued. 'I have briefed Sergeant Hughes and I must say you have a very loyal team behind you so you should feel assured that we will do our best for you daughter.'

Steadying my shaking hands as I left his office, I felt simultaneously overwhelmed by his support and paralysed by the decisions I would have to make to save Emilia's life.

Josh and I resumed our positions staring through the mirror as Angela left after her latest update before he ventured: 'did The Commander speak to you?'

'Yes, he did...'

'I'm not sure how much he's gone rogue. I've heard he's a bit of a rep from his time in Northern Ireland so he gets to push the boundaries more than most.' He fixed me with an earnest gaze. 'You know you shouldn't remain on the case Boss but I'll back you whatever you decide to do.'

'I know… thanks… I'm not going to lie, it's going to be hard watching from a far, when I want to physically drag everything out of her myself but – you're the next best thing. How did you get on in there?'

He seemed to relax slightly. 'She refused to react to any of the charges or evidence put before her, although I think the solicitor was hearing some of this stuff for the first time. She remains determined in her innocence. I don't know if she's deluded enough to think she'll somehow get off, if she trades info about Emilia.'

Ever conscious of being watched, she held the conceit of one with the power of secrets within a faint smile, while the solicitor drummed his fingers on the table.

'Look it might work to our advantage if she's put off her stride by dealing with me, rather than being allowed to play her games with you,' he said as he fixed in an earpiece. 'She might slip up.'

'Or feel free to trip her up.'

THIRTY EIGHT
At a distance

Her eyes followed Josh into the room with an expectant look over his shoulder. He placed copies in front of her of the photos that Michael had shown me.

'This was you when you absconded from the station. And this is you abducting Emilia today at 12.30 pm from St Stephen's School in Wanstead.'

She held his gaze before asking, 'Is Detective Chief Inspector Connelly not joining us today?'

'Do you have an issue with my D.C.I. Paula? Is that why you've abducted her daughter? This is you, isn't it?' he asked, tapping his finger on the photo.

She let her eyes drop momentarily before returning his attention. The solicitor picked up the photos for a closer look. His lack of objection spoke volumes.

'Where did you take Emilia?' He remained calm and controlled.

'Do you have children Sergeant Hughes?' She asked as she began her attempted manipulation.

'Don't tell her any personal details...' I dropped into his ear. 'But push her on her moral shift towards hurting children.'

'See that's the point...' he swerved expertly. 'I was surprised that you took that step: the step towards being known as a child-killer. You'll join that illustrious group, alongside paedos and sex abusers because that's all you'll be remembered for. In fact – over time – the stories will all become muddled. That tends to happen when kids are involved. Paula Wagstaff ... Serial Killer – will be remembered as Paula Wagstaff... Child Killer...' He ran his fingers through the air as though spelling out a newspaper headline. 'Which is a step away from Paula Wagstaff... sexual deviant... and before you know it – Jack and Esme's name will become entangled with yours and with a hop, skip and a jump, they'll be known as the abused kids of Paula Wagstaff.'

She took a deep breath before responding, 'my children are safe.'

'You mean dead...'

'Safe from harm... You can't touch them and you can't threaten me because I've nothing left.'

'But why a child Paula? Why take Emilia? To punish D.C.I. Connelly? Why...? She was only doing her job. If it wasn't her, it would've been someone else.'

'She should have understood as a mother.'

And there it was… to her… I was another unworthy mother.

'But she did...' he continued. 'She empathised with your rage at the death of your son. She understood what blinding grief could do but that didn't mean she'd condone it.'

She looked away to the side. A flicker of doubt perhaps crossing the mask of certainty.

'Find out if Emilia is alive,' I struggled to say before my throat constricted at the thought of the alternative.

'She must have liked you,' he pressed on. 'Emilia...' he added for her questioning frown. 'She wouldn't easily go with anyone. She's a spiky kid. Cheeky but clever, don't you think?'

'She doesn't look like her mother.'

I held my hand to my mouth to stifle a cry. How dare she talk about my child in such an intimate way?

'You noticed?' He replied. 'Split of her dad. You should see them together: peas in a pod.' She seemed to relax for a second into the normality of the conversation, so he slipped in, 'is Emilia alive?' She took her time. He held his nerve.

'She's safe enough...'

I felt sick with relief. Was it enough to tell Pete? No... not yet... false hope... It could still go so horribly wrong. I could see Josh's own hesitation on what to ask next. Where to take her to get the best possible information?

'She must be scared...' he paused for a response. 'I'm sure Esme would be...'

'Esme is safe.'

'But locking a child away... alone... in the woods. That's cruel Paula. Whatever your beef is with her mother, does a child deserve that?' She stared him down, signalling that she would not be baited.

Angela slipped into the room with me and spoke in hushed tones as though Wagstaff could hear through the solid walls. 'Michael's I.D.'d the lorry driver. He's a Romanian national and has a record.' She passed me a print-out with his details and photo. 'Petre Lupa, but he used an alias – Andrei Radu – to get through Border checks. He's already done two years in his country for people-trafficking.'

Fresh alarm rose through my twisted guts. 'Contact The Modern Slavery Unit – see what they know and have them on stand-by. And tell Michael he needs to locate him.'

I returned my attention to the interview room where the stand-off continued. 'Josh... Find out about the driver. We've identified him as a Romanian, Petre Lupa, entering this country as Andrei Radu. He's already done time for people-trafficking.'

An imperceptible nod of his head and a quick jot on his notebook, confirmed his acknowledgement. 'Maybe you had help this time?' he began. 'What about your new mate, the Romanian truck driver?'

Nothing... Josh stretched the silence, knowing that alongside him, I would be searching for a glimmer of reaction in her face but it proved too much for the solicitor.

'What's this about?'

'I've no idea...' she finally spoke.

'Maybe he never introduced himself? Andrei Radu… lorry driver or maybe Petre Lupa… people trafficker... Ring a bell?'

'Where's this going?' The solicitor asked.

She looked up at Josh.

'Didn't he tell you on your cosy little journey back from Calais?' Josh pressed on. 'Was he more than helpful in your plan to hide Emilia? Enthusiastic even...? No wonder. He's probably already sold her onto some brothel full of Eastern European sex slaves. Was that your plan all along?' She continued to deny him any signs of recognition.

I couldn't listen to any more of this and before fleeing the room, left a final instruction: 'stay on this track Josh. I'll follow it through. Angela will stay here with you as support if you need it.'

Steadying myself against the wall in the corridor, I drew a deep breath to purge the toxic reality of what might be happening to Emilia. If she had been touched by anyone – I would kill every one of them. I opened my eyes to find Michael standing in front of me.

'You okay?' he asked.

'No Michael I'm not... but I'd feel a lot better if you have something for me.'

'Yes... but not good... There's no active surveillance on Petre Lupa currently, he's only small fry and the resources are focussed on those higher in the food chain. It's not going to be easy to track him. I'm not saying I can't – but it will take time.'

'Time, we don't have... I'm going out...'

The smell of stale beer caught the back of my throat as I slipped through the door of The Old Axe, down Hackney Road. Charlie Wright was holding court in the corner – a pathetic homage to the old East End style of gangsterhood, still revered in this area.

'D.C.I. Connelly... What a pleasant surprise. A personal welcome 'ome... I didn't know ya cared.' He adjusted himself on his seat, extending his man-spread even further to accommodate his hanging gut. His side-kick-number-one, clinging on by his skinny arse as he threw daggers at side-kick-number-two.

'I don't Charlie... but when I saw you at The Golf Club, I wondered if your probation officer knew you were hanging around with old associates. Breaking parole conditions I suspect.'

'Blackmail...? Not very Ladylike.'

'Never known for my ladylike qualities Charlie – you know that.'

He eyed me up as he rubbed his greasy bald scalp, 'so... as this ain't a social visit – what can I do ya for?'

I smiled an empty smile. 'You can get rid of your two monkeys for a start. I won't hurt you... promise…' He folded his hunk-of-ham arms over his gut and twitched his head at both low-lifes, who scuttled way. I slid into a chair in front of him as he eyed me suspiciously.

'Well Charlie... back in the game...?' I held my hand up as he began to protest. 'Don't worry... I'm not interested in your petty dealings – today... What I need is information.'

He relaxed back into his chair, 'I ain't no grass...'

'Actually Charlie, you are and I've the recordings to prove it. But don't worry, it's no one local. I need to know anything you can tell me about people-traffickers.'

'I ain't into that malarkey,' he replied in cartoonish humour. 'That's all controlled by them Eastern European scum.'

'I know... but as they'll cross over into – shall we say – your market... you could help me get a few of them off the street.'

He chewed his thumbnail as he looked down at his half-finished beer, finally meeting my gaze. 'So, what cha want?'

'A name and or an address where they'd keep the people they'd trafficked.'

'Is it to do with them murders that've been keeping you busy?' He asked, not as mockingly as he could.

I bit down on my lip – the pain distracting me from the rant I wanted to rain down on his head as my panic grew with every second Emilia was not found. 'Let's say it's best you don't know if you don't want any comeback. Now do you have any info or not?'

He revelled in this possible power-play for a moment, before realising he'd best not push his luck. 'I don't 'ave it 'ere but I can find out.'

'I'm after one in particular – a Petre Lupa...' Before he could stop himself, he raised his eyebrows. 'You know him...?' I asked.

He contemplated his answer: 'nar... 'eard a bit... 'e's not one of the big guns but could lead ya to 'em.'

I left my card on the table and scrapped my chair back across the ancient boards. 'You've got until I get back to the station before I get the word out that you've been more than helpful in providing information for our enquiries and I'll send C.I.D. down here to rip you and your enterprise apart.' I grabbed the unopened bag of cheese and onion from the table as I left.

I sat eating the crisps in my car outside the pub for a bit, seeing if anyone else of interest showed up. After counting at least three known associates that would send him back to Wormwood Scrubs, I knew I had enough to secure his cooperation.

By the time I arrived back at the station, George stopped me on my way in. 'I've passed a message onto your team, from – if I'm not mistaken – Charlie Wright.'

'Did he recognise you?'

'Oh yes... he took great delight in letting me know he'd regained his liberty.'

'Let him have his moment George – he'll be back in soon enough.'

Josh had passed Petre Lupa's address onto Susie who was already heading down there. I told Susie to stay where she was and I met her a couple of streets away from the given address in Wood Green: a traditional melting pot of

Greek and Turkish communities with more recent activity centred around Albanian gangs. Every other shop was a kebab shop which paid little heed to what went on inside. We squeezed into her less conspicuous Ford KA and pulled up near the house.

'What's the plan Boss? Do we call for back up?' Susie asked, eager to get on.

'No... I don't want to spook him. If she's not here, we don't want to risk him informing whoever has her.'

'Okay...' she said, as she pulled her bag and a suit jacket from the back seat. She slipped on the jacket and a pair of glasses she rummaged from the bag as well as a file. 'Then let me see if there's anyone there.'

I unquestioningly let her leave the car, watching her fling a lanyard around her neck with some sort of ID card dangling at the end. She marched purposefully towards the house. She rung the bell and banged the door authoritatively until it relented and a scruffy Eastern European man shuffled in the doorway. He looked like he had just woken or was roused from a drunken coma. She nattered away and flashed what I presumed was a fake ID while reading from her clipboard. Her powerful Polly-Pocket persistence threw him and she disappeared with him into the house. The lack of a warrant, being the least of my concerns.

As a reflex, I flinched to jump out of the car but instead made a flustered call. 'Michael... can you check to see if Susie has signed out a firearm today?'

I heard the tapping of his keyboard before, 'yes Boss. Hold on... She's activated an open line on her phone... I can listen in.'

'Put it on speaker now please...'

Susie was in full flow, 'I can have substantial support of law enforcement here within minutes Mr Radu if you continue to be obstructive. I need to be satisfied that the living situation of this house does not constitute that of an

HMO and the legal obligations that are required of it. And as up until two minutes ago, you had no idea what a HMO was, I suggest you let me get on with my job and I can be out of your hair in no time.'

He must have conceded as an acquiescing grunt was heard and a faint, 'stupid bitch,' as she walked away.

'Okay Mike... Hope you're listening in...' She spoke above a whisper. 'I've persuaded him to stay in the kitchen while I look around the house. Contact The Boss so she knows what's going on. She's outside in the car.'

'Are you getting this Boss?' Michael checked.

'Just about...'

We listened to footsteps on what sounded like wooden floors – possibly stairs, soon confirmed by Susie. 'I've already checked the lounge and the kitchen which is clear and I'm now going to the bedrooms. I'm drawing my weapon...' Michael's breathy anxiety was threatening to drown out her narrative. 'First bedroom clear.... like the rest of the house… furnishings are sparse so not many places to hide… mattresses on the floor but no personal belongings.' An unoiled hinge creaked stubbornly. 'Bedroom two... clear... same as before. Maybe we caught them between changeover? Bedroom three... presuming it's his from the eau de stink and suitably disgusting.'

We were left with our imaginings as to the translation of the heavy breathing and groans that followed but it sounded like she was using the camera on her phone.

Michael could not contain himself: 'Come on... Come on...'

'I'm coming Mr Radu...' she hollered, accompanied by hurried footsteps down the stairs before he commenced a rant. 'If the number of mattresses in the bedroom is an indication of the usual number of occupants, then it represents an illegal HMO which your landlord claims he has no knowledge of.'

'Nothing to do with me...'

'Your landlord will be notified – expect frequent visits Mr Radu...'

'She's out Michael... I'll call you back...'

She strode defiantly away from the house clutching her clipboard with Lupa on the doorstep giving her a V sign behind her back. She walked past the car and I waited until he closed his front door before pulling out to pick her up.

'I was listening along with Michael,' I said. 'Some brass front Susie... but at least we know she's not there and he's none the wiser.' Finding her there would've been preferable to where my mind was going with other terrifying possibilities.

She pulled out her phone. 'His phone was charging by his bed. I took shots of some of the numbers he called – I'll forward to Mike.'

We drove back to where my car was parked. 'Let's use mine.'

I settled into the passenger seat and by the time Susie slipped behind the wheel, she had changed jackets and was now wearing casual denim and a baseball cap with the brim pulled low. 'I had a poke around in his room. He'd a wad of passports in a sports bag. About three with his photo, under different names but also another six – all young women: some Romanian and a couple Latvian. I've also sent on to Mike.'

'Let's watch him for a while before we call out full-on surveillance.' We parked back in the spot we previously vacated and did not have to wait long before Lupa surfaced. I called Michael with the details of the white transit van he jumped into, as we tucked in a fixed distance behind as he pulled away. Visions of what Emilia was going through invaded my thoughts until Michael's voice interrupted my concentration.

'Boss... Can I confirm priorities?'

I had to reengage my brain, 'okay... pass the passport detail of the girls on so that the slavery unit can follow that through. Start CCTV tracking of this transit. Cross reference any locations of the transit with any known associates of Petre Lupa from both countries. Get onto our Romanian counterparts and Interpol for any names and those they think are active here.'

'Angela's already been working on that. We're waiting to hear back.'

'Push Michael, please... I don't know how much time we have before they move her.'

'Sorry Boss... will do. I'm also looking to triangulate his phone with the timelines of her disappearance.'

'Great... get back to me as soon as you can.'

I held onto the dashboard as Susie made an emergency stop at a junction. 'It's a dead end,' she said as we peered down the road and watched his vehicle drive through a set of gates. 'Looks like lock-ups in railway arches.'

'Let's get as close as we can.'

We crawled down the road against the kerb and turned the car around when we stopped, preparing for a quick exit. My phone rang as I was about to leave the car. 'Josh...?'

'Boss... she's not giving up any information but she's no longer protesting against any of the accusations. I've no idea if there was an end game or she planned to scare you and return Emilia safely. She only made one relevant comment that, 'it was all in God's hands.''

'Not good...'

'No... Look... I'm on my way to you and I've alerted SCO19 as these gangs may be armed. Hang on and don't do anything yet.'

Susie looked across and knew I was not going to wait if there was a chance that Emilia was inside. 'I'm going in Susie... but you don't have to come with me.' She was out of the car before I finished my sentence.

THIRTY NINE
The Unthinkable

The early evening, winter darkness, offered some cover as we slipped through the gates. We headed for the lock-up with the transit parked outside. The entry gate was slightly ajar, leaving enough of a gap to peek and squeeze through when I was confident the entrance was clear. Susie, with her firearm now drawn, remained close by my side. Our frosty breaths, the only give-away to our presence.

My heart sank; the space seemed unoccupied. I had envisaged at least a huddle of wretches with Emilia held amongst them. As we inched forward in the dim light, we heard agitated voices coming from the back and as we approached, it became clearer that it was two men, mid-argument, in what we could only presume was Romanian. I fired a text to Michael that I was going to send him an audio to translate and flashed at Susie. He texted Susie's phone, informing her that he would send the translation back to her.

Creeping towards a barricade of pallets, dividing us from the action, I crouched on the floor as near to the edge as I dared with my phone held high in their direction, holding Susie's in the other. She remained alert, sprung and reassuringly calm, when I could no longer guarantee my own professional detachment.

The translation began to come through; sporadic and disjointed but about decipherable.

Crazy bitch... won't come back for her... move her...
Don't need this shit... not like others... police heat...
Shipment due... he'll be pissed ... No more cock ups...
Sort it out... Won't cover...

One of them sounded like he was walking away – towards us. Susie had already retreated to the shadowy edges where I swiftly joined her. The argument continued so we made our way back out, only daring to speak once inside the sanctity of the car.

'What now Boss...?' Susie asked as she strapped in.

'Get down...' I slipped down in my own seat, keeping the view of the gates from my wing mirror still in my sights.

I called Josh. 'Where are you?'

'At the junction of the road. We've an address for an associate known to the Modern Slavery Unit and they already have him under surveillance.'

The Transit was at the gates. 'I think that's where Lupa's heading now.'

We slid further down as the Transit sped past and followed when it reached the junction. I put Josh on speaker as his car slipped in behind us. 'What do we know Josh?'

'The address we have is Dalston Lane. Phone activity has been picked up from his mobile at the time of Emilia's abduction, with a frequent unknown number which could have been Wagstaff as well as this known associate. It did show him around Dalston Lane an hour later.'

We let Josh's car overtake us. I opened my glove compartment for a phone charger and was caught by a waft of the pink grapefruit spray that Emilia blasted copiously, before bounding out of the car. I held the bottle to my nose and inhaled.

'Boss... Boss... Did you get that?'

I turned to Susie, 'what...?'

'Josh gave the postcode for a known associate. He's going to head straight there while we follow Lupa and hopefully end up in the same place.'

'Josh... sorry... can you repeat that...' As he did, I tapped the code into the car's Sat Nav and watched him overtake Lupa and speed off out of sight.

I was nudged to the edge of insanity as we crawled in rush hour traffic along the North Circular Road. I lowered my window in an attempt to clear my head, only to be rewarded with the carbon-rich air, clogging my throat.

I could not fault Susie's advanced driving as she weaved expertly far enough behind, staying out of sight, without losing the target. It was pointless attempting to concentrate on anything else. I was fixated on the moving dot on the Sat Nav as it nudged urgently towards its destination.

As the dual carriageway morphed into a high street and eventually a residential road, we had to hold back until we heard from Josh. 'Lupa in view... He's out of the car...'

We turned into the road and squeezed into a parking space with Lupa in our sights.

'We've a unit in the gardens covering the rear...' he continued. 'Lupa has entered number 42.'

We spotted Josh step out from behind a bush on The Green opposite. We joined him in the shadows. 'What do we have?' I asked – unashamedly frantic.

'The blinds have been pulled down but two men have been in there arguing with no one else entering – until Lupa. Are you ready?' He asked me directly. I nodded. He placed his radio to his face and instructed; 'go...! go...! go...!'

A unit appeared from another part of The Green; the lead, a man-mountain with a battering ram. The unit swarmed through the door and spread up the stairs and into the back while we burst into the front room. A cacophony ensued of cries of, 'police!' with a responding chorus of frenzy and threats.

Lupa stood defiant with a gun pointed at Susie who had responded in kind. 'Deal with him,' I said as I ran out of the room into the back, where two armed officers had met the fleeing men, head on.

As they crashed into the kitchen table, food-encrusted crockery, splattered onto the tiles. A comatose young woman sat with her head on the table – unmoved by all the action. After checking aimlessly through any body-sized cupboards, I bolted upstairs towards the chaos and hit a human wall of hysteria.

A moving mass of arms and legs flayed around on the

landing as officers tried to prevent any from scrambling down the stairs and attempted to bring order and calm. I barged through the throng, on my way, searching every face for recognition.

Failing to find Emilia on the landing, I pushed through to the bathroom and on into the bedrooms. All empty until the last one. Between the bed and the wall, a body was huddled tight. All I could see was a mop of brunette hair like my Emilia's. I bent down and touched the top of her head. 'Emmie...' I dared to whisper. As she raised her head I knew, even before seeing her face. 'Don't be afraid,' I tried to reassure the girl, who did not understand a word I was saying. 'You're safe. One of the officers will help you.' Her eyes were empty. Her expression frozen. She lowered her head once more and pulled her knees tighter to her chest.

I ran from the room and jumped down the stairs, two at a time and headed for the lounge. Lupa was on his knees with his hands cuffed behind his back with Susie standing over him. Josh was beside the door as I entered. They looked at me expectantly and I shook my head. 'Out...' I said, unequivocally.

'Boss...?' Susie looked across to Josh for back up.

'Both of you... Now…!'

Josh nodded at Susie and as she joined him to leave, I held onto her arm, 'give me your firearm.'

'Boss...' Josh pulled forward and held out his arm. 'Boss... No...'

I held Susie's gaze and she hesitantly removed her weapon and handed it over to me. 'Out... Now...' I repeated.

I slammed the door behind them and turned my attention to Lupa. He raised his head and cackled, 'don't try and do crazy bitch act with me,' his accent as thick as mud. 'I know you English can't do nothing. Your hands tied like mine.' He attempted to raise his bound hands and continued his manic screech.

I walked over purposefully, wrenched his head back by his hair and held the gun to his temple. 'I'm not any old crazy bitch Petre... I'm a fucking crazy, mother bitch and if you don't tell me where my daughter is now, I'm going to presume that you don't know and I'm going to blow your brains out and my colleagues there, will only be too willing to help me cover it up.' I pressed the gun harder against his temple.

'Okay... okay... Nice lady... maybe we do a deal? I'll tell you big man and you let me go?'

'You're not going anywhere Mr People Trafficker. Your choices are to walk out of here and spend your time at Her Majesty's pleasure or your brains to be scraped off this nice sofa to join you in a body bag.'

Beads of sweat, sat like oil on water on his greasy brow. 'That's not fair. I'm not big man.'

'And I don't fucking care. I'm not interested in fairness. I'm only interested in finding my daughter.' I pushed the gun harder. 'Now for the last time. Where is she?'

'Up... up there...' he squealed, nodding his head to the ceiling.

'Upstairs...? No, she's not. Don't fuck with me... I've already checked.' He cowered as I pushed the gun harder.

The head kept nodding, 'no... no... the roof… in the roof...'

'The roof...?'

Josh and Susie leant against the door as I burst through. I brushed past Josh and could feel Susie close behind me as I bounded up the stairs. Everyone had been cleared and I stood on the landing alone, until Susie stepped up beside me.

I looked up to the ceiling and Susie followed my gaze, 'shit... the loft...' She slipped her gun from my hand as I picked up the long-handled hook by the side. Susie stood at my shoulder with her gun aimed at the hatch as I unhooked the door and pulled down the extending ladder.

'Let me go first,' Susie insisted, already halfway up before I could object.

I followed at her heels as she stepped into the loft. It looked empty at first glance. I turned on my phone light and swung it around the space. Piles of insulation were stacked up in one corner and Susie was soon on it, pulling bales to one side. I joined in until we saw a bundle of white sheeting against the edge which I grabbed hold of and whipped back.

'Please God... Emmie... Emmie...' She looked up at me with pleading eyes as I pulled away the duct tape from her mouth and cut the plastic ties restraining her wrists and ankles.

'One of them's up here...!' She screamed.

'What...?' A heavy weight slammed into my side and I bounced off one of the rafters before crashing to the floor. I felt Emilia's arms around me as the vibrations from a gunshot pierced the air.

'Mum...' I heard Emilia's sobs in the darkness. 'Mum... You're bleeding.'

FORTY
Planting A Seed

'Sign your name here please.' He pulled the book towards him after I finished. 'Mrs Whitehead... Are you a relative?'

'A friend...'

He had little interest in hiding his indifference. The female guard I followed through a series of security gates and checks was no less engaging. As I entered a visitor's cubicle at my own pace, she greeted me as though we were meeting for a spot of brunch. The stench of stale sweat, proved an aid to anchoring me to the here and now.

She was bursting to interact: 'back walking already Amy... and only with a slight limp. I am impressed.'

The reduced swelling in my spine may have returned the use of my legs but the codeine pills I was now regularly popping – didn't touch the sides. It took all my concentration to sit without exposing my discomfort. 'Well, you know what they say: what doesn't kill you makes you stronger or should that be, 'who?''

Her defiant demeanour was in contrast to her physical state. Sunken eyes, punctuated her gauntness and her current fragility, belied her deeds. I had a flash of her in the school playground: eager to please; helping out wherever she could; visible yet invisible. I knew the person in front of me was the same woman but whether it was the impact of her incarceration or the cancer of her deeds, she had truly transformed into an unearthly creature.

'Have you come to gloat…' she said, mockingly as though another failing.

'I can't imagine what there is to gloat about,' I replied. 'The lives you've destroyed can never be recovered – even those who've survived will bear their own mark for the rest of their lives.'

She enjoyed displaying her disinterest. 'Curiosity then...?'

'To a degree... yes... You see I don't know what you're waiting around for. There's enough evidence to convict you – even you'll have to admit that now.'

'I don't care about being put away. People will understand my motives... what drove me...'

'Perhaps... while you remain tucked up here... an enigma... But once you're in that court room, you won't be given the space to cultivate your eulogy. A clever barrister will peck away at your version… expose your sentiments as psychotic delusions… ridicule your experiences… humiliate you to a pathetic wreck. That will be your memorial.'

She chewed her lower lip and nodded rhythmically. 'Surely you'd find that satisfying.'

I inhaled my true response and pushed on. 'You've no family left to protect or to impress even. To your fellow inmates and guards, you're a nobody. Your grandiose crimes have no currency in here.'

She tilted her head to one side, as though I was the one being observed. 'You could never let things go, could you?'

I did not want to engage with her. To feed her self-importance. To be manipulated into an exchange of her choosing. That tone took me back to the bunker: my sense of hopelessness versus her conviction of absolute control. Even behind the reinforced glass, I wobbled with vulnerability that she would find a way out.

'That's how you ended up in your current state – you couldn't keep your nose out.' She eyed me with self-amusement before letting on her in-joke. 'You never asked me if I intended to kill you.' She waited crossed-armed and lent back in her chair. 'The truth is...' she said before springing forward with her face near the glass: 'I didn't care.'

I studied her twisted features and for a moment thought the unthinkable – that she could plead insanity. Incarcerated somewhere for the criminally insane. Having her every need catered for. Therapists on tap. A guaranteed audience for her delusional rants.

'Here's the thing Paula... You see... while you're stuck in there and I'm out here, I have the opportunity to speak to the papers and I'll be telling them all I know about Paula Wagstaff – the serial killer. I'll make sure to enlighten them about what a terrible mother you were. How your neglect, caused the death of your son… How fortunate that he died in the arms of someone who cared for him. His real mother…'

'No...' she banged on the glass, momentarily causing me to flinch.

'How badly you treated your daughter after his death. Wishing her dead in his place and driven by resentment – took her life.' The banging continued in rhythm. 'That will be your legacy Paula – if you insist on hanging around. Or… If… you were no longer here…' I held her manic gaze as I bargained. 'I might be more inclined to tell a more sympathetic story…'

The banging stopped and she held her hand to the glass before running it down the pane as though clawing her way through.

FORTY ONE
Patched Up

I licked my parched lips as my eyes fought against the blinding artificial light. A synthetic tang clung on in my mouth and was thick in my nostrils.

'Mrs Connelly... Mrs Connelly...'

Something blocked the light, encouraging my lids to flicker open. 'Mrs Connelly... I'm Doctor Brennan. How are you feeling?'

'I don't know...' I looked around the room. 'Why am I here?'

'You were stabbed on duty. Don't you remember?'

I closed my eyes and felt Emilia's arms holding me and her shouting something... I couldn't make it out. I looked back up at the Doctor. 'Emilia... is she okay?'

His smile did not reach his eyes. 'She's fine. She's with your husband and son outside, waiting to come in. But before they do... Mrs Connelly... unfortunately I need to inform you that you lost the baby. The knife ruptured the womb.'

'Baby...?'

'I wasn't sure if your husband knew so we haven't told him.' He rolled onto the back of his heels as though he were ready to sprint out of the room. 'Didn't you know?'

'No… no… I didn't… I don't know… I put on a bit of weight I guess but thought….'

He smiled uncomfortably and patted my hand, 'I'll come back to check on you later.'

I reran his words in my head, until they finally connected that he was talking about me. I had no awareness of anything else being said but turned towards the door as it swung closed behind him and I let the silent tears flow.

I touched the bound wound on my stomach, numb from a presumed infusion of morphine. The hollowness within my fragile body, replaced with grief, twisting every organ into a knot. My body began to shake as the emotion refused to be contained. I heard the alien sound of my sobs and felt a sliver of release. I knew I would never tell Peter about the lost child. I could not bear the thought, through my own paranoia, of his judgement coming between us.

My relieved family were eventually allowed in and bounded through the door. Jude taking the lead – his boyish mannerisms exposing his genuine concerned for his mum. Then Emilia... held back by Peter as she looked like she was going to dive onto the bed with me. Peter slipped unassumingly beside me and held my hand; looks exchanged on both our parts of private sadness, regret and relief. The discussion, looming: was it time to pack it in?

A week dragged by before Josh managed to slip past Peter's sentry and he looked surprised and relieved as he pulled up a chair. 'Mmm... That looks tasty,' he said, eyeing the Shepherd's Pie I was toying.

'Smells more inviting than it tastes. What's the goss Josh? Spit it out.'

'How do you know there's anything to tell?'

I pulled a familiar – cut the crap – face. 'Nothing about work has reached my ears in the past week so I'm gagging for some news.'

He was uncomfortable and tense. 'I snuck in to see you today because there's a bit of information that I wanted you to hear from me before you saw it in the news.' I remained silent. 'Paula Wagstaff committed suicide in prison last night.'

We looked at each other. He seemed as confused as if he'd just found out.

'How...?'

'She did it with a belt. Not hers but not hard to get hold of if you've got something to trade. But this was a bit of a surprise...' He spread out a Sunday tabloid on the bed. 'Here... Amy Whitehead's interview on, "the making of a serial killer..." Didn't think it was her kind of thing?'

'No...' I read through the first paragraph. 'Says here... that despite her actions she thought "Paula Wagstaff's intentions were to protect her children." Who'd have thought...?'

'Not sure how I feel... I mean it's like she got away with it... like she got the last word...'

'The killing stopped Josh and people are safe...'

'I suppose... although I'm not convinced you believe that for a moment...' he said, as he picked up a spoon from my tray. 'Are you eating that jam sponge?'

Printed in Great Britain
by Amazon

67061405R00180